ECCLESIA'S TABLE

ECCLESIA'S TABLE

MASON S. HAYNIE

To those for whom the system is not working.
And to those who wish to change it.
You shall not always be faceless.

Contents

The Last Call
Rosalie N. Aranda

Overture: The Show

From Savyer

Seven stand with prisoner hands
Bound by chain and circumstance

One, a traveler
Whose wandering mind led him away

Two, a bystander
Who preaches fear against one leg

Three, her own abuser
Giving up body for bread

Four, a great deceiver
Radicalizing the dead

Five, a firm believer
In her temple alone

Six, a blind follower
Sheepishly watching the throne

Seven, a fallen leader
Wolven pride and woolen pull

Forty years
And one thousand full

Yet all disgrace The Table
And give up on the fable
When grace for another
Resigns with The Other

And the eager announcer announces,
With information new,
"Ladies and gentlemen
Have we got a show for you!"

Chapter 1: Demon Eyes

He was crying before they came in, but he hid it well at first. Yet here he was again, weeping as if the city were already lost. The others didn't know what to do,

they never do in the face of some emotion

but he couldn't blame them. A real Leader wouldn't exhibit such vulnerability, especially not in front of his *Symvoul*. He was grateful that at least his dirty blonde curls hid the unbecoming creases that populated his forehead whenever he cried.

The bearer of the instigating bad news lifted his head and adjusted his left leg.

"Leader, your anxiety is reasonable," said he, penitent as can be. "But you needn't be so concerned. All of the offenders have been centralized; our...demonstration made sure of-"

"There *may* not be any more unmistakable terrorists, but terror itself is in danger of full bloom," said a third person, his strangely hourglass frame extending as he sat himself up. He spoke with the hardly concealed scorn of past affronts. "The seed has already been planted in their hearts."

"You're both right and you're both wrong!" said an ardent fourth. He was excited just to be there. "There is much to be done, but much already *has* been done. We can celebrate the small victory even as we strategize for the final one, yes?"

The other three in the room who had yet to speak sat silently in their seats, as they always did.

"Verily," said Leader. The brief exchange drew the congress' attention away long enough for him to wipe the water stains from his otherwise blemish-free face. He stood up. He wasn't normally a pacer, but governing wasn't normally this stressful. He walked to where each member of the *Symvoul* was seated. And then he went beyond. He kept walking until he completed a full cylindrical lap across The Temple. They didn't usually hold their meetings within the confines of these translucent pillars, but given the circumstances, Leader felt it appropriate to physically gather at the heart of their society: The Table.

"When my grandfather first started building this, he knew exactly what kind of wood he wanted to build it with," Leader said as he let his hand drag across The Table's top. The rest of the *Symvoul* settled into their seats, prepared to hear the all too familiar story.

"Wolfwood, he called it," Leader continued. "And not just for the differing tones of gray, but because of its toughness."

Leader slammed an open palm against the aging surface. The ardent one jumped in his seat and mouthed a smiling "oh my" to his neighbor.

"A toughness to match the fortitude of his philosophy. A philosophy so rigidly loving and inclusive...it's only because he was so committed to it that it was able to persist. And now...now I grieve because The Table is being defaced in its very essence."

Leader collapsed into his chair and held his well-defined jaw in his hands. Each of his supporters strenuously searched for words to support him, but he beat them to it.

"Lieutenant, you've done what I've asked of you, but the city is no less on the verge of collapse."

The penitent one hung his head once more. The scorned one saw his chance to slither in.

"Leader, we must act now. There is no room in your heart and no room in our rules to execute the prisoners, but perhaps we could more simply...send them below."

Leader looked at his advisor with widened eyes and a fierce brow. His shoulder-padded friend was once his sole confidant, but recent behavior revealed the threat of liability residing in his heart. Still, what he said was not entirely an impossibility.

"It would be unconventional, but–"

"I've got it! The *prophecy* is the true answer! Woohoo!"

Everyone turned their heads to the source of the outburst, towards the seat farthest away from Leader. The ardent one. The scorned one rolled his eyes. They all knew that the newest member of the *Symvoul* was annoying in disposition, but they wouldn't have suspected him to go so far as to interrupt Leader. None of them had ever done so, and they assumed that the action didn't bode well. But Leader made no inclination - he was listening.

"What prophecy?" asked the scorned one.

The ardent one looked at each of them incredulously, his pudgy mouth agape.

"Come on...my goodness! No need to jest, my friends! You know it well. *Seven stand with prisoner hands...*"

The penitent one allowed himself a stifled chuckle. "Well...that's not a prophecy..."

"How is it not?" asked Ardent.

"It's clearly metaphorical," replied Penitent. "Those are not specific people, just representatives."

Now it was Ardent who allowed himself a heartier laugh. "Six of those seven 'representatives' match the descriptions *exactly*, and they're all in the same room together as we speak. Need I remind you, Lieutenant, that you were the one who penned them there. I know you're not naive. That cannot be a coincidence."

"Atios 6:11," interjected Scorned. The reference was all he had to say for his intended audience to understand. But Ardent shook his head.

"I've taken the time to calculate the numbers..."

"Of course you have," Scorned said with another eye roll.

"It's been approximately fourteen thousand, six hundred days. Realistically, we could be one thousand full any day now..."

"How deeply have you considered your calculations?" fought back Scorned. His hands gripped his edge of The Table. "By your own admission, we only have six of the supposed seven needed to complete this 'prophecy.'"

Ardent smiled. "Well, rather than sending them 'below,' as you stated, we could bring someone above. That would meet the criteria of the first prisoner quite nicely."

Scorned loosened his grip. He was surprised by how well Ardent had thought this through. But he could see what he was doing, and he would wait for the logical moment to strike back.

Ardent took out his woolen kerchief and dabbed under his arms. The *Symvoul* was taking place in the cool of night, sure, but he knew his apparently singular convictions placed him on the hot seat. The glaring white with purple trim of his new robe was appropriately glamorous, but right now, it didn't appropriately hide sweat and nerves.

"Leader, Lieutenant, and everyone else, how we handle this threat is imperative to how our civilization will function going forward. Ever since...ever since Mahu's disappearance, our jurisdiction has been questioned. Rightfully, perhaps..."

Scorned hastily stood with a prepared defense, but Ardent held out his hands with intentions of de-escalation.

"Now, I know that that is not public information and that no conclusions have been officially made yet..."

Penitent shifted uncomfortably and crossed his arms.

"...but as someone who's spent a lot of time with our citizens lately, Inner and Outer, the rumor mill has done its job. If you want to keep our way of life preserved and our people safe, it's not enough to just pull at the weeds. Rogues have disgraced The Table with their lack of hope and their disregard for neighbor. That seed of disgrace must be uprooted."

Penitent felt a restlessness fester within his gut. What Ardent was saying was completely compelling, but the potential outcomes were unprecedented. He could see persuasion in Leader's water-blue eyes. But he couldn't quite voice his opinion; he wasn't used to doing so.

"My son," Leader said. "What are you suggesting?"

Ardent leaned in. He noticed everyone else did the same.

"When have we ever used The Kolosaio?"

"Absolutely not!"

Scorned voraciously leapt up and kicked his chair back. As it flew across the room, he flew to where Ardent sat and pounced upon him. He swung his lithe limbs across Ardent's plump body to little effect, but Ardent did little in response - he had never been in such an encounter before. Scorned realized he could leverage his nature better by using the jagged ends of his nails to dig in. The cuts were shallow at first, but soon the edges of his fingers became laced with blood. After satiating himself with how well he carved up Ardent's stupid face, he lowered his sights and-

Scorned's body was rocked so hard that he lost complete control of his limbs and felt his head wobble back and forth in the air before he hit the ground. Looking skyward, he noticed something under The Table that he had not seen before. In fact, he was pretty sure no one had ever seen it before, but he was too dazed to get out the words necessary to alert the rest of the *Symvoul*. Besides, Penitent had his elbow firmly lodged on his windpipe.

"What in the world are you thinking, man?!" Penitent yelled into Scorned's face.

The three silent ones stiffened even more.

Leader rushed over to where Ardent helplessly lay. He was still conscious, and Leader realized he must have been in enough shock to keep from screaming out, though he was sure to feel the sting soon. Leader cradled Ardent's head in his arms.

"My son, my son, oh, how undeserving of this pain you are!" Leader's weeping warned of a return, but Ardent stared him in the eyes with a demand.

"Let's vote."

Ardent shot his hand into the air, conviction sustaining the adrenaline in his veins.

"Those for The Kolosaio, raise your hand."

Penitent kept his elbow where it was, but looked around in astonishment. How had it come to this so quickly? Momentum was being ridden like an unrelenting gust. He kept his hands down and knew that Scorned would do likewise.

Leader raised his hand. Once he did so, the three silent ones followed in unison.

"So be it." Leader gently lowered Ardent's head down and proceeded to disrobe. His cloth had already been painted by blood anyway, so he used it to dab at Ardent's wounds and then helped him to his feet. Penitent got off of Scorned, who quickly started massaging his neck. They all returned to their seats.

"This isn't what I want," Leader stated, to himself more than anyone. He looked towards the heavens. "This isn't what any of us want. But it may be what Ecclesians need. Savyer, I wonder if I've failed you more and more with each setting of the sun. But if your words are prophecy, then who are we to deny what must come to pass? Perhaps our greater duty would be to make sure of it."

Leader turned to look at each member of his trusted *Symvoul*. They were all broken in their own unique ways. A flawed foundation may not be ideal for an unyielding building, but when it was all one had, it had to work. Still, some cracks ran too deep.

"I will talk to each of you individually after our congress as to what your roles going forward will be. But know that we shall waste no more time on defensive measures and passive announcements. By tomorrow evening, all will be well in the Sanctums."

Penitent anxiously rubbed his left leg. He knew that once Leader set off in a direction, nothing could alter the course. It was a quality he jealously admired - it had served their city well - but despite how dangerous the world around them was, never had they been in such a precarious setting. Now he feared what his misguided intrepidity would accomplish. Scorned feared his impending conversation with Leader.

He had only recently taken the time to re-prove his loyalty; he knew their rapport would not be able to survive this blow. Maybe, for once, a lack of defense would be the route he took. There was enough blabbering in this *Symvoul* now anyway. Ardent was comforted by Leader's words, and he tried to flash his trademark grin to show it, but the minor lacerations across his lips discouraged the act. It was nice finally being listened to and taken seriously. He had earned his place here, and he would be sure not to squander it. The three silent ones remained silent, trading facial emotion for unwavering obedience. It was nearly fourteen thousand, six hundred days ago when they made their pact: alone, they could never make a difference, but united, they would always have the final say. All six chosen members of this *Symvoul* had contrasting motivations for being there. They all thought they held these inclinations close to their chests, but Leader saw it all. He knew their hearts. It was his gift. And he loved them anyway. Because that's what his grandfather would do. And it was his life's work to be more and more like Savyer. And in this most perilous time, he knew Savyer would do anything he could to keep hope alive. So that's what he would do.

"Let's see what the wolves decide."

Chapter 2: The Fire

The tension was concrete.

The warmth of the fire could not ease the slight of that truth. Dread of confrontation and conversation rested behind the lips of each of the three wanderers.

One of them, of medium height, sat far away enough from the center of the pit that her face was just beyond the exposure of light. She half-hoped that would be enough to hide her visible scowl, but the flickering produced shadows that betrayed the repetitive bounce of her leg anyway. Another, the smallest of the three, held his malaise in the quiver of his bottom lip. He could not stand the silence and would have loved to be the first to speak, but the depths of his disbelief made it impossible for him to do so. The final, tallest member was indiscernible. He sat painfully close to the fire, gravely holding secure the most blank of facial expressions. The only motion he made was the occasionally necessary stoking of the flame.

Surrounding them was the ecological void they had known their entire lives. Sure, at this point they were enveloped by something resembling evergreen trees and other similar-looking pines, but the incessant familiarity of desert terrain was just as close as it had always been. Endless days were filled with harrowing heat and scarce means for survival. Supplies were makeshift, made of ancient gears and sickly twigs. As for food, there always seemed to be just enough sheep, but the inordinate amount of wolves

did you hear that

in the world made it increasingly difficult to find proper sustenance. And if the troubles of day weren't enough, the frigid chills of night were even more dangerous. Traveling by night was a death wish if one didn't burrow into sand or soil, particularly since clothing and any fabric for making it was hard to come by. Having proper kindling at the moment was the second largest grace the group had come across in the last few weeks. But the light of the fire only illuminated their dire need for reconciliation and healing.

Of course, to them, the state of the world was not one demanding complete nihilism. It was certainly challenging, but how can one understand the depths of one's own depravity when there is no alternative? When the world never ceased being a wasteland, how could one complain about the weather on any particular day? A good day in this life consisted of sheepskin, dead lambs, functional limbs, and a manageable source of heat. In the physiological sense, this was a *good day*. It was the needs to belong and to be heard that weren't being met.

Even so, it was that hope for something *other* that was their greatest remaining adhesive. These three wanderers had been stoked by the mystery of a kind of Promised Land. The changing landscape and a scent none of them had ever smelled before told of something brimming with potential along the horizon. That sense of unfamiliarity and bewilderment had immediately felt like something positive to each of them, and it had become their sole focus for the past one hundred and eighty days. That scent had grown ever stronger as they were led out of the desert and into the forest, and the greenness of plant life around them was the confirmation that more sentient life had to be close. Yet as close as they were to solving this puzzle of survival, it appeared that the final test they would have to pass would be to understand the nature of the trauma they had just experienced.

"What, then?...Shall we just pretend that *nothing fucking happened?!*"

The question hung like drying rags beside a dying ember, unable to warm up fast enough to be useful. Amaru felt a second of regret for speaking out - it's always hardest to be the first to do so - but her resolve was hardened by the slightest of winces she saw flicker across her leader's face.

"Better learn to stop talking like that, considering where we're going."

"*Goddamnit Moshe*, that'll hardly matter if they won't even take us in!"

Moshe took a second to consider the weight of that statement

they truly might not take us in...

before:

"Of course they'll still take us in," Moshe said coldly. "That's what they do for anyone who knows *how* to get in. And now we know how. That's what matters, right?"

A pause.

Moshe kept his gaze focused on the fire in front of him. Ironically enough, it was his proximity to heat that kept him from getting angry. He was disappointed in Amaru for confronting him like this. Amaru couldn't possibly understand the heaping of stress that comes along with being an involuntary leader. As much as any fellowship can be democratic, there's always someone who assumes the weight of each decision that gets made more so than the rest. They had made a mistake. Moshe could admit to that. He wouldn't have been sitting there naked while his clothes dried or used their last drops of water to clean his face were that not the case. But their resolve was unchanged: make it to this Promised Land they knew was nearby. Why dwell on complications they could have done without if they found a way around them regardless?

Amaru started pacing back and forth, a habit of hers that Moshe knew meant she wasn't done. Five steps that way, five coming back. She would do this for a total of three cycles before responding,

"We know how. But that's *exactly* the fucking problem. Won't they want to know *how* it is that we know? What do we say then? And - you know what - no. That's *not* what actually matters right now. What matters is that-"

"Amaru, I said to watch your tongue," Moshe replied. It was getting harder to keep his cool: the fire remained. "We really can't afford for you to slip up like that."

"Can't afford for *me* to slip up like that?! You're the-"

"*And* if they ask how it is that we know, we can just say that we've heard tidings from other travelers."

Moshe began to fasten his grip on the twig he used to

you two really ought to stop

stoke the fire.

"Perfect," Amaru said curtly. She had begun to take steps closer to Moshe's direction. "And when they ask why it is that we haven't joined up with any of those travelers?"

Although irritating, Moshe was getting used to Amaru's interrogative form of arguing. She had begun to ask these paranoying questions more and more lately as she started to develop something of her own voice within the group. Moshe supposed it was part of her acclimating to the changing horizon, but compounded with the pressure of that day, it was really starting to get to him.

"We'll just say that we work best as a smaller group!"

"Oh, *clearly* that is the case with-"

Moshe leapt up with stoker in hand, immediately imposing his superior physique. Just as Amaru started to ready her stance-

"Stop it!!"

The two of them had almost forgotten that Reenu was right there with them.

"Please listen to me," Reenu said. He was careful to lower his voice, and subsequently, the guard of these two alpha figures.

"As much as I want to talk about what happened, I don't think any of us are ready to do so. Amaru, you have to respect that, especially for Moshe's sake."

Amaru tried to hide a sneer, but she was at least more successful in lessening her stance.

"I don't really think we can make any proper judgments with how fresh...it...is and how emotional we all are. For now, we just have to do what we've always done: keep going. You want to know what *really* matters? We're here. We're safe. We're together. That's the formula that's been working for us. That's what always has. No matter what happens tomorrow, we *need* to make sure it stays that way. We'll work out these morality kinks when we need to...and that's all I think we should say about this...for now."

Moshe and Amaru were both listening intently. Once again, Reenu was right. As unassuming a countenance and naive a mind as he had, when he had something to say, it was hard to argue with. Moshe and Amaru exchanged glances of ebbing conflict and growing realization. After all that the three of them had been through, they often found it best to shelf problems of perspective for a later date. If things went as they usually did, they would have the chance to address this one later, when cooler.

Amaru sat back down, this time a little closer to the pit. Moshe resumed his place front and center, assertively stoking the flame. It had died down to near exhaustion.

With the three of them back to stability, Amaru felt it opportune to make one final point:

"Moshe...that whole rule about getting rid of some of the words we use just to come across as more respectable?"

"Yes?" Moshe softly inquired.

"It's fucking stupid."

Forty-seven minutes had passed. When the knowledge of the sun and the moon and their paths is a matter of life and death, telling time becomes one of the more intense senses. What each of them were also painfully aware of was that each of those minutes was spent unspoken.

The phrase "time heals all wounds" is pretty universally regarded, but it is also incorrect. It takes more than time. Perhaps an open heart or two. With that and the rising moon in mind, Moshe gathered his inner courage and spoke.

"I don't know what you all have been thinking about, and I don't want to try to guess. But being in front of this fire, surrounded by these lush, green...towers of nature...well, it's giving me perspective."

Amaru and Reenu both had their ears and eyes wide open. Any time that Moshe was about to admit a wrong, he started with something melodramatic like this.

"It reminds of me of the dream we'd talk about eras ago. We dreamed that we would be somewhere else. That we could experience something other than yellow sand and empty hours that make up empty days. No one else really understood this dream, huh? They called us odd for talking about it so much. Impractical, even."

The tension Reenu felt inseparable from was beginning to ease. Amaru, on the other hand, still remained taut and focused. Neither of them were able to hear the shifting leaves happening not too far away.

"Isn't it just absolutely wild to think that our parents couldn't even conceive of what now lies before us? The idea was so foreign to them that their worlds weren't prepared to handle it. But...we're in a different world now. We're in a different world now, but our old rules still seem to work. Reenu..."

Reenu had been inching closer to Moshe as he went on. At an arm's length away, they were almost face to face. Amaru, too, had subtly moved inward, though more so to avoid being left out of sight.

The shifting grew nearer.

"...you're right. We're here. We're safe. We're together. And we *will* keep it that way. But maybe to do so, we're going to have to adapt to some of the rules of this new world. That includes dropping some of those words they call bad, if you don't mind."

Reenu could see the logic in that. He nodded. Amaru, knowing that was mostly for her, still didn't like it.

"Whatever other rules there are, we'll take them as they come. And whatever questions they ask of us...well, we'll be as honest as we need to be."

Moshe reached his hand out and caressed Reenu's face. He knew that was something he liked, and hoped it reassured him. It did.

"And Amaru..."

Amaru had been staring at the fire, now barely more than a few cinders, but she looked up at the sound of her name. Her intention to remain stubborn was still there, but she didn't want it to be. Just as long as Moshe said the right things.

"Amaru, I'm sorry. I shouldn't have gotten - shouldn't have let my anger get the best of me."

Amaru scoffed a bit, but kept it inside. That shifting from responsibility to passivity was just like Moshe, and that was part

wait, what was that

of the whole mess in the first place. But before she could say anything in response,

"I know that it's your tendency to place blame on yourself for things beyond your control. Me too. It turns into shame eventually, right?...*don't let it.* There was not much choice in what happened. And, well, *we're so close.* That dream that's kept us together is almost fully ours! For all that we've gone through, I wouldn't trade any of it if it meant that we couldn't have this now. A fire, each other, and an *actual* future. A real tomorrow."

At this, Reenu couldn't contain his excitement. He reached out his arms, allowing Moshe to hold his hands. He was aware that Moshe was addressing Amaru, but the thought of an end to a fraughtful journey elevated his emotions to something like joy. He then turned and beckoned Amaru with his eyes, hoping that she would accept the invitation and make the embrace complete...

But Amaru hesitated. A real tomorrow? There had not been much in her life that could have even *sounded* too good to be true, but this definitely fit the bill. Maybe that's where part of the conflict came from. She wasn't ready for such a shift, even if it was satisfying. Still, here were her two true companions, awaiting her choice to make amends and continue on. That made her feel much warmer than the red embers that were quickly becoming ash beside her.

She gave in.

The three of them held hands tightly, a quarter lifetime of understanding passing between their wordless glances. This silence was different from that of the past hour: this was a silence to deeply savor, were it allowed to last its proper length. Unfortunately for this trio, that was not the case.

The first howl lit up the night with its tangible ferocity. The second came from the opposite direction, this time behind Reenu instead of Amaru. The encampment was then lit ablaze with another dozen or so cries of animal hunger, instantly catapulting the three of them into stances prepared for a fight.

"*Shit!*" Moshe hushedly exclaimed. "There's fifteen of them."

"I fucking knew they'd be back!" groaned Amaru.

"They're still a half-mile out or so, and they're *Nubili*," whispered Reenu. "If we leave now and don't stop, we'll be fine."

Each of them quickly scanned the trees for the best way out. There were many paths they could take, but fifteen wolves from contrary directions made choosing one difficult.

Another convulsion of howls.

Moshe instantly turned his head southeast.

"There."

"Would have been nice to be well-rested before the big day," Reenu half-jokingly half-complained.

"Well, once again, choice is taken out of our hands, so come on," Amaru countered. "Grab our cover and let's go."

Reenu ran and slid toward their supply of sheepskin and picked them all up. Amaru completed one final scan before hurrying on her way. Moshe stamped out the faint, ashen remains, and then the three of them were gone.

The feeling of wearing sheepskin is simultaneously familiar and perpetually itchy.

It certainly does nothing for one's mood after a long night of *scraping* - which is the word Moshe, Amaru, and Reenu used for their process of quickly traveling while synchronously covering their tracks. They had developed quite the system over the years: Moshe's keen sense of direction placed him at the head of the formation, Amaru trailed and made sure to smear each of Moshe's prints as she went along, leaving Reenu in the most challenging, most pivotal position. Being the lightest and most agile on his feet, Reenu would have to hop backwards while brushing his hands across their path to doubly ensure that they couldn't be followed. Although the team often performed this operation with ease, the long night and the itch of the sheepskin made Reenu rather grumpy.

"Sure as goodness won't miss having to wear *these* anymore," Reenu moaned.

Moshe and Amaru looked in light displeasure at each other, both not desiring to respond, but feeling it necessary in order to keep the youth's morale up.

"Funny thing, isn't it?" Amaru said flatly. "We've worn the skin of sheep our entire lives, and it still never got even relatively comfortable."

Moshe suppressed a slight chuckle.

well, of course not. why would it feel any better if the texture never changed

"They've always served us well when it comes to wolves. And the good thing is," Moshe added, "we won't *ever* need them anymore by the time the sun goes down."

Amaru and Reenu nodded in agreement. They had made great progress over night. The soil had grown ever more fertile and the land ever more hilly. They knew they had to be close. It made sense that the soil would be ripe for life and that the hills would serve as protection. The fact that daybreak was nearing was all the more reason to be hopeful. On the other end of one of these hills would be their longed-for destination.

It was atop one of these hills that Amaru found the courage to ask:

"I'm not saying we should take a break, but shouldn't we at least talk about what we're going to do once we get there?"

Puzzled and wary, Moshe replied, "You're right. We shouldn't take a break. Whatever is on your mind, say it as we move along."

Amaru was a bit annoyed since she actually did want to take a break, but she continued:

"Well-" Amaru had to catch herself as she nearly stumbled over what she thought was a rock but was actually compacted dirt, "we're not entirely sure how these people will react to us. I mean, it could be a trap after all."

Moshe didn't respond so Amaru kept going:

"And even if we do get in, we might not be fit enough for their society. These people must be survivors. Perhaps that's something they could hold against us."

Moshe kept quiet.

"And don't you think it's possible that there's actually *nothing there at all?* The grounds seem favorable, but it could just be some big myth, right? Haven't you taken the time to think of these things?"

Moshe stopped and sighed, causing the others to halt with him. Of course he had thought of these things. It was all he had been thinking about. He just never let see his worries for fear of spreading that anxiety. Once again, Amaru was showing that she didn't understand the complexities of being a leader.

"We're the most perceptive group out here. We'll know it's a trap once we get there. We're also the most able people we've ever known. They wouldn't kick us out for that. And..."

At this thought, Moshe hesitated. He was being presented with his deepest fear, and he had to mindfully prevent himself from falling too deeply into it.

"...if there really is nothing there...well, we'll just figure out what to do once we get to that point. *If* we get to that point. Anything else?"

Amaru tried to think for a second, but Moshe almost immediately kept going. He believed that the only thing that could truly stop Amaru's questioning was arriving with the dawn. They headed down the next slope.

"You see, Amaru," Moshe said as they lessened in pace so as to counteract the fall of the slope, "we've lived most of our lives as wanderers. We've gotten good at it. What we're not so good at is thinking of something *better*."

Amaru's buzzing mind slowed in its intensity. She hadn't considered this before.

"It makes sense to me that you would be so...inquisitive and doubtful...because those are two qualities that have kept us alive so far. But now that we're becoming a part of something new, it's possible that those very qualities might be what hurt us in the end."

Reenu, who had been enjoying the green of the ground and the brightening yellow of sunrise, now focused a bit more on Moshe's words. He was concerned that his thoughts would turn into more of an attack on Amaru's character.

"We *are* going to something better. There's no doubt about that. Anything's better than where we've been. And part of what makes it better is that it *has* to be a very established place. They obviously know how to run things for them to exist in the way they do. Who are we outsiders to question them?"

As Moshe's argument grew more elaborate, the wanderers instinctively stopped at the bottom of the slope to give it more thought.

"Reenu, Amaru, I don't often share the reasoning behind my decision-making with you. You've always trusted my thinking, and I'm grateful for your loyalty in that. But those are some of my thoughts in regards to this journey we've been on. I can't fully say that your concerns are completely out of line - this is a new experience for all of us, after all - but I do ask that you trust me. Because, after all of the surviving we've done, what's the point if we don't *try* to do something better? It's got to be leading to *something*, right?"

Moshe was doing his best to keep his emotion from getting the best of him. He had built great internal walls for the sake of leadership; he was unused to such vulnerability. He wasn't aware that this openness was exactly what his companions wanted from him for so long.

"Moshe," Reenu answered, "we *do* trust you. Not every decision you've made has been perfect, but we know you're doing your best. We've supported you all the way, and we'll continue to do so."

Reenu looked at Amaru, hoping that she would have something to add, but something strange was streaking across her face instead. It was a complicated mixture of guilt, uncertainty, regret, and love, and it was preventing her from speaking. Different parts of her face were twitching, and Moshe understood that she would not be able to say anything in the moment.

"And...as for yesterday..." Moshe reluctantly began to confess-

But Reenu's ears perked up.

"Did you hear that?"

The moon had completely snuck away, and the sun had come to re-place it. Along with it came the various sounds that accompany the life of a rising culture: a mechanical humdrum, and yet, full of life. The three wanderers were hearing these strangely juxtaposed decibels for the first time.

Rather than saying anything to commemorate the event, each of them felt something different. Moshe felt relief and let out an aching breath to show so. Amaru felt a cold sweat escape from her palms, and she started to smush them together while wondering what these foreign noises meant. Reenu felt the need to run, and so he did.

They ran up the next slope, knowing that it could only be a few more in between them and their new home. Down they went again, this time throwing less heed to their descent, but finding that momentum only helped to carry them further faster. On the next hill, each found them-selves with enough time to have their final thoughts

there is something out there for us after all

please don't let me mess this up

no more sand...no more wolves...

before ascending the final hill. And once they made their way, absent of breath but full of expectation, they were greeted with a sight they never could have predicted.

Ecclesia was a phenomenon. Settled securely at the bottom of a chasm of green surrounded by ridges and cliffside, it would still be a couple miles' walk down to get there from where the three of them stood. But their bird's-eye view gifted them with a sense of what life must have been like down there in that valley.

What was most noticeable from their perspective was a massive coliseum that looked to be a mile in diameter in the northwest section of city. Moshe assumed they used the stadium for some kind of games or events, but he wasn't entirely sure what that even meant. He couldn't wait to find out. Opposite that behemoth was a towering citadel that reached out far above anything else. Amaru assumed that this building was where their governing bodies made important decisions

is this a democracy...or something else

for the lives of the people. In between these two structures was perhaps the most deeply green tree they had ever seen. They were still getting accustomed to that color in the first place, and they found it odd that there wasn't any fruit on the tree as far as they could tell, but it must have provided wonderful shade for one and for all. Aside from that contrast of juniper, stark white from the many mansions that crowded the areas between the two main structures made the place feel nearly overpopulated. In front of the tree, and almost exactly central within the city, was a rectangular building that seemed to be held up by pillars lining every side. They could not tell what that site was for, but Reenu assumed it might be some kind of trading grounds. On either side of that building were two marvelous fountains that somehow seemed to be endlessly pushing water

the technology here must be astounding

out of their cores. They knew that was the first of many observable mysteries to come. Another peculiarity they could see was that the city seemed to be divided exactly in half (Moshe estimated that the entire city must have been a few miles in diameter) by a stone wall. Everything on the closer side of it was too low to the ground for them to see, but considering that half was where the gates were, they knew they would experience that side first. And the gates! They had to be at least forty feet high along with the rest of the outer walls. The walls themselves looked like they were made of jasper stones, shiny yet almost translucent in the way that they gave off light. In fact, the entire city seemed to be exploding with light, though it felt impossible to tell where the source was exactly.

The scene was almost too categorically shattering to comprehend, and it was far too breathtaking for any of them to articulate any singular thought. When one comes across architecture of previously inconceivable metaphorical and literal heights and depths, it can be the kind of experience that denies language and fundamentally shifts a worldview bred from previous hierarchies and a lifetime of ordeals and affairs. For Moshe, Amaru, and Reenu, these internal shifts were just beginning, born out of sheer spectacle.

The three of them continued on, unable and unwilling to express themselves. As they sank closer into the bottom of the valley, the ground beneath began to feel as if it were sinking. The soil was nearly oozing in its fertility, welcoming the newcomers just as much as it was convincing them to stay. Reaching the joining of slope and plateau, they noticed that dead, lengthy palms were laid on either side of the solid gold path to the front gate. They found it odd that such a commodity of the desert would be the gesture of welcoming to this countryside of beauty, but perhaps they were a relic of sorts for these inhabitants. A reminder of the past pointing the way to a more desirable future.

Forty paces from the gate.

Moshe - who had fallen behind, distracted by the glare of the palms - regained his composure and quickly but casually proceeded to the front of the group.

Thirty paces from the gate.

On his way there, he stole a glance at each of them. Reenu had his mouth slightly open, clearly in wonder. Moshe noticed that his lips were dried to the point of cracking. He let a smile pass from his lips, believing that they would never thirst again.

Twenty paces from the gate.

Moshe's observance of Amaru was not as pleasant. He could feel the stiffness of her body, even from a few paces behind. As he passed her, he was instantly drawn into the hardness of her eye contact. She would not let his eyes go, but it was not in anger or concern. Her eyes shimmered in a way that he hadn't seen before. Was it fear? He couldn't understand. She suddenly stopped walking, causing Moshe to do the same. It was then that he turned his face forward, and realized that they had arrived.

The tension was concrete.

The brilliance of the pearly stone gate before them could not ease the slight of that truth. Dread of confrontation and conversation rested behind the lips of each of the three wanderers.

But silence was all that passed between them.

As much as the three of them had prepared for this day, they were unsure of what to do next. How could it be so quiet here when they had seen that the place was teeming with life? Should they knock? Yell? What was customary for greetings here? Was someone observing them on the other side of the wall, waiting for one of them to make a move?

Being in the back, Reenu was growing impatient. His habit of awkward wincing was begging to be itched, but he dared not show it. He didn't want to start off on the wrong foot here.

Amaru felt empty.

Moshe looked forward, stoically waiting. He had always been the one to act when it was necessary, but now, he felt almost paralyzed. Being on the literal doorstep of a journey's end can be exhilarating, but the feeling of "what next?" can just as easily sour the taste.

Moshe's nose started to wrinkle. He had figured that they would be adjusting to strange smells for a while, but this one was uncannily

burning?

familiar. This scent was one of those insidious sensory experiences that made it hard to discern between the physical and the mental. Was he really smelling something or was it just in his head?

Before he could turn to see if his companions were noticing the scent, it had left. It must have only been in his head then.

Just then, a person-sized slab of the stone gate began to roll away. It looked like it was somehow going into the gate - another small convenience of this land that amazed the three of them - without having to fully move aside. But it didn't move quite far enough for anyone person-sized to squeeze in. Instead, slivers of a face and the right side of someone's body came into their view. It was then that they realized it was time for them to be asked the question they all knew was coming.

"What's the password?"

Reenu gulped.

Amaru looked down.

Moshe said,

"Salvation."

Chapter 3: Relief

69 DBK

"Welcome to Ecclesia."

The stone gate rolled away, and Moshe, Reenu, and Amaru were greeted with an abundance of life.

There were hundreds and hundreds of people crowding the streets before them. People of all shapes, sizes, and genders. It was a melting pot of hope, and it made each of these wanderers feel close to home. But as quantitatively abundant as the area was, it didn't seem like the same could be said qualitatively. The streets were dingy and didn't look to be taken care of much. There were no impressive buildings around, only small shelters and ratty blankets stuffed with sleeping people. Was this why it was impossible to see everything *this* side of the dividing wall from the valley's top? Moshe wondered if those in control kept everything

how could this be

hidden so as to not detract from the main event: the enigmatic grandeur on the other side of the wall. Moshe looked at Amaru and knew from the way her eyelids tightened, like a wolf scrutinizing its prey, that she was thinking the same thing. If the city kept its more obscene sectors hidden from the outside...

what else could they be hiding

Then Moshe had another thought:

maybe there's some greater good

It *was* possible that there was some kind of benefit to the layout here. Maybe seeing the ghetto upfront was a final reminder of the wasteland they all came from, making the inner utopia all the more enticing. That didn't really explain *why* there were so many people still apparently living here, but who knows? Maybe there were actually *a lot* more people on the inside. It made sense that such a haven would have more people on the inside than the outside, even if it had to be regulated somehow. Moshe wrinkled his nose again. Being in the dark was not in his wheelhouse. And he knew that first impressions were often wrong.

Moshe didn't have time to progress past this internal conflict - the man who let them in started speaking:

"Peace be with you!" The man then started to approach Moshe with open arms. He grabbed Moshe's forearms and planted a strong kiss on both of his cheeks. This kind of physical affection was not new to Moshe, but he was still surprised to be welcomed that intimately by a stranger. Nevertheless, it *was* comforting.

"Peace be with you!" the man repeated as he did the same to Amaru. Their embrace was more awkward, mostly due to her resilient frigidity. Still, tenderness like that was her most prominent love language, so even *she* was slightly warmed by it.

"Peace be with you!" the man proclaimed with a sense of finality as he arrived at Reenu.

"And also with you!" Reenu had remembered that that was supposed to be the customary response here. The other two felt a bit embarrassed about not doing the same.

"My, you all look a bit confounded! I'm sure it's partially because the glory of Ecclesia is something you've not seen before, but if it's also from the weariness of your travels, then I understand. It's been a couple decades since I've really been out there, but I too was once on the road like you. Then, I-"

The man caught himself, looking a bit ashamed for nearly self-propelling into a long-winded story.

"Forgive me, I should have started with my name! I'm Duman. I am one of the gatekeepers *and* the *official* tour guide here at lovely Ecclesia. I'll be showing you around in a bit and doing my best to make you feel as comfortable as possible! But first: what are your names?"

"My name's Moshe."

"Katir."

"Uh...my name's...Reenu!"

Reenu's slight pause threw Duman off for a second, but he recovered with:

"Moshe...Katir...Reenu...Katir...Reenu...Moshe...Reenu...Moshe...Katir. Apologies if you find my repetition odd! As you can imagine, re-membering thousands of names can be a bit, well, confounding! *Never-theless, I'll do my best, that's all we can do, yes? Yes!"* Duman nearly hopped in joy at the rhyme's delivery. It was clear that he had practiced that line many times before, likely as a tool to keep himself and present company entertained.

Moshe and Reenu *did* do their best not to look at Amaru. Her name change was never discussed. They were sure it was a defense mechanism, but what for? It was not like the Ecclesians could do anything with that fragment of information. If they *did* want to keep a low profile in case things went south, having to remember to address her by her false name only made things more complicated. Moshe was understandably annoyed.

"Katir" was doing *her* best to analyze Duman without him noticing. He was a short, slightly round man with pinkish skin and many sweat spots on his nicer-looking cloths. It looked like he was wearing three or four layers of clothing, with the top one featuring little connective cir-cles lined up and down its center, something that Amaru had not seen before. His pants looked to be made of some kind of wool, but again, it was not like anything Amaru could properly register. Hanging out of them was a little golden chain that was attached to something that was ticking inside of his left pocket. His shoes were as aggressively black as they were shiny, and the entire outfit made him look a little silly, albeit definitely higher-class. Outside of his appearance, it was already obvious to Amaru that his defining characteristic was his exceeding exuberance, and that it would become grating very soon.

"Well, *ahem*, before we go any further," Duman said with modest indignation since his clever tercet went unacknowledged, "as much as Ecclesia is a community that *can* accept all people, it's important that I ask you some preliminary questions. After that, I'll lead you on a tour of much of the city. How does that sound?"

Moshe's right eyebrow quickly and subtly lifted at this. He realized that this must be the questionnaire they had heard-

"Sure, that sounds fair," Moshe replied. "Ask away."

Reenu's brow dropped a bead of sweat, which Duman noticed.

"Oh, no need to worry Reenu, it's really just a couple of diagnostics! Survey data for those in charge. See?" Duman pulled out from one of his pockets a scroll of parchment lined with columns of what looked like previous travelers' responses. Most check marks landed in the first column, with less in the second, and only a handful in the third. Moshe wondered what the odds were that the first column was the one they wanted to be in.

"We wouldn't turn you away based on your responses, especially since you knew the way in," Duman warmly reassured them.

Reenu showed a half-smile, but he dropped another bead of sweat. Duman was dangerously close to what made him most nervous, and his perceptiveness made lying seem impossible.

"Actually, that *does* bring me to my first question..." Duman thought aloud as he pulled out his pen, looking down at his paper as if he didn't know the questions by heart.

Reenu took the opportunity to cast a glance of muted panic towards Moshe. Their eyes met and almost telepathically communicated their thoughts:

what if he asks me how we know

don't worry, I'll-

"How *is it* that you knew the password?" Duman directed his inquiry towards Reenu.

"As a matter of fact," Moshe interjected, "Ecclesia is fairly well-known out there. I mean, some people think of it as less than myth, which is forgivable, but really, I think it's just common knowledge now. Most groups we came across knew."

Moshe kicked himself for subconsciously adding that last line.

"Ah, that's interesting. How come you three never joined any of those groups? Sorry, that's not part of the survey, I'm just curious." Duman stated this nonchalantly, but still had his pen hovering closely over his paper.

"Well," Moshe cleared his throat. "Since most people don't find Ecclesia possible, a lot of them just didn't want to come with us."

"Yes," Duman said while forming a peering look, "it is quite the shame that some are so deluded by their harsh living conditions that they can't accept good news anymore. They might be even worse off than those who have never heard of Ecclesia!"

"And," Moshe started with the anxiety that accompanies reluctant candor, "just for the sake of honesty...we've had a few...unfortunate conflicts with others in the past."

Moshe, Amaru, and Reenu were instantly reminded of some of those conflicts. Most of them were attacks from scavengers. There were so many in the wasteland; resource scarcity bred them. But there was also the group that forced them to join up. It was a kind of indentured servitude: Moshe, Amaru, and Reenu had to work for them in exchange for protection. It wasn't necessarily a bad circumstance, but it was more so just the fact that they *had* to work for them that led to struggle. It also didn't help that this particular group had a number of people who were unfair and abusive. There was also the couple that they came across that was dead set on advocating for this abnormal approach to romance. What was it called again? Monogamy or something like that. And then there was-

"Ah, that's...interesting. It actually brings me to my next question, which I'll ask each of you, starting with you, Moshe..."

Moshe prepared himself for what felt like a tide-changing inquisition.

"Have you ever killed anyone?"

The question carried with itself an air of banal execution one might expect from someone who never had to subject themselves to such violent ends. Amaru instinctively turned her head away for a split second upon hearing its bald delivery. In that instant, she noticed a red-headed woman a couple hundred paces off talking down to a man much bigger and bulkier than she was. They were in between two walls that left them hardly any room to move, as if to discuss something secretive or deeply personal. That didn't stop the red-headed

peculiar color for someone's head to wear

woman from yelling at him as if everyone in their vicinity needed to hear it. The man himself looked sulky and shameful, but that didn't appear good enough for the redhead. Amaru sympathized, wondering if these two ever had to face the minor trauma of revisiting past bloodshed.

"Yes," Moshe said as blankly as the question itself was handled.

Duman turned.

"Katir, have *you* ever killed anyone?"

"Yes." Amaru followed in Moshe's footsteps.

Duman turned once more.

"Reenu, have you ever killed anyone?"

"No, I have not."

Duman let his gaze linger on Reenu for a second longer than the others. Despite giving the truth, Reenu felt somewhat contrite and worried about not being on the same page as his companions. That gaze of Duman's only intensified his concerns. But before they could brew any longer, Duman returned to his friendly countenance and said,

"Well, not to worry! We understand that, sometimes, violence is necessary. You come from a world of darkness and despair, and that gives freedom to many people to live out their inner, most violent desires. Some of those people just can't be helped. Self-defense against those types is admirable, particularly when it is the result of protecting your own, uh, family, if I may use that word for you three."

The three of them felt relief, appreciating that Duman didn't question them further despite also finding it odd that he didn't even ask them about their motivations in such encounters.

"Thank you, sir, for-" Moshe started.

"Just Duman is fine," Duman insisted.

"Oh," Moshe let out a small, nervous laugh. "Thank you Duman for being understanding. And yes, we *are* a family." Moshe hoped that the word had the same definition here as it did for them.

"Of course!" Duman delighted. "Now, just two more questions! It's clear you know that Ecclesia is a place of salvation, but what does that *mean* to you?"

It was a good question. Moshe recognized the genius in asking a question so brief that would also provide so much insight into their expectations. He just hoped that his expectations were properly aligned in this case.

"I believe that this is a place of rest. A place where the suffering, violence, and inequality of the world ceases to be because everybody here has...exactly what they need."

Moshe started out with confidence, but the ghetto around him eroded that sense of triumph the more he went on. He'd have to ask Duman about that soon.

"I believe it's a place where we won't have to worry about wolves or wearing this awful sheepskin anymore," Reenu spoke with a smile.

Duman guffawed at Reenu's light-hearted note.

"That surely is a benefit here! *And* you'll get to wear much more unique clothing - like mine!"

Duman held his arms above his head and did a quick spin for them to take in the splendor of his various cloths. They still weren't sold on his look, but they could see how nicer clothes led to a happier outlook on life.

"What about you, Katir?"

Amaru had been trying to formulate a proper answer. Should she speak truthfully about her doubts? Moshe said they would be as honest as they need to be. It was still hard to tell if this was a place that prefers its citizens to accurately express themselves or if hiding her questions was better. She went for the latter, just to be safe.

"I'm, uh...I'm just glad to be here and not out there," Amaru stumbled over her answer.

"Well, certainly! I promise you that Ecclesia is a much better alternative to living out in the wilds. In fact, it may be the *only* alternative!" Duman was nearly shouting with excitement.

There was something in his eagerness that was infectious. It had begun to work its way into the hearts of these wanderers, and it was most definitely a welcome tone for them to embrace. There are few things that do a soul more good than to be genuinely excited about something. It was a feeling none of them had ever felt so strongly before. Moshe smiled at his companions, knowing that, even if Ecclesia did not live up to their considerable conjecture, at least the purpose and meaning they were presently experiencing was enough to lift some of the staggering spiritual weight they had all been carrying. At least a little bit.

"Now: my last question. Well, it's really a no-brainer at this point..." Duman methodically articulated.

Moshe, Reenu, and Amaru all leaned in towards Duman in anticipation.

"Would you three like to know more about Ecclesia?" Duman asked, grinning like a child on their most memorable *ekatomeres*, friends and family huddled around them in celebration.

Moshe answered this one without any hesitation:

"Duman, we've come to this city in search of relief from the troubles everyday life constantly threw at us. We *need* a path that leads us to hope. Please, show us the way."

"Now you're talking!" Duman exclaimed, showing his appreciation for melodrama. "Just a second!"

Duman quickly ran a handful of paces back to his post at the stone gate, hurriedly digging through a small chest.

Moshe turned and looked at his friends. Reenu smiled unabashedly. Moshe knew that Reenu would fit right in here. Positivity would be just what the young man needed. To transition into adulthood without the usual accompanying cynicism

what a thought

made Moshe excited for what Reenu would become. Looking over at Amaru, Moshe thought he also saw the fleeting remains of a smile. Perhaps Duman was growing on her after all. Moshe could only hope that Amaru would somehow let her guard down after a lifetime of building up emotional walls of steel against anything outside of

eventually

them.

But for now, whatever smile she was gathering faded into a frown, and then a subsequent groan, as she looked at what Duman was bringing their way.

"Take off your sheepskin and come with me!"

Amaru supposed the clothes they were given weren't all that bad. The simplicity of their silken robes was at least highly favored over Duman's extravagant, woolly layers. Each of their robes was a stark, block color: hers was red, Reenu's was blue, and Moshe's was white. Now that she had gotten over her initial distaste for the cloths, she turned her mind to what struck her as odd about them.

"Hey, Duman," Amaru initiated.

"Oh! Yes, Katir?" Duman, along with Reenu and Moshe, was surprised that *she* would be the one to start conversation.

"Is there any particular reason for the specific colors we are wearing?" Amaru had been so used to wearing the dull and dirty whitesmoke of sheepskin and whatever rags they could gather that the shock of vibrant colors made her question

perhaps these colors are codes

their purpose.

"Well, actually, for the most part, I'll usually just pick clothes based on the size and gender of new travelers," Duman started, "but with you three, I felt that these colors reflect what I know of your particular personalities. Red for the fiery Katir, blue for the thoughtful Reenu, and white..."

Duman had stopped leading them to take the time to look Moshe in the eyes as he said:

"Moshe, if I may be so forward with my diagnosis, I believe you are a man seeking innocence and purity. The weathering of the world had eroded your hopes, but now Ecclesia has rekindled that flame!" Duman exclaimed.

Moshe nodded, the right side of his lip turning upward slowly.

Amaru noted Duman's

he notices a lot

attentiveness.

"Besides," Duman continued, "I think these colors look nice on you, don't you? Red, blue, and white - a great combination!"

Reenu also nodded, beaming.

"Now, let's continue on!"

A few moments before, as the sun passed its zenith, Duman had taken them to their first stop. On the way there, Reenu observed the way people interacted with each other. For the most part, it looked as if everyone kept to themselves. There was the random couple or even a threesome that had walked by, but there weren't any groups larger than that. Even those "groups" kept their conversations at a barely audible hum, looking with wariness at Reenu and his friends. Reenu was disappointed that the environment didn't incite more friendly exchanges between others,

i suppose old habits do die hard

but maybe these people had yet to break out of their shells and open up to people. He was determined to do so once he got the chance.

Their first stop was a cylindrical booth that was only fifty paces or so along the main wall. Outside it was a colorful sign that said "Ecclesian Essentials." Inside it were a lot of different, small collections of parchment that Duman called "tracts." The little booklets they picked up were fascinating to them, as they contained "pictures" (another term that Duman had to explain) of some of the great sights on the other side of the wall. Moshe saw that there were larger booklets there as well, but Duman didn't acknowledge their use or importance. Apparently, being this booth's First Attendant was another one of Duman's many

he has his hand in a lot here

roles. Duman had also told them that they would not be visiting the other side that day, but that he'd have a special surprise to tell them at the end of the tour.

Currently, Amaru was flipping through its pages and taking in its wonders. The stadium, the citadel, the mansions. They all looked even more impressive in the detail that the pictures held. She was even able to get a closer look at the temple with the pillars that they couldn't really see all that well atop the valley...

Amaru noticed something.

Inside the temple was an elongated structure that was was about waist-high with small columns underneath it. She turned to the next page, which displayed this mystery in greater immensity. The sight of its mahogany grooves and the sense of longing emptiness embedded within its presence caused her heart to feel as close to welcome as she had felt so far. Emboldened by the success of her previous inquiry, she decided she would ask Duman about this, but it was at that moment that they had arrived at their next location.

"Here we are: The Troei Café!"

According to their tract, The Troei Café was what Moshe and his friends would have more plainly called "the feeding grounds" in their previous community. To be fair, this place had much more pleasant amenities than what they were used to: an orderly line where food (of mushy, chunky consistency, Reenu dismally discovered) was served by workers with nets on their hair, dozens of rows of wooden benches for visitors to sit on, and even designated bins for disposing waste and washrooms for, well, for also disposing waste. It was surely a step up from sandy, raw meat and sandy, raw asses, but Duman sensed that none of his present company were all too impressed. He could tell their minds were preoccupied.

"As your tracts mention," Duman said, "The Troei Café is where you will get your two regular meals each day. Admittedly, it used to be three, but there's been such an influx of travelers lately, we've had to ration down to two. The world must be getting harsher out there, eh?"

That question was Duman's trite attempt at a quip to lift their spirits, but he knew it didn't work. Duman sighed.

"Come. I think it's time I address your concerns. Let's move on to your living quarters, and then I'll tell you why we must keep you all on this side of the wall. For now, at least."

Duman always hated this part of the job. As someone raised (not born, as he often let those he guided know) within Ecclesia's secure walls, his optimism was as unsophisticated as it was absolute. His elders taught him to love others as himself, a philosophy which fostered his cheeriness and brought fulfillment to his life. There was the odd happenstance of turning people away or letting his mind wander and dwell on what lay outside his comfortable life, but he always returned to a peace that made him quite the encourager. That's who he was. A people-pleaser, through and through. Telling others of unpleasant things was enough to make his stomach sick.

"So, ehem," Duman cleared his throat. It always constricted and grew muculent when he had to do this.

"As I hinted at before, overpopulation has become a real problem."

Reenu frowned. This sounded bad already.

Amaru caught that Duman was twiddling his pen back and forth between the fingers of his right hand.

Moshe, as usual, was listening intently. These next few words might mean the difference between he and his companions making Ecclesia their home or moving on once again.

They were all sitting uncomfortably on the floor of their "living quarters." It had taken a while to get something properly situated for the three of them, and it wasn't until nightfall that Duman was able to bring them to their "new home." The empty tent was barely large enough for three people to lay down side-by-side in, so having a fourth member present made for a difficultly close conversation. Duman was speaking freely since, as complicated as this information was, anyone nearby was already acquainted with it. But the few feet that separated each of the tents would make holding private conversations impossible later on.

"When Ecclesia first started, it was quite exclusive. The first settlers, led by a practical man named Prames, believed that they were a unique people, that discovering the perfection of this valley meant that it should belong to them alone. So Prames and his family lived in earned luxury. They worked hard to make it what it was, but they never let anyone in. They're the ones responsible for the fortitude of our walls. They built it to last for eternity. But as generations went on and Ecclesia developed, one of Prames' descendants, Savyer, saw the goodness of the land, and decided that it would be even better if *anyone* could live here."

Moshe felt a wave of gratitude pass over his heart. Savyer's generosity led to the integral hope of Ecclesia that gave his friends a chance. But he knew there was more to the story.

"Yet as good-natured as Savyer was, he was also realistic. He knew that not *everyone* would make Ecclesia a home. It's just not sustainable. Additionally, it's unfortunate, but not everyone is fit to live here," Duman said with a sinking chest.

Reenu's heart beat faster. He was afraid that that was a possibility. The minute amount of confidence he had was wavering.

"Savyer set in place certain resolute rules," Duman said with a sense of growing credence. "He calculated what Ecclesia could handle, and came to the number of one thousand. That's how many inhabitants we can have living within the Inner Wall. At least, that's how many space and resources will allow for."

Moshe's right eyebrow cocked.

"Duman, that's a number I'm not even convinced that I could understand," he remarked. "Surely that's enough for everyone this side of the wall?"

"Unfortunately, it's not," Duman uncomfortably admitted.

This time it was Moshe's heart that sank.

"Savyer constructed a massive, beautiful Table that-" Duman realized that these travelers might be unfamiliar with that word. "-it's a flat, wooden surface with legs underneath it. We use it for our weekly feasts and..."

Duman's voice trailed off as Amaru's eyes shifted back and forth as she focused on his description of The Table.

that must be what I saw in the tract

Reenu's fading optimism was momentarily halted by

do they use sheep or wolf legs for this table? Or...people legs...

confusion, but he did his best to keep up with Duman's explanation.

"The Table is how we've been measuring how many people live on the inside. And right now...well, there's only about seventy spots left. Give or take a couple."

Moshe's eyes widened.

Amaru scoffed.

of course

Reenu, who had been leaning forward for most of the conversation, collapsed backwards in anguish. In doing so, his head inadvertently peeked out of the tent and instinctively turned to the right. In that instant, he noticed an older man sitting by himself on the outskirts of the living area. He had a clearly worn stick beside his left leg, which looked to be smaller and less shapely than his right one. He looked forlornly at those passing him by, often attempting to raise a hand as either a sign of welcome or of need. Reenu wondered if the man's heavy glance was because he knew that he would never belong on the other side of The Wall.

"So what you're telling me is," Moshe began with suppressed indignation, "that the *hundreds and hundreds* of people living out here, as well as the wanderers like us who all arrive with a dream for a home, for refuge from the world, are all vying for just a *few more spots*?" His last three words held a regrettable amount of angered emphasis.

Duman had been working on "putting his foot down" (a phrase which his boss had explicitly used in warning during their most recent meeting) on the last few groups he guided, and he decided now was the time to do so.

"Our current Leader has *always* held to Savyer's rules with zeal. They are resolute. They cannot change. If we just willy-nilly let everyone in, how would we be able to survive and do the good for others that we've been doing?"

Moshe was taken aback by Duman's vigor. Perhaps their guide had as many layers underneath as he was donning atop his skin. He seemed to have a grasp on the complexities that accompany leadership. As put off as Moshe was by reality once again caring little for his group's situation, he also felt a kindred spirit in Duman. But still...

"I see the logic there, but then again," Moshe rebutted, "how do you make that decision? How could *anyone* just choose who's in and who's out?"

Amaru's palms started to sweat again. She always respected when Moshe would

fuck yeah, Moshe

stick up for them, but she was also a little nervous about him showing such backbone so early on.

"Well, that's the thing, Moshe," Duman's tone found some of its original cheer as he transitioned back into the good news. "*We* don't choose. *You* do."

"I don't follow."

Moshe's confusion had intensified. He looked to Amaru to see if she understood, but she had the same look upon her face. Duman's ambiguous statement also caused Reenu to sit back up, now completely enveloped in the tent, wearing a similarly quizzical expression.

"Moshe, when you three first arrived, you acknowledged that Ecclesia is a place of salvation, correct?" Duman asked.

"Correct," Moshe answered.

"That was always Savyer's intention, and it still is true. However, with salvation comes a process that we call *sanctification*," Duman said with a spark in his eye.

Amaru spoke up.

"And that process is basically how we earn our spot then?"

"Mmm, I wouldn't say that you necessarily *earn* your spot. It's more like the way that someone accepts a gift. You can be given something for free, but it's up to you to take it."

The group's confusion persisted.

"I'd love to explain how sanctification works, and I usually do, but tomorrow - and here is that special surprise I mentioned earlier - tomorrow is our hundred-day gathering that we like to call...well, The Call!" Duman was clearly excited about this event.

Again, the group chose to listen and hope that Duman would make sense of himself at some point.

"Oh, it's an absolutely splendid time! The idea was actually propagated by our current Leader, and it's just ingenious! Basically, *everyone* out here is invited inside and brought to a seat at The Table. Well, not *exactly* at The Table, but pretty close to it! There will be a feast for the current nine hundred and thirty or so, and everyone else will get to have some of the leftovers, which, trust me, is much better than anything at The Troei. Then, Leader will speak, giving a short message for all to hear and an explanation of sanctification, as well as a time of grace and understanding that we call Q&A, where you can basically ask him anything."

The group was tantalized. The more Moshe learned about how this society worked, the more curious he found it to be. Amaru found the prospect intriguing: it was a risky and potentially vulnerable move for their governing body to make. She liked it. Reenu was excited about actually getting to meet with and talk to others and see what life was like on the inside.

"And I just think," Duman continued, "that the timing for the three of you is just *perfect*! I mean, Leader can properly introduce himself *and* sanctification just in time for you all to make it in and stay together. What a dream, right?!"

They all *did* find it convenient that circumstances were aligning themselves in such a way. Well, it *could* be convenient for *them*, at least.

"Anyway, it's getting late," Duman said while pulling out and looking at the ticking object in his pocket. "I apologize that Ecclesia has the limitations that it does, but it's simply the best way for things to work out. I suggest that you all get a good night's rest in preparation for tomorrow. It's going to be quite the treat!"

With that, Duman hurriedly opened the flap of the tent and made his way out.

His retreat was so quick that the three of them had yet to fully convert from confusion to awareness of what was going on. Amaru snapped out of it first and immediately cast a look of offense

just like that then

towards Moshe. When he saw her eyes, he snapped out of it as well, and followed after Duman.

"Duman!" Moshe did his best to project without yelling. He was not sure if he was successful, but he *was* able to get the guide's attention.

Duman turned around, startled.

"Er, yes, Moshe?"

"Now," Moshe panted, having caught up to Duman. "As a leader, I appreciate structure and rules. I get that they can be necessary to make things work. But, don't you think it would be helpful to everyone this side of The Wall if the living conditions were at least somewhat improved? Inner Sanctum is a land of plenty, right? There must be some way to allocate your spare resources."

This wasn't Moshe's most pressing question, but he felt that it would be a good litmus test for Duman. He believed the guide was compassionate, and he wanted to see just how far the rules would stretch.

Feeling pity, Duman responded,

"Believe me, Moshe, if there was anything that could be done, we on the inside would do it. We don't want it to be this way. You'll understand more tomorrow, but for now, hear this: as much as Ecclesia is a place of love, it is also a place of *truth*, and here is the simple truth of it all...the world is cruel and unforgiving. Ecclesia is the only chance I know of that offers something else, but that doesn't make the rest of the world any less dark than it already is. Some will get to fully partake of Ecclesia's glories, but maybe the rest will at least have something they couldn't have anywhere else: hope. Don't you think that's worthwhile?"

Moshe nodded slowly. He had to admit that this hope was what kept he and his companions motivated for so long, but he had also believed that the end was something that could justify the means of getting there in the first place. He was learning that maybe the desire for something greater was just as, if not more, valuable than the object of desire was itself.

"It is," Moshe stated. "I just...alright." Having not been in a position of deference for a while, he felt a pang of sympathy for his companions. Not wanting to press the issue too much, he would let this one go for now. At least he knew that there were kind people like Duman here, and that the rules were firmly planted but built out of benevolence.

"It's hard to accept, yes," Duman consoled, "but additionally, think about this: there really aren't any rules for the people living *outside* The Wall. If you keep the peace, you're welcome to stay here. We don't offer much, but it is enough to keep surviving. It looks unruly simply because, well, people seem to like it that way. We let everyone express themselves freely, and this is what it looks like."

Duman motioned to the ghetto around them. In doing so, it caused Moshe to fixate on a woman who looked to have been looking at him first. In that occurrence, he noticed that she was wearing a robe that was similar to Amaru's in color, but invitingly darker. It also fit her body more tightly, accenting her voluptuousness in inquisitive ways. Her eyes seemed to beckon Moshe, but it was also just how starkly clean she looked that was refreshing amidst the rest of the slums. He turned away before he could observe her any further, but he still felt her stare follow him.

Moshe appreciated the freedom that Duman described, but he wished that the environment felt more communal. Maybe a greater sense of unity would generate interest in cleaning up the place. Maybe that was something that he and his companions could change if given the chance.

"Maybe it reminds them of of their past homes or something. Cognitive dissonance."

"What do you mean?" Moshe asked.

"Oh, forgive me, I suppose that is not a term people outside The Wall would use," Duman atoned. "Cognitive dissonance is that uncomfortable feeling when what someone believes contradicts their behavior. Some of the people here want a new life, but they aren't quite living it yet."

"Hmm," Moshe considered the concept. "I can see how it'd be hard to transition into this new life. Maybe I'm just still too shocked to feel that effect, but I'd imagine...we'll have to deal with that growing pain a bit."

Moshe was thinking of Amaru as he said that, but he did not want to say her name. Something in Duman's eyes told him he knew who he was thinking of regardless.

"Yes, all do," Duman reassured. "But your awareness of that fact already makes you more ready for Ecclesia. And the clear kindness you feel towards your neighbors means you're fitting in awfully quickly." Duman smiled in genuine kinship.

Moshe smiled back. He was starting to believe again. He knew his group had the compassion to work things out on the inside and the strength to shift the system to help out those on the outside. It was all a matter of time. And timing.

Feeling satisfied, Moshe let Duman go.

"Thank you, Duman."

"Peace be with you, Moshe."

As Moshe re-entered his tent, he was greeted with a familiar view. Amaru and Reenu sat in the center of the tent, holding each other closely. Their love had always displayed itself in physical ways, bred by the harsh cold of desert nights and the purity of passion that results from touch. This particular embrace, however, didn't feel as warm as it usually did. It was more like the kind of embrace a parent provides for a child after waking from a bad dream.

"What's wrong?" Moshe asked.

"Really?" Amaru flatly returned the question.

"What?" Moshe resisted. It always bothered him when Amaru would answer his question with a mocking one of her own. As if he were supposed to always understand what was going on. He preferred to give people the benefit of the doubt, letting them explain rather than trying to assume what went on in their heads. Maybe that was part of the problem now.

"This place won't last," Amaru relented, knowing Moshe was either going to keep playing dumb or possibly never get what was wrong.

"How's that?" Moshe asked, annoyed that he had to prod her forward.

"Duman claims that Ecclesia has been fortified well on the outside, but he doesn't acknowledge that it's the *inside* that's the freaking

fucking

problem. There's no way that everyone here can be fine with how things are run."

Amaru was confident in her assessment of this society, but Moshe knew that his intuition and bit of additional

cognitive dissonance

information was enough for him to make a fairly strong devil's advocate case:

"You're probably right, Am- uh...Katir. But we don't know everything yet. Duman said they wouldn't have it this way if they could help it. He could be lying, but he seems pretty genuine to me. Do you not think so?"

Amaru felt herself to be a strong judge of character, which is why it bothered her that she had to agree with Moshe on this.

"He does seem genuine. But that's the other thing. All we know is what he's *let* us know. As bad as things look to us when we've only been here a day, don't you think it's more likely that things are worse than they seem?"

Moshe sighed out of tiredness from the day's events and the heft of Amaru's pessimism, as practical as it was. They were all running on a lack of sleep. Irritability was inevitable. He decided that what was best for them was for him to end the conversation as quickly as possible.

"Yes, that's likely. That's why..."

Moshe brought his voice to a whisper.

"...we're going to remain as careful as we always are. Tomorrow, we'll go to this Call meeting and simply continue to observe. We've got to lay low as much as we can. I'd like to have answers as soon as possible, but nothing will raise their suspicions more than antagonistic questions. That's why I didn't put any pressure on Duman just now."

"Ok, that's fine," Amaru said at slightly louder volume than Moshe. "What *did* you learn from Duman then, if anything?"

cognitive dissonance

"He mostly just said we'd learn more tomorrow," Moshe replied, thinking about what Duman said about hope. "He also said that, outside of normal decency, everyone is pretty much allowed to do what they want out here."

"That's-" Amaru felt her rebellious spirit rise and restrain itself, "...probably not true."

"I'm sure there are some caveats," Moshe admitted, "but it got me thinking: after we lay low for a bit, what do you say we try fixing up the place a bit? Being good citizens and neighbors couldn't hurt, and it'd be a great way to lift morale and get to know people."

"Verily to that!" Reenu exclaimed with enthusiasm. They had all heard people use that term when they visited The Troei earlier. Context clues made figuring out its meaning pretty easy.

"Sure," Amaru complied, though she already had other motivations in mind.

"Moshe," Reenu said, "do you think we could talk to people tomorrow though? At The Call."

didn't you just hear me say we have to lay low

"I'd imagine everyone will be a bit cheerier then. It might be the ideal time to get on people's good sides." Reenu was trying to be practical, though his heart was in the prospect more than he let on.

"We'll see. I'm just..." Moshe clamped his fingers at the bridge of his nose in pain. The pain of remembering. "I'm just a bit hesitant. You...remember."

It had been a thousand days since the three of them were a part of any semblance of a society, but that experience with corruption, distrust, and power in their indentured servitude was intense enough to leave its mark of bitterness on Moshe and Amaru. Reenu still admirably clung to his youthful idealism.

"I understand," Reenu frowned.

"But we'll see," Moshe comforted with a hand on Reenu's shoulder. Such a fine line it was between encouraging open hands and mistreated ones.

"For now, I'm just glad we're not sleeping in sand, as...*shitty*..." Moshe said with a whisper and a wink, "...as this tent is."

That was something they could all agree on.

"Even so...let's keep watch tonight. You two sleep first. Katir, I'll wake you in a couple hours."

Amaru and Reenu nodded and got into enjoyable enough positions, exhausted and grateful for their leader's courtesy.

Later that night, as the second hour of her watch was nearing its end, Amaru smelled something.

It was a scent that she was oddly familiar with, yet it felt out of place here.

is that...burning

She quickly scanned her sleeping companions and the raggedy fabric of their tent, but was unable to find the source. Curiosity and concern led her outside.

As she entered the cool breeze of the night, she looked around and saw that not a single person was outside. There was no sign of smoke anywhere, and there was no light other than the lanterns that sat sporadically atop the Outer Wall. The scent was perplexing: Amaru had taken steps in every direction from their tent, but it never got any stronger or weaker. It was as if it followed her, mocking her in her state of puzzlement.

Frustrated and unsatisfied, she retreated back into their tent. She was at least glad that she was able to rule out any possibility of imminent danger, but the scent itself was nearly suffocating in its persistence. She would ask Reenu what he thought in a few minutes once it was his turn to keep watch.

But as quickly and insidiously as the scent had appeared, it then ceased.

Chapter 4: Stygiophobia

68 DBK

Arah was a man of habit. He knew it, too.

This morning was going like any of the other nine hundred and thirty-two mornings he had spent living this side of The Wall. He would wake up before dawn hit...only to move the flap of his tent with his foot, see the persistence of night, and without thinking, fall back asleep. A couple hours later, the heat and the outside bustle would cause him to wake once again so that he could mentally curse himself for sleeping in as per usual. Each of those curses would reciprocate an aimless prayer for forgiveness, which would remind him to read some of The Manual. For whatever reason, that was a pattern that he could never fully integrate into his routine - reading The Manual. He always found himself having to catch up to the daily readings, but he did his best.

After that, Arah would turn his focus to his physical needs. A circuit of push-ups, sit-ups, and rock lifts (he gathered the stones from outside the gates, much to Duman's chagrin, but he convinced the tour guide that he needed to keep his strength up in order to be "more fit for Ecclesia") helped keep his wiry frame toned before he headed to The Troei. He used to head to the café first since his past life centered around finding sustenance as quickly as possible, but he trained his body to ignore that empty ache in his stomach for discipline's sake, and he was proud of himself for that. It helped that the gruel at The Troei quickly outlived its appeal.

Since bathing water was hard to come by, Arah typically chose to amass his rations of drinking water over the course of a week in order to keep himself looking decent. He had always been concerned about his looks. He felt that his presentability equated with his rationality in the minds of others. A level head was worth a lot here. Of course, washing his hair came at the cost of cracked lips (which irritated him more than anything), but it was worth it. His locks were approaching a mane-like status, and he was convinced that others whispered, or at least thought, about his hair whenever he passed them by. He tried to believe that his hair care wasn't a case of vanity; it simply made him distinct...and helped hide the flatness of his nose and the dull, nearly-black brown of his eyes.

Once he returned from The Troei, Arah would secretly and quietly meditate back in his tent. This was an activity that was silently looked down upon from other members of the community ("fill your mind with The Manual, don't empty it" he often heard), but it had always helped him clear away the thoughts of lust, laziness, and loneliness that parasitically dwelt within him. As impeccable as Arah was at keeping his body in shape, his mind never seemed to work that way.

For better *and* worse, Arah was a man of habit.

This morning, it was in the midst of his usual meditative practice that he was met with a welcomed interruption:

"Ecclesian hopefuls! Whoever will turn from their ways and answer The Call shall be saved! Come and have a seat at The Table!"

----

mass of wolves
hopefuls!
bloody sheepskin

ways and answer

are you ok

a seat at

Moshe, let's go!

Moshe awoke in a pool of sweat. He hadn't been able to sleep in the past three days and he didn't expect to be able to rest well this time either. The nightmare was unexpected, though. He had never been one to dream at night. He often thought of himself as a dreamer of the day - someone who let his imagination flourish while awake. That was a more productive and useful way to live. His brain didn't operate during sleep; it was too wasteful to remember his jumbled-up collection of strange imagery and disjointed events. Especially when they were terrifying.

Moshe turned his mind away from what he didn't want to think about, and was able to instead feel bad about his sweat pooling under the cheeks of his companions.

such a waste of water, too

He had to get up.

As his senses recalibrated and consciousness fully returned, Moshe became aware of the insistent murmuring and scattered steps of a large crowd outside. He swiftly pulled away the flap of his tent and saw nearly everyone in their makeshift neighborhood making their way towards The Wall. The gate of pearl had opened up; a couple of Ecclesians in black and white robes were attempting to regulate everyone coming in, but the force of their eagerness was too much to handle. He let a thought of a curse pass through his mind and then cursed himself for that thought.

this must be The Call!

"Reenu! Amaru! Wake up!"

Then:

"I mean...Katir."

Not fully conscious yet, he supposed.

Arah typically didn't like his clockwork customs going unfinished, but he instantly forgot about everything once he heard Duman's announcement. There was something about the collective buoyancy in the air during the rush of these occasional gatherings that caused him to abandon the discipline and patience he had worked so hard to achieve. He changed into his cleanest-looking rags and made his way toward The Wall.

His aim was to be as close to the head of the pack as possible. He assumed that those in charge would probably appreciate punctuality considering how organized they had to be in order to maintain Inner Sanctum. His brisk march was briefly halted by a bitingly familiar sight: the beggar.

There was nothing like an accidental glimpse of the beggar to bring Arah down. His subconscious always directed his face into a frown when he saw the broken and unclean man. Part of him wanted to go over to the man, kneel down, and use his comparatively brawny arms to help bring the man to The Table. He knew he could, and he also knew that it *would* look good to others. But that was a selfish motivation - how much good would actually be done if his heart wasn't in the right place? And besides, falling behind was a risk he wasn't willing to take. The longer he spent in his lowly tent, the more desperate he became to become a true citizen. Weighing out the pros and cons, his hesitation only lasted a couple of seconds before he kept on marching.

But he hoped someone would come by and help the man.

"Alright, you're all clear to go. Take in the sights a bit and then have a seat near The Table. The Call will begin at sundown. Peace be with you."

The peacekeeping security guard who cleared Moshe, Reenu, and Amaru had been friendly enough in her tone, but being so thoroughly searched would always be an off-putting experience for the group. It felt more like the Ecclesian leaders were preparing for a hostile takeover than a hospitable greeting. Moshe obliged because he understood the need

maybe she just doesn't know

for safety, particularly since the amount of people flooding in made it easy for someone dangerous to slip on in if the guards weren't being careful. No need to take such a risk.

On their way in, they were each given a map of the area and a "single-use camera" (which was what they used to take pictures with, apparently). They were encouraged to take a picture (with themselves smiling in it) of their favorite part of Ecclesia as a way to capture that memory, but Moshe suspected that these pictures would also function as a visual reminder of what could be theirs one day. Still, they had to be choosy since each camera could only produce one picture. Most people made their way straight to The Citadel, content to wait in line for an incredibly long time just to make their momentary visual souvenir one that showed off the building's proportions. Moshe and his companions took one distant look at The Citadel and the mass attraction that it abscessed and wordlessly decided that there were probably other meaningful places to visit. Each of them thought the same thing,

lay low

but it was Moshe and Amaru that were the most pleased to not be visiting The Citadel right away. Large crowds made them both anxious, a shared bend in their personalities that was not unmerited.

Although each of the mansions showed off the exact same architectural design,

compliments to Prames and his people for consistency

one of the residences they came across had a quaint mat in the front that cemented its homeliness with the statement: "This house is a home." Amaru rolled her eyes at its cheesiness, but something about that earnest sentiment melted Reenu's heart.

"Guys, can we take my picture here?"

So the others agreed. Amaru tried her hand at picture-taking while Moshe took in Reenu's joy. It ended up being a little off-center, but not bad for someone's first time.

"One day we'll share a place just like it, huh?" Reenu asked with an air of fact.

"That's the dream," Moshe answered with a smile.

"Well, just as long as we can have a mat that's not so...silly," Amaru pulled her punch a bit when she saw Reenu's eyes widen at the start of her request.

"I like it a lot," Reenu said, intending no room for argument.

"We'll get something that's fitting for all three of us. Fair enough?" Amaru insisted anyway.

"Fair enough." Reenu would get his way eventually (as he often did), but he let Amaru stick to her typical contrarian manner without putting up any further of a fight.

Moshe was just glad that Amaru was speaking as if one of these houses *would* be a home for them soon enough.

The sun started lengthening the shadows of the Ecclesian hopefuls, but neither Moshe nor Amaru had found the right place for them to take their pictures. Moshe initially wanted to take his at that impressive amphitheatre he saw from the hill, but The Kolosaio was closed for the day. Moshe was mostly just curious if the arena was used for entertainment or if it had a more militant function. One could tell a lot about a culture by how their resources were managed.

The group's inability to find Moshe's picturesque point on the Ecclesian map was frustrating but not surprising. Reenu and Amaru were well-acquainted with his

minor

perfectionism. That was a relative term in the context of their living conditions, but Moshe always found a way to make each clothing rag and every lamb's leg reach their utmost potential in effective use for the group. He wasn't ashamed of his perfectionism either: it was created from the need to be that way, and he didn't feel any need to be any different. He was willing to take on the conflict his obsessivism generated with Amaru - she thought it made him come across colder than he intended to be. She was certainly feeling that way now.

"Moshe," Amaru said with an obviously pacifying tone. She had noticed his grip on the map tighten as they walked along the main road. His head was buried in it to the point of near negligence for what was in front of them. His frustration intensified as the map suddenly became enveloped in a blanket of darkness, making it harder for him to see what was worth exploring. The same shade caused Amaru to look up and notice where they were at.

"Why not take your picture here?" Amaru asked unassumingly.

Moshe looked up. His grip lessened as he slowly breathed in and let out a long sigh.

"Yes, this is fine."

Truth be told, Moshe was quite content with taking his picture underneath The Tree of Origin. The map told them that it was the first thing Prames and his people had planted in Ecclesia, and the speed at which it grew was the miracle that led to the rest of development going so smoothly. It was the most alluring of enchantments that Ecclesia boasted: the rich green of its endlessly entwined branches gave it a gravitas that matched the ten-foot breadth of its greying trunk. It seemed like the perfect location for people to gather around and reflect or relax, but the bustling smorgasbord of activity the day offered made for an empty, quiet scene here. Deep within himself, Moshe appreciated the tree's currently unattended state and its perennial beauty, but he had to fight being upset that he had his head so far down into his map that he didn't even notice them come across it.

Just as Moshe lifted his camera and tried to frame the shot so that he could properly capture the tree's charm, he saw his companions looking back at him with warmth on their faces. Amaru, who had always chosen to love him despite their differences. Reenu, whose loyalty and love never ceased, even along rocky ground. His heart let go of the acridity it was brewing.

"My dears," Moshe said. "You belong in this picture, too."

Reenu and Amaru didn't have to conjure up smiles for the picture - they were already genuinely doing so. The landscape that the picture afforded was greatly reduced by their inclusion, making it so that The Tree of Origin had a small role to play, but Moshe didn't mind. He knew that this was the best version of his picture that he could get.

The camera clicked.

Contentment.

"It's sundown!"

"YAHHHH!"

Someone in the distance had made that ecstatic indictment of the sun's setting, which was quickly accompanied by the unrelenting roar of thousands. The rush for The Table was on.

Moshe had started to make his way toward the rush when Reenu uttered,

"Wait, but Amaru, you haven't taken your picture yet!"

"I know," Amaru admitted. "It's ok. Maybe I can take it inside."

Amaru hoped that her disappointment didn't show. She *was* actually getting excited for the place she had in mind. This sense of positive expectation was unexpected for her. Perhaps she was beginning to see the potential Ecclesia had to offer.

Still, the masses would not wait. So the three of them went off to join the fray, and eventually, enter The Temple.

The Temple was as voluminous on the inside as it looked from the outside, but even so, the Ecclesian peacekeepers (in his attempt at talking to one of them, Reenu found out that they were called Kohen, but that was about as much information as he was able to get before he was told to "keep moving") were having trouble fitting everyone inside. Fortunately enough, the walls and the pillars were made of a translucent material, so anyone who couldn't be seated inside would be able to at least see what was going on from the outside. But Moshe wanted to make sure that he and his companions would be on the inside.

"Moshe, we don't have to be so pushy. We'll get inside eventually if we're meant to," Reenu whispered into Moshe's ear. He had always been uncomfortable with his own physicality whenever it was used for aggression.

"Reenu, I'm pretty sure that we'll want to be inside for this. The information being shared is something that *we* haven't heard before. According to Duman, most people know it already, they just like coming for the spectacle, the excitement of it all. We don't always have to get our way, but right now, we need to. Right, Katir?"

Moshe looked at Amaru with emphatic inquiry in his eyes; he really needed her affinity right now to reassure Reenu. Navigating the crowds was stressful enough.

But Amaru was struggling to maintain her gentle yet assertive demeanor. Like a static stream passing between piles of rock, slipping between everyone was suffocating. She felt as though everyone's desire to get inside would soon outlive common decency; pushing and panic were only moments away, and then

what do we do if the crowd breaks out into fights

panic would ensue and their "lay-low" strategy would be jeopardized. But she complied.

"Ye-...yeah."

Reenu closed his eyes and took a deep breath. They had assumed their *scraping* formation, with the added element of interlocking arms so as to not get separated. He was glad that *he* didn't have to be the one pushing through everyone, but he still couldn't bear their narrow confines much longer. As he opened his eyes, he felt a hand on his shoulder stop him.

Unnerved, Reenu let go of his hold on Amaru's forearm and stood frozen.

Whoever was behind him probably expected him to turn around, but since he didn't, no motion was made. Instantly aware of the pressure that left her arm, Amaru looked back at Reenu. Her eyes looked at the presence beyond...and then returned to him with reassurance.

"Excuse me," the man in black and white asserted, "I noticed that you three have not been here before. Come with me."

The Kohen sat them down fairly close to The Table, with just a few rows of people in front. The limited space meant that everyone had to sit cross-legged, but no one this close seemed to mind. Front-row seats are always windfall.

Seeing The Table up close, Amaru noted the differences between the real thing and the picture in the tract. Reality presented a much more worn edifice, but that sense of use and overuse was much more comforting and less imposing than the perfection that the picture offered. It was no wonder that everyone around them seemed so cheery. Well, everyone except for the person directly next to them, whom Reenu tried his best to engage.

"Hello there! Peace be with you!" Reenu said with vigor.

The man's jolt betrayed his bulky build. Though, if Reenu had been paying better attention, he would have noticed the man's body language told of someone on edge. Eyes darting back and forth, arms held close to his chest, left hand fingers massaging right hand knuckles, a slight rocking of the torso.

"Oh, I'm sorry to have startled you! It was not my intention. I'm just excited to be here. What about you?"

The man's eyes, initially widened with apprehension, began to retract as he analyzed Reenu and evaluated his harmlessness. Moshe, who was also somewhat surprised by Reenu's exclamation, saw that the man's eyes were

why so little sleep in a place where you don't need one eye open

bloodshot.

"Uh, yes. It's always pleasant being here at these gatherings. I guess. Peace on the other hand..." the man said tersely before he trailed off.

"Oh...so you've been here a number of times then? How long have you been here at Ecclesia?"

"Oh, I don't know...six hundred days or so? Yea, that sounds right," the man said while his eyes returned to their regularly scheduled flickering, as one who hopes to escape a conversation by finding someone else that they could talk to. Moshe noticed this even if Reenu didn't. Still, he found it odd that, even though the man's face looked like he wanted to leave, his body seemed resolute in staying where it was.

"Wow...is that how long it takes?"

"What, uh, what do you mean?"

"Well, to get in? I mean, surely you've been outside The Wall this whole time if you're still coming to these Calls, right?"

"I mean, sure. Sure, I've been outside this whole while. But, well, you know..." the man's nerves were allayed by his confusion.

"No, I don't, actually."

"How can you not? It's different for everybody."

A sharp scream that quickly became a fading whine turned everyone's heads to the northern side of The Temple. Moshe nearly readied himself into fighting stance, but he cooled off once he saw that it was only Duman. He had approached a sturdy-looking wooden structure that came up to his chest; upon it was a metallic device that seemed to be where the sound emanated from, as it amplified Duman's voice,

really gives him a boost of authority

filling up the entirety of The Temple instantly.

"Hello everyone! Peace be with you all!"

Duman's excitement was much more harmful than Reenu's - it caused the one-two punch of the scream-and-whine to come back harshly. Duman quickly stepped back and returned with a reserved tone.

"Welcome to our 70th edition of The Call. As is customary for this event, dinner is ready and shall be served immediately. After that, we'll hear our usual Epainos Report from Zacchaeus, followed by a wonderful teaching from our beloved Leader, as well as a brief Q&A. But for now, enjoy your *psomi fantastikos!*"

Duman's final phrase garnered some hum from his metallic device, but it was overpowered by the applause of the people who were looking forward to the immediacy of their dinner. A couple dozen Kohen (though Amaru saw that these Kohen were all women) were making their way through everyone with silver dishes. They handed out the plates silently with beaming faces, responding to neither gratitude nor greed. Upon arriving at Moshe and crew, Reenu gave the one who served him his biggest

"Thank you so much! Peace be with you!"

but her countenance remained unaltered.

Figuring out what was entering their bodies had always been a matter of life and death, and so, Moshe evaluated his plate with expert discernment. Atop the plate sat a golden-brown half-globe that was warm to the touch and smelled like comfort. Moshe pulled it apart and saw that its insides were starkly white and fluffy. When he lifted it up, he also noticed that its undersides were glazed in an invitingly dark red that tasted sweet

and clean and beckoning and she wants me to fol-

Moshe shook his head. His heart was beating faster. He had to stop thinking about *her,* so he turned his attention to Reenu and the bulky man, who had resumed their one-sided exchange.

"-sure, it's pleasant bread and all, but it pales in comparison to what *they* are eating."

The bulky man motioned to the citizens seated at The Table.

They were far away enough that their conversations could not be understood, but what was clear were the emotions that adorned their faces. Contentment. Peace. Kinship. Identity. It was all there, all easily divined by the cross-legged masses surrounding them. Every single one of them looked as if they had forgotten any semblance of past misery and replaced it with joy everlasting. The Table was full of greens, reds, yellows - foods with flavors that Moshe and his companions could not ascertain. Upon turning her eyes from her plate to The Table, Amaru's *psomi fantastikos* felt sour and heavy in her mouth. She returned her gaze to her plate in hopes that the sweet taste would return.

"Well, one day, we'll get to taste what they're having too," Reenu said with unbroken optimism.

The bulky man was astonished by Reenu's sentiment.

"How long have you been here?"

"We actually arrived just yesterday."

"Ah. Makes sense."

⸺⸺⸺⸺⸺⸺⸺⸺⸺⸺⸺

Dinner was ending, but Reenu and the bulky man weren't prepared to stop their conversation. Reenu had gotten him to open up a bit more about his experience in Ecclesia, and, from what Moshe could tell, the man might have even been warming up to Reenu's extroversion.

"Now do you understand why so many people," the bulky man said with abandon before succumbing to a whisper, "don't like The Call?"

"I guess," Reenu half-relented, "but so what if the information is repetitive? It can't be any more repetitive than what living out *there* is like if it only happens every hundred days."

"Sure, people do *need* repetition in some ways, but there comes a point where they don't *want* it anymore. You can only hear the same old things so many times before they start hitting your ears without actually getting inside." As the bulky man laid this last bit of reasoning out before Reenu, he began to feel a tinge of guilt as he saw Reenu's eyes lose some of their fire. Of course, that tinge didn't compare to the tidal wave he was feeling already, so shaking it off wasn't an issue.

Ironically, the bulky man's final statement caught Amaru's attention. She had been lost in her habitual analysis of this new location, so when she finally looked at the bulky man, she realized that something about him seemed familiar.

"Excuse me, what did you say your name was?" Amaru asked as if she had been part of the dialogue all along.

The bulky man looked at her with guarded suspicion.

"I actually didn't," he said indifferently.

"Reenu, he hasn't told you his name yet?" Amaru impatiently asked.

"Well, no, I guess not. And I hadn't told him mine yet...but now he knows," Reenu admitted, looking at Amaru with widening eyes.

fuck

The bulky man folded his arms and leaned back.

"Well, shit," the man uttered with surprising brazenness. "Reenu's the name, is it? If she's with you...she must be good people as well."

Moshe instinctively leaned into the three-way talk as means of showing that he too was part of the group. An assertive member, at that. The bulky man looked at him intently, but then he relaxed into a knowledgeable grin.

"Sir." Reenu's worry wasn't settled by the man's openness. "Aren't we not allowed to say words like that?"

"Not sir. My name's Matthias. You three should probably leave."

"Hello again, everyone!"

Duman's face was gleaming more than ever as he re-greeted the masses.

"Good news! I figured out how to stop that awful noise that happens whenever I come up to speak. Always making progress here in Ecclesia, am I right?!"

A few people clapped. More hollered out of long-awaited relief.

"How was dinner?!"

A lot more claps this time.

"Oh, perfect! I heard that the *psomi fantastikos* was even better than usual! Of course, the *ecclesia eidikos* that those at The Table eat is always exquisite, but that's as expected."

Some uncomfortable shifting in the crowds.

"So, ahem," Duman reluctantly began with a familiarly sickening stomach, "I wanted to address what everyone was worried about first and foremost. Unfortunately, yes, after last *ekatomeres'* record-breaking efforts...there are only about seventy spots left here at The Table."

Moshe was surprised he didn't hear a single groan from the thousands of people there, but the air was certainly tense. Perhaps it was because that truth was obvious - a mere glance at the community of The Table and the glaring emptiness of that final section of seats was undeniable.

"And yes, we do still take in people almost every week. That may seem counterproductive when there's so few spots left, but that also speaks of the beauty and power of Ecclesia's message. We are the only beacon of hope in this wasteland of a world, and as long as there is space and time, you *all* have a chance to be welcomed in. Verily?"

"Verily!" the masses recited in lively response.

Their forcefulness strengthened Duman's spirit.

"The hardships of your past can be undone! Verily?"

"Verily!"

"Life can be as it was always meant to be: full of light and harmony! Verily?"

"Verily!"

"And you can live free of the chains that *survival* casts upon you, free in the promise of *thriving* before you! Verily?!"

"Verily!!"

With each declaration of the crowd, Moshe attempted to show more enthusiasm in his cries. Amaru did the same, though she felt that the hive mind responses were absolutely ludicrous, even if effective. Out of the corner of his eye, Reenu noticed that Matthias stayed silent. His abstinence was unnerving - it got into Reenu's head, crowding his mental space with his final words:

you three should probably leave

After Duman continued in his grandiloquence for a couple more minutes, he introduced a man who carried with him even greater pomposity. He stood tall as he walked on-stage from the shadows, his strangely hourglass frame accentuated by his outfit of black and his considerable shoulder pads. As peculiar as his appearance was, Moshe couldn't deny that his very existence exuded dominance.

"Thank you, Duman, for that wonderfully elongated introduction," the hourglass man said coldly. "And yes, everyone, - eh, peace and such - let's congratulate Duman for adequately opening tonight's events!" The hourglass man said with unexpected animation.

Strong applause. Duman had done his job well, and he was being properly praised for it. Sheepishly, Duman stood up from the seat he just found and gave the crowds a hearty smile and wave.

"For those of you who don't know, Duman has been training under me recently in order to help lighten my load as my duties...expand. Though, if you didn't know that, you probably don't know who I am either," the hourglass man paused in calculated forethought.

A smattering of laughter. As expected.

"Let me introduce myself. I am Shedim, General Speaker for Ecclesian Events and Head Stomio for Leader. As you can imagine, Leader's routine is packed with balancing care for both sides of The Wall, and so, it is *my* responsibility to sift through the most important obligations for him and speak on his behalf when necessary."

Amaru was curious as to how much "Leader" actually had to handle when the balance of care seemed so

top-heavy

but she kept her thoughts at bay.

"This being The Call," Shedim continued, "you will all be graced with Leader's presence and expertise-"

Claps and hollers here and there.

"-very shortly. That makes my job easy today, but let me first remind you of the few, simple rules of this assembly: firstly, do *not* interrupt Leader as he is speaking. His wisdom far surpasses any of ours, so to interrupt would not only be unthinkably disrespectful, but you would also be doing *everyone* a disservice. Admittedly, you've all been wise enough to never do this before..." Shedim paused again.

Less laughs this time.

Reenu's eyes locked with Matthias' before the latter quickly looked away.

probably leave

"Additionally," Shedim carried on, "if any of you plan to leave, that's completely fine. You'd be missing out, but that's on you. Just be sure not to be a distraction as you go. A Kohen will escort you and whatever belongings you have on your way out. Finally, please keep in mind that during the Q&A, because there are so many of you and so little time, we only allow one question per inquisitor. So do pick the most important one you have. Now please, join with me as we sing 'Ecclesia: Our Only Hope.'"

Everyone promptly stood and looked directly above them. As far as Moshe could tell, there was nothing to look at above them, but he joined in. It seemed like a symbolic action that they all took seriously.

"Grace for the other
Strangers and brothers
A seat at The Table means
Warmth and community..."

The song went on. By the next runaround of the verse, Moshe, Amaru, and Reenu were able and willing to sing along. The melody was pleasant in its simplicity, and it reminded them of the few light moments of fireside songs that they had shared when they could. Singing really did foster community. Even if this tune's redundant nature sucked out the enjoyment somewhat. Reenu saw that Matthias himself was mouthing the words, though he held them with a sense of retrospection.

"You may all be seated," Shedim said as the song concluded. "Now, our wonderfully shrewd Lieutenant Zacchaeus will come up and give a brief Epainos Report. Lieutenant..."

Everyone sat a little straighter as the Lieutenant made his way on stage. Moshe felt a sense of appropriate regard sweep across The Temple. Clearly, this man had earned the regard that he now commanded. Though, curiosity dominated his mind:

why the need for a military

Lieutenant Zacchaeus stepped up to the podium. Reenu frowned, noticing that the limp that hindered the man's left leg made for an encumbered trek.

"Hello, hopefuls of Ecclesia. Peace be with you all," Lieutenant Zacchaeus stated. "Thank you all for taking the time to be here today. All of us in the *Symvoul* love to see turnouts like these. It helps us know that we're truly...making a difference. Anyway, I'll keep this brief. As has been the case for the past one thousand eight hundred and twenty-five days, I'm happy to report that there is *still* no need for any active military operations."

Cheers.

"That being said, we've been as diligent as ever in keeping our groundsmen strong. Training is crucial to being prepared for any kind of oppressive efforts. Our scouts tell us there are no signs of any violent masses outside our walls, so there's no need to worry, but you never know when the enemy might attack."

Some nods and just as many affirming groans.

"For now, you can all continue to rest easy and simply focus on your means for salvation..." Zaccheaus looked down and hesitated. Amaru thought she saw a bit of remorse in his eyes, but it quickly dissipated into martial determination.

"Now, without further ado, please stand-"

Immediate, ubiquitous response.

"-as we welcome the gracious Head of Ecclesia - the man who governs over all with wisdom and competence - please welcome: Leader Saios!"

The roar that deafened The Temple could be heard for miles outside of Ecclesia. If this isolated society *did* have any enemies nearby, they would have been either sprung into action by the sound of vulnerably joyful people or terrified by the sheer magnitude. As such, even from the back of The Temple, Arah's eardrums were in considerable pain. He was already annoyed by the fact that he ended up way in the back (he had been sidetracked by the request of a Kohen who had noticed his obviously strong build and needed help with carrying loads of dishes; by the time he finished, the crowds had settled in and kept him out), and the excessive decibel level only made his mood worsen. If it wasn't for the excitement of Saios' imminence, he would have considered leaving. Now, there was not a chance.

If Zacchaeus commanded regard, Saios commanded *reverence*. He was taller from his shoulders and upward than anyone Moshe had ever seen. His face was chiseled and without blemish; Amaru could not understand how not even a trace of life's weathering left its mark anywhere on his head. Even the dirty blonde curls that crowned him were perfect in their careless mess. He didn't need the shoulder pads that Shedim boasted, for his upper body build looked as if his muscles hadn't stopped tearing themselves apart since his adolescence. Arah would have felt jealousy if he didn't feel awe. Sensibly, Saios' robes looked better taken care of than anyone else's; the brilliant white laced with stripes of purple and gold was either meticulously cleaned or made new each time he wore them. Yet in all of his undeniable gravity, most anyone who saw him would say that it was his unshakable smile that inescapably made its way into the hearts of all. It was not plastered or overly animated like Duman's, it was not always attached to his visage in obvious denial of reality, it was simply *real*. And it invited others to do the same. Moshe, Reenu, Amaru, *everyone* there was amazed. If leadership qualifications were based on physical presentation alone, there could be no one else that better fit the role.

But then he spoke.

"Peace be with you," his voice effervescently, effortlessly boomed.

"And also with you." Everyone had been holding their breath in subconscious expectancy, and so, a collective sigh of relief quietly accompanied the unified sinking of chests.

"When I was growing up, I was a much different person. You all know that my grandfather was Savyer, and his reign has been considered The Golden Age of Ecclesia. Truthfully, it was. He maintained the perfect balance of inclusion and boundaries, of love and justice. He created this beautiful Table and implemented policies that made it the holy symbol that it is."

Saios looked longingly at The Table. Everyone followed suit.

"He was a remarkable man. Unprecedented in his impact. His is a model that I've done my best to emulate. But it was not always that way."

Saios' face hardened, mingled in memory.

"'Even good seed can lead to bad weeds.' He told me that once. You might think that having Savyer as my grandfather would make me good by...moral proximity alone. But that was not the case. In fact, if anything, my grandfather's positive influence had the opposite effect on me. Call it being unintentionally spoiled, call it not having experience of the outside world...I make no excuses. I was rebellious."

People gasped. Moshe wondered if this was new information. Regardless, he was as captivated as everyone else.

"There was something about his...impeccable integrity...that I wanted to puncture. I wanted to see where the holes were, where could I poke that would make him tick. I'd pick fights with other Ecclesians. Any time I heard him moralizing to someone else, I'd loudly interrupt with my own rebuttals. I don't know how many people I led astray by doing that. I even-"

Saios' thought caught in his throat. As his eyes began to moisten, not even the proverbial pin drop made a sound. He sighed, regaining his composure.

"Perhaps my greatest offense towards him...involved The Table itself. When my grandfather first started building it, he knew exactly what type of wood he wanted to build it with. The name doesn't matter anymore, but it was located a couple days east of here. He told us that not only was it the strongest wood he knew of, but its location was a sort of oasis for him. He told us that when *he* was young, he was sent there by his father to meditate after being particularly troubled by the nature of Ecclesia's exclusivity. It was at this place that he first thought of creating something like The Table, so in a way, returning was a bit of a home-coming for him. He'd finally seal the promise of hope that he made to himself."

Moshe knew where this story was
the promise would be broken
going.

"He took a dozen of our most capable men with him. Though my body was still juvenile, Savyer wanted me to go with them as well. I suppose he thought that this place of peace would change me somehow. Eventually, he would be right, but I went with evil intentions. It was dusk of the second day when we arrived at the site, so my grandfather decided to let everyone rest for the night before we got to work. The place was so peaceful that even the all-wise Savyer let his guard down. No one was watching the grounds as the moon rose to its peak. And so...do you know what I did?..."

Saios had reduced his voice to a mere whisper. Whether or not the question was rhetorical, Saios' conversational delivery made it seem like he was talking privately to each and every person there, which is why some people responded with an impulsive

"what?"

No one expected anger to flood their Leader's eyes as he shouted:

"I burned it all down! The beauty, the trees! All of it! My work of destruction undid my grandfather's work of hope *instantly*! And I didn't even care. I truly...didn't...care."

The ferocity with which Saios roared these confessions sent chills up Reenu's spine. His heart was also touched - it was hard not to feel for someone recalling such crushing guilt. Saios returned to a more self-reflective tone.

"The next morning...I was awakened by sharp cries. Everyone was mourning. I wasn't surprised, but the weight of what I had done was starting to find me. I went outside from my tent and saw Savyer. He was looking at the barren field before him. His hands were clenched. I expected him to be fuming. I *wanted* him to be fuming. But he turned and he saw me...and he opened his hands. In his palms were a couple of seeds, the burnt soil from where he picked them up still half-covering them. With affection in his voice, he said, 'Even good seed can lead to bad weeds...but those weeds can still be redeemed.' I knew exactly what he meant. *I* was the weed corrupting my grandfather's plans, and he knew it. He knew it but that didn't matter. He still wanted what was best for me. He wanted me to come back to the right path. My heart broke. I collapsed into his arms, and from that moment on, I vowed to follow in his footsteps."

Cheers rang out. This was the kind of story everyone was looking for. The story that Moshe, Amaru, and Reenu *needed*. They had joined in with the clapping just as emphatically.

"*That* is why we should *all* follow after him! Give thanks to Savyer!"

"Thanks be to Savyer!"

Everyone was on their feet at this point.

A neighboring follower could not keep his excitement to himself. He looked at Matthias in unadulterated joy and said,

"What a wonderful history our Leader has!"

"Oh, yes, definitely! The story..."

A strawberry blonde woman passed by Matthias amidst the buzz of the ovation. She placed a small device in his hands and told him

"ten minutes."

Matthias' eyes widened

already?

as he finished his sentence

"...never gets old."

"I know that some of you may question the way we operate," Saios said, his eyes full of compassion. "It is understandable, but do realize that *everything* we do has a reason. Even if it is a symbolic one. And what it all comes down to...is salvation. That's why you are all here, right?"

"Right!"

Reenu, having forgotten about the unease of Matthias' presence, was all ears. Now was the time when they would finally learn how to be Ecclesians.

"You all want a seat at The Table, and I want you *all* to be here with the rest of us."

Saios' eyes fell.

"But the way is narrow, and space is limited. Know that. Know that even as I explain salvation here and now, it is with both delight and anguish: delight that some of you will take the opportunity, and anguish that not everyone will."

Amaru's eyebrow raised. She assumed that Saios would be quite particular about the words he uses, but that sentiment was questionable. Was salvation a matter of choice or capacity? Why wouldn't everyone want it? She eagerly awaited the Q&A.

"You see, after my fiery conversion experience with my grandfather, I made it my life's work to imitate him. And like I said, we should all imitate him. But in my zeal, I took it a step further. Space at The Table was filling up quickly, and Savyer was feeling the stress of maintaining our ever-growing community. Recognizing that Savyer's way was the best way to live, *I* was the one who suggested to him that we place a limit on who we let in."

Small gasps in the crowd.

"Of course, being the excellent mind that he was, he knew a limit was necessary, he just didn't see how he could make such qualifications. Choosing who was in and who was out was not my grandfather's forte. So, at a meeting with his *Symvoul*, I proposed that *his life* be the model by which salvation occurs. Admittedly, he was uncomfortable with the idea at first, but everyone else in the council felt so passionately in favor of it that he relented. And so, I interviewed the man day and night, spending every free moment I had with him so I could truly understand what made him tick. Ironic that in all my previous antagonistic attempts at figuring out what his weaknesses were, it was in those moments of genuine discovery that I began to see him and his vulnerabilities. Those days were when I fell in love with him."

Saios had to stop himself from getting choked up again.

More sporadic cheers.

"What I came up with in all my research of Savyer and his character was something now known as The Trial."

Moshe involuntarily winced. After the struggle of their desert lives, he was not eager to engage in another trial of any sort. Though he had already assumed that salvation would not come easy.

"You see, Savyer was very rigid when it came to his citizens pledging allegiance to Ecclesia. He believed that salvation could be given to those who simply believed in what he offered. And I whole-heartedly agree with that! But true belief is born out of testing. And that's what The Trial is. Just as my grandfather was tested in his journey of remodeling Ecclesia, so too must you be tested. For forty days, your allegiance will be proven in several ways. Firstly, you must read The Manual twice a day, morning and evening. It contains wisdom, stories, and rules for how Ecclesian life functions, making it imperative to know in order to be properly Ecclesian. Secondly, you must pick up two pieces of refuse and dispose of them adequately before each meal. How you treat the land outside The Wall is indicative of how will you treat the land within. Thirdly, you must talk with others in your community at least twice a week about the things you have learned in The Manual. Neighborliness and sharing are two of the essentials of Ecclesian life."

Moshe was intrigued by these eligibilities. He had never been in a situation where the *kind* of person you are outweighs what you can do. That shifting of values would be difficult, but he believed in its potential.

"And finally, as you progress throughout The Trial, you will all be individually tested in ways that are unique to you. Ecclesians celebrate the diversity of life while recognizing that each person has their own inner struggles pre-salvation. Those will be tested for the sake of determining integrity."

Moshe, Amaru, and Reenu each felt cold at that last qualification.

what will mine be

"Each of you will be given a *senton* to track your progress on. At the beginning of each day, bring your paper to the Kohen Office right next to the entrance at The Wall. A Kohen will mark your *senton* if you were truly successful, and discard of it if you were not. Do not fear, though, for that is not your only chance. You will receive a new *senton* so that you may try again. Chances are unlimited until space is full, so I encourage you all to do your best as you get shaped into a rightful Ecclesian by the pure objectivity of The Trial. I hope the best for you all."

Saios took a step back and bowed. Everyone stood up and cheered. He felt a little silly making the gesture, but he knew that the crowd loved to see him do so. It was also just a humble way to show that his message was over.

"Please, please be seated. Now, does anyone have any questions?"

For quite some time, not one hand rose.

Silence lasted for a few moments longer. That inelegant stillness was born out of sheepishness and fear. No one wanted to be the first to ask, the first to admit if there were any holes that needed to be filled. Would that be a mark on Saios' clarity or on the asker's

does everyone else get it except for me

intelligence? These were the variables swimming through a number (the majority, even) of attendees' minds. Yet as awkward as it was to be the first to ask, a handful of people also realized that allowing the silence to persist was perhaps even more awkward. A short-haired young woman proved her bravery by standing up and asking:

"So, if we're supposed to bring the, uh, *senton* to the Kohen Office every day for it to get approved, how are *they* going to know we did what we're supposed to?"

"Ah, yes," Saios seemed pleased by the thoughtfulness of the question. "A good insight, miss...?"

"Diora, sir."

"Ms. Diora. Pleasant name, by the way."

Despite all eyes turning towards her when she started speaking, Diora didn't feel the blushing heat of embarrassment until then.

"Well, Diora, I can say that we initially did rely on a code of honesty. Savyer assumed that everyone who wanted to be Ecclesian would be truthful in their record-keeping since that *is* the norm in Ecclesia. But after being...well, burned on a few different occasions, we've increased the roles that Kohen play in monitoring events that happen outside The Wall. If someone is lying about the faultlessness of their *senton*, there is always a Kohen who can verify that."

Moshe sensed forming tension amongst the people. He understood why they'd dislike tighter security, but if that meant a safer community, it seemed worthwhile to him. Saios must have also felt the tension, for he said,

"Security *has* tightened over the years, but it's truly for the greater good. And to make sure the people who truly deserve Ecclesia will have it in its perfect state."

Diora nodded, not without some discontent.

"Thank you, Leader Saios," she said as she sat back down.

Saios smiled and nodded back to her. "Peace be with you."

"And also with you," everyone replied.

Relieved of the pressure of inauguration, a boy who could not have been older than eight

wow, I haven't seen anyone that young since I was his age
immediately stood up.

"Hi Leader Saios, I'm Paidi. Um, I have a question for you." The kid was certainly shy, but the sight of him made the entire assembly feel a bit warmer.

"Sure thing, little Paidi. And everyone, isn't it great to see youth like him willing to speak their minds?" Saios motioned toward Paidi with wide-open arms.

The crowd strongly cheered, with many people waving at Paidi. It didn't make him feel any less self-conscious, but he went through with his question anyway.

"Um, I've always tried to be a good boy for my parents. I know that makes them happy. And I know that would make you happy, and that would mean that I could maybe sit at The Table when I'm older someday. But, also, I don't know if that's true."

Saios looked at Paidi intently. No one was sure where this was going.

"I always thought that if I'd be good enough, then my parents would always be happy. And if everyone was good enough, then maybe that means everyone could be happy. So, Leader Saios...how come so many people aren't happy? How come even when I'm good, bad things still happen?"

The boy's lip began to tremble as he struggled to get out his thoughts. He had clearly pondered this question heavily. Moshe believed it was a question that everyone there had probably considered throughout their lives. He knew that he had. He still did, in fact. It had yet to be met with a satisfactory answer.

"Oh, little Paidi. You have a sweet soul. May you be joyous and followed by fortune for all your days."

Saios said this with his arms raised above his head, as if he were conjuring something beyond them. Amaru could tell from the looks she saw that this expression was something important. She didn't fully understand it, but something about it felt...sacred. Regardless, she could admit that it was a nice gesture, even if it didn't mean anything.

"It pains me to know that you haven't always been happy. A good boy like yourself deserves to be. But the fact of the matter is this: no one is ever always happy. Bad things have happened to everyone, you are right. I'm happy to say that the Ecclesian lifestyle has remedied those severely human ailments in ways that you will understand the day you come sit with me at The Table. But until then, know this: the pains of life are what make us stronger. All of you sitting here today are here only because you have overcome adversity. That is what has taken you this far, and that character that you all possess is what will carry you all the way to the end!"

Everyone cheered. What Saios said was true, and they all believed it in their hearts.

Paidi was happy that everyone else was happy, and so, he began to sit down. As he got on one knee, his eyes lit up in remembrance, and so he got back up and asked,

"Oh, but what about the people who don't make it to the end? The people who never get to Ecclesia, even if they're super good?"

Silence returned. Moshe hadn't considered that logic in the moment, but it made perfect sense to ask.

Saios himself was taken aback by the inquiry.

"...mmm..."

Shedim hurried quickly to the stage. Saios saw him coming and stepped slightly to the side as he approached the podium.

"Little boy, I'm sure you remember the rules, but let me remind you of them: we only have time for one question per person. Thank you, but your time is up. Next question."

Shedim half-bowed towards Saios and hurried back to where he sat.

Paidi's self-consciousness returned. He sat down as quick as he could and wondered why he even had such a thought in the first place.

Saios returned to face the crowd. He looked down in pensive thought for a moment. Then,

"Paidi, do not feel bad for asking your question. Even if it was against the rules, I appreciate the sincerity of your heart. Just be more careful from now on. And I'll just say this...people will do what people will do. It's not up to you to save everyone. Just do what's right and...it'll be ok."

A small smile slowly formed on Paidi's face.

"Now," Saios' tone of authority and accessibility returned, "does anyone else have a question?"

"Yeah."

Everyone turned to look for the audible source of self-assurance. A few rows in front of Saios, a strawberry blonde woman stood up.

"What the *fuck* is going on with *KAMNOS*?"

Gasps!
did she really just say that
how dare she say such filth in the presence of children
hoo boy, is she in for it now
who even is this chick

The strawberry blonde's (whose lesser hair color was falling out even in between her two statements) demeanor was unfaltering in spite of the myriad of horrified faces that surrounded her. Aside from the pervasive inhales, no one dared voice any of their opinions or concerns over what she said so as to avoid being lumped in to the eventual Kohen wrath that awaited her. Besides, deep down, even without confession...they too wanted to know the answer.

The sole possessor of fury in the room, Shedim, quickly got over his shock and bolted up. Fists and teeth clenched, he steadfastly marched towards the podium, prepared to unleash himself on this disrespectful philistine; before he could, however, he was met with an equally resolute open palm signaling him to stop.

"Shedim," Saios said determinedly, "it's ok."

Dissatisfied, Shedim
if I was speaking, there would be no such...

relented.

"Young lady, what is your name?" Saios asked in earnest.

"A question that is neither useful nor important," she replied as if in recitation. "But that method seems to work well for you: distraction earned by sympathy and supposed interest. I asked *you* a question point blank, and considering that this *is* a Q&A, I don't think I need to ask it twice before I get an answer. No, not just *an* answer - the truth. So let's hear it."

Saios leaned back, inadvertently motioning his lower half forward. To some, it might have come across as conceding. To others, it might have looked as if Saios was looking for the right words to say. The strawberry less-blonde interpreted the body language as another one of his blasé power moves.

"*KAMNOS*," Saios intoned. Some people were even surprised by him mentioning the word.

"People, we need not fear the word itself. The idea behind it, however...yes, this is something I've been meaning to address. Tell me, miss, what have you yourself heard abo-"

"Please, not this bullshit. Just tell us what we need to know," the strawberry lesser-blonde said behind grit teeth.

That one sparked some murmurs. Moshe could sense the discomfort festering.

Saios' eyes narrowed.

"It would be helpful to know what misconceptions you're personally dealing with, but I'll speak plainly if that's what is needed."

Saios cleared his throat as his personage cooled and re-introduced authority.

"I know that there is a rumor circulating amongst some of you outside of The Wall that Ecclesia is operated by this...*KAMNOS*. A great and evil furnace - I can only imagine whoever came up with the idea must harbor some kind of internal evil themselves. The fact of the matter is that it's simply not true," Saios said reassuringly.

A shrill, singular beep rang throughout The Temple. Though confusion spread from Saios to the Kohen to everyone else, the strawberry least-blonde held her indignation.

"*Goddamnit*, how do you explain the burning smells then?"

"hey, you watch your tongue!"

"yeah!"

"there are children here!"

The unrest of the crowd led to outbursts. Most people were fed up with the dialogue time that this woman (and the more she turned around to look at her opposers, the less blonde she became) was privileging for herself. Moshe himself was annoyed, not because he wasn't curious about the burning smells, but because he didn't feel that the woman's approach was conducive to helpful intercourse. Looking to the sides, he noticed that a handful of Kohen were readying themselves to step in. He was thankful knowing that this woman's interference would be nearing its end.

"It is true that Ecclesia runs on the power of several underground furnaces, but we use natural resources *only*," Saios answered calmly. "Stone, wood, we've even been testing different liquids and have found that some of those are conducive to power as well. Nothing involving *people*."

Reenu gulped in horror.

wha- do...do people actually *think that is...*

But judging by the lack of surprise on people's faces, he knew that must have been the rumor. Furnaces powered by...human bodies? *How depraved!*

No one else seemed concerned by the hideous thought. They were too focused on the pestering woman with her incessant presence.

"What about the missing people?"

"just sit down already!"

"think about others!"

"yeah, we've all got questions, too!"

The unrest grew to previously unreached decibel levels.

At this point, Shedim couldn't hold himself back. Risking the ire of Saios, he ran for the podium and proclaimed:

"Ma'am, you're gonna have to sit down now or one of the Kohen will escort you out of here. We all know the rules: only one question per-"

"Oh, fuck off Shedim. We deserve to know! This isn't a trivial concern! This is *actually* life and death, and I'm not risking ignorance on this one!"

As the strawberry woman shook her bouncy curls in defense, Amaru began to notice something. Aside from taking a liking to her obvious backbone, the blonde had completely faded out and fallen to the floor. The now dark red that shone from her head caused her to remember where she saw the woman before.

"Men!" Shedim yelled out.

Five Kohen closed in on the redhead. As they formed a semi-circle around her, she kicked the nearest one in the groin, grabbing him as he doubled over and tossing him into the two behind him.

Though Shedim maintained his place at the podium, Saios spoke from the side.

"Ma'am, please give this animosity up and step down. This time is meant for everyone to come closer to the truth, and I have only given the truth. If you don't believe me, you can ask anyone else who has a seat at The Table-"

"Yeah, of course everyone *there* is going to back up what you say! You're all on the inside! You all got what you want! None of you are in danger of burning fore-"

The man who sat behind the redhead was the most annoyed by her perturbation. After sitting as patiently as he could for the last few minutes, he decided he had heard enough. He ran his hand through her bouncy red curls and yanked back as hard as he could. With this action, The Temple erupted.

Some cried out in her defense, some in hysterical relief, many were simply confused. There was none more disconcerted than Reenu. The litany of new information, coupled with the cries of the masses and the sudden disorder had proven too much for him. He was frozen. If he had been able to gather himself better, he might have heard the metallic beeping right next to him that increased in intensity and tempo after the redhead was pulled down. Instead, he looked over to his newfound friend in hope of finding understanding. Instead, what he found was a beeping device in Matthias' hands and tears upon his face. That was the last thing he-

BOOM!

With this action, The Temple erupted.

Chapter 5: Wisdom

Roots and darkness.

All Amaru could see when she opened her eyes. Aside from the smarting headache, she felt

there...there was an...ungh...

fine.

Roots and darkness. But the darkness was giving way to amber light.

As she stumbled along, she angled her head upward so she could look down. She was able to see her arms pinned together, wrapped in rope as she was led along. Whatever was covering her eyes prevented her from seeing any more than that, though. Including whether or not her friends were still with her.

Panic suddenly gripped her.

With a glottal

my throat stops like it's been hours

yell, Amaru began to thrash about to the left and the right. Almost immediately, she went down, tripping over the sturdy roots that necessarily directed her steps and made her path unstraight. Her head smacked against one of these roots, intensifying the headache she felt, the source of which she now recognized as coming from a large bump west of her left temple. She also realized that both her hands pulsated with the warmth of inflammation.

"Ow! Oh, fu-"

"Hey, hey, hey!"

Amaru was grateful that the man's rough interjection prevented her from letting loose an unseemly word, but she froze since that voice was entirely unrecognizable.

"Alright, everyone get back up, we're almost there."

Now *there* was a voice that she *could* recognize, but there was a steel to it that masked whatever personality it emanated from. Regardless, her head was swimming to the point where making any more sudden moves would be a painful waste.

Her escape attempt was not *completely* in vain, however. When she fell, a number of people fell with her. She ascertained that the rope around her hands was connected to four or five other people, including one behind her. That became more clear as they all stood up, though it seemed that maybe a couple of those people were still unconscious, as the pull of the rope felt like some were being lifted up instead of standing by themselves.

As she stood up, she was surprised by a swift

smack!

on her rear end. With a grin in his whisper, the man who initially yelled at her when they fell leaned into Amaru's ear and said,

"You *earned* that one, doll."

The force of it felt like more than mere punishment, as if her judge found a degree of pleasure in the prospect. Anger welled up inside Amaru, though she knew she was powerless to respond at the moment. Fortunately, she didn't have to, for she heard a rush of air that was followed by a searing

thwack!

and a cry of pain from her offender.

"Bukshee, *you* know better than that! You *cannot* steep to such base actions. We'll discuss this inordinance once we get back. For now, just keep your hands to yourself. Onward!"

That second voice was becoming clearer to Amaru as the troupe resumed their march through the roots.

Roots and darkness. But the darkness was giving way to amber light. And the light was revealing more and more of the path that they walked.

BOOM!

In an instant, The Temple became a cesspool of fear, excitement, adrenaline, and the purity of mass hysteria. The inciting event itself produced a fair amount of destruction and flames, but the physical damage was reparable and momentary. The same could not be said for what was psychologically incited at Ecclesia's seventieth edition of The Call. Safety became an illusion.

Amaru was tossed from her spot as though she were weightless. Her flight was interrupted twenty feet later by one of The Temple's supporting pillars. Stars flew as she did her best to reorient herself.

Moments before the explosion, Amaru had stood up. She was considering coming to the redhead's aid after the man behind her pulled her down. There was something about the brass way in which she spoke that was inspiring to Amaru, but she hesitated helping since she knew that wouldn't be a good look for her and her friends. A moment later, she was in the air.

Amaru hesitantly reached for her left temple, but the throbbing she felt on contact instantly bred regret within her.

Moshe...Reenu...where are you

A woman wrapped in failing, ratty rags cried out in delirium as she rushed towards Amaru's direction. Amaru didn't have enough of a chance to fine-tune her senses and move out of the way before the woman inadvertently laid her out flat on her back. Now looking up at the dark-skinned woman who clumsily lay atop her, Amaru realized that for all the analyzing she had done so far, she had yet to make any prolonged eye contact with anyone in Ecclesia. The shock of the encounter caused the dark-skinned woman to still her screaming and look back into Amaru's eyes. The change from resting in security to flitting in uncertainty was unceremonious. Amaru almost felt comforted by the exchange, but the woman quickly resumed her grievous scream, pressing her arms against Amaru's chest to give herself leverage to get up. As she took off running amongst the throng, she left most of her remaining rags atop Amaru.

That strange encounter was enough to jolt Amaru into fully returning to herself. She was now acutely aware of the stampede of footsteps that surrounded her, and quickly realized that the pain in her head and the loss of her friends was secondary to the very present danger of potential trampling.

Amaru attempted to get herself up, but each time she placed a hand on the ground, it was greeted with the crushing weight of a wayward foot or pushed away by a swinging leg.

Collapsing, Amaru cried out:

"Help! Can someone hel-"

This time it was a knee to the jaw that stopped her efforts. Dazed and flat on the ground once again, Amaru nearly resigned herself to curling up and hoping for the best, when she suddenly felt herself being lifted up.

"Come on, woman! Let's go!"

Standing up straight, Amaru was able to look squarely into the eyes of her deliverer.

They were the eyes of the redhead's offender.

As simultaneously swollen and constrained as her hands were, Amaru felt the slightest tinge of gratefulness for her nerves as their caravan of ignorants continued on amongst the roots. She knew that, for her, nerves were often the precursor to sweaty hands.

She was also comforted by the near confirmation that both Moshe and Reenu were with her. Years of *scraping* made it so that she could easily recognize the footsteps of her friends. She couldn't tell if they were fully conscious, but she assumed they were not. They would have responded to her danger whistle if they were: a low-high-low melody that was both recognizable and inconspicuous to the untrained ear. Either way, it made sense that both of them would be keeping quiet. She'd do the same for now, but if the opportunity came, she hoped she'd be able to do what she had to.

Suddenly they halted.

Someone up front was walking towards them.

The sound of unraveling melted into a soft plump on the ground.

A couple more footsteps and the sounds repeated.

Amaru steadied her breath and clasped her hands together.

Now she saw a pair of feet in front of her.

As they prepared to relieve her of her binds, she slipped right out of them.

Immediately, Amaru was grabbed from behind, both arms wrenched upwards and behind her.

"Maybe we should put the rope back on this one," came the increasingly grating gravel of Bukshee's voice. Amaru noted that he was the one right in front of her.

"Bukshee, relax. That won't be necessary. Isn't that right, Moshe?"

"She'll cooperate. Right, Katir?" Moshe said with striking calm in his voice.

Amaru recognized that her breathing had picked up since she was pinned. Slowing down, she said,

"Yes. I was just showing you that I could have gotten out of those binds this whole time if I wanted to."

The strain on her arms increased.

"Oh sir, it's really ok," Reenu hastily insisted. "I think she'd be more...responsive if you let the sack off her head, too."

Silence.

"Really sir, now that we're here, why not-"

"Alright, alright. Babu, release her."

Relief accompanied the flood of rushing blood in Amaru's arms as she was let go. Free to make any motion she desired, Amaru took the sack off herself.

In addition to her companions, a smaller man with a clear snivel on his face stood with crossed arms. Next to him was a taller, stockier oaf who looked at her with inquisitiveness. They both wore the recognizably binary cloth of the Kohen, though neither the outfits nor their wearers carried the dignity that others in the position seemed to have. Amaru looked to the left of them and smiled at Moshe, but it quickly became a frown as she noticed Reenu and his injured body. She didn't know the extent of their situation, but she was still comforted by their presence. Being with them was always better than being without. They both smiled in return, but they braced themselves with a grimness that she didn't expect.

"So, defend yourselves. Tell me...why *aren't* you three responsible for the explosion?"

Bukshee and Babu parted, and behind them was the source of that command. Amaru then realized how precarious their situation was.

In front of her stood the wonderfully shrewd Lieutenant Zacchaeus.

"This is your *fucking* fault!"

The man was confused. Why was the woman he was trying to save suddenly being aggressive with him? Also, what was his fault? It didn't really matter - he was now focused on getting out alive, as Amaru had lowered her shoulder into the man's sternum, sending them both out of the path of the throng and onto a nearby pile of rubble.

Amaru pinned the man's arms down, stretching them out above his head. On top of being dazed from getting decked, the man was sur-prised that the wild woman planted on his chest was strong enough to hold both his arms with one of hers. Surprised and terrified.

"Why would you do that?!" The pervasive uproar of panic around them made it so that Amaru *had* to yell in order to be heard. She appre-ciated the opportunity.

"Wha-wh-..." the man stammered.

Amaru lifted his arms up with hers only to slam them down again, tightening her grip.

"You pulled that redhead's hair. This chaos is because of *you!*" Amaru adamantly declared.

"Woman, calm yourself!" The man resisted. "You're being hysterical. I have *nothing* to do with the explosion! I pulled her down because I wanted peace. I wanted things to return to order."

Amaru lessened her grip. The man made sense. He likely wasn't the cause - he seemed pretty harmless. He definitely didn't have much strength. Unless...

Amaru's grip tightened to the point of breaking the man's skin.

"Ow! Goodness! What is your *problem*, woman?" The man was clearly in pain.

"You did what you did to be a distraction. Isn't that right?! The red-head had some valid concerns. She was making a scene and you decided to stop her so that the explosion itself wouldn't be stopped. That's it, huh?!"

Amaru felt the man's blood warm itself onto her fingers. Though her grip didn't lessen, the man wasn't writhing at all. It was as if a sudden realization overpowered the sensory agony he was experiencing.

"Maybe *I'm* not the one who was the distraction..."

Amaru's eyes widened.

Immediately, she got up off the man and started briskly walking away.

From the ground, the man yelled out:

"Excuse me?! Where are you going? I just tried to *save* you and you violently attacked me! I should report you to the Kohen!"

Amaru didn't turn around, scoffing at the
hypocrite
idea.

Getting up and clutching the forearm that was bleeding, the man continued:

"In fact, I think I *will* do that! Woman, what is your name?!"

Amaru stopped. Turning around, and with all sincerity, she curtly told the man:

"Amaru"

and walked off. She was committed to finding her

"well, you better clean up that mouth, Amaru!"

friends, but first she had to address her suspicions. Knowing Moshe and Reenu, they would have been smart enough to go back to their living quarters. Out in the wilderness, they'd always go back to their designated safe place when getting separated like this.

Amaru found herself going against the flow of people trying to escape The Temple. If she was right, the culprits would be doing the same. Of course, that didn't make it any easier. The mass hysteria had not died down. If anything, it only intensified. People were speeding by - more willing to push others in order to get to safety. All of the budging and shoving was starting to annoy her, so rather than giving in and shoving back, she decided to make her way to the nearest pillar and hide behind it for a few seconds.

It was there that she saw what she was currently trying to remember.

Aside from the bitter breeze, the forest felt like a prison. Nature has a way of imposing seclusion, and in the middle of the night, lined up across from men with torches and uniforms, Amaru had a feeling that she and her friends could very well be prisoners soon enough.

Lieutenant Zacchaeus was eyeing each of them up and down. Aside from Bukshee and Babu, there was a line of five stoic Kohen behind him. The ones on the sides held the torches. Were it not for them, they would have been in blinding darkness. Amaru thought that this was an intentional tactic on Zacchaeus' part: the minimal light behind him made it hard for his potential prisoners to discern any of his physical tells while illuminating Amaru and her friends quite well. Whatever path they decided to take, Zacchaeus could tell where they were going.

He stood in front of Reenu first.

A leaf fell from above and haphazardly made its way down to Reenu's right shoulder.

Reenu whimpered, but tried not to move.

Zacchaeus delicately picked the leaf from Reenu's shoulder, oozy blood stringing itself upwards until the leaf was far away enough to break the syrupy connection.

"Babu, get this man some bandages. Wrap up his shoulder and apply the *keftikos* gauze to his side," Zacchaeus said tenderly.

Reenu thanked Zacchaeus with his eyes, but Zacchaeus could tell that Reenu was too scared to do or say much else. That was good.

A few ginger steps to the left and Zacchaeus now stood across from Moshe.

Moshe held his gaze sternly. Moshe himself had a two-pronged scratch that criss-crossed over his right eyebrow, but it wasn't deep enough to bleed. The two of them stood silently for an uncomfortably long time, neither willing to budge. Zacchaeus discerned that this one must be the leader, if they had one. He'd hold on to that assumption until differing evidence presented itself. With a nod, Zacchaeus moved on.

"I'm sorry for Bukshee," Zacchaeus told Amaru. "He and Babu aren't actual Kohen. That kind of behavior wouldn't happen if they were. They're in a volunteer training program that gives 'em the opportunity. Part of their Trials. Though, it's not looking good for Bukshee, if we're being blunt."

Zacchaeus looked back at Bukshee gravely.

Arms crossed and head down, Bukshee stood on his back leg and tapped his foot. Amaru couldn't quite see his face, but the man's body language gave off a mixture of anger and fear. He knew he'd have to start over.

Amaru couldn't hide her surprise. She had been in similar positions of captivity, and never had she experienced any ounce of compassion from her captors. Apologizing was another level.

"I heard stories growing up about the concept of wisdom," Zacchaeus continued. "Wisdom as knowing what the right thing is. Wisdom as knowing *when* to say or do the right thing. Wisdom personified as a woman. I always found that interesting. The men around me were the ones who got things done, the ones who made the decisions, yet they conceded wisdom to her womanly form. Ironic, I thought. Is it because women were hardly listened to when men made their decisions? Or maybe it's because women often made better decisions when given the chance."

Zacchaeus stopped, as if pondering a thought he spoke but didn't create.

"I'm giving you a chance, Ms...?"

"Katir," Amaru said while softening her glance.

"Katir." Zacchaeus stopped again, this time looking intently at

shit, does he not believe me

Amaru.

With a sharp breath in, Zacchaeus resumed, more briskly this time.

"I'm giving *you* a chance, Katir, to tell me what happened. In fact, let me tell you what *I* know, and then you can tell me what actually *is*. Is that alright?"

Zacchaeus came off as entirely interested in Amaru's perspective, though weariness caused his shoulders to sink by the end of his thoughts. Amaru knew the man would not accept any sheepshit at this point. It had been a long night, and his lame leg had done a lot of walking.

"Yes, sir," Amaru committed to the truth. There was nothing to hide, after all.

"I honestly don't care what you call me, but I prefer just Zacchaeus.

Anyway, I know that you three - Reenu, Moshe, Katir - you arrived just a night ago. Quite the time to show up, huh?"

Zacchaeus' eyes looked for answers in Amaru's. She had yet to give him any.

"Normally, we wouldn't suspect hopefuls as new as you to be part of an explosive attack like this. After all, you've just gotten here. How could you even know anything of how we operate? But then again, normally, we don't have explosive attacks like this. So it's, uh, new territory for me, honestly. And when faced with something as foreign as this, wisdom tells me to fall back onto what I know. And this is what I know: there *is* a group that's trying to tear Ecclesia down. I'd tell you their purported name, but..."

An idea struck within Zacchaeus.

"...well, do you know what it is?"

Still, Amaru's eyes held no answers.

"It doesn't matter then," Zacchaeus cautiously relented. "Of course, everyone in Outer Sanctum is trying to get to The Table, so it follows that this group would have a hard time recruiting any hopefuls...unless they got people *truly* on the outside..."

Amaru knew where this was going.

"It just seems mighty convenient that you three show up *just* in time for The Call. *Just* in time for this attack. Now, I'm not saying the responsibility is *completely* on your shoulders; after all, Reenu looks to be bearing more of it than you two - let me know how that *keftikos* works, son. But I'd be willing to abstain from any kind of punishment if you could provide me with some information. If the three of you were co-opted into this coup, I get it - you're in a new place and you've always had to be skeptical and cunning to survive out there. All I'm saying is...giving me some kind of light for my path would go a long way for y'all."

Amaru carefully considered what Zacchaeus was implying, but-

"Sir, with all due respect, just because we're new doesn't mean we're dangerous. We don't know anything about this, and we believe in the promise of Ecclesia. We already *want* to be a part of this community,"

Moshe butt in. Chest held out, he wanted to make it known that intimidation wouldn't work on this trio.

"I'm asking the lady, Moshe," Zacchaeus stared him down.

Moshe took a step back as a sign of acquiescence. He knew his tendency was to defend his friends, but he also hoped that Amaru could handle herself.

"Looking at you three, I'm not sure I have much reason to be suspicious," Zacchaeus admitted. "But you're my best lead right now. Multiple people identified y'all as being front and center of the explosion. Also, there are a couple reports of someone looking like you...Katir...attacking a man shortly after."

Moshe held back, but Reenu's eyes showed surprise.

fuck

Amaru's head hurt as she remembered that exchange. Not the best decision on her part in hindsight.

"Duman also let me know that you've got a *fire* to ya. Something that might lend itself to this particular situation," Zacchaeus cocked his head to the right. He could see it on Katir's face that he was making progress.

*I knew *that bastard was more attentive than he seemed**

Amaru's head was pulsing.

Zacchaeus massaged his left leg. His patience was fleeing with the night.

"Look, if *more* incentive is what you need...I could easily cut you a deal that would make anything these...terrorists are offering like morsels at a feast."

Moshe's right eyebrow raised.

Amaru's curiosity had her brain racing, sending another pulsation from the back of her head to the front. The pain caused Amaru to hold her hand up to her left temple.

And that was when she remembered.

Hand to her head, Amaru steadied herself as she briskly swung around the pillar. In between all the people stampeding their social courtesies away, she realized she had full view of The Table. Completely abandoned, the sight of it wasn't nearly as welcoming and domestic as it appeared a few minutes prior. The dark grey bark seemed almost sickly with no one inhabiting it.

But, as it turned out, it was not completely abandoned.

About a quarter of its length in from where Amaru was standing, two figures stood beside The Table in a fashion similar to when Amaru first saw them, though this exchange was distinguished by its haste.

It was the redhead, and, as Amaru speculated, Reenu's new "friend": Matthias.

Admittedly, Matthias looked to be in pretty bad shape. Amaru picked out that a lot of blood was flowing from his left hand, most of the front of his rags were completely blackened and patched with red, and the front half of his already closely cropped hair was singed to the scalp. Aside from that, Matthias seemed to be leaning against The Table for support while the redhead clasped his hands.

Suddenly, Matthias dropped to the floor.

The redhead then started looking around in alarm. But Matthias seemed to be moving around from where he lay. Or maybe he was wriggling in pain. Amaru couldn't tell. The sea of people obstructed her view.

That was when she realized she had something with her that could aid in focusing her view: the camera.

Pulling it out, Amaru saw that the redhead was indeed peering around with suspicion, though it didn't seem that she was overly concerned with Matthias' well-being. Instead, she came across as more of a lookout, particularly since Matthias looked to be attaching something underneath The Table.

Within the next five seconds, Amaru juggled the type of conflicting thoughts that pause time and extend the present.

who are these people
are they planting another explosive
putting it under the table is risky shit
what do I do
stopping them might be useful for us
would I be stopping something that should be

Sometimes, when faced with a binary decision that requires more information than is presently available, the wise thing to do is to find a middle ground. Amaru did just that - using her one and only shot of the camera on the correspondence that she couldn't keep her eyes from so she could make a well-informed decision when needed.

Unfortunately, at that point, the sea of panicked people had only grown, swarming around the pillar Amaru hid behind, sweeping her up and away from where she was at. This made taking the picture more difficult, and she wasn't sure if she got a clear enough shot to be useful. As the picture developed and its image started to surface, Amaru felt a pull relieve her from the crowd she was entangled in. When she turned to see who it was, the hope that it was one of her friends quickly faded. It was a small, snivelly man with a bloodthirsty glare in his eyes.

"You're coming with me!"

Another blow to the temple, which led to darkness. And then roots.

"A deal? Who do you think we are that we would be interested in that? We only want to be citizens like the rest of you."

Moshe reclaimed the helm of conversation. He saw Amaru holding her hand to her head and realized that the pressure of the situation might be getting to her.

Zacchaeus slowly turned his eyes over to Moshe. He saw that Moshe was going to force himself in to view no matter what, so he figured that he might as well address him for now. Satiate his need to be heard.

"That's exactly what I'd be offering."

Moshe's eyebrow raised again, but he didn't speak. In this duel of wits, holding back was not weakness, it was strategy.

"You could go along with The Trial and do your best," Zacchaeus continued. "But as you might imagine, the success rate of that process isn't exceptional. What Leader Saios *doesn't* underline at The Call is that just as The Trial is different for everybody, so is the *way* to salvation. If you give us something that results in real progress towards solving this mystery, I could make it so that you, Moshe, will be saved. You and your friends."

Reenu shifted from side to side. The bandage on his shoulder was applied tightly, so the motion caused him to wince. But it wasn't as upsetting as the feeling in his stomach.

Moshe still wasn't budging. Let the man speak until he was done.

But Zacchaeus didn't say anymore. He hoped that he could incite any kind of reaction with the information he revealed to them. When none was given, he slowly walked back to the line of Kohen and became enveloped almost completely in the darkness. Moshe couldn't tell exactly, but it seemed like he was digging through some kind of pouch. When he fully returned to the light, he held three *senti* before them.

"As a reward for providing crucial information for the survival of the Ecclesian community, I could personally sign off on each of these *senti* without you having to go through the whole 40-day ordeal. We value security and maintenance above nearly all else, so as much as this may feel like an unfair shortcut, it would most definitely be earned."

Zacchaeus walked in front of all three of them as he made this statement. Finally arriving back at Moshe, he waited in anticipation of an answer.

"That is quite generous of you, sir," Moshe treaded lightly. "Unfortunately, I meant what I said. We *truly* don't know anything about this."

but I do

If Amaru's head had been swimming in pain before, it now felt like it was drowning. The picture she had could be enough to clear them, but she couldn't keep herself from the conflict of her thoughts.

our freedom means the imprisonment of others
perhaps they deserve it
they very well might be threatening
they're clearly dangerous
but are they dangerous to the right people
who are the wrong people

Amaru looked around. Being taken here - in the seclusion of night, heavy trees, and twisted paths - certainly didn't feel right. But this was the Lieutenant himself. If corruption lay with *him*, then she wasn't sure that any of it could be trusted. Amaru kept looking around. Her eyes landed on Bukshee. She hadn't really examined him yet. Her first glances told of someone embittered by punishment, visibly controlling his breath and calming himself down. But now, he seemed eerily still. He looked stoically ahead, and Amaru realized this drastic change must have happened once Zacchaeus gave them their offer.

...when to say or do the right thing...

She made the call.

"You mean *psomi* at a feast."

Zacchaeus looked back at Amaru. He was prepared to interrogate Moshe further, but he was glad that the woman spoke up.

"What was that, Katir?" Zacchaeus asked as he limped back her way.

"You said that this deal would make anything the terrorists offered us like morsels at a feast. You should have said like *psomi* at a feast."

Amaru put her hand back down to her side. She now stood with her chest out, fiercely preserving eye contact with the Lieutenant. From her peripheral, she knew that Moshe had turned towards her and was probably offering a look of warning.

But she knew what she was doing.

"Sure, Katir, like *psomi* at a feast. If I had it my way-" Zacchaeus apologetically started.

"Spare me that, Zacchaeus. If you had it your way, we would have some information for you. We would take the deal, and you would be able to get to doing your job well. But we don't. And we won't accept any shortcuts. We are going to do The Trial just like everyone else because we don't deserve it any more than anyone else does."

The whistle of the wind that coursed through the company had never been more apparent.

The Kohen straightened themselves.

Reenu's stomach felt worse.

No one was more disquieted than Moshe, who had feared that Amaru would pull some kind of brash stunt like this. After a moment's silence, he took a step forward, but Reenu grabbed his hand and held him back. He beckoned Moshe to look at Zacchaeus.

The Lieutenant was allowing a smile to spread across his face.

"The wisdom of a woman," he said before taking a step back and bowing to Amaru. Now no one was more disquieted than Amaru. Zacchaeus came back up, rubbing his leg.

"Every night, my mother would tell me, 'My child, if you will heed my words, the treasure of the world will rest upon your soul: seek wisdom and she will guard you.'"

Looking over at Moshe and Reenu, Zacchaeus' smile persisted, "Boys, you have just been guarded."

The Kohen marched forward in unison until they stood right behind Zacchaeus. Babu and Bukshee followed suit. Zacchaeus handed out the *senti* to his ex-prisoners. They were blank.

"We all want the easy way out. Yet we ignore her when she's staring us right in the face. You two keep listening, and you'll all get there soon enough. I'll have one of my Kohen escort you back to your living quarters. Sorry, but you'll have to put the rope binds and sacks back on. I wish you all the best of luck in completing The Trial. Remember that it is *indeed* a road that you all must travel. Individually. Verily?"

"Verily," Amaru confidently said.

Chapter 6: The Idea

57 DBK

"Well, you can have it like this or you won't have it at all," the server at The Troei said in her typically banal manner.

Reenu winced. He hadn't meant to offend her, but in his experience, she was someone who made offense a regular practice. Reenu found it odd that someone could give off an air of apathy with her dry-as-sand eyes and her lethargic work ethic while also being hurt by the quaintest of suggestions. He had been eating at The Troei for nearly two weeks now, and he found that both menu items *could* be improved if those in charge would accept his advice. *Casu* was a creamy, smelly substance curdled from the sheep of the surrounding forests. Adah and Adinah told Reenu that Zacchaeus had a faction of Kohen go out to the nearby flocks to harvest their natural resources. Judging by the blotchy, blue discoloration and rigid outer casing of the food, Reenu had a feeling that workers at The Troei probably had it sit around for a few days before serving it. Between he, Moshe, and Amaru, Reenu was often the one who handled the culinary side of things. Mostly, that just meant getting creative with sheep. By now he knew how to get the most out of them (merinos were his favorite due to both their tenderness and long wool), and he knew that they could do much better with what they had. Though, he supposed that if the woman who served him nearly every day did not entrust him with even her name, there was not a chance that she would hear his helpful feedback. Still, a good meal does a person well, and for the sake of quality of life, Reenu persisted.

"I'm sorry, ma'am," Reenu respectfully insisted. "I'm not trying to be selfish. It's just that, well, I want what's best for us *all*. Don't you?"

"Eh," the server said with unchanged eyes as she slapped the *casu* onto Reenu's stone platter. "You've got your firstmeal now, so move along."

Reenu looked down at his portion. Today wasn't particularly special or taxing, but for whatever reason, he just couldn't stomach his firstmeal this time around. His plans for the rest of the day were quite simple, and he didn't think he would need the energy that this stomach-threatening sustenance provided. In line next to him was a kid who looked about the same age as the one who spoke

poor kid

at The *Last* Call the other week, a term some dwellers of Outer Sanctum were facetiously using as of late. Reenu wasn't sure if his next action was a necessarily helpful one, but he knew the kid would appreciate it.

"Hey there," Reenu said as he bent down to be eye-to-eye with the kid. "Would you like my firstmeal today?"

The kid's eyes widened as he slowly shook his head up and down. Reenu gave him his platter and began to walk away. The act was part generosity, part urgency. Reenu knew he was not in the right mental place to adequately converse with anyone. He felt weighed down, and when that happened, he didn't want to let anyone in on what he was feeling.

"Listen, sir."

Reenu stopped and turned back around. The server's eyes were different now, slightly more animated.

"This job...it's a part of my Trial. It's not my place to change how things work. I'm just meant to serve to the best of my capacity. I do what I do and no one gets hurt by it. As far as I know. But Leader knows best. He and his *Symvoul* know how to allocate resources. Sorry if I've been rude to you, I don't mean to be. I'm working on it."

Reenu slumped, instantly feeling irritation

still healing

in his right shoulder, though he was grateful for the apology.

"It's ok, ma'am. I'll see you again."

Reenu headed for the usual spot, walking past people he regularly saw in their usual spots.

still understanding

At the usual spot, Moshe and Amaru sat with Adah and Adinah, their self-proclaimed "new best friends."

Amaru had never traveled the week-long journey of strangers to best friends before, and she had a hard time believing the validity of the path that the two young brunettes seemed so sure of. The girls explained (multiple times) that aside from looking similar with their twig-like torsos, pronounced forearms, and freckled faces, they were also magnetized by each other's flowery personality. That much was obvious - Moshe was surprised that the two weren't sisters based on how uncannily they doubled each other, though Adinah was certainly bolder than her near-twin. Both could talk. Amaru had never been a fan of bigmouths, but their first few days at The Troei were unexpectedly insular. It was as if no one wanted to come close to the

so much for camaraderie through circumstance

newcomers.

Was it possible that their encounter with Lieutenant Zacchaeus had propagated throughout Outer Sanctum? Did people suspect them to be culprits of foul play? Or, perhaps even worse, were they considered to be advantageous having met the Lieutenant and been proven clean? Amaru could see how the appearance of leverage would make them less desirable in the company of hard-working, equitable outsiders. For those reasons, as well as their youthful, feminine charm, Amaru appreciated the two girls' company. They were supposed to be talking routinely with others about what they learned from The Manual anyway. But best friends was a stretch. She already had those.

"It seems like an awful harsh punishment, though, doesn't it?" Adah asked, her head turned slightly down with eyes peered up. They quickly scanned back and forth between Moshe and Amaru, who were sitting on the wooden bench across from her, and Adinah, who sat by her side. They always returned to Adinah.

"I mean...cutting it off...I wouldn't ever want to cut off any part of my body, especially not one I use so regularly," Adah reiterated.

"Oh please, Adah," Adinah said as she rolled her eyes. Hers hardly drifted to either Moshe or Amaru. "This is Simadi we're talking about here. Don't be silly. This is *supposed* to be a more metaphorical section of The Manual."

Adinah was confident, but Adah wasn't sure where that assurance came from.

"How do you know that?" Adah asked earnestly.

"Moshe," Adinah turned her eyes to him momentarily. "What's the exact wording?"

Moshe had his Manual open to the exact page. Simadi 9:43. He had had a feeling that this particular passage was going to foster discussion. He began reading, slowly.

"'If your hand causes you to betray your neighbor, cut it off. Better to be without it than to be a bringer of fire.' Verily?"

"Verily," the three girls said in union.

"Come on Adah, don't you see it?" Adinah pleaded. "A *bringer of fire*? What could that literally mean? Betraying your neighbor will, what, instantly create flames? Besides, cutting off a hand really isn't practical...there'd be a lot more lefties around if we all took this command literally."

Adinah's confidence didn't waver, and it started to comfort Adah. Amaru was glad she wasn't the one asking questions for once.

"Yeah, that makes sense, but...why even use that language in the first place?" Adah countered.

"Well, it's poetic," Adinah persevered. "It's beautiful, even. I mean, we all know that betraying each other is wrong, but now we've got some exciting imagery to go along with it," Adinah said, eyes glinting.

"Ugh, I've never understood that about you, dear friend," Adah said with a frown. "Your propensity for the gruesome."

"Hey, it's effective, isn't it? No one wants to be a cripple."

Adinah's three listeners each nodded their heads in agreement.

Adah turned her head to the left, eyes widening as she did.

"You don't suppose that this verse...is why *he* is the way he is?"

Each head followed suit, but to their surprise, it was Reenu who landed in their line of sight. Amaru was confused.

"Adah...are you saying there's something wrong with Reenu? Those scars are from the explosion, you know that." Amaru kept her ire more than skin-deep this time around. For now.

"Oh no, just beyond him. You know..."

They looked again, this time seeing the beggar, sitting alone with an empty platter and his trademark worn stick.

"Well, if you're still trying to be literal, it's his *leg* that's messed up," Adinah wryly suggested.

Moshe didn't like where the conversation was going.

"I don't think we need to talk about that man. It's all speculation, anyway, right?"

Before anyone could respond-

"Hey, guys," Reenu said as he sat down next to Amaru.

"Hey, Reenu."

"Hey."

"How's it hanging?"

"Hi there, friend."

Amaru saw something she didn't see in Reenu's eyes very often. Lack.

"Where's your firstmeal?" she asked.

"Not too hungry." Reenu said, looking off towards the beggar as he spoke.

Moshe turned his eyes back to the beggar as Reenu did so. They both noticed a man with exceptionally long hair and exceptionally distinct muscles talking to

at least someone *is*

the beggar.

"Even if you're not hungry, it's wise to keep eating. You'll heal quicker, you know that." Amaru didn't like pestering Reenu as if he were not her equal, but she would always do her best to take care of him.

"I'll be fine, don't worry," Reenu said flatly.

Amaru doubted that, considering her temple was still the cause of many headaches.

"Oh hush yourself, Katir," Adinah dismissively stated. "Reenu's a big boy."

The wink in her tone went unnoticed by Reenu.

"Uh, anyway," Adah kept moving along. "Have you all heard much about how the reconstruction is going?"

Now Amaru looked away.

"I haven't heard anything since the initial report...other than hearsay," Moshe asserted.

"Right," Adinah agreed. "Well, today's the day, isn't it? They said we'd get an official update every five days, at least."

"I'd not worry about it then," Moshe insisted. "I'm sure Leader and the Kohen have it all under control." He was trying to get back to The Manual, as was their duty to do so.

"Yes, I'm not worried," Adah obliged. "It's just...upsetting to me. To think that some...radicals out there would desecrate Inner Sanctum and The Call in such a-"

"Some people just want to ruin everything for others." Adinah had a way of addressing Adah's concerns before they were completely vocalized. When they met the girls, Moshe thought it was a rude trait of hers, but with time, he saw that it came from Adinah's depth of understanding Adah's fears and desires. He admired that, sometimes even longed for it. It also usually led to a rapid-fire back-and-forth between the two.

"To successfully ruin such a joyous occasion..." Adah started.

"That only comes once every hundred days..." Adinah continued.

"Well, these people aren't only violent..."

"They must also be capable enough to surmount authority..."

"And if they were able to pull that off..."

"What else could they accomplish?"

The group let that thought hang in silence for a moment. Moshe knew that the girls had a propensity for gossip, and this time, their wayward tongues were searching for something distressingly close. Reenu still didn't pay much mind to the discussion at hand, lost in his head, but Amaru wondered if something more mutinous was brewing.

"Listen Adah, Adinah," Amaru said as she straightened her spine. "We didn't have anything to do with it. Ok? We've already been subjected to some pretty intense questioning; we don't need anymore. We get it. We're the newcomers. People are suspicious. But we'd have been found out by now if we really did something wrong. So please, don't go on about this...stuff...anymore."

Adah and Adinah sat back, huddled a little closer to each other. They had not experienced any of Amaru's ardor before. Moshe feared it was devolving into paranoia instead.

"Um," Adah quivered. "We don't know what you're talking about, Katir."

Amaru stopped. She allowed herself to sit back, wiping her hands against her thighs.

"Sorry," Amaru said. "Moshe, just...get us back on track. Can you read the verse again? What was it...Simadi 9:43?"

Moshe nodded.

"'If your hand causes you to betray your neighbor, cut it off. Better to be without it than to be a bringer of fire.'"

No one said anything, pondering the wisdom hidden in the passage's rhythmic integrity.

Then-

"Bringer of fire..." Adah repeated.

"Speaking of fire," Adinah said. "What do you guys think of *KAM-NOS*?"

Amaru sighed, forcefully pushing out air as a sign of derision.

"Alright," Moshe said, standing up. "We're gonna go back home for the day. Reenu, Katir."

Reenu and Amaru both stood up.

Adah and Adinah looked at each other in confusion.

"Girls, we'll see you again tomorrow. Peace be with you."

"And also wi-..."

But the three of them were already on their way.

"Would you like my firstmeal today?"

Being next in line, Arah overheard a short-haired, boyishly handsome young man offering his sustenance to the kid next to him. Of course, Arah himself did not wait in line for the purpose of consuming *casu*. He hardly ate at all these days, but he did stick to his routine of accompanying his obtuse friend Lipos and giving him *his own* firstmeal. Lipos was as simple as he was large, and both were qualities that unnerved Arah to no end. This was not an instance of opposites attracting; Arah saw the value and valor in acquainting himself with those who were unlike him. It taught him understanding and empathy. That's what he read in The Manual, at least.

As they sat down at their usual spot, Lipos immediately transfixed his being onto his double portion. Lipos was one of the few people who didn't mind the limited amount of utensils that The Troei offered - he never used any.

Arah breathed in. There was no need to panic. Lipos was just going about his conventional slurping and chomping. It was what he always did. Arah breathed out. It didn't matter how disgusting it was for Lipos to not notice the *casu* that dripped past his pudgy fingers and sludged its way to a halt on the underside of his forearms, casually joining encrusted *casu* from firstmeals past. It shouldn't matter. Arah closed his eyes and tried to control his breathing.

The mouth noises stopped.

"That was nice, wan't it?"

Arah slowly opened his left eye. Lipos' hungered face was still hovering above his platter, but his light brown eyes shone as they looked up at Arah with thirst. Arah internally cursed himself. He was afraid his unintentional piety was showing.

"I'm not sure. What are you talking about?" Arah asked.

"That young man in line. He gave the boy 'is firstmeal. What a pleasant delight. 'Specially after what 'appened with that kid at The Last Call. What was 'is name again?...It started with a 'p' or somethin'..."

Lipos wandered off in aimless thought. Arah could have ignored Lipos' statement until he moved on to a more interesting subject, but he decided to ignore judgmentalism instead.

"Paidi, I think."

"'Eah, that it. 'ard to believe what 'appened to 'im. Just a boy at–"

"Lipos," Arah interrupted. "Do you mind if I...leave?"

Lipos was confused. Arah had never asked anything like this before.

"Where are you goin'?"

Arah pondered.

"I'm...just going."

But as Arah stood up and turned around, he only went a few paces before coming across another agonizing dweller of Outer Sanctum.

The all-too-familiar beggar sat before him, looking up with his light gray eyes.

Arah looked down at him, a multiplicity of thoughts coursing through his mind. But one prevailed.

"Hello."

<u>FOS 3</u>

¹*There was a group of young travelers who spent their lives careening from place to place. ²When one member of the group grew tired of the place they had established, they would say to the others, "Come, let us leave such and such! A greater adventure lies in the unknown." ³And so it was that this group became settled in their restlessness, unable to call a single corner of the world their home. ⁴It was in them that they must settle it all before they could settle down.*

⁵*One day, the group's restlessness had fully lodged itself beneath their skin. ⁶Sustenance and covering became deficient. Friends in prolonged company with one another became bickerers filled with strife. ⁷Their self-appointed leader was considering the abominable: casting lots to decide which one of them would take the fall and be eaten first. It was a horrid suggestion, but one that the group now found themselves at the debased level of contemplating. ⁸It was that very evening that another way was provided for them in the form of a stranger.*

⁹*They came across a poor, dying old man. The man himself lay sprawled across the sands in front of them. Yet even in his condition, he still possessed more than them. ¹⁰As they circled around the man, the shade that the sphere of their bodies provided caused him to look up at them. Silence was all that passed between them. The group exchanged uneasy glances with each other, unsure of what to do next. But before they could decide, the old man cracked a frail smile. ¹¹Though he had only rags and morsel, he gave freely and willingly all he had to the trav-"*

Moshe closed his Manual and sighed.

His chest was heavy, a feeling he did not

convicted?

often feel.

how many times did I- we pass by other travelers on our way here...and *yet, here is this old man giving to people who need less than even he does...we always did what we did because we had to...it was too risky to subject ourselves to others...not after we'd been burned so many times over...the generosity this book prescribes...it's radical...it's not realistic...but...is it right...**

He did not like the feeling.

maybe that's it...it's idealistic...no one could actually meet such a standard...as romantic as Inner Sanctum is, I wonder if they actually meet them...

Moshe vigorously rubbed above his right eyebrow, causing the residual "X" scab to open up again. He had a bad habit of picking at the places where wounds were. Amaru always got on him for that, complaining that that was what prevented him from healing as quickly as she and Reenu. But he did so now because he was frustrated. On the one hand, digging into The Manual had been more joyous than he expected. It had only been ten days, but he was nearly finished with it already. It was packed with wisdom and philosophy that he had never considered before, and that degree of unexpected education provided his soul something it always struggled for: purpose. Meaning. He now had the necessary tool to truly better himself, the absolution he needed to actually move forward instead of falling back into old cycles of mere survival. On the other hand, learning and doing are two different things.

Moshe put his Manual where he usually lay his head at night. He figured that was enough for now. It was incredible how The Manual always packed so much to think about into so few words. He wondered if that phenomenon was always how it was with reading. Picking up on the Ecclesian characters had been easy enough for him, but that was because he ardently applied himself. He didn't see that same effort from his friends, and he believed that was why they were having a harder time grasping the written word. Worried that this would eventually cause them to fail their Trials, he made it a habit to read aloud to them each morning and evening. This system of delineating the information they needed to know was quite bonding for all three of them, he thought.

A melody: high-low-high.

Moshe smiled.

Amaru and Reenu entered the tent, both smiling to different extents as well.

"How's Diora?" Moshe asked.

"She was quite informative, actually," Amaru answered. "Apparently she became eligible for the Diados Program a few days ago."

"Really? At her age? I would not have assumed she'd be able to yet." Moshe's interest was piqued.

"According to her, it's a little different for everybody," Amaru suggested. "It's not just based on how many times you've failed The Trial; it's also based on - Reenu, put my Manual over there, thanks - it's also based on how much effort you've put in. I guess the Kohen help determine that."

"That makes more sense," Moshe realized. He had come to value Diora's tenacity based on the conversations she had with his friends. He hadn't spoken to her much himself; he limited most of his time to the boundaries of turning pages. He looked at Reenu, noticing his

still?

distance as he plopped two copies of The Manual down in the corner of their tent.

"Yeah," Amaru continued on, "she just had the first meeting with her mentor. She said the man was very kind and great at listening. He didn't pass any judgment on her past failures, and she said she even told him about her unique addiction, whatever that is. She's still not willing to tell us. Anyway, she said he basically just went over what he thought would be a helpful section of The Manual for her - Mati 5, apparently - but with some greater insight into it than she had heard before."

Moshe cocked his right eyebrow.

"Seems like learning from an expert on the subject could be useful. What do you think, Reenu?"

Reenu was laying on his back, clearly elsewhere. Blinking a few times, he responded,

"Oh, yeah. It sounds useful,"

before returning to his prior mental space.

Moshe looked at Amaru, who was already looking at him. Her eyes lay half-closed, not out of tiredness, but out of the tiresome way Reenu had been behaving. Moshe understood. It had been a few days of this. Reenu had moods like this from time to time, but neither Moshe nor Amaru knew how to properly navigate these labyrinths of emotion. Part of it was his age, but there was always a very real and present uncertainty at the heart of him. Moshe found it best to let him be and not address anything, but Amaru was impatient. It had been a few days. Moshe breathed out.

time for the indirect approach

"Katir, what do you think?" Moshe asked, eyes fixated on hers.

"About?" Amaru asked, confused.

"Well, we're about a quarter of the way through our Trials. But the question remains for us all: is this a place worth living in? I know you've been skeptical, I think we all have. But I think we can talk openly about it now. We're fitting in. We've got people, friends. The standards haven't been too challenging, but they *have* been different. But at this point, I'm only more convinced that we're all able. We *can* do this. But do you think we should? Do you still doubt?"

Moshe was not as convinced about Ecclesia as he made himself out to be, but he knew that his level of certainty would be enough to prod Amaru into a rebuttal, even if only to be contrarian herself. Which is why he didn't know what to say to her actual remark.

"I'm getting there, I think. I still have plenty of questions, but reading The Manual has helped me see the virtue in this lifestyle."

A pause.

"Oh. Well, that's...good to know. I'm glad you're opening up," Moshe said while looking in Reenu's direction. He looked back towards her.

"But it's still good to be critical."

"I know," Amaru stated. "It'd be nice if we could get more of a look into Inner Sanctum. Everyone out here seems pretty unwavering in their devotion, but I'm curious as to whether or not everyone's perspective from the inside is just as faithful."

Another pause. Still no reaction from Reenu. Amaru was getting annoyed.

"Actually," Amaru pondered out loud, "I wonder if Diora could figure that out for us."

Moshe noticed a slight shifting of the shoulder from Reenu.

"How's that?" Moshe asked.

"She could ask her mentor about Inner Sanctum life. They've established a connection, and she's fond of us, so I'm sure she could get some information out of him."

Amaru's leg started bouncing out of excitement.

"That's worth considering. You'd just have to be careful not to push it too far," Moshe asserted.

Reenu faced towards them completely. They both looked at him, hopeful that he would break free of his internal self-shackles. His eyes heightened before he placed a lone finger over his mouth. They got the hint.

From outside,

"...named Amaru. She's about this tall, a little younger than you, light brown hair close to her head. Witnesses say her eyebrows are very pointed and intense," said a gruff voice.

"I don't know anyone named Amaru," said a more timid but irritable voice.

"Perhaps she's using a different name," retorted the first voice. "Hiding her identity. Do you know anyone who matches that description at least?..."

The three of them sat up straight, equally puzzled. It sounded as if the voices were right outside their tent.

Amaru acted with haste.

She reached down the front of her robe, retrieving something from one of the folds. Placing it in Moshe's hands, she started for the tent's flaps-

Reenu grabbed her by the arm.

It was their first physical connection since Reenu closed himself off a few days prior. Concern spread across his face as he motioned for her to stay inside.

who knows what they want you for

Using her free hand, Amaru dug into the skin above her left eye and ripped out most of the pointed brow she bore. Reenu let go in surprise. Amaru winked at him and smiled, as if to say

i do

As she exited the tent, Moshe looked down at what she had left in his hands.

It was the picture she had taken the night of The Last Call.

Amaru stepped outside at the right moment. There were two Kohen interrogating her tent neighbor. She realized that none of them had talked with any of their direct neighbors before. For whatever reason, it seemed as if they were never around, and when they were, they did not seem interested in conversation. Amaru had ascertained that this woman, of middle age and cross scowl, lived by herself and rarely ventured outside her tent. From the liable look in her eyes, Amaru guessed correctly that the woman was in the middle of giving her up. Amaru struck first.

"Hello, advocates," Amaru said, using the more deferential term for the Kohen. "Is there something going on?"

The Kohen swiftly completed an about-face, allowing Amaru's cantankerous neighbor to casually sulk her way back inside. She hadn't wanted to talk to them in the first place.

"Good evening, miss...?" started the first one.

"Katir," Amaru said unflinchingly.

"Miss Katir," he resumed. "We're looking for a woman named Amaru. She's about, well, your height, and-"

"Yeah, I heard you from inside actually."

The second Kohen scribbled

probably don't like being interrupted

something down on what looked like a finer, dark blue senton.

"Why are you looking for her?"

"A man named Jaben claims this woman assaulted him during the terrorist attack at The Call," the second Kohen stoically stated.

Amaru feigned a gasp.

"That sounds awful!"

"She's also guilty of utilizing some unseemly words during the assault," said the first.

fuck yeah I am

"Well, she deserves to be asked about that, I'd say."

"Ma'am?" the first Kohen half-asked, half-confused.

"Well, I'd imagine she didn't assault this man for no reason, right?" Amaru suggested.

"You never know," said the second. "Regardless, any kind of physical assault is a criminal act, and she-"

"She should be taken in, yes. But if you ask...Jaben if he perhaps...provoked her into action, it might help with your search. Motivation."

The two Kohen paused, both staring intently at Amaru.

"You don't know her?" asked the first.

"Nope," Amaru reassured them. "Just an idea."

She hoped she didn't come off as too cute about her ignorance, but she thought that badgering them with a Shetland's trail would be enough to get them off her scent.

"Ma'am, your eyebrow is bleeding."

Amaru held her hand up to where it stung.

"Oh, right," she said. "Accident at The Last Call. I tend to scratch at the scab."

Amaru heard some muted shuffling from inside her tent. She suppressed a smile.

More staring from the Kohen. The second one wrote some more.

"Alright, ma'am," said the first one. "We'll let you get back inside. But just so you know, as a comfort for all citizens, we've got plenty of Kohen on this. We'll find her before the night is gone."

At this, he motioned with his arm to the rest of the living quarters.

Amaru saw that a few dozen Kohen were traveling in pairs, and she knew that what they said was true. Everyone was going to know to look for her. Her hands began to sweat.

"Looks like you will," Amaru agreed. "And I'll be sure to keep an eye

brow

out as well. Good luck."

The second Kohen smirked, already walking to the next tent.

"There is no luck," the first Kohen sternly reminded Amaru. "Rumai 8:28."

Amaru nodded. Looking out at the small multitude of advocates before her, she saw one who seemed marginally out of place. He was a taller, stockier man, and his uniform was surprisingly too large for even him. His walk was irregular and he looked awkward holding his senton.

looks like they even have some of the amateurs on this...wait a second...

Amaru bent down and peeked her head back inside their tent. Moshe and Reenu looked as if they had remained unmoved throughout her whole time outside, albeit stiffer.

"Guys, it's Babu!"

Moshe blinked. Reenu paid no mind.

"Who?"

"Babu, the kind Kohen-in-training we met in the forest. He's wearing the black-and-white! I'm going to go congratulate him."

It had been fifteen minutes. Amaru had yet to come back. Silence persisted between Moshe and Reenu. It reminded Moshe of that night by the fire - what was only a couple weeks ago now felt like a different life. It wasn't completely reminiscent though, for this time, Moshe was going to say something.

He was looking at the picture. He was surprised that he had yet to analyze it before, but he supposed he never had a reason to ask Amaru about it, even though she told them the morning after The Last Call that she had it. They had all just gone about focusing on The Trial. It was strange for him, he'd typically analyze every little thing they came across. He realized now that it might have been helpful to have done so earlier.

He recognized the redhead from The Last Call instantly. The picture was too blurry for him to make out her distinctive facial features - a pudgy nose and rounded eyebrows - but her hair was undeniable. There was also another being in sight, though half of their body was under

The Table?!

This had to be it. Moshe couldn't tell what they were doing, but the fact that the redhead and her companion were at The Table was proof enough. People of Outer Sanctum weren't allowed to be that close, and after the commotion she deliberately caused, Moshe knew she was up to something counterproductive to the greater good. Or at least counter-cultural. Either way, Moshe was emboldened.

"Reenu!" Moshe exclaimed.

Reenu lay still, facing away from Moshe, sullen as he had been before Amaru left.

"Reenu," Moshe said more calmly, "did you know about this picture?"

Still.

Moshe was starting to get frustrated. He tossed the picture in front of Reenu's face.

"You see that, right? I'm not just going crazy," Moshe said, simultaneously lowering his voice to a whisper. "This is *evidence*. This is exactly what Lieutenant Zacchaeus is looking for, exactly what could clear Katir of any allegation."

Moshe thought for a moment.

"Reenu...why would Katir hold on to this?"

Reenu lay for a moment longer before picking up the picture and

progress

looking at it. He still said nothing.

"I don't understand, Reenu. She knows how risky it is to hold on to that. It's risky for all of us just having it here. Is she...planning something? Why wouldn't she tell us? I-"

"Moshe," Reenu interrupted purposefully, now facing Moshe. "Just ask her."

Moshe stopped. In the mad rush of his brazen mind, he truly hadn't considered the obvious tactic: talking. Communication. It was what he was critiquing Amaru for abandoning, and yet, here he was following her model. Once again, Reenu was saying the most without saying much at all. It chipped away at Moshe's pride, but he was mostly just glad that Reenu was speaking again.

time to go for it

"You're right, Reenu. I should. And I will. I think it's...Almos 12:25 that tells us that good words between friends can bring down walls. Something along those lines. But I can't right now."

Moshe paused as Reenu sat up. He had hoped that his break in speech would be enough to draw Reenu into the conversation more. He was right.

"What if more Kohen come by? If they came in, they'd find the picture right away. There's nowhere in here to hide it, so we've got to get rid of it. And the safest way to get rid of it is to freely give it to a Kohen. They have no way of knowing Katir's part in it, and it'll give them the *actual* criminals they've been looking for."

"But Katir has it for a *reason*. We can't just give it up without knowing why she has it. Don't you trust her?" Reenu said, wisely bringing his voice down to match Moshe's.

"I do. You know that. I've trusted both of you with my life countless times. But we've got to do the right thing right now. It's how we stay safe. If Katir were here, I'd talk to her. But she's out there. We can talk to her when she gets back, but for now, we've got to make a move."

Moshe felt his earnestness grow. He became more convinced that this apparently minor object could have major implications for them. But Reenu was having none of it.

"No, Moshe. You've got to respect her choice. She's earned it. Remember what Lieutenant Zacchaeus said? He recognized her sensibility."

"Reenu, come on. He only met us that one time. Besides, she can still make mistakes. Anyone can."

"Including you."

Moshe's eyes tightened.

"Reenu. Give me the picture."

"No. Not 'til Katir comes back."

"Reenu, give it to me."

"No."

Moshe scooted over so that he was directly next to Reenu. Reaching over to grab the picture from Reenu's right hand, Reenu swatted him away with his left. Moshe sat stunned for a second, but he quickly recovered, wrenching Reenu's left arm out and away while pinning down his right wrist with his forearm. Moshe quickly grabbed the picture and scooted near the entrance.

"Ungh, what's wrong with you?!" Reenu said, raising his voice at Moshe for the first time.

"Me?! You're the one who's been sulking for who knows how long! What's wrong with *you*? Are you not appreciative? We've made it to the place we always dreamed of! We sacrificed so much to get here...and I've *always* done my best to protect you and Amaru. Including this!"

Moshe gestured with the picture and proceeded to open the flap of their tent. If Reenu wasn't going to be on his side, fine. They'd had some disagreements before, though he was more used to that lot coming from Amaru. He'd get over it, though - they both would. But before he could leave,

"Including Mahu?"

Moshe gripped the flap tightly, creating a small tear in its fabric. He turned around slowly and deliberately. He cautiously placed the photo on the floor in between them. He nodded at Reenu, looking at the picture. Reenu looked back and forth between the picture and Moshe.

pick it up?

Moshe nodded.

Reenu leaned in, outstretching his arm toward the picture, and then-

"Yes, of fucking course including Mahu! That was *all* about you. Don't you dare try to put that on me, man! What did you think was gonna happen? No, what do you think *should* have happened? Go ahead, man. Tell me. I'm really listening now."

Moshe was seething. Reenu shrank back onto the floor. He hadn't heard Moshe cuss in close to a month. He had forgotten how terrifying and powerful the temper that occasionally came along with those words could be. He quickly lay back down, once again facing away from Moshe.

Moshe immediately felt regret.

"Reenu," Moshe retreated to a whisper. "Reenu, I'm sorry. I really didn't mean to yell. You just know how I get about...I didn't...I've just been wanting to know what's going on with you, really. This isn't about me. I'm concerned for you. You haven't talked to us. I thought this was everything you wanted. You were so cheery at first, so typically optimistic. I just want to know what changed."

Still.

come on...you fucking idiot...you know better than to let them in...how could you blow up like that...

Moshe looked at the picture. He looked at his Manual. He picked them both up and went outside.

"Babu...Babu!"

Babu looked up from his *senton*, completely bewildered. The toughest part of his new job was all of the writing he had to do. It was as if Lieutenant Zacchaeus wanted them to document *everything* they saw or did. Babu knew he had always been more of a slow sheep than a witty wolf, and since writing Ecclesian characters was a completely new concept for him, he had been pretty slow on the uptake. His fellow Kohen and really everyone else in Inner Sanctum was patient with him, but he couldn't help but feel like a burden most days, especially since this new project of theirs was such a trial-by-fire exercise in writing. His partner Etair thought it would be best for Babu to get some practice in by being in charge of the *senton* while he asked the questions (mostly because Babu couldn't really ask any questions regardless), but they were both aware that this arrangement meant they would be reaching their quota much later than everyone else. Thus, Babu poured out all of his focus onto his *senton* and the intricate shape his left hand held as he struggled with creating the characters. Which is why he was shocked to hear someone calling his name. And it was even more shocking that the voice came out of the prisoner girl from The Last Call.

"Babu," repeated the out-of-breath prisoner girl as she caught up to him. "Babu, it's me...Katir...do you remember me?"

Babu smiled warmly yet suspiciously and nodded.

At this point, partner Etair's attention had also been taken from the Ecclesian hopeful he was interrogating. He decided to speak up.

"I'm sorry, ma'am," he said. "Who are you?"

"Sorry, sir," Amaru replied. "I've known Babu...since he was training to be a Kohen. I just wanted to congratulate him for making it."

Babu smiled and nodded again.

Amaru had two burning questions and decided to ask the more polite one first, though she feared for what the answer might be.

"Where's...Bukshee?"

Babu frowned.

"Oh, yes," said Etair. "Babu's old friend. He wasn't deemed fit for the position."

"Oh," Amaru said, contemplating. "That's...too bad."

"In fact," Etair continued. "I heard that he took it pretty hard. He's supposed to be leaving Ecclesia right about now."

"What?! Where is he going?"

"Well, nowhere basically. We all know there's nothing else out there."

"Why would he want to leave then?"

"I mean, I certainly wouldn't. Maybe he couldn't handle the disappointment. I don't know, I guess it's not right to speculate...man, we sure haven't had anyone leave in quite a while, though..."

But Amaru was already making her way to the entrance gates.

"Thank you...thank you."

Arah walked off. His conversation with the beggar was a complicated mixture of enlightenment and disheartenment, but he figured he shouldn't have expected anything less. In retrospect, he realized that that was probably the main reason why he hadn't talked to him before.

As Arah returned to his tent, he sat down, eager to meditate. Routine was good. He had been given so much to think about, but getting back to his routine and clearing his mind through meditation was probably the best first step before he would sort through any of it.

He sat still, stretching his legs to form a diamond shape, placing his hands on his meaty calves.

He closed his eyes.

A deep breath in-

But there was still the image of the beggar sitting before him.

A deep breath out-

But he remembered the creaking of the beggar's exhales as they talked.

A short breath in-

He imagined him hobbling around, asking for *casu* from anyone who was willing.

A short breath out-

A short breath in-

A short breath out-

A short breath in-

A short breath out-

He couldn't do this.

Arah stood up. Now was not the time for quiet reflection. It was the time for decisive action.

He walked over to the footlong pool he had dug out. That was where he stored all of his drinking water before using it to bathe his lustrous hair. Looking into the pool, he saw his reflection. He realized that he actually hadn't looked at himself in a week or so, surprisingly. His hair had become more unruly, but his lips were not as cracked as before. He smiled.

Scooping up some water with his hands, he made for his tent's entrance.

the routine's about to change

The gates stood with an impenetrable gaze. Bukshee looked up at them with a bittersweet grin. He thought it ironic that one could forget entirely about the preeminence of the pearl luminescence once they decided to leave Ecclesia. But he knew that this was the right decision. And he was ready. But he was definitely not ready for the pink, pudgy man with his pithy sayings who stood between him and separation.

"...how should I say it...*why believe in a fable*...hmm...*when you can sit at The Table*...erhm, maybe not...oh! Bukshee?"

"Hey, Duman," Bukshee said flatly. He had not interrupted Duman talking to himself before, and he hoped that the occasion could have been enough to distract him so that he could sneak past him and pull the lever himself. Not the case.

"Bukshee! What a splendid surprise! It has been a minute, hasn't it? Why, I don't think I've seen you since...mmm...two Calls ago? How's training been? Are you official yet? Oh, and how's Babu?! He's such a sweet frien-"

"Duman, I'm leaving," Bukshee said. He was at least glad he was able to cut Duman off one more time before *he* was off.

Duman quickly blinked three times.

"Ecclesia. I'm leaving Ecclesia. Now. Let me out."

Duman gasped and took a dramatic step backwards.

"Whaaaa-"

"Bukshee!" yelled another voice.

He turned around. Amaru expected an instinctive groan and snarl to escape from Bukshee, but his actual countenance surprised her. His eyes were bigger than she remembered, and he carried a convinced dejection in them. They looked deeply into hers.

"Hello...Amaru," he said, the second word more of a mouth shape than a whisper so that Duman, who was still so shocked that he went deeper into his gatekeeper's booth to frantically retrieve something, couldn't hear.

Now it was Amaru's eyes that grew wide.

"Who...how..." Amaru tried to ask.

"I figured it out from the Kohen's questioning. The physical description. The...scrappy disposition. It was too obvious, really," Bukshee said bluntly, maintaining unrelenting eye contact.

Amaru smushed her fingers against her palms. She wanted to say something, but she knew she had to be careful. The past animosity between them made her situation as uncertain as it was precarious.

"Nobody knows. No need to worry."

Amaru relaxed a bit, but she stayed on guard. She had not felt this defensive since, well, since the last time she was in Bukshee's presence.

"I had...to let it go," Bukshee continued, finally lowering his eyes as their dejection was replaced with shame. "After I was...discharged...I fought back. I couldn't accept the decision. Not over such a small, stupid exchange. It made me furious. Especially towards you. I spent a couple days asking around, looking for any way to find you. I was glad for this Kohen search. Glad that you could receive some comeuppance of your own. But..."

Duman returned, panting and with a shaking finger on a passage in The Manual.

"Bukshee, Bukshee, look at this. In Atios 21-"

"Duman!" Bukshee yelled. Duman stepped back. Bukshee's arms had instinctively folded when he yelled, so he had to pause a moment to consciously release them. He now spoke to both of them at once.

"I wanted to hurt someone. I didn't know what I was going to do to them, but it was going to be bad. It took a door getting slammed in my face for me to realize that *that* is what I need right now. I've got to be alone. I've got to figure out what's going on inside of me. Away from everyone else."

Amaru looked at Bukshee, who was looking away from both of them. She was trying to grasp his reasoning. Whenever she wanted to hurt someone, she just did it. They always deserved it. She was learning from The Manual and her conversations with others why that was wrong, but she couldn't help but feel like this time, *she* was to blame. She deserved it. She felt paralyzed by this newfound moral dilemma. Duman, on the other hand, was driven by his panic to act. He held his arms out and away, effectively blocking the lever that controlled the gate.

"Duman, let me go," Bukshee stated.

"Bukshee, please!" Duman said through a constricting throat. "Ermh, you don't know what will happen once you're out-"

"No, Duman, *you* don't know what's out there. You've lived your whole life inside. I was born and raised by the wilderness. It's time I go back to my roots for now."

"Bukshee, you don't know what you're asking-"

BWAK!

Bukshee clubbed the side of Duman's head with a open-palmed right hook, leaving him dazed and sprawled out on the floor. He reached over and pulled the lever. As the gates opened, he turned to Amaru and said,

"At least I got to do that before I left. Do you mind closing the gate once I'm on the other side?"

Amaru, still paralyzed, though she was now transitioning from guilt to the fear that accompanies leaving things unsaid, said,

"Sure."

Bukshee brushed the pearl slabs before him as he walked out. After pausing for a second in between the two stones, he proceeded on. But—

"Bukshee!"

Bukshee looked back in response to Amaru's cry.

"I forgive you," she said as she pulled the lever.

Bukshee nodded. As the stones obscured more and more of him from view, he said his final words:

"Peace be with you."

"And also with you."

Reenu was fast asleep by the time Moshe returned to the tent. Moshe exhaled, releasing a tension that had been building up during the last few steps before he entered. He *had* to make things right with Reenu somehow. They had never experienced a divide like this, and he didn't like it. It was preventing them from being together; neither person's needs in the relationship were being met. He would have Amaru spend some time alone with Reenu at some point. She was better at seeing his heart.

Moshe lay down next to Reenu. He took out his Manual. It was quite dark, but that didn't matter. They could all see quite well in the dark. The Manual was such a massive volume - he'd had trouble knowing exactly where he left off because of it. Until now. He realized that having some kind of marker to keep his place was extremely helpful. Though, he also knew that this particular marker was one he would not be able to keep. He'd have to give it back once Amaru returned and they had a talk. He took out the picture and placed it next to him.

He didn't like being interrupted mid-chapter, but such were the events of the day. He was happy to get back to Fos 3 and beyond. But after reading it, he realized that if he had finished the chapter earlier, the lessons he learned would have helped in his conversation with Reenu. He put The Manual back down. He yawned vigorously.

reading seems to wear me out

He closed his eyes, allowing sleep to capture his consciousness. His conversation with Amaru would have to wait until tomorrow.

---

[9]They came across a poor, dying old man. The man himself lay sprawled across the sands in front of them. Yet even in his condition, he still possessed more than them. [10]As they circled around the man, the shade that the sphere of their bodies provided caused him to look up at them. Silence was all that passed between them. The group exchanged uneasy glances with each other, unsure of what to do next, But before they could decide, the old man cracked a frail smile. [11]Though he had only rags and morsel, he gave freely and willingly all he had to the travelers. The travelers looked at each other, surprised by the generosity of the old man. [12]But their philosophy told them that generosity was vulnerability. They kicked the man repeatedly until he was unconscious, and then, dead. They took his body along with them, each traveler thrilled by the prospect of a considerable supper. [13]Thus, while it is profitable to give with little prejudice, it is also wise to give only to those who have proven themselves worthy.

Chapter 7: In My Pocket

47 DBK

it was the eyes that he rememb-

Moshe woke up flailing, frightened, and in a cold sweat. He thought he was having an abhorrent dream, but he couldn't remember it. This was becoming the norm for him. His dreams, though he knew that he saw things that could not be forgotten, were now phantasms he had to chase when he'd awaken. Growing up, he remembered being taught that dreams, whether terrible or strange, were *gifted* to people. When interpreted correctly, they would provide moral instruction, directions that led to progress and change. He remembered the Dream Assemblies - meetings where dozens of people would come together for the sake of interpreting a single dream. He hated them. As a youth, he could only remember three dreams, and none of them could be discerned by the community. Even so, he played along. When asked by another about a dream, he would provide some kind of lip service answer, but he had never been one to truly divine their meanings. And whatever the moral consequences were of the un-dreams that he had been having as of late were completely lost on him. The physical after-effects and extreme disorientation, however, were not.

What made this particular instance singularly disorienting was the place he was in.

He did not know it.

Moshe immediately closed his eyes and

feel

felt.

He did not leave them open long enough to see anything other than red, but that did not matter. He could handle wherever he was, but the uncertainty of who his captors were was what caused his survivors' instinct to kick in. If they saw that he had awoken, they would have reacted.

controlling the reaction of an oppressor is the key to escape

So Moshe felt.

The quiet was what stood out first. There was no whistling wind or shuffling commotion of nearby neighbors. There was nothing to hear at all. His body, chilled by the muted air from his conspicuously missing robe, lay atop something even more plush. The hungry pain in his lower back told him that as plush as the surface was, it was not very deep in its support. He silently, purposefully inhaled through his nose, picking up a spicy, earthen scent that nearly caused him to cough from its strength. It reminded him of some of the little trees they passed by coming into Ecclesia.

From these senses, Moshe judged that he was in someone's living quarters, albeit with much finer amenities than any tent he was used to. The abrasively engaging scent was too omnipresent for him to detect if anyone else was in the room with him, but the silence led him to believe that was not the case. Frankly, the details that he was able to pick up were actually inviting. Whoever it was that was holding him there, they wanted him comfortable. He was not even bound in any way. He was not used to that. Confidence sprung up from within. Who knows - maybe he wasn't even being kept there by anyone?

Moshe opened his eyes.

The room was dark, its faintly warm glow administered from two mini-flames was held in place by cylinders on a small table. More focused, Moshe could tell that the room's aroma emanated from those objects as well. There was a reflective surface that nearly covered the whole wall opposite of him. He could see himself in it, naked, though his robe was neatly laid next to him. He appeared to be on some kind of elevated platform composed of stitched-together robe material that was white, purple, and gold, and softer than any other robe he had felt. Aside from that, the room was barren. The walls were sturdy, like the stone elements that made up Ecclesia's outer walls. Instead of the flap of a tent, there was a rectangular stone that was

a way out

in the corner of the room and separate from the rest of the wall.

Moshe looked at the other corner of the room.

He first saw the dark maroon robe. It was lying on the floor as if it were just recently and eagerly tossed aside. As his eyes moved upwards, he saw silken white legs, one crossed over the other. Those legs were attached to wide, feminine hips that were designed with purpose. The hourglass led to overly round, luscious breasts that crested and fell slowly and rhythmically. Two graceful, delicate hands did just enough to cover those breasts, coming together in the middle and creating a mesmerizing crease as fingers interlocked. Her smile was enticing; her lips looked as if they had never believed in the parching powers of the sun. Her cheeks were high and taut, her nose even daintier than her hands, and her eyebrows smooth in their curvature. Moshe saw that she also had hair that was almost miraculously held up in place atop her head, but he had stopped his comprehensive analysis of her beauty by the time he got to what really beckoned him.

He knew her.

It was the eyes that he remembered.

Moshe's heart had always been beating, but now he felt it pound.

The woman sat before him like a gift waiting to be opened. Waiting to be taken. If this was a kidnapping, the lines between captor and captive could easily be blurred from one moment to the next.

They sat there together, staring at each other in endless fixation. Moshe did his best to keep his gaze eye-level. The woman did the same but with an ease and a confidence. Though she kept herself hidden and just barely in the dark, she was relaxed. Realizing her modesty was half-baked, Moshe blushed and frantically covered himself with his robe. She smiled.

Moshe did not know what to
what am I doing here
who are you
why is this happening
say. For now, he would keep his cards close to his
breasts
chest and not say anything at all. He tried to control his breathing and imitate the woman's coolness. His heart slowly ceased its pound-

"Would you like to have me now?"

The pounding intensified.

"Excuse me?" Moshe asked.

"Come, now, Moshe. We are here together," the woman insisted. "We can have our fill of each other, if you so desire."

Moshe shifted his robe.

"I don't understand...what's going on," Moshe continued in his stupor.

"There's nothing to understand," the woman continued in her seduction. "There is only you and I and now. Now, what will you do with that?"

She started to move her fingers, deliberately changing the pattern of their interlocking. Back and forth they went. Moshe grew, uncomfortable. The questions he had seemed to be fading into the background of his mind. Coming to the foreground were wolf-like instinct and desire.

He knew the longer he sat in this non-verbal stupor, the easier it would be to let himself stay in the moment. And the moment was full of alluring promise. He managed a question.

"I...I do not even know your name...and yet you know mine. How is that?"

"Ambree," Ambree said. "Though that is not my first name. It was given to me because

it's beautiful

of its beauty. And I know yours because you told it to me."

Moshe felt the pounding stop for a second.

"...when did I...tell it to you?"

Despite not moving an inch on her stool, Ambree remained as relaxed as ever. The only motion happening on her side of the room came from the coaxing repetition of her breasts rising and falling. Rising and falling.

"At The Troei. We were talking about Jensio 5, but then it went into more personal matters."

Moshe gulped. Ambree continued.

"You told me of your relief that the search for Amaru was over, though no one knows why. But you also lamented over your relationship with Reenu, for it has only gotten worse with time. It has now been ten days since you last talked."

Moshe was shocked. There was no way he would have revealed all this to her. Or anyone for that matter.

but how else could she know all this

"Moshe, my darling," Ambree said in a sweet, dripping tone. "Do not feel heavy if you don't remember this. I don't expect you to. You were in quite a stressful state. But now, you don't have to be."

Ambree let her fingers recline, each hand now completely separate and resting on their respective breasts. Moshe acted quickly.

"What else did I tell you?"

For the first time, Ambree's seductive expression changed. She donned an inquisitive, thoughtful look and let her eyes wander the room, which only made Moshe more intrigued in her personage. But her original composure quickly returned.

"Hmm, not much else," Ambree insisted. "You mainly expressed your desire...for this."

Ambree allowed her legs to uncross, slowly and automatically spreading themselves wide.

The pounding intensified.

Moshe looked away from Ambree. The fortitude of his mind was failing him. As far as he could tell, the position he was in was simple. It reminded him of something he read in Brevos,

ask and it will be given to you

though he couldn't imagine that this was the right context for that truth. But maybe it was. Maybe his inner desires were manifesting themselves into realization. A reward for his striving. Their absolute solitude insisted that whatever act he partook in would be safely hidden from view. There was no threat here, no way of being found out.

What Ambree may or may not have known was that Moshe struggled deeply with lust. Not just of the physical variety, but with the very *essence* of lust itself. He longed *intensely* for what he did not yet have. Absolution from the choices he had made. Belonging in a place where he did not have to bear the weight of leadership. Relief from the anxieties of everyday living. These were the major lusts of his life, sex was just the easiest one to fulfill given the current opportunity. Because he could not achieve his primary desires, the base ones and their ease had a firm foothold within his ego. He had always struggled with a lack of contentment in the present tense, and his tendencies were to either shelf the issue until further notice or give in to the darkness it fostered within him. But in this moment, his body disagreed with his heart. And there was something odd about the way Ambree had opened up. Every part of her had seemed so effortlessly fluid up to that point, but that single action came across as something more...mechanical. He retreated into denial.

"No," Moshe stated. "This is wrong. This isn't what I want."

"How could it be wrong?" Ambree pushed back. Her legs now rested firmly and squarely apart. "Your desire and what it leads to is utterly and completely natural. A man and a woman. The oldest ritual in history. Do not deny your sensual inheritance."

Moshe sat up and scooted to the edge of the bed. He placed his hands rigidly atop his knees, still careful to keep the robe safely in his lap. He needed a counter-emotion, even if it was just a feigned one. He decided to try to convert his lust into something it was the neighbor of: aggression.

"It's just as natural that I end you with fire and put out the threat that you are to me. Does that make it *not* wrong?"

Ambree remained unmoved.

"Ooh, a little anger starts to show its face. We all know what that leads to," she said with a wink. "Passion. And thank you for acknowledging my implicit...danger. It's quite tantalizing, isn't it?"

Moshe felt his robe move a little. He suppressed it, hoping Ambree didn't notice. The curves that crept around the corners of her lips said otherwise. She moved on.

"Nature or not, you do *need* this. From what you were telling me, there's been a lot on your plate. Let me clear some of that off for you. Let our union be the release that helps you keep going."

Moshe looked down. He *knew* he needed some kind of release. He was losing his companionship with Amaru and Reenu. They had all been doing well enough throughout their Trials, but in doing so, he felt the divide between them grow ever deeper. Each of them was having a hard time coming together like they used to. In integrating with Ecclesia and the lifestyle of Outer Sanctum, they were all transforming into different people. Moshe was not ready for that. It had always been them three through everything. But he was beginning to see that, for their own good, it might be best if he let the sheep freely roam the ground.

To be true Ecclesians, maybe each of them must finally become true individuals. It made his heart heavy and his body

release is...good

ache.

Moshe shook his head, both in response to Ambree's rhetoric and as a physical shaking away of his thoughts.

"No," Moshe stated again. "There is release...in different ways."

"And what might they be?" Ambree asked. Moshe couldn't tell if she was fabricating interest or if she truly sought an answer.

"The Manual. Have you not been reading lately? Its wisdom is joy. And it says not to 'engage with fleshly lusts.' Brevos 2:13, right?"

Ambree's eyes flickered, falling from Moshe's for a split second.

the footing I needed

"It also says in Niroc 7:9 that it is better to satisfy your needs than to 'burn in passion.' Ask yourself, Moshe: are you burning inside? And if you're not burning for me..."

At this, Ambree leaned forward and let her hands release her heavy breasts and run freely down and up her toned, cream-white legs. She lifted her head up and looked at him with her beckoning eyes half-closed.

"...then when will you *ever* be satisfied?"

Moshe's robe flung from his lap. He chose not to scramble and grab it for fear of looking weak, but now they were both completely exposed. Both participants scanned the other, both feasted with their looking. Moshe didn't know what to say once again. Her well-laid propositions, coupled with her well-crafted body, were too much for rationality to have its way. And she countered his defenses with his own scriptural techniques.

if even The Manual says it's permissible...

Ambree stood up and took steps towards Moshe. She was resolute, but she also looked

annoyed...

"Moshe, listen to me," she said as she grabbed his head behind the ears and held his face close to hers. He could now smell her body, its blossoming scent becoming unbearable.

"I want you. I love a strong leader."

She looked down at the lower half of his body and grinned.

"...And you want me. There is nothing to fear here. No need for apprehension. This doesn't have to be ongoing. It is just one night. Why not try it?"

She smiled at him, knowing her seduction was nearly complete. Moshe placed his hands on her stomach...and gently pushed her back, creating the distance he needed to stand up.

"If you break the law just once, are you not a criminal?" Moshe asked.

Ambree took a step back. She had to recompose herself after his slight rejection, but she was still determined. She would go about with deference. She sat back down on her stool, legs spread, but Moshe noticed that her legs were not as inviting as they once were. They were tense.

"There is no law against this," she insisted.

"Maybe not in Ecclesia, but *I* am committed," Moshe said.

"Oh, please," Ambree said with a chuckle. "To Amaru?"

Moshe looked away.

"I've been studying her. She's got an attitude, but she is beneath you. And have you two even done anything in the time that you've been here?"

Moshe blushed. When he looked back at Ambree, he thought he saw her lip quiver for a moment. There was certainly something changing in her

a different mood

eyes.

"What about you?" Moshe asked. "Are you not with someone?"

Ambree froze.

"No," she stated.

"When was the last time you were with someone?" Moshe continued his interrogation.

Ambree's eyes softened, but her lips were unwilling to part. Her legs moved closer together.

"Wait...have you *ever* been with someone?"

Ambree's chest went from an elegant elevation to panicked heaving. She began to look around the room. Moshe frowned, confused by her reaction. She suddenly fell off the stool. Moshe leapt to her. When he picked her up off the floor, he saw tears forming in her eyes.

"Fine...just fucking fine! I don't want you. I don't want anyone."

Ambree and Moshe sat opposite each other on the bed. Once again, they were deep in analysis, but now with different intentions. Moshe noticed that Ambree's eyes were developing that decaying, glazy redness that one gets after crying for minutes on end. She had not been a very violent crier, but her tears left their ubiquitous marks on the bed and in her eyes all the same. She was huddled into herself, robed but with visible gooseflesh erecting the previously hidden hairs on her legs and arms. Moshe looked at her with heaviness and

what a poor, tortured creature she must be

pity. Ambree noticed that Moshe's body had almost expanded due to a new sense of alleviation. He was not obnoxious about it, though; instead, he postured himself in a more sympathetic way than before. He gave off the impression that he stayed only for the sake of listening, and that gave Ambree a sense of well-wishing that she had not felt in a long time. It helped that his hazel eyes had transitioned from a look of strategy to a look of compassion. She supposed she could talk to him.

"I'm asexual," she said.

"I'm unfamiliar," Moshe responded instantly. "But I'd like to learn."

Ambree allowed her frown the introduction of dissipation.

"It means I'm not attracted to anyone. Female or male. Or otherwise."

"Ah...so you really meant it, then?"

Ambree nodded.

Worry let itself into Moshe's mind.

"Is that...the right thing to...*be* here?"

Ambree's frown returned, mixed with conflict of thought.

"No. I mean, I think some might say it's helpful. But I don't know if anyone would say it's *natural*. And I think that's what matters."

Moshe was confused.

"That makes sense, but it also doesn't. I know that The Manual warns against...'fleshly delights'...but like you said earlier, attraction is natural. How can both be true at the same time?"

"Sounds like *cognitive dissonance*, right?" Ambree aligned, suppressing a smirk.

or was it a scoff

Ambree realized her arrogance. "Oh, sorry. If you haven't heard that phrase here yet–"

"I'm familiar," Moshe declared.

"Okay. It is confusing."

"Is that why you've taken me here?" Moshe guessed.

Ambree subconsciously adjusted her place on the bed, shifting in the direction away from Moshe.

"Yes."

"To prove you're not bound to your...asexuality?"

Ambree's lip quivered, leaving her with only the ability to nod.

"Ambree," Moshe said, eyes growing in understanding. "Why do you think it's so wrong to be yourself?"

Ambree forced her lip to stop quivering and began to speak:

"I've always known that I'm asexual. My siblings all fell in love with the other adolescents in our tribe, but I never felt anything. I thought something was wrong with me. Faking it became so easy that I almost started to believe the lie. But whenever I was with someone, regardless of what my body did, my mind was always disengaged. When our tribe...dissolved, I vowed to stay true to who I was. There was no more need to keep it hidden. But then I found my way here. I've been here for two years. I've never been able to figure out why I can't pass The Trial. I've not really told people I'm asexual, but I've assumed that it complies with the rules. After all, The Manual tells us that fleshly delights are one of the main reasons why people are hindered from becoming true Ecclesians, truly like Savyer. I don't know, though. It doesn't seem like anyone really believes that."

Moshe was trying to keep up with her details, but at this point, he had to interject.

"How's that?"

"Well, if you noticed at The Last Call, most of the Inners there came in pairs. One male, one female...

hmm

...and not a lot of singles. Hardly any, really, other than the men in leadership. It got me wondering if my problem is that not being with someone prevents me from understanding the love that every Ecclesian *has* to emanate."

Moshe believed he was still listening, but the overriding section of his thought space was starting to formulate a theory.

"Why did you choose me, then?"

Ambree paused, collecting her words.

"I'm not entirely sure. I mean, I don't really get how anyone *chooses* this kind of shit anyway. But I knew that you were new. And new people are more susceptible to losing track of their moral convictions when they're in a new place. So I studied you and your friends. That's why I know all those things I said earlier, by the way. We've never had a conversation before."

Moshe half-heard her but responded anyway.

"I hear you. Thanks for explaining."

"How did you choose?"

Moshe paused, collecting his thoughts.

"Choose what?"

"Amaru. How did you choose to be with her?"

There was a plea in Ambree's eyes. Internally, Moshe laughed the kind of laugh that one generates in the face of something that's not supposed to be funny. But it was somewhat comical that the same eyes that nearly seduced him and made him a victim were now looking to him for saving. Now that they were fully robed, the power play surrounding who was in whom's pocket had shifted. He did not relish the fact

why does everyone end up looking to me for advice

and he felt sorry that the advice that he could give was something he knew would not be satisfactory for her. Nor was it truthful.

"I don't know. I guess attraction is just something that...happens."

Ambree looked back down. Her eyes told a new story. Moshe had seen them tell of lust, curiosity, desire, sorrow, and even friendliness. Now, they told only of defeat.

"Okay."

Silence returned. Minutes passed, neither of them willing to move. Half an hour ago, concession looked like the first person to give in to fervor. Now, concession was giving up on conversation.

From afar, Moshe heard the faint bleating of sheep. He realized that they must truly be *inside* the stone of the outer walls if he was close enough to hear their incessant baaing. He also realized dawn must be arriving.

"Ambree, I've got to go."

Ambree didn't look at him.

"Okay."

Moshe's conscience berated him, but he stood up. He walked towards the loose stone wall and put both hands on it when-

"Moshe, is there any hope for me?"

It was a last-ditch effort. It was a final straw. It was a question attached to the crumbling ashes of a worldview nearly irrevocably broken. And Moshe said,

"Yes. If you're willing to change."

The day was beautiful. When Moshe exited the wall, he was greeted with the glory of a burgeoning sun that painted the rows of tents and pathways before him in a warm pink. The quiet he now experienced was not stressful, rather, it was peaceful (aside from the few sheep he still heard). He only saw a couple of people walking about, some just barely coming out of their tents.

i should get up at this time regularly

He heard the stone wall behind him shift back into place, but paid it no mind after a deep breath in, his nostrils filling with a dry but pleasantly neutral scent, and a deep breath out, his muscles relaxing and encouraging him to walk forward. He had not realized how tense he had become, but the encounter had lasted for a couple hours, so it made sense that he would need to stretch himself out some. That time was mostly dominated by a dubious silence, but now, he appreciated the semblance of stillness that the day's awakening bestowed upon him.

After calibrating his sense of direction, he found a small clearing devoid of tents or trash, and stopped there to continue his stretches. He raised both arms up behind his head. His night had been dominated by a dismal story, but he believed it could get better. He lowered his arms and moved into a deep lunge. He was grateful for the experience, for it taught him how to love someone who was vastly different from himself. He reclined from the lunge and reached down to touch his toes. He also learned how to exhibit self-control, and that, perhaps, was the most exciting exercise of it all. Whether the woman with the beckoning eyes knew it or not, she had given him the tools he needed to overcome the lust he had been plagued with his entire life. He returned to his normal walking pose and proceeded to walk home.

i've passed my Test

Chapter 8: Abigail (See)

37 DBK

Reenu was heading home, engrossed in the day's early rays. He had been slipping out of the tent before the arrival of the sun for the past month. As far as he knew, his friends were unaware of this daily respite. Oh, how he wished he could tell them! He knew that Moshe probably took the blame for his silence and that Amaru was probably just mad, but even though it was neither of their faults, he still could not speak. It was a tightening of the chest that prevented him from doing so. It was the culture shock. He believed in the authenticity of the people around him and in the benevolence of the authority above him, but...was he just *expected* to accept it completely? The transition from cynicism (an attitude that he disliked despite its usefulness) to idealism could not be so fluid.

And so, he left every pre-morning to think. While Moshe thought about The Manual and Amaru thought about her interactions, Reenu thought about philosophy. He thought about ways that Inner and Outer Sanctum could be more united, yes, but he mostly thought about where it was that *he* fit into the equation. Not that he necessarily doubted that Inner Sanctum could be the haven that he and his friends desired, but he didn't know if he would be ok living there while all others suffered out here. What was special about him that he deserved a seat over anyone else? Is "whoever tries hardest" the best measurement for merit? These were the questions he pondered in his heart. They bogged him down and kept him inside. He couldn't tell other hopefuls because he couldn't trust them. He couldn't tell his friends because they seemed to be adapting much better than he, at least on the outside. Back and forth the thoughts went, and though his morning escapades were nice, they had yet to provide any clarity. But today was different. He tried *not* thinking. And he found that to be the most consoling exercise of them all.

...

So as he walked back under the splendor of the day, he prepared himself to finally speak. He opened the flap to the tent, which had truly become a home to him now that he reflected on it, and-

"Reenu, it's time to *freaking* stop. You've been playing this dumb quiet game for weeks on end. It's not getting you anywhere. I'm sorry if this has all been too much for you. I'm sorry if Moshe or I said something you didn't like. But being closed off like this isn't good for you. How are you going to pass The Trial if you're not talking to anyone?"

Amaru had grabbed Reenu's arm and pulled him inside. The assertive grace of her movement was not a surprise to Reenu, but he was alarmed by how quickly she had pivoted his body

am i growing oblivious

underneath hers. Now straddled atop him, Amaru pinned Reenu's wrists above his head with the girth of one forearm, a favorite maneuver of hers. Reenu could tell that Moshe was not in the room, but he would not check to be sure. He dared not turn his head away from the fiery eyes of the one atop him. Rather, his eyes began to well with pardon.

"Is that why you're concerned?"

Amaru's grip lessened.

"Well, yes. I-...you can't *not* make it in if Moshe and I do."

"That's the only reason?"

Reenu saw Amaru's eyes change, and he knew her heart was coming forth.

"I...*need* you to talk to me."

With that, the two of them shared an intimacy of mutual, long-repressed tears. As water silently flowed between them, it hit Reenu that this had been the longest stretch in their lives that they had not really talked. To think that it was all due to his own inevitable internalization! His heart sank because of what he had done to her. To rob her of their verbal commiseration was cruel. He wished that he could now find the words to help her understand. But that was not the only thing between them that was missing.

Their eyes changed. The wide-open moment of vulnerability melted into a half-cocked gaze that promised something more. Amaru increased the pressure on Reenu's wrists, but not in malice. She lowered her face to be next to his, smelling his vanilla breath as his mouth automatically parted. Their cheeks touched - his unnaturally smooth in youth and hers dry and rough but still welcoming. It had been their first affectionate contact since before Ecclesia, and all that had been building within them would now be released because of it.

Reenu was smiling. He and Amaru were headed towards The Troei for their weekly hangout with Diora. Amaru was daring, occasionally brushing her arm against his. His body had almost forgotten how flirtatious she could be. But he knew they had to be somewhat careful. They had yet to come across anyone else who had romantic involvements, or at least no one was willing to show it. Reenu found that

why not express love when you have it

odd. And meeting with Diora, they would be extra careful. She had hinted at being perpetually and reluctantly single, and Reenu had a feeling that had something to do with her "unique addiction." It didn't help that the two of them were still reveling in the makeup of their morning union. It was hard not to be bubbly, especially after such a long time. Reenu decided to direct that joyous energy into the mood of their time with *i'm sure she could use it*

Diora.

She was sitting by herself at the Cafe's northwest corner. Reenu looked at Amaru, puzzled. That was not their usual spot. They could tell from afar that she was in an agitated mood - her hands were planted firmly on her knees while her fingers tapped away in arhythmic motions. Her eyes were red-rimmed and scanning the landscape as quickly as they could. They momentarily landed on Reenu and Amaru, but before Reenu could finish waving to her, her eyes flit towards the next subject. Reenu and Amaru knew this kind of behavior from past

wolves

experiences, so they instinctively paced themselves with caution, slowly sitting down on opposite sides of her.

"Hey, Diora, want to get in line?" Amaru deliberately asked.

Diora's eyes finally settled on her newfound company. She eased up a bit.

"Oh, no...I'm okay."

"Are you sure?" asked Reenu. "You look hungry, and it *is* lunch ti-"

"Yeah, I'm fine. If you two want to eat, go ahead."

Reenu and Amaru looked at each other. Though *casu* hadn't gotten any less disgusting over time, the monotony of consumption made it so that now they barely even thought about how it tasted. It was purely sustenance. But the adrenaline that their prior passion birthed had kept them pretty sustained.

"I think we're good," Amaru estimated. "What's going on?"

"What do you mean?" Diora's eyelids resumed their twitching.

"Just...is there anything you want to talk about today?" Amaru tried her hand at assuaging.

"Why would there be?"

"Diora, you look to be in a bad state, okay? You're so jittery. And your eyes. It's pretty obvious. What's bothering you?"

Amaru's eyes showed her puzzlement. She had not expected such tenacity from Reenu. It was not in character, but he continued his charge.

"You've been keeping inside. Being closed off like this isn't good for you. That's why you joined the Diados Program, right? To talk with someone..."

Reenu trailed off as his mind instinctively connected the dots.

"That's what changed, isn't it?"

Diora looked up at him, mystery in her redness.

"The Program. We wanted you to ask your mentor about Inner Sanctum life...and since then, you've stopped talking to us. You know something you don't want to tell us?"

Diora's frantic ocular pacing resumed.

"You owe us. We're your friends. Whatever it is, you can't keep it from us. Just like your...addiction."

Reenu was controlling his tone, but Amaru was still shocked by his unwarranted forthrightness. Amaru surely agreed with the truths he was speaking, but he was in the same position merely a couple hours before. Maybe he just saw how effective her approach had been...

or maybe he's projecting

Either way, addressing her about her "addiction" like this was not tactful. She knew they both had wanted to know for some time now, but that was something that could only be revealed on her time. It hadn't stopped either of them from asking almost every week, but in her current state, it was an inappropriate ask.

Diora doubled over, hiding her face in her hands. Amaru and Reenu felt bad for their friend, but they both knew how important it was for her to speak to them. Eventually, they *couldn't* let her have her way with this one. Then her back straightened. As she sat back up, her hands wiped away the red from her eyes, now replaced with a hardened determinism.

"So, the boy has the courage to speak now, eh?"

Amaru and Reenu stiffened, readying themselves for the unprecedented.

"Well, friends, speak to me now about this: *why* do you want to know about Inner Sanctum?"

Diora was now leaning back on her bench, arms crossed. She had the look of someone who would wait an eternity for the answer she desired, but were she to get an answer she did not desire, her arms would be crossed forever.

"Who *doesn't* want to know?" Amaru asked.

Reenu looked at his friend-lover, expecting her to go on. Over-explanation seemed like the safer route here, but perhaps there was wisdom in her moderation.

Diora looked both of them hard in the eyes. In Amaru, she saw a stubborn dedication to her own prudence. In Reenu, she saw someone who was trying to be like Amaru. That would do. She released her arms, smiling as she did.

"Friends, let's go."

They stood in a secluded stone alley, lost from the rest of Outer Sanctum in its intricate environmental anagram. To get there, they had to traverse the infamous Torched Tents. This was a living quarters area and wooden guard tower in the eastern side of Outer Sanctum that had disastrously burned down some time ago. The rumor was that an Ecclesian hopeful living there had finally given up...and decided that others should, too. His fiery murder-suicide cleared a hundred tents' worth of land before it was able to be put out. Rather than revitalizing the haunting landscape, it was decided that the area would serve as a visual reminder of hopelessness, a sort of negative reinforcement to press on. It was pretty rare for anyone to actually visit the memorialized scene, though; in fact, neighboring tents were moved farther away so as not to be daily reminded of the tragedy. Upon first hearing this story, Reenu found it despicable. Taking away choice from others particularly irked him. But it was not long before he and his friends had heard fragments of another story - that the Torched Tents were somehow related to the mysterious person furnace: *KAMNOS*. Amaru had once asked Diora if she knew anything about this rumor, but she hesitantly affirmed the opposite, claiming to not know about either backstory. That's what made their travel through the maze of debris all the more befuddling.

After covertly passing the tents and collecting ash along the way, the threesome had to squeeze through the wreckage of the tower in order to get to the alley. It was dark and quiet, and only went for a few paces before they reached a

dead end

wall. Diora stood at the wall, looking it up and down as if for clues. Reenu and Amaru looked at each other. They had always considered Diora to be odd, but this was turning out to be their oddest day with her yet. They were both worried.

"Diora, why are we here?" Reenu asked, patient in tone.

Without looking back at them, Diora answered:

"You know, whenever I tell anyone about my 'unique addiction,' there's a pretty predictable conversational path that I expect to take. I'll hint at it, they'll ask politely for more information, I'll decline. At that point, they give up. They tell me that it's my burden and I don't have to share it if I don't want to. And I accept that sentiment. But on the inside, I don't. If we all keep our burdens to ourselves, how could we ever get better? And so, I've come to realize that most people don't really want to get better. And most people don't want others to get better either."

Diora placed her hands over specific grooves along the stone.

"And yet you still haven't told us, despite our persistence," Reenu noted. "When will you and why won't you?"

Diora took her hands off the stone and turned around, her grin as big as it was the last time she heard one of them say the right thing.

"There is no such thing, other than maybe exposing people. I do love doing that. But it was all a *shibboleth*."

Reenu and Amaru simultaneously perked their eyebrows up.

Diora chuckled, "You two are cute. It's a way for me to tell that you're worthy. And you are."

With that, she kicked aside an indistinct piece of thin wood in front of them. Inside was a six-foot drop that led to a long tunnel of darkness interspersed with weakened torchlight. Reenu and Amaru looked at their friend, who grew more enigmatic as the day went on. She hopped down and motioned for them to follow.

"People get scared off by that word. They think that you're somehow...broken. I guess, in a way, it's true. But what they don't get is that our faults are what give us the sight to see how similar we are."

Diora had been going on about her false addiction for more than a few minutes. Walking alongside scattered torchlight on a slight decline had become disorienting, and Reenu and Amaru had little idea as to how long it had been or where they were going. They would have been perturbed were it not for the extended soapbox their friend was on and the warmth she now spoke with. Still, they knew how dangerous walking into a situation nearly blind could be,

always see, through one sense or another

so they had ceased walking, planting themselves squarely in the shadows. Diora didn't notice for a second, but when she did, she briskly walked back towards them.

"What's going on?" she asked them.

"That's funny - shouldn't you be answering that for us?" Amaru asked in return.

"Well, we're underground," Diora simply answered.

"Such a secret path makes for secret motives," Reenu added.

"Definitely. We don't want to be found out," Diora said.

"And why not?" Amaru asked.

"Well...we're *underground*," Diora repeated.

"That's not helpful," Amaru impatiently intoned.

"You'll understand soon," Diora insisted. "Just trust me."

Diora started to walk off, but her friends didn't follow. She sighed and turned back towards them.

"We're a secret non-group that's fighting against the tyranny of Inner Sanctum through semi-planned guerilla warfare and subtle, exploitative insurgence. We're the ones who started the fire."

Diora had hoped for more than surprise from the two of them, but her hopes were only half-met.

"Like I said, we're underground. Come on."

Reenu gathered tremors in his chest. He didn't think of himself as the rebellious type, and he still believed in what Ecclesia had to offer. He was greatly unsettled by the thought of being co-opted into whatever movement was taking place, but when he looked at Amaru, he saw a different emotion on her face. There was a peacefulness

almost a...joy

that was as relieving as it was curious. He knew he was safe with her, but he could tell from the glint in her eyes that they did not have the same expectations for this experience.

Reenu cupped one ear and pressed it forwards. Voices became clearer with each step.

"-doubt that this will work-"

wait, i know this voice...

"-allow it, but do you have any better-"

"-another explosion would surely-"

Reenu gulped and grasped Amaru's hand tightly. Amaru squeezed back and rubbed his shoulder. It was a nice feeling that he realized was only nice because his shoulder was no longer tender. The scar would never go away, however.

They turned a final corner and were immediately greeted with the end of the hall and everyone in it.

The room had clearly been carved out to fit a simplistic architecture that would support smaller gatherings. Six pillars adorned with torches stood thirty feet high between floor and concavernous ceiling. On the ceiling was writing that Reenu did not understand, but it looked to be some kind of a phrase. On the walls were drawings that depicted all kinds of graphic events, from the violent to the sexual. The room itself was circular, with three thin layers of descending step leading to the marbled center of the room. In that center were two very familiar faces,

Matthias? at least, I think it is...

the redhead!

and upon each ascending step sat another dozen or so congregants. All eyes were turned towards the three new intruders.

"Diora, you bring with you two new members of the disenchanted?" the redhead asked.

"Yes, Abigail," Diora said. "These friends of mine are not like the others."

Abigail looked both Reenu and Amaru up and down.

"What are your names?"

"Katir."

"Re-Reenu."

"And you two are lovers, I suppose?"

Abigail motioned downwards. Reenu and Amaru didn't realize they were still holding hands. They separated, but Amaru figured there was no point in denying it.

"Yes...and there is a third."

All that could be heard was the faint flickering of flames. Reenu was stunned Amaru admitted that,

she didn't even say her real name

for they had yet to find anyone else in Ecclesia who loved like they did. Days ago, Moshe had suggested to them that they keep it quiet after he had some encounter in which the nature of their relationship was nearly found out. And for a moment, not even these underground revolutionaries seemed to know what to do with the information. But Abigail spoke up.

"Really?" she half-asked. "A romantic trio? Why, I've never heard of such a thing...you'll fit in well around here!"

Everyone cheered ferociously. Well, almost everyone. Amaru was laughing out of relief, but Reenu noticed that the man opposite Abigail was looking at them with sorrow. Reenu thought this was Matthias, the bulky man he conversed with at The Last Call, but aside from his size and bloodshot eyes, there wasn't much left that looked right. His left hand was missing its inner fingers and most of the outer ones. His head was completely shaven, his chest completely bandaged, and he leaned against a crutch under his right arm. But the more they stared at each other, the more Reenu knew. It was him.

"Yes," Amaru affirmed amidst all the ovation. "And in fact, my name is not Katir. It's Amaru."

Wondrous gasps emanated from the crowd. Abigail smiled.

"Ah, the only person in Outer Sanctum with a warrant."

Everyone laughed. Amaru felt sheepish, feeling that her revelation was ill-timed.

"Well, as long as you keep the pseudonym, you'll fit in well around here. Please have a seat anywhere you'd like as Matthias and I finish our discussion."

"Hardly a discussion," Matthias sulked.

"Matthias," Abigail said, almost paternally. "Just because I disagree with you doesn't mean you're not free to speak your mind."

"Why speak if no one is listening?" Matthias grunted.

Abigail placed her hand on her breast, offense clearly drawn across her face. That motion caused Reenu to notice that her breasts and the rest of her body were barely covered. The robe she donned was torn in a way that was not overly sexual, but it was definitely protesting modesty. In fact, nearly everyone there seemed to wear their robes in similar fashion.

"Please, Matthias, I *am* listening. If there's anything I do, it's that."

"Then why aren't you hearing me when I say you're being too aggressive?!"

Matthias stumbled a bit backwards and placed what was left of his hand on his forehead.

"Reio, support him," Abigail commanded.

A boy younger than Reenu immediately stood up and went over to Matthias in order to steady him.

"Matthias, The Last Call was costly...but effective. You deny that?"

Matthias half-shrugged. "The job was done."

"Exactly, Matthias," Abigail said. "But it was only part one. Why half-ass it and back out at this point? After what it cost?"

"*Because* of the cost!" Matthias shouted while Reio struggled to keep him balanced.

Matthias turned towards the crowd.

"I know we've all rejected The Manual, but do you remember that passage...'violence creates violence?'"

Immediately: "I'm pretty sure that's not in The Manual, but-"

"Aban!" Abigail leered. Aban ceased speaking.

Matthias continued on, "Regardless, it is true. Clearly, I was nearly blown to bits in the process. Many others were injured, many of them innocent. And Paidi..."

Nearly everyone hung their heads low at the mention of
is that...the kid...
that name. Something adjacent to guilt strangled Amaru's thoughts. Reenu gulped and squeezed Amaru's hand once more.

After a few moments, Abigail breathed in and spoke again.

"Yes, of course. Paidi. The least deserving of death among us all. But Matthias...that is *exactly* why we must continue the path."

Matthias' eyes sharpened and he opened his mouth, but Abigail pressed on.

"There is no great movement without sacrifice, no necessary evolution without giving something up. I laud the diversity amongst everyone here, but the one thing we have in common is that we want to see things change, right?"

A few people murmured their agreeances before Abigail ceased them with the closing of her raised fist.

"The problem with everyone up there is not that they aren't good enough. They are truly valuable creatures, but they don't want to change things themselves. *We* do. *We* are willing. It is up to us to make Inner Sanctum no longer 'Inner,' but something for all. That is what we are here for and that is what Paidi died for."

The nods around Reenu and Amaru were growing in their fervency.

"Matthias, do not forget that we have already reached compromise. This was the less violent of the two proposed plans, and so far, it is working. You've been a big part in making it work. Of course, it is still contingent on there being another Call, but I'm sure the ego of Leader and his lackeys will win out over good judgment. We *will* be able to use the microphone when the time comes."

Matthias looked weary, and Reenu was not sure if it was because of his physical condition or because of Abigail's rhetorical confidence.

"Matthias, I deeply appreciate and value your assistance in our methods," Abigail let her arms hang limply at her sides while she said this. Her palms faced outwards as she concluded her inclusion.

"And I know you would not stand for the other plan. So please, will you continue to see this through?"

Everyone waited. Matthias took his time, and Reenu was struck by the pervasive energy of the room. It was as if he could feel the collective desire of reconciliation escaping the pores of each individual and being sent towards Matthias.

"Alright," Matthias conceded.

"Everyone!" Abigail shouted. "Let us praise Matthias and his prudence!"

A clamorous mixture of affirmation and nonsense filled the room, though it seemed to be at a very aware and controlled volume.

"I think we can call the discussion for now," Abigail decided. "We will meet again in ten days as developments arise. Feel free to mingle with each other and enjoy yourselves."

One couple had been romantically entangled for at least a half hour. The woman's body slid back and forth across the pillar opposite the entrance due to the brute strength the man was handling her with. Another couple, two males, did something similar, or at least as similar as they could. There was a knee-high rock formation outside the pillars that looked to be imitating the dimensions and style of The Table; on it was bizarre food that was not quite *casu*. Most everyone was talking in differing group sizes and differing emotional capacities, but the other ten or so people were wrestling fiercely in the center where Abigail and Matthias had spoken not too long ago. It was beautiful, living chaos, and Amaru loved it.

She kept her distance, though. These people felt wild and free, and as enchanting as those adjectives had always been to Amaru, they were also the ingredients that concocted volatility. Amaru scoffed at the thought.

how strange it is that our desires are so close to our demise

Besides, as much as she was interested in learning more about the people around her, she always went to the source. Abigail was facing a wall, etching something into it. Reenu had disappeared only a few moments after the meeting was adjourned, but

hope he finds someone to talk to

Amaru was not worried. There was not much room for him to get into any serious trouble, and there was only one way out. She'd meet up with him soon enough. For now, it was time to talk to the red-headed ringleader.

As Amaru approached Abigail, the redhead immediately dropped her pebble, turned around, and aggressively landed a kiss on her lips. Amaru backed away immediately, eyes wide with shock. Abigail laughed.

"I'm so glad you told us about your love trio," she said. "That's going to open up *so* many possibilities."

"There are still rules to our love. It's the three of us," Amaru informed as she wiped her mouth.

"That's disappointing," Abigail said, frowning before immediately enthusing, "But the less rules, the better. You took one off the board for us: monamory."

"Don't you think openly kissing whoever comes across you is a little like the greeting kisses some of the people up top do?" Amaru asked, hoping to playfully shoot down Abigail's contrarian confidence.

"Sheepshit," Abigail mocked. "That's politeness. That's the physical epitome of wanting to be *nice* to others but not giving enough of a fuck to do anything meaningful with those relationships. A lip-kiss...that's intimacy."

Abigail went in for another, this one slow and gentle. Amaru did not back away.

"You claim the less rules, the better," Amaru said, "but you've got to have some kind of structure here. How can a leader lead without a system in place?"

"I'm not a leader," Abigail insisted, allowing hints of hurt to enter her yellow aphrodisiac eyes. "Maybe *de facto*...but everyone's got equal voice here. Anyone else's direction is just as valid as mine."

Amaru twisted around Abigail and leaned against the wall, covering whatever it was she had been drawing or writing before.

"Matthias didn't seem to think so."

Abigail picked up her pebble.

"His plan is not better. It's as simple as that here. No one is willing to go his way."

"And that's determined by a vote?" Amaru asked.

"We don't vote," Abigail said. She was starting to write again, but strangely. She would write from the left side of Amaru all the way until she reached her skin, and then she would keep writing on Amaru's right. She went about this for a few rows.

"With voting, no one really wins. All you get is a split room." Abigail motioned to both sides of Amaru as she said this.

Amaru got off the wall and looked back at it. She asked Abigail what the writings meant.

"On each side of you, I wrote opposing statements. *I believe, I don't believe. I follow, I don't follow. I lead, I don't lead.* That's what voting leads to. Which is why, like I've been saying, we let anyone do what they want."

Abigail drew a line through each of the statements.

"What about when people have conflict? Does no one ever hurt each other?"

Abigail placed a hand firmly but lovingly on Amaru's right shoulder, massaging it slightly.

"That's what Inner Sanctum doesn't get. They think that holding onto a reward is what will motivate people to be better. But when you take the reward out of the equation, there's nothing to hurt each other for."

Amaru smiled. "There is truth in what you say. But I still find it hard to believe that this way of life is sustainable."

"And you should!" Abigail laughed. "Doubt is the core of it. Please, sit with me, my legs are fucking tired."

They both sat down, cross-legged and open-hearted. Amaru felt Abigail's transparency radiate as brightly as her hair. She figured that she had the right to ask what she wanted, and even if she didn't, Abigail couldn't be offended. There was hardly such a thing as *right* with her.

"What's this plan Matthias is so afraid of?"

Matthias sat alone, hidden behind the clump of wrestling rascals. He would have left already, but Reio was one of those rascals, and he was supposed to help him out. Ever since The Last Call, he was resigned to depending on some wooden crutches that Abigail had fashioned for him, but he hated them. After a few days with them, he decided he would never use them for walking, though he still kept them with him for self-defense. Each passing day convinced him more and more that he was in danger. His wounds made him look far too suspicious, which was why Abigail advised him to stay underground for the time being. Reio would help him walk around and heal faster, but Matthias was growing stir-crazy, and admittedly, paranoid. He couldn't shake the feeling that Abigail was changing, that there was something powerful being born from within. He wanted to tell others about it, but he was afraid that no one would side with him - they all loved her! Besides, she hadn't done anything truly anathema yet.

The clump was dissolving, so Matthias peered into what remained of it, hoping to find Reio. Matthias grunted when he couldn't find him. Unfortunately for him, his peering led to direct eye contact with someone on the other side of the clump: Reenu. Matthias groaned and looked away, but he knew Reenu was advancing.

"Matthias," Reenu said once he stood before him. "...my...my word. I..."

Aside from the speechlessness, Matthias sensed Reenu's disturbance by the way he held his hand to his mouth and slightly trembled. Most people he had seen in the past couple weeks presented a similar reaction, which was part of why Matthias had to stay underground. He was growing tired of the reaction, but he tried to show grace to Reenu. He knew he meant well.

"Yeah, kid. You should have seen me at the beginning," Matthias said with a half-grin.

"I'm so sorry," Reenu atoned earnestly.

"Fuck sorry," Matthias said bluntly, eyes hard. "This ain't got nothing to do with you."

"I-I know..." Reenu backpedaled. "I just mean...you shouldn't have to be in this state."

"It was my choice," Matthias admitted. "Part of...the plan."

"What *is* the plan?"

Matthias inspected Reenu. He already knew the kid had an inquisitive side to him, but he was still surprised by such a forward question. It was as if he had already assimilated himself.

"Uh. Abigail was the distraction. And then I was. I had the explosive device that Rixi made from parts he scavenged. We didn't know how much damage it would cause, but that didn't matter. As long as it provided enough time for Abigail and whoever else - it ended up being me again - to plant the microphone under The Table."

"What's that?"

"What?"

"The...microphone."

"Oh. You remember the device that Duman and the others spoke into that made their voices loud enough for everyone to hear?"

"Yes."

"It's one of those."

"Okay," Reenu said. He stopped for a second, allowing himself to think. He wanted to know more, but first:

"So, you could have died, then?"

"What?"

"You didn't know how powerful the explosion would be."

Now Matthias paused, scratching his skin-patchy chin with the nubs of his left ring and pinky fingers.

"Yeah, I guess so. We didn't think it was a lethal operation."

Matthias' response bewildered Reenu. He almost didn't know what to say.

"So...you...are fine with that? Or...?"

Matthias looked to the left.

"Everyone here realizes that, in the grand scheme of it all, our individual lives are fairly insignificant. We live in endless sand. As far as we know, this is the only place of structure and security out there."

"So shouldn't that make life here more treasured?" Reenu asked. The underground was becoming more confusing than above.

"It is. Which is why it's more important to us to change things than it is to be cozy." Matthias said, now looking deeply into Reenu's eyes.

That brought a form of clarity. These people were very different, but

Reenu could see something noble in them. That didn't mean that there weren't any problems. In fact, Reenu thought that, if anything, these people might be even more dangerous than anyone up top. But as long as they stuck to something noble.

Then a terrible thought struck Reenu.

"So...if that's what the first step required...what about the next one?"

"There are a couple ways this can go," Abigail said. For the first time, Amaru saw something like indecision upon her face.

"If they decide to have The Call once more - which I'm counting on, the fucking hubris that drips off their grimy balls - then we will remotely turn the microphone on during dinner."

Amaru blinked. "And what does that accomplish?"

Out of the corner of her eye, Amaru saw Reenu walking towards the cavern entrance, supporting another man as he walked. She had never seen Reenu go that slow before. She smiled and nodded at him,

he is making friends

but Reenu returned her glance with an empty look. The frigidity stung her.

"Exposure," Abigail said, a wild furor in her eyes. "Everyone will be able to hear what they really talk about when they eat. And I'm sure it will be as disgusting as the *casu* they insist on stuffing us with."

"And what if it's not? Or what if they don't ever have another session of The Call?"

Abigail's face hardened. She searched the few crevasses that lined Amaru's eyes.

"The microphone also has another explosive attached to it. This one's much more powerful."

Amaru's eyes widened. She searched the fire of Abigail's golden eyes. She hoped to find humanity.

"You're willing to randomly kill an unknowable amount of people at The Call? Do you not know how traumatizing that would be?" Amaru found herself smushing her palms together.

"It would shatter their paradigms," Abigail said. The fire was gone, but the flame remained. "No, I'd rather not kill if I don't have to. It's their structures that need to break, not their bodies. But I- we're undecided about whether or not to execute this step during The Call or just...whenever. Blowing up *just* The Table could do the trick, but..."

Abigail looked away, ideological distance separating her and Amaru. She slightly shook her head a few times as she finished:

"We're not sure if that's enough to get the message across. Sometimes violence is the necessary, ugly measure to take."

Amaru thought this over. She wasn't completely wrong. Violence had been her own way of life as well. Before Ecclesia, it was something she hardly thought about. When they needed to, they would kill. They would brutalize, even. She remembered how she and her friends had escaped from their owners long ago, back when they first decided to live on their own. *They* - she would not even think their names now - had been vicious and unfair to her and her friends. It got to the point where she began to see Reenu *believe* what *they* were saying

useless...unfit for living...if only we had ten sheep, we could get rid of you...

about him. She thought that their bond was enough for him to break free of the slander, but his mind was conditioned to go the opposite way: he started to *love them*. Reenu believed his captors were the ones keeping him safe in a world he didn't think he could handle. When Moshe suggested escaping, it was Amaru who wanted to go beyond. They plotted and exacted their revenge, picking off their captors one by one during the only time they could get them

their last sexual favors

alone. At the end of it all, the three friend-lovers gathered the bodies, dismembered parts and all, in the center of the camp and burned them. Amaru had never been more proud. She thought it was her life's accomplishment - they had worked together and overcome their oppressors! Victory through bloodshed! Fire with fire! But Reenu's reaction told her a different story. In front of the glaring heat from the melting corpses, Amaru initially thought Reenu was sweating, but his shudders and shakes soon made her realize that he was crying. All of the other indentured servants had fled, leaving the three of them alone. Moshe had them make a pact: this act of severe violence would be their last. Reading the teachings of Mati helped concretize her newly developed desire for pacifism. She saw that, on a small scale, death needn't be the answer. But she also saw how changing the scale changed the answer some.

"Besides, nothing is as ugly as *KAMNOS*," Abigail snarled.

Amaru stiffened. Even the sound of it induced bodily fear.

"Alright," Amaru conceded. "You *need* to tell me more about that."

Reio and his newfound friend-lovers took off running. He was beyond excited to try some of the group intimacy that the new short-haired woman suggested. He couldn't help but feel like he was forgetting something, though...

Matthias sighed. "There goes my way out of here."

Reenu watched five young, angular men frantically scurry towards the cavern entrance. In another context, Reenu would have gleefully gone with them. Wherever they were headed, it looked like fun. And more importantly, it looked like they would have fun together. But here, their enthusiasm scared him. It was ferocious, and it reminded Reenu too much of the destructiveness he and Matthias were discussing.

"I can help you out," Reenu suggested.

Matthias looked up at him. His eyes softened. "Sure, kid."

Reenu took Matthias' hand and wrapped him over his right shoulder. He grimaced.

"Actually, can I have you lean on my left side instead?"

They walked in silence for a number of paces. Each step was laborious. Reenu took a step with his outside foot, then Matthias with his. Reenu would take a step with his inside foot, then Matthias with his. Then they would be still for a moment before moving on. Matthias had given Reenu a lot to mull over; it weighed heavily on him. Matthias felt bad. He remembered the kid having an endless natural reservoir of optimism when he first met him. But that was then. He wasn't sure if it was daily life in Outer Sanctum or if it was his own dour thoughts that affected Reenu, but he didn't like it. The crushing of the soul is the unfortunate expense of time long spent in unfortunate places.

"So..."

Matthias readied himself for another question.

"...I understand that, if it exists, *KAMNOS* is truly despicable and unjust. But...do you believe it?"

"Believe what?"

"That it exists."

Reenu felt Matthias quiver against his body.

"Huh...no one's ever asked me that," Matthias said. "I think we all assume it does. Why wouldn't it? No one ever hears from people who leave...and the burning smells...what else could it be?"

"Well, it doesn't *have* to be a furnace that's powered by the bodies of...what did you call them? Derelicts?"

Matthias grunted in half-agreement. "That's not what *I'd* call them but that *is* what they're called."

"Right," Reenu continued. "Well, what's the proof that Ecclesia *has* to run on burning bodies?"

Matthias didn't say anything.

"And," Reenu continued. "The people who leave...what if they just don't come back?"

Matthias gave a small laugh. "Kid, Ecclesia is fucked up. But it's not *that* fucked up. Even those who've lived here and hated it would probably come back after a week out there."

good point

"Maybe they all just died out there then."

Matthias' head tilted side to side, mulling the idea over. Reenu shifted him over to alleviate some of his weight.

"When I was little, I believed everything that bigger people told me. We all do that, huh? I still don't really question people that I think know more than me, but...who was the one who told you about *KAMNOS*, Matthias?"

Reenu felt Matthias turn stiff.

"Abigail."

Reenu nodded. "I'm not saying she made it up, but I just figure, with as brutal as she's willing to be, I...I don't know."

Matthias pressed down, forcing Reenu to stop. Reenu turned towards him, and they met with intense eye contact.

"You're right, Reenu. We don't know. And we may never know. But I do know that this place is for the placeless. And even if we don't always get it right, we at least acknowledge that we don't have to. You may have a point, but I don't know if anyone will listen to it. For now. It's worth looking into, but I don't think you should suggest that to anyone else. Understand?"

Reenu nodded and gulped. He made to speak, but Matthias preempted him.

"Because even if Abigail is in the wrong...we still give names to the nameless. Faces to the faceless."

"Do you have a name?"

Amaru and Abigail had nearly caught up to Reenu and Matthias -

mostly because they were going five times as fast. They had just come into view, and it would be only another minute before they reunited.

Abigail laughed, a heartier laugh than Amaru expected from the nearly frameless woman.

"No, that would ruin it. Some have suggested we be called The Underground, but that's somehow both cheeky *and* tacky."

Abigail playfully hit her companion's shoulder and Amaru laughed a little.

"A name makes us an entity. Might not sound like a bad thing, but then we'd be easier to find. Last thing *we* need is a reputation."

"Isn't the point to be known?"

"No, the point is to *know*," Ambree laughed again, this time at her amateurish wordplay. "We want people to know there is another way without the obligation of joining another group. That defeats the purpose."

Amaru felt like she was starting to get it, and it made her glad. Abigail could see the joy spreading across her face. She turned and grabbed both of Amaru's hands, halting them in the process.

"What it comes down to, Amaru, is this. There are two types of people: seekers and dwellers. Dwellers find a place of their own and call it home. They don't need to upturn anything or even renovate, really. But seekers are never satisfied. They endlessly search for truth and the way to it. As far as I'm concerned, most dwellers are content with living up top. Most seekers find their way down here. That's all it is."

Amaru had never felt more understood in her life.

Reenu tossed aside a fragment of burnt tent.

"Do you think we should–"

"Not now, Reenu," Amaru said bluntly.

Once they got back into their own tent, Reenu immediately burst out, brimming with words to tell.

"What a peculiar place that-"

"Lower your voice," Amaru whispered.

Her command completely ceased the rapid-fire of Reenu's thoughts, which benefited them both.

"Well...what should we do?"

"About?"

Reenu blinked. "That whole thing."

"Probably nothing, for now."

Reenu shook his head, aghast.

"Wh-...why not? How *could* we not? We stumbled upon an entirely new world - it demands a response!"

Amaru eyed Reenu.

voice down

"I don't think we're on the same page about it."

"Well, what did you think of it?"

"I think we found *it*."

Reenu's surprise persisted. It wasn't like Amaru to buy in to something so holistically.

"How can you say that?"

"Isn't it what we've *actually* been looking for? A group of people coming together but not really in charge of one another. Engaging in whatever they want but never bringing harm to one another..."

"You mean people coming together under the pretense of disgruntled unity. Engaging in whatever they want without fear of consequence, willing to harm others when necessary."

They stood there on opposite sides of the tent.

"Yeah, I think we need to get on the same page before we do anything," Amaru said.

"How can you be ok with such extreme violence, Katir? You remember what Moshe said-"

"Yeah, and I remember how he went back on his word, too."

Reenu took a few terse steps towards Amaru before utterly embracing her. The hurt was still present.

"I know, but we both know he's sorry."

"He ought to say it, then."

"I know."

Amaru pulled back so she could look at Reenu.

"Reenu, I will always do everything I do for you. For the three of us. That's why I'm committed to helping you see the good in...those underground."

Reenu smiled, he knew she was trying. They kissed and lay down next to each other, holding each other's hands and their collective future loosely. Then Reenu had a thought.

"Well, we should at least tell Moshe, right?"

Amaru didn't hesitate with that one.

"Not yet."

Chapter 9: The Ultimatum

28, 27 DBK

Lipos sat across from Arah, incessantly blubbering atop his double-portion.

Arah smiled. The breakthrough was finally happening.

He would let his friend stream tears into his food for as long as he needed. Ever since conversation with the beggar became regular, Arah had begun to understand people better. Before, he only felt confusion in light of others' mistakes and weaknesses. As bodily disciplined as he was, it was hard to relate to the exterior shortcomings that so many other hopefuls in Outer Sanctum were plagued with. But now, he understood that everyone had their own specific pratfalls that kept them from being their best. *His* failures weren't any better, just different. The way into Inner Sanctum was not about being perfect - it was about overcoming your *own* imperfections. A slight distinction in thinking that made for a much lighter burden. And actual empathy. And Lipos was the fleshy culmination of his philosophical shift.

"Ah just...Ah always dun et this way. Et's 'ard not to," Lipos managed to say in between sobs.

"Why's it hard, Lipos?" Arah asked.

"Wah not eat 'til I'm not 'ungry?" Lipos looked up at Arah with red-rimmed eyes, his chin gently grazing the top of his *casu* mountain.

"What about others? The more you eat, the less those around you can have."

Lipos sniffed. "Ah know. Et's just..."

"Do you think this is why you don't have any friends?" Arah asked, unwavering.

Lipos froze, blinking and taking a moment before he sat up straight. "You're mah friend."

Arah lowered his eyes. "Yes, any...other friends."

Lipos blinked again. "Well, ah suppose. But ah don't need any other friends."

Arah audibly breathed out his nose. "Right, but...I just mean to say that maybe your overeating is connected to all your problems. You're stuck in this cycle that keeps you out of Inner Sanctum. It makes you miserable, and yet, you keep doing it. It's why everyone else you know is already inside and you're still out here. In fact, I'm sure it's why they didn't stick aro-"

Arah stopped. Lipos' eyes were watering again. Arah thought up colorful curses for himself.

"I'm sorry."

Instead of responding, Lipos lowered his head and continued to eat his double-portion. Arah ran his hands through his now greasy and unkempt mane, unintentionally pulling out a clump as he did so. He tried, but he couldn't handle the self-destructive negligence any longer.

"You're lucky you ended up here."

Arah stood up and walked briskly away. As he did so, he saw the trio he often saw but had yet to approach. They were a newer group, but they possessed an obvious bond that currently brewed extreme jealousy within himself. Their eyes were closed and they held their arms out towards each other. Arah couldn't be sure, but it looked as if the tallest one had his eyes slightly open.

Moshe, Amaru, and Reenu held their arms out and open towards each other. Seated at their new usual spot, plates of *casu* atop both benches, they synchronously drew their breaths and allowed their chests time to expand. Ten seconds of tension. Then, a letting go and a relaxation of posture. On one side, Amaru sat with her back shrunk in and cheer on her face. Her legs rested peacefully in a fairly wide stance. Next to her was Reenu. His face was as still as Amaru's legs, and his vacant gaze contrasted with the clear emotion on hers. Finally, Moshe. He sat across from his friends, and as such, he had to reach a little farther to join with them. But he managed to interlock his fingers with theirs, as was their new custom. He gave his friends a face of receptivity.

Another long breath. The idea was not to hold it for a certain amount of time, but rather, to try and breathe at the *same* time. To move in between the inhales and the exhales together. Reenu coughed as if he incidentally fell into smoke. This was only their third time attempting this exercise, and Amaru's tendency was to hold it in too long. It was her idea to do this. Moshe agreed that it would be worthwhile to attempt, though he found it odd that she would not tell him where the idea came from. Just trust me, she said. He tried not to give it much thought - he was trying to trust more, and he knew her heart was in the right place.

A final, much-needed

thanks

breath. Now, it was time for looking. This part felt unusually

but I suppose we never had the luxury of games

game-like, but Moshe went with it anyway. After the third breath, the trio would instinctively look at one another, and whoever made eye contact would keep it. The first two times, it just happened to be Reenu and Amaru (which Moshe made sure to tease them about afterwards). But now, it was Moshe and Amaru. They would hold each other's gaze for as long as they did.

Moshe knew that his first facial expression was probably one of shock. He felt a little embarrassment at that, for Amaru still held the buoyant smile that comes after a light laugh. It was infectious, and caused him to beam immediately. Over the last forty-one days, he had seen his friend undergo a true transformation of demeanor, but particularly during the last ten. He concluded that it came out of the life-giving properties of The Manual and its teachings - she had been opening up more to its tenets and asking more questions as he faithfully read them to her and Reenu. But he also *knew* that this change was the result of her finally believing in the hope that he had so painstakingly sought to provide for them over the past however-many hundreds of days. And in all those days, he realized

i don't believe i've ever seen her smile like this

and it was a smile that made her endlessly beautiful.

Moshe wrinkled his nose. He tried to hold it back, but he couldn't. His eyes became moist, and a second later, they let tears fall rapidly. Amaru nearly squealed. Reenu slightly edged backwards in perplexity. Moshe let go of their hands and wiped underneath his cheeks. He tried apologizing but could only laugh at himself. And, he realized, to beg pardon was to squander the grace of the moment.

They resumed their limb-locking and closed their eyes. This concluding act was meant to allow each of them time to reflect individually on their time together while still being connected. They would then go about the rest of their day, now that each of them had their own regular routines. For whatever reason, they had yet to discuss the meaning of these experiences so far. Moshe thought it was because the experience itself did not warrant many words, or maybe they just hadn't found the right words for it yet. Regardless, they let the intimacy last for as long as it would. But Moshe was nervous. He didn't know where Amaru's idea came from, and he never saw anyone else do anything like it. Reenu shifted. Moshe knew there was nothing wrong in what they were doing, but he had begun to understand how important social perception was. Even if it just *looked* like they were doing something wrong, it could negatively impact their lives and their chances. So, he made sure to leave his eyes slightly open, just in case.

He had her pinned with both arms pulled back and away from her body and a foot planted firmly on the base of her neck. Naked, face-down in the molding dirt, Amaru snarled. Three others stood around her, each snickering and relaxed, but ready to step in and deal more damage. One of them came from behind and kicked her exposed crotch, making her convulse as much as her confinement allowed. The others laughed. He did it once more, this swing of the leg eliciting a pitiful whimper. The others started doubling over, holding their stomachs in euphoria and strange sympathy. The offender went in for a third help-ing, but Amaru shot her right leg straight into his gut. As he doubled over in pain, she lifted her heel into his jaw with crunching precision, causing him to stumble into her overhead oppressor before collapsing. Amaru used the will of her body and the push that adrenaline pro-vided to swing her arms down to the left, her captor landing broken-nose-first into the ground beside her. She was unable to stand herself up quickly enough - the other two charged into her and grabbed her arms. Amaru's legs went wildly kicking as they lifted her into the air and slammed her down into the ground. Dazed from the new throbbing in the back of her head, Amaru let a few punches strike her body before rolling her legs to her chest, leaping to her feet, and falling back down with elbows landing directly on each of their spines.

The five of them lay in exhaustion. Amaru breathed heavily while the others struggled to breathe at all. Then she laughed - a deep belly laugh that spread to the rest of them. Amaru spanked the two spine-tapped ones as she got up.

"*That* is the spanking you *all* deserve," Amaru continued laughing. "What terrible strategy! Pali, Via, you can't just stand there while one person does the work. Epi, you of all people should know that the rear, though not visible, is *exactly* where someone would defend themselves from - for that very reason! And Krati...work on your grip, man. Seriously."

The boys hung their heads. Amaru rolled her eyes.

"Okay...you *are* all improving, I'll admit. But you'll get your asses whooped even harder if you try wrestling with the others any time soon. So...just keep practicing for now."

Each boy nodded his head. They all turned and saw Abigail coming their way. Amaru walked over to her abandoned robe and put it back on. The boys started running in the opposite direction, but Epi stopped and turned back.

"Same time tomorrow, Amaru?"

Amaru put her hand where her eyebrow used to be and closed her eyes.

"Sure, Epi."

And off he went to rejoin his friends.

Abigail arrived with a devilish grin drawn from cheek to cheek.

"Fucking up the little ones again?"

Abigail leaned in for a kiss, but Amaru pulled away, causing the pair of cracked lips to brush against her neck instead.

"They've got much to learn," Amaru insisted.

"But they've got the *desire*. A beautiful thing, ain't it?"

Amaru nodded.

Abigail's face hardened. Her eyes narrowed as she took Amaru's face in her hands.

"What's going on?" she asked.

Amaru looked at her ally with open eyes.

"Nothing," she said as she shook her head.

Abigail let go, a little more gruffly than was pleasant.

"You know I don't do that shit. Tell me or don't - it's your choice."

Amaru nodded, breathing out a heavy sigh from her nostrils.

"Will you be here tomorrow? For the meeting? There are some...interesting new developments that you might want to know." Amaru knew there was sincere longing in Abigail's questions, but her voice betrayed that intention in favor of steely indifference.

Amaru kept her eyes close to her chest. She knew that Abigail wouldn't understand, but she also wanted to try and make her. But she feared the alpha woman's anger. And she knew that no matter what her response was, it would come.

Abigail's pudgy nose started to twitch.

"I get it," she sarcastically insisted. "Your hope is not yet broken. Fortunately for you, I am not worried about that. For it soon will be."

Abigail walked off, confident in her indignance. Amaru tried to do the same.

The gray, wooden pitch of a tent collapsed under the pressure of age, bringing down the tattered remains of fabric and releasing fading ash into the sky. Reenu winced in reflex. He had always been easily startled, which would have been a useful reaction outside of Ecclesia were it not to lead to the freezing response that he experienced. Amaru was fight, Moshe was flight, he was fright. His friends teased him about it, but it was a legitimate insecurity of his. Were it not for them, it would have only been a matter of time before his innate fear response led to his anticlimactic end. That thought passed his mind every time he was startled, though it now held greater weight considering the context.

He sat alone with broken and burnt tents, but far enough behind any so that his robe would not be covered in soot. Legs outstretched, he tried to remain as still as possible. Not a single one of these tents was whole, which served as both a convenience and a fatal flaw. He would likely be able to see anyone who came near, and thus, fulfill his given duty, but it was possible that he could be seen first.

at that point, why have a lookout

He didn't expect anyone to come; it was not a popular scene. However, if someone *did* traverse this deeply into the Torched Tents, they would likely be Kohen. And then, he wouldn't know what to do. Did it make any sense to fight? If he took off, he would be abandoning his friend, and she would surely be discovered. All he could really do, if he didn't freeze, was either go willingly and place himself in justice's hands or create a diversion, but he couldn't think of anything effective. An excuse coming from the lips of an unconvincing liar was like small talk from an uninterested party. He had been waiting there for several hours now. He didn't mind it at first - he was the one who volunteered a few days prior - but today felt different. On the eve of such an important day, he would have preferred to spend the entire time with both Moshe and Amaru. But he recognized that they had their...commitments. In all fairness, he probably *could* be down there with Amaru if he wanted to, but it didn't take long for him to realize that those weren't his people. He knew that their company and...voracious way of life gave Amaru joy, and so he encouraged her to join with them whenever she pleased, but he was beginning to see the enabling folly of his consolation. She was spending more and more time underground. It was getting risky. But so far, there had n-

A shambling cacophony.

what was that

Reenu's chin went up. His eyes cautiously went over the details of his anemic landscape, but his alertness was for naught. He spotted a dust cloud reaching for the sky as it floated above a mangled pile of fabric and wood. Another collapsed tent.

It was then that Reenu noticed the wind. It had strengthened considerably since he had got there, which explained the frequency of falling tents. Reenu silently rubbed his chest with both hands. Truth be told, a part of him hoped that someone was there. Friend or foe, abundant human contact was becoming foreign to him once more. He had recently lamented the loss of Adah and Adinah, the nearly-twin girls, from his life. Moshe suggested they stop interacting; he was worried that their chattersome ways would be problematic. Reenu was saddened by the thought that Moshe was probably right. Were that the case or not, Reenu feared that the lack of regular social interaction was even more harmful to his health.

He heard rumbling from behind him and turned his head. He smiled, seeing Amaru punch the plank aside and rise out of the alley's ground. She was not as happy about seeing him, it seemed.

"Aren't you just absolutely, wonderfully excited?!"

Moshe stopped and stood still. He was. He would never express it with the exuberance Duman hardly ran out of, but he felt a newfound confidence and peace that he took as his sign of true change.

"I am certainly looking forward to it," Moshe replied. He resumed re-stocking. The two of them had been cleaning and filling up the tracts at Ecclesian Essentials. There had been a recent influx of hopefuls, and supplies (as well as tents, much to Duman's dismay) were running low. Moshe felt the throb of cognitive dissonance when the latest large group arrived. Fifteen or so. He observed their chummy devotion to each other and found it electrifying, but he knew that it would be a long, narrow road for a group that size to all make it into Ecclesia. Especially after tomorrow.

"As you very well should be!" Duman exclaimed as he vigorously rubbed Moshe's shoulder. "With all transparency, most people do not pass their Trials on their first go-around. But I have no doubts about you."

Moshe stopped again.

"Why do you think that, Duman?" Moshe sought confirmation more than understanding.

"Hmm. Unfortunately, it seems to be an issue of effort," Duman continued without missing a beat of his tract-replacing. "Most people get here and are unable to 'kick the old wolf,' as they say. They don't realize that change is born from positive action *and then* it results in a positive heart. Or, maybe they do realize that and would simply rather not spend the energy. It's a courageous last step. But you - my good man! -

you have always been so helpful and conversatory with others. Conversatory? Conversational? Who knows? Ho ho! And consistently reading through The Manual with your fri- what was it, *three times through already?...*"

At this, Duman also stopped his duty to thoughtfully give Moshe a glance.

"...yes. No doubt in my mind."

Moshe was well-pleased with Duman's commendation, even if he had heard that same explanation several times over at this point. He smiled. He started placing the tracts on the shelves quickly and accurately. For the first time in his life, hard work was paying off generously. When it was just the three of them, hard work was a *necessity*, not an attribute of character. It was a means for survival, and the reward was another day of suffering in the sun. When he had a home, before he left it with his friends, hard work went a little beyond survival since it was useful for maintenance. The threat of death was not the everyday constant, but its accolade was repetitious non-meaning. The days were not memorable because they were not distinct. And now, his time had finally come. He had freed his friends from oppression and led them to the Promised Land. All in a life's work. He had no qualms about being ready for his recompense. He could imagine that everyone else around him had similar journeys of adversity, but they were unable to take that courageous last step. He was.

Moshe stood outside his tent, hand on the entrance flap. He had nearly entered, but he realized that it would be best for him to wait. The sounds from inside were muted, but he could tell that Reenu and Amaru were nearing the end of ardent lovemaking. Let them enjoy it - he hadn't done so in quite some time. He convinced himself that it was mostly just an issue of timing and safety - it was yet another activity of theirs that might be considered morally ambiguous - but the last time he was with them felt different. It was only a week ago, and their first time attempting anything as far as he knew, but their energy was not as...sensitive as it had once been. He didn't tell them, but something about it felt...disjointed. He didn't really have the language for it yet, and so, he kept it to himself. They didn't seem to mind. Besides, Moshe believed their new bonding ritual was doing wonders for them that sex never had.

A slight whimper from Reenu and a mutual release of breath. Moshe ascertained that he need only wait another minute before it was safe to enter. No need to risk opening the flap and having someone nearby see anything unseemly. He turned around and looked out at all that surrounded him.

The sun was setting. Moshe never felt positively about this daily ceremony before Ecclesia. What was different now? Walls. The towering walls that surrounded the settlement must have kept both the cold wind *and* the hot air out. The temperature had never been perfect, but the weather's threats were nullified in Outer Sanctum. And it led Moshe to realize...

the sunsets...the reds and the oranges...they are beautiful

Moshe's eyes came down from the sky and rested on someone who was already looking at him. His right eyebrow went up momentarily, coming back down as he quickly recognized the man. Even though they had never met, the man was well-known in the community. It took Moshe a moment to recognize him because the reason for his fame was waning: his hair was not the impressive, midnight-black curtain that it once was. He stood in perfect line-of-sight with Moshe, though many tents away. He had a pleasant face that was neither intimidating nor encouraging, and he was simply, half-heartedly waving. Moshe waved back at his distant neighbor. But as they finished their remote greeting, someone stepped out of the man's tent. As she stood up, she started speaking to the man before turning and facing Moshe as well. Moshe felt the intensifying beat of his heart. Even without the up-do maroon of her hair - for she was now strikingly bald - her cheekbones and eyes were a combination that he would never forget, along with the rest of her visage. Ambree looked surprised for a moment, but her familiarly curved smile returned. Moshe didn't hesitate.

"Friends, h-how was your day together?"

Reenu was mid-fastening his robe when Moshe burst in, so he quickly scrambled to finish the job before relaxing after seeing who the invader was. Amaru sat wide-legged and was clearly pleased to see the distracted Moshe.

"My dear Moshe, we had a great time with Diora, as per usual," Amaru reassured him.

"Ha, 'usual' may be an overstatement," Reenu countered, snickering at Amaru as he did so. Amaru playfully smacked his rear.

"Fair. Since she...opened up, at least," Amaru corrected herself.

"Great," Moshe said. He was managing a smile, but he was also peeking back outside.

Amaru and Reenu looked at each other.

"Is everything alright?" Reenu asked Moshe.

"Yeah," was his answer, closing the flap once more.

"How was *your* day, Moshe?" Amaru asked, trying to ignore Moshe's aloofness.

"Oh, yeah. It was fine," Moshe blinked a couple times as he settled himself. "Mostly just helped Duman with getting everything back in order at Essentials."

Amaru and Reenu looked at each other once again before giving in to temperate laughter. This time it was Reenu who spanked Amaru. Moshe was confused.

"What?" he asked.

"We made - oh, what was it that Adinah called it?" Amaru asked Reenu, teasing him with the tone of her voice.

"A bet," Reenu reluctantly admitted.

"Yes, there it is. Anyway, I *knew* that's what you'd be doing."

Moshe frowned, still not quite understanding the intent of their laughter.

"How did you know that?"

Amaru rolled her eyes. "*Because*, Moshe. That's exactly what you'd be doing. Always making sure everything is going smoothly. 'In order,' like you said."

Moshe's demeanor remained constant. He crouched awkwardly beside the entrance flap while the others lay on their sides on the opposing corner of the tent. He didn't feel obliged to make himself more at home. Not until he got some clarity. He didn't like feeling like he was "figured out."

"Assumptions are deadly, friends," he said.

Reenu clammed up a bit. Amaru rolled her eyes, less blithely now. In light of her recent, lively escapades, Moshe's stoicism was coming across as less strong and more dull.

"Relax, Moshe. It's just fun. We just know you, obviously. And we missed you."

Moshe nodded and allowed his body to soften. He stretched out his arms and crawled up next to his companions. He turned his head away from them as he yawned.

"Besides...that's what you'll be doing on the inside after tomorrow, right?"

Moshe stopped his yawn. When he turned his head, he saw Reenu looking at him. Reenu was sitting up and leaning over Amaru, a certainty in his face that Moshe had never seen before. Moshe returned the gesture.

"We'll *all* get to straighten things out in there after tomor-"

"No, Moshe," Reenu insisted. "*You* will. You know Katir and I aren't the types to do that sort of thing. We don't take charge."

Moshe countered quickly, not letting the seed of doubt be planted. "Maybe not in The Citadel, but there will assuredly be other important roles for you two. Reenu, every meal I've ever had that's come from your hands has been better than *casu*. I know you can do something about that. And Katir...you're one heck of a fighter. The best I've ever known. I'm sure Lieutenant Zacchaeus would be delighted to have you support him."

Reenu and Amaru let the ideas circulate their thoughts. Neither of them had considered the ways in which their expertise could be maneuvered into something that could benefit all citizens. They had been stuck on the ways the system had been failing them, not on how they were perhaps failing the system. They maintained their open hearts for as long as they could.

"These aren't just images of wishful thinking, friends," Moshe continued. "I've thought about this. I've had discussions with Duman about this. He's been clear not to make any promises, but he's always encouraged the possibilities. We are on the brink of not only making Ecclesia our home, but making it a better home for everyone else. And the past forty days...they call it The Trial, but really, it was a refinement. We needed that time to understand The Manual. To figure out the needs of those around us. To be purified of the animal habits that the desert bred in us. To be more like Savyer, even. As lofty as that may sound. I know it was frustrating to wait even longer, but I count it all as worthwhile. Don't you?"

Moshe looked down and saw that his hands were outstretched once more, reaching towards his friend-lovers with longing. He saw it in their eyes. They, too, were longing. And it was the next words that were spoken that sealed that longing just as much as it sealed their dividing.

"Moshe, if I'm with Zacchaeus, and Reenu's making *psomi*, and you're in The Citadel...then we're not together. And if we're not together...how is this our home?"

The question gave word to the feeling that the last forty days had been manufacturing through its underlying relational strain. It deadened the air like time does to youth. And it killed their pretense like time does to the old. Sometimes a simple, transparent question can be more cutting and destructive than a detailed argument. Moshe held fast to the reason in his head, but the question would linger in his heart for weeks. He tried to recover against its weight.

"Katir, just because we might not always be together from here on out doesn't mean we have to change our relationship. It's just where life is taking us. When we sought safety in the sand, we followed the direction of the wind, knowing that it led to the most traveled path. Right, Reenu?"

Reenu nodded even as his eyes threatened welling. Moshe looked away so he could fight his own wave of emotion, but it still found a way into the tone of his voice and his burgeoning, passionate plea.

"It's not so different in here. We've got to...roll with the punches. We've got to take what we can get, even if it means less time together. Because at least we know we are all safe. We are all doing well. In Inner Sanctum, that will always be true. And besides...the *time* apart we've spent here hasn't caused us to *drift* apart..."

Moshe wanted to say more. He wanted to make his friend-lovers feel as confident as he did in what was to come. He wanted to tell stories of times past. He wanted them all to sleep peacefully before tomorrow came. But mostly, he wanted to ask for *their* reassurance that they believed in his last statement so that *he* could. But it was that sentiment that kept words from coming out of his mouth. And it was the defeated looks on their faces that gave him not the answer he desired, but the one that he feared.

Somewhere between the dream of reality and the nightmare of delusion, Amaru spoke. Moshe was drifting off (or maybe he already had?), but he did what he could to listen. Why did she always have to speak at the most inconvenient times?...

She said something about the underground. She's working with them? She is them? Moshe couldn't shake the sleep dust from his eyes hard enough to understand. But she made it seem pertinent. Reenu looked tense too, so it must have been. Something was wrong. Amaru messed up. She realized it, and realized she wanted to pass her Trial. This admittance was her form of repentance. She hoped that coming clean would be enough, but she didn't know. She was apologizing. Moshe was halfway forgiving and halfway chastising. How could she endanger the group like that? Did she not realize what a foolish decision that was? Or was it? What even was underground? Moshe told her to not worry. It was a mistake, but everyone is allowed at least one...

Moshe fastened his robe tightly. These days he was even less aware of how he looked than when in the wilderness, but he thought it might not hurt to clean up a bit. He pulled his hair back from his brown eyes and pushed the fringes behind his ears. He had forgotten where in The Manual it said this, but he was pretty sure that external cleanliness was considered a reflection of internal purity. If not, it made sense at least. He rubbed some of the caking dust off of his face.

Reenu and Amaru were similarly getting ready. Reenu's hair stayed short, so he didn't have to worry about that, but he made sure to do some morning stretches. He was convinced the activity made him look taller. Even if it didn't, the faux confidence worked well enough. He certainly needed it this day. Amaru rubbed the sides of her face as if she could miraculously massage the wrinkles into oblivion. She turned and looked at Moshe. As she did, she felt the smooth length where her left eyebrow used to be. They exchanged light smiles in remembrance. It was quite the surprise that it had yet to grow back.

Looking at his friends, Moshe felt an unusual joy cultivate within himself. He had done all that he could to lead them to this day. The Trial they each experienced was nothing compared to the trials outside Ecclesia's walls. He felt they would be ok. The joy was unusual because it was parental. But it was also unusual because it was not uncontaminated. His mind filled with a flash of the previous

what was it she said

night. He knew Amaru had admitted some-

the underground!

Moshe's heart froze.

but...was it a dream?

He looked at her as she helped Reenu finish his stretches.

it probably was...a nightmare...the manifestation of my irrational fears...

Moshe reasoned that either she said what she needed to or she didn't need to say anything at all because it wasn't real. He felt they would be ok.

Arah sat alone. He was not surprised that Lipos didn't want to sit with him anymore (well, maybe a little), but the fact that he was not there *at all* was quite unexpected. He would have sworn that his fat acquaintance would have at least found another to leech portions off of, but he was nowhere to be seen. Arah had always been patient with him - if not internally, then definitely externally. He had never insulted him until yesterday, but as harsh as it was, perhaps it was exactly what he needed to make a change. Arah wanted to believe that was the case.

But now he sat alone. By himself at The Troei, a place he had always loathed. He accepted some *casu* with the thought that Lipos would come by at some point and that an act of kindness might warrant forgiveness, but as the sun passed its zenith, he realized that would not be happening. A month ago, he would have told anyone that he didn't mind being by himself. In fact, he often thought that solitude was what brought him the clarity and space he needed to be the best potential Ecclesian he could be, allowing himself to focus on that which is good and lovely and true and not on that which is present. Arah shook his head, trying to rid himself of dark thoughts as he got up to throw away his *casu*.

What was even more troubling was the beggar. They had grown

closer over the past few weeks, at least in the teacher-pupil sense. Arah wasn't sure if they could be considered friends, but he knew he had learned a lot from him. He learned about the plight of the disabled and how to let go of vanity. Arah took these lessons to heart, feeling more peaceful than ever. Dichotomously, he also felt more antipathy for the way people like the beggar were treated in Outer Sanctum. He thought of a conversation they had once

how can we be made new if no one wants us to

almost daily. And to think that he once felt similarly repulsed by people like his new frien-...teacher. But it wasn't those lessons that were presently troubling. It was the fact that, just like Lipos, the beggar wasn't around. In all actuality, Arah hadn't seen him in several days. It was unusual, and it made him antsy. Could that anxiety be part of what led to his poor treatment of Lipos yesterday? Arah looked down at his *casu* as he held it above The Troei's trash receptacle. His hands started to tighten around the feeble plastic tray. He let out a sharp cry as he slammed the tray into the trash with a startling

SMACK!

The Troei was busier than usual that day, but the bustle of the throng ceased ubiquitously, replaced by apprehensive looks towards Arah. He grew red. He noticed his hands were shaking. To the average stranger, it may have looked like the man with the once-glorious mane was retreating quickly out of embarrassment. But as Arah took off running, it was not humiliation that motivated his one-track mind, it was mission. He needed to find his friend.

Last Judgment. It was a term jokingly used throughout Outer Sanctum in reference to the end of someone's Trial, but it sure felt appropriately haunting. The three of them walked in a single file line: Moshe in front, Katir in the middle, and Reenu at the end, occasionally looking behind him out of habit and curiosity. As they drew closer to The Wall, they saw a variety of expressions pass them by. Rejuvenated by the promise of The Last Call, this was Last Judgment for a lot of people, and because of that, The Wall was lined with passionate dissonance. Reenu saw a young, dark woman holding a screaming child and walking past him at a dejected pace. Amaru could hear the anger in a man's voice as he received the bad news. Moshe felt the wind stirred up by a number of teenagers who excitedly ran past him, unknowing of their fate, yet hopeful.

rejection is prominent

the path is narrow

fucking shit

They were still fifty yards away. The three of them unanimously decided not to rush; if they were accepted, their patience would lead to joy. If not, their haste would lead to misery. No need to spoil it.

"WOOHOO!!"

Moshe stopped walking, now thirty yards away, causing Amaru and Reenu to come alongside him. They focused their gazes on the Kohen Office at the entrance of The Wall. A man with fierce eyes and a strong chin was jumping up and down in a clumsy embrace with Duman. Amaru was able to recognize him since she had once pinned him down, proximity allowed her to remember the heat of that moment. She let disgust show on her face before quickly replacing it with a tepid smile.

"Looks like people actually do make it in," Reenu said to no one in particular.

A four-note, brassy harmony quickly chimed before the sound of clanking metal overtook it. Five Kohen stood on each end of the opening Wall, serving as a flesh barricade designed to prevent anyone ineligible from rushing in. Moshe thought this was

if anyone tried to rush in, it would only be a matter of time before they were escorted back out

overkill, but it made the event feel prestigious for the hopeful-turned-citizen. A grand entrance reflective of a grand accomplishment.

But as the man with the chin began to smugly make his way in, he saw that he would have to briskly step aside. Marching in perfect time was a diamond-shaped squadron of twenty or so Kohen with Lieutenant Zacchaeus himself at the head. In the center of the black-and-white battalion were three ragged prisoners, shackled together and recently beaten.

The marching ceased once the last member of the diamond formation made it past the circumference of The Wall's entrance. The gates of pearl then swung shut, underlining the tense silence with a reverberating boom. Lieutenant Zacchaeus leaned on one leg and looked around. He had a captive audience in front of him and a small contingent of trained underlings behind him. His face was sorrowful but resolute, and his lower lip stood out even more than usual as he made his announcement.

"Derelicts!" he yelled as he pointed back towards the three captives. The Kohen behind him stepped out of the way so that everyone near could get a clear view of the damned.

"Let it be known amongst you Outer Sanctum hopefuls," Zacchaeus continued and started to regally hobble around. "It is better to have never even heard of Ecclesia than to have been a citizen and betrayed her. Derelicts receive the strictest, most experimental judgment because they have had the good life and rejected it. So, please be considerate and consider this: even if you have passed your Trials..."

With this, Zacchaeus looked back at the man with the jaw. He looked smaller than before, and he gulped when the Lieutenant laid his gaze upon him. He took a step away from The Wall.

"...you must still count the cost. You must still be the Ecclesian you proved you can be. Inner Sanctum is not all *kataplik faito* and peaceful living. We are a community that wants to make the world better. Just as you are training yourselves into being that kind of person *now*, so you will continue on the other side of The Wall. Kohen!"

The Kohen straightened up and marched past Zacchaeus, heading directly towards the gates.

"My men will now complete the judgment that derelicts deserve: permanent banishment!"

The uneasy quiet returned. It was a mixture of people not knowing how to react and Zacchaeus not knowing how to finish. Reenu saw that the Lieutenant was clearly in an emotional state, but it was not exactly like the indignation of General Speaker Shedim or the determinism of Leader Saios that Reenu remembered from The Last Call. There was a true sympathy hidden on the many lines across his face. The Lieutenant felt the heaviness of the quiet start to weigh down on everyone there. He mustered up a conclusion.

"Ehm, peace be with you."

"And also with you!" said the multivocal echo.

After another moment, everyone returned to their pre-disturbance affairs. Zacchaeus turned around and signaled for the The Wall to be opened aga-

"Lieutenant!"

He turned around once more and saw his three overnight once-prisoners walking briskly towards him. The young, skinny one led the charge, while Katir and the mouthy one followed right behind him.

"Reenu, was it? Nice to see you again," Zacchaeus said with the faintest of a nod and smile.

"Oh, yes, thank you for remembering," Reenu gave a quick smile back before his concern returned. "Lieutenant, what happened with them?"

"The derelicts? My goodness, weren't you paying any attention? That whole demonstration was an explanation!" Zacchaeus rubbed his forehead in exasperation, though there was a tinge of half-joke in his expression. "Katir, didn't you lend this boy any of your wisdom in the past forty days?" The faint smile returned.

Amaru felt herself redden for whatever reason. In response, she put her hand out.

"Nice to see you again, Lieutenant."

Zacchaeus took her hand and gave it a firm shake.

"Likewise."

"I think Reenu wants to know the specifics, if that's possible."

Zacchaeus looked past Katir to the source of the remark.

"Moshe," he said. They exchanged nods. Zacchaeus took a step back so he could look at all three of them. He put his hands on his hips and furrowed his brow.

"I'm afraid I can't give any. We keep criminal detail to a minimum. The only time the public is made aware of the ins and outs is if the crime directly endangers the community on a grand scale."

"Ah, so transparency is your policy only to the extent where it can get your point across, then?" Katir asked with a wink.

"Never afraid to kick against the pricks, huh, Katir?" Zacchaeus said this with a smile that quickly turned into a frown of realization. "Regardless, it's something of a newer policy. We've discovered that when someone does something...inadmissible on a public level, it encourages others to follow suit. I forget the fancy word they made for it, some kind of mob mentality thing. And, well, I'm the Lieutenant. My job to keep the peace and all."

"And thank you for that, sir," Moshe said. "Perhaps some time in the near future we shall come and help you do so."

Moshe felt pride and confidence in light of that statement. It was something that was both true and becoming true. But Zacchaeus was unresponsive. He looked at each of them passively.

"Right, well, good luck to each of you on this sunny Last Judgment. Hope to see you all soon."

Moshe blinked. That response was odd, trite, and even bordered on rude. Once more, Zacchaeus motioned for The Wall's gates to be opened. As the chains started clanking, Katir decided to leave Zacchaeus with one final, burning inquiry.

"Lieutenant, whatever happened to the search for this Amaru woman? We were receiving regular updates and then they suddenly just stopped."

"Believe it or not, Jaben dropped the charges. He said that he had forgiven the woman in his heart, there was no need to make her pay." Zacchaeus leaned his head side to side in careful consideration. "Maybe that's why he made it in today."

They all turned and saw Jaben running through the gates, arms held in unhindered prospect.

"Does that mean..." Katir cautiously approached this question, "that...Amaru's debt is forgiven? Does she have a shot at peace in Inner Sanctum?"

Zacchaeus paused and thought. There was dodgy understanding in his eyes.

"As much as anyone else does. Verily?"

He started walking and The Wall started closing.

They stood in line. A short, stodgy man walked past them glumly. There were about five more people in front of them. The Kohen Office was designed similarly to The Troei. It was built into The Wall - dirty glass that had become barely translucent with time covered most of the opening that hopefuls saw, leaving enough room for people to pass their *senton* to the decider of fate.

Four people left. A taller, darker man this time. Just as glum.

Reenu peeked around the final four as best he could. From what he could tell, the process was swift. Give the *senton* to the Kohen. The Kohen leaves momentarily. Within a minute, he would be back with the news, good or bad. So far, so bad.

Three left. A woman. Stoic. Reenu gripped his *senton* tightly.

Moshe reached over and embraced Reenu's tense hand. His affable face exuded warmth and reassurance, a mask he often wore. They had previously decided to let Reenu go first since he was showing signs of being the most nervous. But now, Moshe pulled his friend backward and swiveled into position. He decided that him going first would ease the pressure put on his friends. If he was accepted, there would be elation and a realization that their chances were up. If he was not, then even if *they* were not, they could all try again. But truthfully, Moshe felt that he might have been the most nervous. It was an odd feeling for him. He was so used to being the comforter - who could comfort him now? Nerves hardly came into play when he struggled with his friends through the desert. He understood now that tripping up at the finish line would be more crushing than any previous failure.

Two. Another face of disappointment.

when will it end

Amaru grabbed Moshe's other hand. It slipped out almost instantaneously, slick with sweat. She did not believe that any of them would make it. Whatever improvements they had made...could they have been enough? Forty days. What difference did that make? She did not believe.

One.

They all instinctively let go. Hands free, they were now close enough to see the muddied outlines of the Kohen inside. Just like being in the presence of a wolf, looking afraid now would not help. Confidence must be projected. Standing a few feet in front of the pearl wall, there was nothing else that could be done. No time to fear.

It was now Moshe's turn.

He stood unmoving for a number of seconds. His head became as air, weightless and unbound. He didn't know what was happening, but he could not be free of it. His head started to tilt back, and involuntarily, he saw the sky. The sun was bright and generous. The few clouds that surrounded it kept the gravity of its glare from fully downpouring onto hopeful and Ecclesian alike. Moshe's head lolled forward before it shambled its way back into place. He took the courageous last step forward that he needed to take.

All previous exchanges with the Kohen had been silent, so Moshe did the same. The Kohen faded from sight. Moshe placed his hands on the ledge to steady himself. It felt like he was breaking down from the inside out. He slumped his shoulders as his strength left him. His friends were a few feet behind him but they felt absent. He was alone in his apprehension, unattended to in his anxiety. A horrible memory of a days-old conversation invaded his thoughts. He and Duman were discussing a concept new to him: imposter syndrome. It was a feeling that Duman told him many hopefuls struggled with. Even those who did everything right still *felt* like they were not right enough. He wanted to ask Duman if feeling that way was a crime in itself. There was nothing in The Manual about it. But he did not dare ask, for Duman had put to language a feeling that occupied his late nights and long days frequently. It was the peak of this feeling that now caused his body to nearly give up in collapse.

...

A signed *senton* slid into the space between his hands.

"Brother," said the Kohen. "You are now a citizen of Ecclesia."

Moshe was unable to lift his head. The words, though they promised absolution, were heavy with expectation. He thought he heard the euphoric cries of his friends behind him, but they were far too distant to really be there. He saw the *senton* and everything he wanted within its freshly-written ink mark. Had he truly made it in or was the delusion of his desire lying to him?

The jolt of brass notes provided him the answer. He picked up his *senton*, thanked the Kohen, and looked back at his friends. They both clapped and smiled and offered him looks of sincere commendation. Love, even. The clanking of metal had never sounded sweeter.

As the gates opened, Moshe proceeded to the entrance. Others nearby gave him varying degrees of congratulations; some, however, looked

some people would always prefer to see you burn than succeed

away. He now stood twenty feet away from the threshold into Inner Sanctum. He was just out of earshot of the Kohen Office, but he would wait to go in until his friends stood beside him. Hopefully, the guards of the gate would not pester him to come inside or close it on him before Reenu and Amaru could make it over.

The harmonious notes rang out once more! They were becoming more pleasant with each arrival. Reenu was running towards Moshe with open arms. The impact of their embrace was enough to knock

Moshe back a few steps, but it broke Moshe down to the point of watery eyes.

"I honestly didn't think I would make it in," Reenu said from Moshe's bosom.

"I *knew* you would," Moshe affirmed. He held Reenu back so that they now looked at each other. "You are Reenu. You are the most gentle, compassionate person there is. You *are* an Ecclesian."

Reenu's eyes were watering, but not out of complete satisfaction. Moshe saw that there were still fragments of disbelief within, and he knew that some of that was

imposter syndrome

his fault. Moshe wanted to say more - he wanted to give his friend-lover release. But he didn't want to bring the occasion down with past troubles. The present was too irresistible.

Amaru saw her friends from afar and sighed. She knew what was coming for her. She rubbed her temple. With nonchalant reluctance, she handed her *senton* over and started walking, hating that she had to give Moshe and Reenu the bad news.

Moshe and Reenu separated themselves from each other and looked in confusion at Amaru as she firmly strode towards them, hands hidden in the confined wrappings of her robe.

"Katir...where is your *senton*?" Reenu asked.

Amaru gave a slight, harmless scoff at Reenu's naiveté.

"I don't need it. I need a new one," Amaru said.

"Why?" Reenu asked.

Amaru gave him a look that said

you know

Reenu's eyes began to re-water. He ran towards the Kohen Office, determined to be sure of his lover-friend's fate.

Amaru cast her head downwards. It was too painful to look directly at Moshe, a man she had loved and had failed. Moshe took a step towards her, allowing their foreheads to butt softly against each other. All emotion muted from his voice.

"I thought you told me about working with some...derelicts in a dream – a nightmare last night. But that was real, wasn't it? It's true?"

Amaru sniffed as her nose and mouth began to tremble. She placed her hands on Moshe's shoulders, head still down.

"Yes. It's true. I met them and I believed in their purpose more than anything I've believed in my life. I still think what they think is right and that we could be a part of them happily. But I also realized too late that I will always choose you two over them. I'm...so sorry that I messed up. It's my fault, I know. Especially knowing that you two *deserve* Inner Sanctum. It hurts to know that I'm the problem here. But...we can try again. There are still spots left. I know what to do now. And why. We can try again, right?"

Moshe took a step back and slowly lifted Amaru's chin so that it was level with his. Another emotional face sat vulnerable before his. And likewise, there was disbelief.

"Yes, of course. *You* can."

He was off. Resolute strides toward Inner Sanctum. He beckoned an evermore confused Reenu to come with him. Amaru stood as if she had been knocked down into sitting, frozen in shock. The man she had followed and loved and defended and disappointed was leaving. It was the experience of a sheep being left behind as the rest of the herd moved away. The lone prey involuntarily forced into the duty of sacrifice. But Amaru resisted the image. She could not let that be her fate. It was not like her.

She ran with force towards Moshe. He sensed her rapid footfall and turned about-face abruptly. When she collided with him, he held up her forearms in a defensive clasp. He pushed her back mildly but with enough violence to keep her at a distance.

"What are you doing?" Amaru asked with disarming tenderness. Her voice trembled out a hurt that foretold of simmering anger.

"I am an Ecclesian. It would be a crime to defect," Moshe said, calmly.

"What? I mean, not really. You've been given the gift. You can still refuse it." Amaru wasn't sure of the accuracy of her claim, but it made enough sense. Moshe wasn't on the other side yet.

Moshe nodded his head thoughtfully. "I'm not aware of all the technicalities of this law yet. Perhaps I should ask Lieutenant Zacchaeus the next time I see him. But Katir, you're missing the point ag-"

Moshe felt his fingers grip his palms. Reenu arrived. He had run up to them so that he was nearly in between them, but he stopped and backed up a couple steps when he felt the concrete pressure of tension in the air. Moshe waited a couple seconds, breathed deeply out his nose, and continued.

"Technicalities aside, I *am* an Ecclesian. You know it to be true."

Amaru understood and looked down, overcome. She felt a snarl grow and she looked back up at her opponent.

"What, then? You're just going to leave us? We have to fend for ourselves now?" Amaru felt the heat of an uncivil war brewing, but it was bloodless for now.

"No. Reenu is an Ecclesian, too. He'll be coming with me. Reenu?"

Moshe extended a hand and a smile towards Reenu. Amaru looked his way as well. Reenu saw both sides and hated it. He had never needed to choose between his two life-companions before, and he couldn't believe that it had come to this. He wondered where things went wrong, what was that initial point of dissension? Yes, Amaru took the risks that led to this specific disjuncture, but Moshe should have known that *of course* she would. She would never be able to buy in to a system with the structures that held up Ecclesia. And Reenu knew he would always be the one in the middle. Indecisive. But he remembered that conversation around the campfire and the mantra of his that Moshe had then affirmed but now seemed to

we're here...we're safe...we're together

throw away.

"Moshe...I..."

Reenu knew tears were falling, but he kept them out of his voice.

"You've almost always led us in the right direction. I've always followed you. But...if we're not together...how is this our home?"

Moshe retracted his hand as if embarrassed, but the three of them knew it was out of hurt. He hardened his voice.

"The road to salvation is traveled individually. Verily?"

Moshe considered turning around and being on his way about that very road, but he saw Amaru's leg bouncing and her eyes tightening.

"Wait...what was it? That verse in...I can't remember. About making peace..."

"Mati 5:23-24?" Moshe inquired. His voice was lighter as he asked, and he felt a beam of pride in his own remembrance and Amaru's faint recollection.

"Yes. *'If you are given a gift and still hold onto a grievance that someone has against you, make peace with that person first.'*"

Moshe's right eyebrow went up. He knew where this was going.

"You are not a true Ecclesian," Amaru attested. "Sure, you read The Manual habitually. You talk with others regularly. You never told us what your damned Test was, but you clearly passed it. But you don't fully obey..."

Moshe's eyes glanced at their surroundings. He was worried that others heard

an expletive, really? even now?

Amaru. He hoped that everyone would stick to their humdrum busyness, but it was not so. People were starting to gather, likely drawn by the gate being open for so long, but they were beginning to notice the commotion. And Amaru was not stopping. No, she grew in intensity as she went on, inching closer towards Moshe.

"You still need to fucking apologize to us, my dear. Or have you forgotten that in your quest for self-righteousness? You broke the vow. You broke the only real boundary we held each other accountable to, and you haven't said a damned thing about it. You don't know the damage that's done to Reenu and I. Why do you think I can't trust this place? How can I when I can't even trust one of my own lovers?! And, actually, fuck what it's done to us for just a second. Because, more importantly for you, there's still goddamned Mati 5:23-24. You're contradicting that rule. You're not fully obeying. And because you're not fully obeying, you're not a true Ecclesian. You are *not* a *true* Ecclesian!"

Moshe waited a couple seconds, breathed deeply in through his nose, and-

A swift kick to the chest and he was flat on his ass, recovering the wind he lost.

"Fuck your stupid breathing exercises!" Amaru yelled.

She lunged towards Moshe and lifted her leg for another front kick, only to be stopped by Moshe's hands. He twisted her foot in a half-circle and she landed flat on her back.

Roars. Reenu turned. A festering multitude had enclosed the space between the Kohen Office and The Wall. They were surrounded. Reenu saw on their hungry faces that they did not intend to maliciously intervene - they merely lusted after the present entertainment - but it didn't make their presence feel any less threatening. They would cheer with each blow, regardless of who it landed upon. Reenu was horrified as he became enmeshed in their mass.

Amaru lifted her other leg and brought her heel down hard just below Moshe's left wrist. She heard a pop, a yelp, and cheers before she felt release. She then rolled into a backwards somersault and leapt up into an offensive stance. She saw Moshe on his knees clutching his arm, his left hand spasming in eerie, irregular directions. She saw the opportunity for a breath and a query.

"How can we be made new if no one wants us to?!" She used all of her vocal strength to be heard over the constant clamor of the crowd.

"The Diados program is-" Moshe started through grimaces, barely audible.

"Fuck your Diados program!" Amaru screamed, loud and clear.

The cheers and jeers propelled Amaru towards Moshe. Just as she got to him, he swung his leg out, launching her into the air and landing on her head behind him. Moshe turned around. Amaru was up, but she was dazed. Moshe brought his right hand down across her face in a back-handed slap, then proceeded with a flurry of jabs to her chest and stomach. Eventually, Amaru was able to deflect one and fiercely seize Moshe's left arm. He screamed in pain as she spun him around and launched him a few feet, landing on his stomach. He attempted to use his left arm to stand himself up, but he was terrified to find that it was completely inoperable. Amaru grabbed him by the waist and flung him so that he was on his back. A few kicks weren't enough to keep her from positioning herself on his chest for a number of uppercuts to the gut. Moshe felt the wind leave him once again and his head lolled back so that he saw what would really grieve him.

Unable to hear the mechanical motion over the crowd's bloodthirst, Moshe saw that the gates were halfway closed. He had spent years trying to find the way to salvation, but it might have been lost forever if he didn't act fast. Still out of breath, Moshe let out a pained,

"Amaru."

Amaru looked at her friend's face. There was weakness. It was the closest thing to regret that she had ever seen Moshe allow.

"Amaru."

His voice was shrinking. Amaru didn't know if it was from physical suffering or mental anguish. But it drew her in. She lowered her face so that it was just above Moshe's.

"Amaru."

He said her name once more and she knew that he was sincere. Whatever he wanted to say, she would hear it.

"Yes, Moshe?"

"I'm...leaving."

Another explosion. Moshe mustered all of his strength to leave his friend with a parting punch to the temple. This explosion - the cracking of her head - hurt worse than the first. She slumped off of him, unconscious. Moshe quickly got up and ran. Reenu galloped towards Amaru.

"Katir! Katir! Oh no, oh no, oh no, oh no..."

Reenu landed next to his friend and turned her over. Her temple was gushing out blood in pulsating waves, split open as it was. Reenu looked up for Moshe.

But he was gone. And The Wall was closed.

Arah arrived at the Kohen Office, not to turn in his *senton*, although it was his Last Judgment as well. He had been inspired enough by Leader's message at The Last Call to start over, despite having heard something similar ten times before. But it was his interactions with the beggar that had changed his heart on Ecclesia as a whole. He was beginning to see the system's shortcomings, but if anyone was to have seen his missing friend, it would have been the Kohen.

The Kohen looked Arah up and down, eyes dulling as he noticed that there was not a *senton* in sight.

"Hi, hello. I'm looking for *ahem* the beggar," Arah stated. He was slightly nervous; he had a feeling that this request was incautious. If the beggar was really missing, there was likely a foul reason at play. The Kohen's half-mast eyes blinked sluggishly, wordlessly.

"H-have you seen him?" asked Arah, impatience growing.

"Sir, now is not an opportune time for this inquiry," the Kohen admitted. "Look behind you."

Arah did as he was told. At least thirty people looked back at him, faces ranging from obliviously worrisome to irritably frustrated. Arah felt bad. He offered a raised hand of peace and a mouthed "sorry" to the line, but received unchanged faces in return.

"So what?" Arah asked the Kohen.

"As you can see, today is a rather large Last Judgment, for obvious reasons," the Kohen said lazily, the last bit under breath. "In order to be timely and make sure we meet everyone's-"

"I understand that you're only trying to do your job," interrupted Arah. "But aren't you guys supposed to be peacekeepers? Wouldn't a missing person fall under that?"

The Kohen stiffened, eyes parting to three-quarters-mast.

"What's your interest in the missing party?"

Before Arah could answer, his attention was taken by nearby roars.

He turned and saw a massive huddle of people gathered around the opened pearly gate of The Wall. Even most of the people in line behind him were hurrying towards the commotion. Arah followed suit.

Rushing over, it seemed as if every other step Arah took was accented by a cheer or a

"Fuck your Diados program!"

gasp. When he made it to the back of the pack, he found it rather easy to slip through the

CRACK!

throng. Pushing his way to the front, the crowdnoise stopped. It was that newer trio, though one of them was running to the closing gate while the other two were center stage. They were clearly hurt, physically and emotionally. Blood. Some people, no longer interested in the scene, had taken to swarming the ten Kohen at the gates with their strength in numbers, but most of them met broken noses and bruises thanks to resilient batons. The gates would not re-open for the remainder of the day. The rest of the crowd started to dissipate, but Arah just stood there, impassably lost in thought born out of the tragedy before him. He knew that the Kohen wouldn't tell him where the beggar was even if they harbored the information. Ecclesia is a system built on individual reward, the incentive strong enough to tear even the most bound of lovers apart.

It's time to leave.

Chapter 10: Dimly Lit

24, 14, 10 DBK

Reborn at the waxing of sunlight. It's the first time Moshe notices the effervescent way the morning star slits past the beige curtains of his bedroom. Time to finally leave its carefree custody.

With a grateful yawn and stretching of the arms, Moshe considerately pulls back his covers, swivels until he sits along the side of his bed, stands up, and considerately replaces his covers. It's all beige - the entire room. Inoffensive. Pleasant. After The Wall closed, Moshe was almost immediately greeted by a swarm of Ecclesians that were eager to help him transition. He couldn't remember any of their names at this point - too many all at once! - but he would be sure to thank them the next time he saw them. He knew they weren't Kohen, but their ivory-white robes laced with golden trim indicated some kind of status. It was they who directed him to the mansion that had awaited him since before he was born, and it was they who told him to rest in it for the next three days.

Internally, Moshe fought against his own disquietude. He wanted to dive into the exquisite waters of Ecclesian culture, not sit around for a few days. But he knew he was to

give thanks to Savyer, for he has given us all things - Rumai 11:36

be grateful, and so, he sat through the "rebirthing process" in his beige home.

The first night, he was anxious. He didn't know what it was like to be alone. Miraculously, he slept more soundly than ever; by the time he arose, it was nearly sundown again. His heart lightened, knowing that the stress of the daily past was behind him.

The mansion was interesting. The architect must have had a vertical mindset - everything was narrow but high. Almost every item and area had a small card with a word and its definition on it. Kitchen, toilet, window, spa. Moshe was mainly resting, but the rest of his time was spent getting acclimated to the amenities.

He also contemplated the meaning of his mandatory recess. Was it to shed off the final layer of the outside world? Was it simply a well-deserved rest? Was it to lessen the culture shock? Moshe worried that rather than being the receiver of the shock, he would be the transmitter. He knew he was coming into a group that was firmly functional - would he be the cog that set it off its rails? The last thing he wanted to do was to be a disruption. Aside from resting, Moshe spent much of his rebirthing reflecting on how to handle himself during his upcoming first impression. Excited, but not too much personality. Interested, but not too many questions. In a way, he would have to stay even lower than when he first entered Outer Sanctum. But only for a time. And the time was finally now.

Moshe tried placing his left hand on the beige doorknob that led outside, but it fumbled awkwardly off and slumped back to his side. He grimaced at the pain's sharpness and used his right instead. After all the thinking he had done for the past three days, Moshe came to what he thought was a rather wise conclusion: he would have to think less. Obviously Ecclesians were thoughtful people, but from his study of The Manual, simply doing was better than thinking. So rather than being swallowed in the engulfing anxiety that plagued him the day he turned in his *senton*, he simply opened the door.

The day was beautiful, the air was crisp. A smattering of people was walking gaily along. All was as all should be. It was all Moshe expected it to be. He took a step forward and felt disturbed by a scratchy substance underneath him.

It was a mat. "This house is a home." Moshe felt a wave of repressed emotion rise from his stomach, threatening his lips and eyes with an - oh!

Someone stood before him, waiting for him to notice.

She leaned on one leg like someone trying out timidity. Her cheekbones were high and her blonde hair radiated beyond its shoulder-length glory. She smiled, head tilted in budding adoration.

"Hi. I'm Fila."

— —

Trudging along in silence. Reenu and Amaru had hardly spoken in the several days following their Last Judgment. Much of that time was spent in recovery. Amaru had developed a severe fever that kept her tentridden; even if she had wanted to talk, it would have been too painful to meaningfully communicate. She didn't want to, though. Reenu had to scrounge for gauze, bandages, and makeshift salve whenever he could. The Kohen were gracious enough to provide the initial dressing that stopped the bleeding and probably saved Amaru's life, but that was all they could do. Supplies like that were always scant. It was twisted, but Reenu appreciated the way his new role as caretaker revealed a resourcefulness within that he was not aware he had. He developed multiple means of finding supplies. He was not entirely proud of them all, but he knew they were necessary. Feeding the glutton extra portions in exchange for an extra pair of eyes. Waiting for distant neighbors to leave their tents so he could rummage through what they had. Things like that kept his sole lover-friend alive.

But they weren't really talking much. What was there to say? They were forced back into a pre-Ecclesian mode of survival thanks to betrayal and circumstance. What was the point in their endeavors? There was none outside of an intrinsic, incessant need to continue. But continuing in Ecclesia? Pressing on towards Inner Sanctum? They hadn't discussed it, but *that* momentum was gone. Reenu saw it in Amaru's sprawl across the floor and Amaru saw it in Reenu's dead eyes every time he came back through the flaps. This place was not a home.

Still, they were stuck there for the time being. Reenu meandered over to Ecclesian Essentials one day just to break up the monotony of his newfound life. Neither of them was interested in the habits they formed during their Trials - reading, meeting with friends, sex - so even a walk to the stupid tract booth was a consoling shadow of an exciting event. Reenu laughed in disbelief at the promises written inside.

[...there are plenty of seats...]

[...will give you a meaning and purpose to...]

[...a dedicated follower of Savyer, and a true Leader...]

His sinking heart was prepared to discard the tract and leave, but the wording of an advertisement for The Troei caught his eye:

[...serving delectable *casu*, a delicacy so delicious that it even makes Ecclesians jealous! But as the saying goes: as above, so below. Here at The Troei, our only desire is to make sure you enjoy what you're craving just as much as you will when you're...]

So Reenu returned to Amaru with a plan, a faint glow of hope.

Amaru was laying down with her hands on her head and her legs split wide. She didn't budge from this position when Reenu arrived.

"Amaru," Reenu stated. "How are you feeling?"

Amaru peeked at her friend from underneath her hands momentarily.

"I don't know."

"Physically, at least."

"Better, I guess."

"Good. Ready to go?"

Amaru took her hands off her face. She looked at Reenu quizzically. Reenu tried to keep the smile from his face as he mouthed the word

underground

Amaru's eyes sank with her head.

"Oh, Reenu. I don't think they'll have anything to do with me anymore. I left them for you and Moshe, and, well..."

Reenu felt the sting of that one, but he knew she wouldn't say more. He continued.

"Maybe not then. But at this point, why not try?"

"Or why try?" Amaru countered with pessimism.

"Because what else are we going to do?" Reenu resisted with apathy and it somehow worked. They exchanged a look that said

fuck it

and headed on down.

So they trudged along in silence alongside scattered torchlight, Reenu helping Amaru struggle along. This time it was Amaru with apprehension in her heart and Reenu with excitement in his. As they drew closer to the end of the hall and that final bend, their silence was devoured by the nonsensical chatter and hollering that made up the moments before this motley crew's penultimate meeting.

Fila climbed The Tree of Origin with grace and ease, like someone who had done so a thousand times before. It was only a few seconds before she was thirty feet up, shaded by the dark green of syndetic branches. She stifled a giggle as she looked down and saw Moshe's astounded face, gaping mouth. His subconscious searched its muscle memory banks for a survival skill that he never had to develop in the wilderness. There were hardly any trees outside Ecclesia, certainly no behemoths like this one. Moshe found it to be intuitive enough: wedge a foot here, place a right hand there, keep going up. And yet the nuance of the movements and the altitude were unfamiliar. The greying trunk felt more comfortable than the deeply brown branches he held his face against for balance. The simmering in his stomach intensified as he ascended. Was he...actually afraid of these heights? Or, perhaps, the meaning of the meeting.

Fila waited patiently for Moshe, though not without hiding her amusement. After a couple minutes, he was in arm's reach.

"Here," she said, extending a hand towards him. Moshe grabbed it with his right and leapt up so that his head was at her waist. He quickly let go and thrust his arm for the branch opposite her, clumsily situating himself atop it. Another stifled giggle as he turned around to face his new friend.

"Looks like you oughta learn about more than just the people here," Fila teased.

"I just need experience," Moshe said coldly, embarrassed.

Fila's smile evaporated. "Sure, yeah."

They both looked around each other for a time. Silence was present, but Moshe could not tell if it was either awkward or welcome.

"Um," Fila initiated. It was awkward. "T-tell me about...yourself, Moshe."

"It's even more beautiful up here," Moshe said, eyes elsewhere.

Fila looked out with him. Though the sun was nowhere to be found from where they were sitting, the sky was still bathed in the blend of orange, blue, and pink brought on by its early eminence. More people populated the streets now, and the concordant sound of commotion struck Moshe as more cordial than the clamor of Outer Sanctum. Fila's eyes flitted over The Temple for a second. She didn't feel the need to ponder; she was already at her most favorite place. Moshe's eyes were squarely on The Citadel. Talks with the people he met in Outer Sanctum brewed regret within him over not visiting it when he had the chance. The architect remarkably designed the building so that, at several points along the way to the top, its continuous ridges would fold inward, making the pinnacle seem very thin and distant. Moshe knew he would visit it soon.

"That's where the big business happens," Fila noted. Moshe's eyes redirected back to her. "Me, I've never had such lofty aspirations. Perfectly content with being the best person Savyer wanted us to be. Got to be grateful for those up top though, right?"

There was a cheerful but tempered honesty in her eyes that Moshe enjoyed. He nodded.

Silence returned. Fila tapped her fingers along the branch she sat on. Moshe could tell she was searching, desperately even, so he decided to throw her a bone.

"How long have you been here?"

"In this tree with you? It's been a few minutes, I'd say."

Moshe made to correct his intention, but Fila held up a strikingly proportioned hand.

"I know what you meant. It's been one thousand days."

Moshe smiled and nodded a few times.

Fila smiled in return, the kind for condolences. "Yes, it's actually something of a special milestone for people here. I'll probably be acknowledged at the *Sympos* - uh, a weekly feast held at The Temple; don't worry, I'll take you - but it's not like a huge celebration of me or anything like that."

Moshe kept nodding. "I see."

Fila frowned. "Is something wrong? Am I offending you? Or...boring you?"

Moshe motioned to speak again but Fila kept going.

"I'm sorry, I don't mean to assume. Maybe you're just a quiet guy and that's perfectly fine. It's just that I've been called uninteresting before and I really don't want to give off that impression because I think of myself as a rather fun girl and if being boring is what's hurting my chances of-"

"I don't see that in you," Moshe interrupted.

Fila stopped, mouth still open from its rambling. She giggled, and the sound was like a brighter rendition of The Wall's chimes. "Oh, great. Thank you."

"I..." Moshe said, nose wrinkling. "I'll...try to explain myself. Three days ago, I wasn't even sure that I *could* be here. And if I didn't pass my Trial...I don't know. I guess we - I - would have just tried again. But then who knows what would happen or what could ever happen. There aren't many spots left, I know that. But then I spent three days in a beautiful, barren house, and now I'm here with you in this glorious tree, and everything feels like it should be so...easy. And it is. Certainly compared to life out there. And yet...I feel like I shouldn't be talking to you."

Fila froze, looking like she was built into the tree itself. Moshe noticed, scrunched his face, and tried scratching his scabbed eyebrow with his left hand before remembering.

"No, not because of *you*, because of me," Moshe tried explaining.

"I think I've heard that before," Fila said, still frozen.

Moshe was not sure what she meant, so he breathed deeply in and deeply out.

"Everyone here - including you, Fila - has earned their place. Ecclesian life is a gift from Savyer, but they at least meet the standards for it. I don't know how anyone who's had to live outside these walls could have escaped from getting their hands dirty, but they have been washed clean somehow. That must be true. I'm...scared that might not be true for me."

Moshe did his best to maintain eye contact with Fila so she understood his words, but he broke away at the last of them. He felt too seen. Fila recognized that as her body returned to its previously unbothered state.

"Moshe, you have read The Manual, you have shared it with others, you have disposed of an appropriate amount of trash, and you have even passed your Test. In that sense, you have done something right. Many things right. But something you may not yet understand is that no one this side of The Wall is better than anyone that side."

Moshe looked at the woman before him with a raised eyebrow and ears to hear.

"The only difference between us and them is that we have been given a chance and taken it. If we thought we were better than them, The Wall would never open. We would be content to live in paradise and forget the past, but trust me, *no one* does that. We *must* continue to reach out towards everyone else and figure out how to make their lives better and encourage them along the way. It's our Ecclesian responsibility to do so."

Moshe felt slight embarrassment once

all my study of The Manual and sometimes it is as if I have forgotten all about it

more.

"So please, if you can, understand that I view you as my equal. And hopefully, a new friend."

Fila extended her hand once more, eyes shining with potential. Moshe shook it gladly.

"I'd give you a proper hug but that seems precarious right now," Fila said. They both laughed.

"My apologies, Fila," Moshe said. "You asked me earlier to tell you about myself. I don't think I've ever been asked that. I wouldn't know where to start."

Fila, feeling motherly and adventurous after how well the sand tide had turned, compassionately inquired:

"Is your hand ok?"

Moshe looked down at his left and went frigid in tone: "No."

"Oh." Fila feared she might regret pushing further, but she did so anyway.

"What happened?"

Moshe thought. He felt as though he could tell his new friend any-thing in the world. The marriage of her empathy and their seclusion in The Tree told him so. But despite what she said about remembering the past...surely there were still parts of it worth forgetting.

"I don't know."

Fila said nothing, trying not to let her body naturally freeze up. Hurt by the obvious lie.

Moshe aimed for redirection once more.

"When again is this feast you mentioned?"

"Tonight!"

Amaru found it delightful that no matter what potentially hostilities intruded the six-pillar room, not a single member there would turn away from their respective fucking, gossiping, and wrestling. There was something ever so inviting in their disunified focus. It was not the carelessness of neglect or fatality of oblivion. It was the recognition that whatever was present *was present*. All else would come to pass. It was also the implicit acknowledgment that anyone who was able to find their way through the dark, damp hall would be welcome. But this premise was not entirely true. There was always one who *would* turn their head at the sight and sound of someone new, and Amaru was staring directly at her as she entered.

The hardness of Abigail's face and body was unmoved by the eye contact as she sat upon her elevated chair. This chair was a new development since Amaru had been there last. It was composed of deathly twigs and compacted *senti*, but it was made to look like a seat at The Table, with its dark brown, oblique top and convex legs. The main differences were the unruly back and arm attachments.

Amaru was unable to keep her eyes up. She stopped walking, but stillness was the only motion that people noticed underground. She felt eyes start to settle on her, but she only noticed one group in particular. It was the boys - Pali, Via, Epi, Krati - that she had been training in self-defense. She remembered the last thing she told Epi. Unnerved, she was prepared to leave and never come back. Reenu noticed her aversion and placed a hand on her shoulder in support. They stood far before Abigail.

"Why are you here?" Abigail asked from across the quieted room.

Amaru was still for a second before wiping her non-existent brow with the back of her hand and answering:

"I thought that-"

"*I* thought that you, the boy, and the square were going to live gay lives up top? See the sights, as it were. Cheer at The Kolosaio. Jerk each other off, metaphorically, at The Temple. Fuck yourselves, literally, in your nice, clean-ass mansions. All that pleasant shit. Hmm?"

Abigail looked at Reenu and Amaru with false inquisition: eyebrows raised, head tilting side to side. They remained silent.

"No? Wasn't that the plan?"

Amaru sighed. "No, it-"

"It wasn't the plan? Really?" Abigail's interest increasing with her sarcasm.

Amaru huffed, getting annoyed herself, her body feeling the exasperation in the dingy atmosphere. "I suppose it *was*, but I don't know if that's what I really wanted."

"Fucking *KAMNOS*, are you kidding me?" Abigail demanded, incredulous. "If you're not going to respect me with straight talk, why even bother with this?"

Amaru shot her hand up to her temple, falling to one knee as she did so. Reenu caught her on the way down, but he was not able to catch himself from the rage that boiled over.

"Dammit Abigail! Amaru is in serious pain! Her temple was split open days and days ago, and it's only just stopped bleeding. She's had a fever that won't go away. And you know what else? This was all because of Moshe - the *square* who rounded off his edges so that he could fit into Ecclesia's ideal mold! And...and I don't know if he's on the other side working hard to help us get in with him or what. The Moshe I've loved would be doing that. But the last thing the Moshe I've loved did was leave a parting wound on my other love's head and then walk through those pearly freaking gates, and I'll be damned if there's anything that hurts worse than that. So we come here - I decided to come here - not because I like you or this place. Fact is, you've always made me uneasy, though I'm sure that's obvious to you. No, we come here because *where else do we go?* Where else could we find safety and help when we need it most? Surely not in the anti-Ecclesia, the land of free voice and unsatisfied seekers?"

Everyone had turned to witness the most verbose rebuke Abigail had gotten in Ecclesian history, and more curiously, her prompt response.

"Just because you two were hurt does not mean I was not."

Amaru looked up from where she knelt. Abigail seemed unbudged, but Amaru knew her rhetorical pattern well enough to tell it was coming.

"I cannot forgive Amaru as of yet, for she left at a most inopportune time. She was not the only one to leave for the ever-failing hope of Last Judgment. And...I thought we were getting somewhere," Abigail admitted, finally repositioning herself on her makeshift chair. "However, who am I to deny her the common goods of the people? Whoever is willing to help out with your injuries will. But not until after the meeting, there is much to discuss. Recommence!"

Immediately, every patron present moved with a precision and haste akin to what Reenu assumed Kohen formations were like. The strange thing was that each person ended up in a seemingly random seat and way of sitting.

creatures of habit

Reenu walked Amaru back towards the entrance so she could sit with enough space to stretch out, but she kept her eyes on Abigail the entire time. Abigail was the only one who remained where she was, downcast countenance complete with the face of a reluctant clairvoyant.

"Let's skip the pleasantries," Abigail said abruptly. "At least for now. Updates will have to come later. I know there have been positive developments with Sef finding sustainable sustenance as well as Siranga's tunneling expansion, but let's start with what's pressing. I have heard an anonymous report that someone was talking with a Kohen about this place."

A collective gasp. Just loud enough to cover up something faint.

"Who the fuck?" came from a grizzly tongue.

"I cannot say who," Abigail answered, slumping down deeper into her chair.

Untenable uproar accompanied by actual boos.

The perfect cover.

Abigail let everyone air out their grievances. It was what she always did when reception was negative. The last couple of meetings were headed towards this anyway. First it was the death of Paidi. Then it was the mass exodus that cut away a quarter of their regulars. Twenty or so in a cavernous space like this made it feel like the desert. Like it was purposefully deserted. The non-group built on its non-unity was finally coming apart. And Abigail knew that treason would be the last straw for many of the remaining few. Unless she started something.

"Alright fuckers, just listen up!"

Everyone did, they always did.

Even if it was too late.

"Things are looking bad right now. They're looking pretty shit. You all know that I hardly go upside anymore. There's nothing for me there, and there's *still* nothing for you there. But being down here, waiting for you all, planning what we should do next, I've found that most of my time has been wasted. By worry. By concern for you. Because, though we have no identity, you have become my family. And I'm no fucking matriarch - I've always let everyone do what they please because I truly believe in that autonomy. It's the only way for us to be peaceable be-ings. But...the time has come for some agreement. You want to know why things are looking bad? How it's gotten to this state? Because we haven't *fucking done anything!*"

If there was every full agreement in that room, it was in the cap-tivation from Abigail's passion. The forlorn had become re-enchanted. Engaged to the point of tunnel vision. But Reenu and Amaru heard the slightest of patterings come from behind them. Amaru side-eyed Reenu, blinking her right eye three times as she did so. Reenu twitched the inner fingers on his left hand. Amaru placed a hand on Reenu's thigh to lift herself up but he held it there. They looked at each other eye to eye now. There was no more subtlety. Amaru stood up, but Abi-gail spoke first.

"It's time! What else can waiting do for us? We go on the offensive because things have got to change. No one else will do it! So, before they can get to us, I say we grab our weapons and take this fucking city."

Looking back, Abigail would not remember whether or not she heard the thwack of the cold baton or Amaru's warbled cry, but what she saw across the soon-to-be-even-emptier room was clear as upside day. Amaru was askew on all fours, palpitating from the strike to her scalp. Fifty Kohen and Matthias were bunched up together in a staggered formation, batons pointed forward. Reenu had turned to face them with hands raised above his head, and the rest of the underdwellers eventually repeated his actions. The lead Kohen spoke the inciting words.

"Everyone in this room is subject to bondage."

The *Sympos* was where Moshe finally understood that not even the decadence of his third dream could live up to the reality of Ecclesia. Out of all the festivities, the first thing Moshe noticed as he entered The Temple with Fila was the floors. They were *spotless*, their wood brown marble causing discernible reflections throughout the room. Moshe looked down at himself in wonder. His eyes could have stayed there all night, as his ears were plenty bewitched by sounds unknown. Understanding or not, what he heard was beautiful. And loud.

"*Orektiko*, sir?"

Moshe was startled by a different kind of Kohen suddenly before him, offering a plate of something with a sculpted smile. He was wearing the usual black-and-white garb, but the ends of the arms were folded neatly back. The rest of the robe was more form-fitting as well, actually. It was a lot of new information for Moshe to process all at once. He stared at the fanciful man with creased, wandering eyebrows.

"Sure, we'll take some! Thank you and peace be with you," Fila said, saving the day and limiting awkwardness.

"And also with you." The server bowed and proceeded to his next objective.

Moshe held the palm-sized vessel with confusion. He slowly slurped it after Fila modeled how to do so. It was delightful.

Moshe remembered The Temple feeling a lot bigger during The Last Call - even though it was stuffed with hopefuls - but that was probably because of the way it was currently decorated. It was also a lot brighter; now, it was dimly lit. The area around The Table remained untouched, but the rest was divided in a sheepshoe fashion composed of five sections with accompanying activities that made them uniquely interesting. The closest was occupied with the most people and was likely the most fun for the average attender. Everyone, paired up, had their backs against each other and knees bent into a squat. They were tossing an object overhead to their partner, and once someone dropped the sphere, they had to go sit down. They would do this until one couple remained, and the apparent winners would be handed a glass they would clink together. They would play this game repeatedly. Moshe was surprised that its simplicity hadn't worn out its welcome.

Fila placed a hand on Moshe's shoulder.

"Would you like to play *tosbala*? I'm sure you've figured out the rules already," Fila said with a giggle.

Moshe didn't want to upset his friend, but the amount of people already playing made him nervous.

"I'd like to see the rest first," Moshe asserted, tapping Fila's hand a few times. She obliged.

They stopped by the next space, where a plethora of servers handed out glasses from behind a stylish little wall. Moshe and Fila took a couple, clinked them together, and drank. The liquid was cold yet warm, bitter yet delicious. Moshe found that he felt light-headed if he drank too quickly, so he made sure to pace himself.

Lining the wall opposite the entrance was the strip that enticed Moshe most. A collection of Ecclesia's most distinguished citizens from days past, from Prames to an empty space notably reserved for Leader Saios. These exquisitely chiseled replicas were glorious, each sitting on a pedestal that placed them a few feet above onlookers. These pillars of greatness were now as the actual pillars of The Temple. They were even made out of the same material. Moshe felt a deep reverence course through his body. It was a quiet, empty, introspective space, and, to Fila, boring. Her patience had waned by the time Moshe made it halfway through the catalogue, a whole thirty minutes later.

"Our history is great and all, but if we don't move on, we won't get to see the rest of what's here. The present! Or play *tosbala* like you promised." Fila did her best to bat her eyes as a sign of light-hearted solicitation, but she could tell her persistence was showing in her strained smile and tired eyes.

Moshe winced. He knew he hadn't promised. And he also felt like he was falling into the exact social trap he spent the last few days preparing himself to avoid. How hard it was to set aside desire for the sake of fitting in.

"Dinner will be starting soon. These statues will be here every week for the rest of time," Fila reassured him. She was right. They moved on.

The fourth section was bare, but it seemed to be where people were congregating to conversate. Fila cajoled Moshe into meeting a few of her friends for a bit. Moshe obliged.

"Apa!"

A tall, narrow woman turned around upon hearing Fila's cry. Moshe could have sworn that nausea passed through the woman's face before the two of them excitedly embraced. Apa was in a light green robe that was even tighter than what the servers were wearing.

"Fila? My, my, another surprise for the evening. I haven't seen you here in-"

"Yes, but it's my milleversary!" Fila hurriedly interjected.

Apa stood blank-faced for a second, as if calculating a response.

"Why, that it must be! Cheers."

The two ladies clinked their glasses, but Apa already had her eyes on the tan, chiseled man beside Fila.

"I know this is a big night for you, Fila, but you have taken *far* too long to introduce me."

Fila blushed. "Oh, I'm very sorry. This is Moshe."

Apa already had a hand extended towards him, further exposing her slender limbs and elegant poise. Unfortunately, Moshe still had a drink in his right. He nodded and tipped it towards Apa, hoping that would suffice. Apa slowly pulled her hand back, narrowing her eyes. Fila couldn't help but notice.

"This is actually his first day after rebirth!"

Apa's eyes returned to their already slim norm.

"Indeed it is."

A brawny hand became a brawny arm that wrapped around Apa's waist. A man to match her glory made himself visible with a sly kiss on her cheek and a couple drinks in his other hand. He gave one to Apa, the two smirking to themselves before he noticed the others before him. At once, his cool confidence was replaced with a paling temperament. Apa noticed.

"Oh, is this unknown news? My, it really has been a long time, sweet Fila. Eras and I have been together for ninety days now."

Fila had a plastered smile that contradicted the strained muscles on the rest of her face. She could only nod, slowly, and then more vigorously. Eras had his lips stretched in a flatline of ambiguity. They each stood gracelessly. Moshe wanted to break the tension. Perhaps a question was appropriate - he was the one with the most to learn anyway. It would have to be about something else. Ecclesia, The Citadel, *Sympos* in general, anything else, really. But he was being swallowed up by the anxiety of the mass of people slowly inching closer towards them. Their incompatible crew of four was being dissolved into the rest of the party. Moshe was ready to move on, but familiarity returned.

"What did I tell you? Not a doubt in my mind, my good sir!"

Duman grabbed Moshe passionately, kissing his cheeks more fervently than Eras did to Apa. It felt like the first time they met, but even warmer. And boozier.

"Peace be with you, Duman." The first smile of the night for Moshe.

"And also with you, Moshe! I've spent half my life welcoming hopefuls into Outer Sanctum, and it really is one of my great sorrows that I hardly have the pleasure of seeing them beyond The Wall. To see you here now - oh! What a joy it is! I see you've already met our most boring love triangle!"

Moshe winced, as did Eras and Fila. Each gave equally tepid greetings to the greeting-giver. Moshe wasn't surprised by Duman's social blindness, but he was surprised at how forthright he was. There must have been something about those drinks.

"We must make sure to assemble together sometime, Moshe, you and I. I'm always busy, and I couldn't tell ya for the life of me what my schedule is like right now, but we must make it happen! Who knows? Perhaps I shall just invite myself over some time, ha! Dinner will be starting shortly, please excuse me as I allow myself the pleasure of just one more drink."

As Duman whisked away, one of the positives of the throng made itself known to Moshe. He and Fila were able to dissociate from Eras and Apa without having to further conversate. The crowd was loud enough and mixed enough for them to make their getaway to the fifth section: the photo booth.

They stood in line, waiting for their chance to stand before the stationary camera that flashed and expunged a photograph quickly enough. Moshe found it interesting that everyone before them was a pair, male and female. Now, in the peace that comes from patience, he met with the courage to speak.

"Fila," he simply said.

"Yes?" Fila responded, the plaster in her smile obviously cracking. This would be tricky to navigate.

"I don't need to know the details, but clearly that couple is affecting you."

More cracking. Moshe reached for Fila's farther arm and pulled her in for a momentary squeeze.

"But that's ok. You don't have to worry about them anymore."

It was their turn for the camera, and both of them were able to truly smile for it.

They didn't ever get to play *tosbala*, but that was ok.

Everyone seated at The Table. Further rejoinings and recelebrations over time lost and found once more. Moshe wondered how large the community must feel considering how frequently and fervently these Ecclesians dined on nostalgia. He was about to do so.

"Get ready for a meal like you've never had before," Fila said excitedly.

"You mean there's something better than *casu*?" Moshe asked with affect.

Fila laughed more robustly than Moshe knew she could. It expanded beyond her typical, cutesy giggle into something more guttural and throatier. She cut herself off before it could continue into something obnoxious, redness expanding upon her face. Moshe laughed both at and with her, even as he considered how he *had* had much better fare than *casu*. Many a time.

The seat to his right became occupied by a heavy sigh: Lieutenant Zacchaeus. He didn't see Moshe, lost in his own thought space, so Moshe decided to speak first.

"My first *Sympos* and I'm honored with a seat next to such a dignitary." Moshe was not usually so playful, but he was feeling...different.

Zacchaeus looked at his neighbor unamusedly before he saw who it was. He thought before he spoke.

"Moshe," with a hand out for shaking. "Aren't you aware that there are no dignitaries here? We're equal now."

"In some sense, but you hold a position of elevated responsibility. It follows that there is implied decorum with it."

Zacchaeus' eyebrows quickly flashed up and down as he sipped his implied drink.

"Amaru and Reenu?" He asked while firmly putting his drink down, looking forward.

Moshe picked his up and put it to his lips. What answer could possibly be satisfying? Satisfying did not mean right.

"Next time."

Zacchaeus lightly, sympathetically scoffed. "For your sake, I hope so."

"The milleversary girl herself!"

Moshe heard the smacking of lips on skin and turned to see the next familiar face.

The same slimming outfit of black and pompous shoulder pads overshadowed the concealed physique of the General Speaker for Ecclesian Events and Head Stomio for Leader. Shedim felt even more paradoxically imposing up close. He held his hands close to his chest in the manner of piety as he listened to Fila recount her last few days.

"And how has your quest for another been?" he asked after waiting enduringly for the appropriate time to divulge what he was truly interested in.

Fila's face must have grown sore from how often it had reddened and plastered that night. Shedim's eyes gravitated towards Moshe, lighting up with realization.

"Stranger, do not keep yourself strange. What is your name?"

"Moshe," hand outstretched.

Shedim clasped it with sinewy strength, both hands enveloping his but without motion.

"It is good to have you here, Moshe. The Table is nearly brimming with your added presence," unabashedly grinning.

He released his grip and regained his regal composure.

"I must make the opening announcements. Fila, I'll see you soon enough."

They both nodded towards the General Speaker as he glid away. Moshe and Fila looked at each other in acknowledgement of the general oddness of the interaction.

"Brothers and sisters, blessed as we are by the labor of Savyer and those who followed after him, we take up the cup that they have handed to us with joy and gratitude!"

Moshe saw everyone lift up their cups in response to Shedim's mantra and hastily did the same. Shedim stood at the podium and spoke into the microphone as easily and carelessly as one might expect after doing so hundreds of times.

"I'll keep this brief because I am starving..."

More laughs here than at The Last Call. Moshe hastily joined in.

"Leader is not here tonight, he is overlooking a rather unexpected development that is happening beyond The Wall. Now, please, there is no need to worry. There is just some minor rebellion from a group that apparently meets underground, but we have

what

strong reason to believe that we can address it before it spreads. By next *Sympos*, it will be a memory."

Moshe let his cup falter. He wondered if he could tell Fila what he was feeling afterwards. Right now, he saw she was saddened by some bit of that news as well.

"As far as lighter news, it is Fila's milleversary!"

A decent number of people cheered emphatically, everyone else joined in unanimity. Fila put her best face forward, stood up, and gave a slight bow.

"Now, we dine!" Shedim exclaimed as he immediately went for his seat, which was not far from the podium.

Hollering spread throughout the room in randomized bursts of excitement. It was as if all consideration of previous information was nullified by the air of gustatory possibilities. It was no time at all before servants appeared from behind every other seated patron, each carrying a covered dish soon to be devoured. For the next three hours, these servants would promptly replace the old with the new - another meal, another vibrant collection of colors, another part of the palette satiated. Moshe was in disbelief. His eyes had become bigger than his mental faculties, he would have to ask Fila what each delicacy was named another time. There was no time to remember, only to partake. And the partaking led to great conversation.

Not long after the first dish arrived, Zacchaeus slipped out as slightly as he could. Someone else replaced him, a burly but surprisingly compact man named Fasi. He and Moshe hit it off with a little help from their drinks.

"But there must be some conflict?" Moshe asked, his voice falling off the high of laughter from a particularly funny joke Fasi told.

Fasi chuckled. "Wh-why? Is your soul so depraved that you need something to harm it?"

Moshe felt Fasi pat his back in jest, but it was as if he was patting it from another room.

"No, no. I mean, I surely hope not?" returning the pat. "But what is life without conflict?"

"Paradise?" Fasi smiled and clinked Moshe's glass with his.

Moshe rubbed his chin. "Sure...I guess I still cannot fathom it. Even as I feast."

Fasi saw the earnestness in the newcomer's eyes and gave him something to chew on. He leaned in like he was revealing secrets, but his voice did not actually lower enough to be effective.

"There *are* still problems."

Fasi started pointing out where.

"*She* eats too much."

"*He* can be petty."

"*They* don't have any kids."

"*I* like to gossip," pointing at himself and beaming. Moshe laughed.

"But...these are all small things," Fasi insisted. "I've lived here for nine years. The first half of that time was spent pondering your very question. And I think you're right: people *do* need something to struggle against. So I say, let these small things be if it helps with the big things. Besides, everyone here truly deserves this place and we do our best to help the hopefuls- Moshe, what's wrong?"

Moshe put a hand on his face and felt tears slipping down. He rubbed himself instantly, embarrassed. He meant to speak to show he was fine, but his vocal cords felt thick. He had finally found the answer, the way to live in harmony. If such wisdom graced all inhabitants of this land, it made sense why they could flourish.

"Sorry," was all he could muster.

Fasi placed a hand on his thigh and smiled, emanating warmth.

"I understand. Enjoy these moments. The beginning is so sweet. Maybe another drink to go with it?"

Fasi stood up and half-stumbled towards the bar, leaving Moshe in a peaceful state.

It was then that Moshe noticed Fila's company. Or lack of it.

She hadn't spoken a word throughout their meal. Moshe felt bad, knowing that he should have been paying more attention to his partner. He would make up for it.

"Fila, is everything alright?"

Fila looked up from her plate, despondency fleeing.

"Yes, of course," matter-of-factly. Moshe probed further, courageous.

"Was there something about that underground business that was...troubling?"

The outer rim of Fila's eyebrows went up.

"What do you mean?"

"What Shedim said. About the underground group in Outer Sanctum."

Fila shook her head knowingly. "It will be a memory. I just...I thought Leader would be here."

Moshe felt his pulse fall from rush to gait. He rubbed his new friend's thigh.

"Don't forget: I'm here."

Fila showed a smile but it didn't lessen her burden.

The night was winding down, though no one had left yet. There was no rush, after all. Moshe had the pleasure of introducing Fasi to Fila, and the three of them joked and confided in each other old stories and future hopes. A couple of hours went by like rest. Moshe learned much about the people and culture, and he knew he would love it even more as time went on. There was such a positivity embedded into the atmosphere, and it was not fictitious. His new friends helped him see that this was a positivity that was *chosen*; optimism couldn't fix all of the world's problems, but it could fix the present tense. Moshe wondered whether or not choosing positivity in his past life would have made all the difference.

Shedim was at the podium.

"Brothers and sisters, blessed as we are by the labor of Savyer and those who followed after him, we have taken up the cup that they have handed us with joy and gratitude!"

Everyone placed whatever they had in their hands down on The Table. Each pair of hands were clasped with a neighboring pair, fingers interlocking.

"I'll keep this brief because we're all nearly comatose at this point..."

The laughs were nearly comatose, too.

"This was another wonderful *Sympos*. They always are. There are no further announcements other than what must be visually obvious to you all..."

Moshe looked around to see where everyone was looking. They all faced Shedim's direction, but their eyes went lower, towards The Table. He saw.

"There are only *seven* seats left at The Table when you include your honorary children who will one day make fine Ecclesian citizens. It seems likely that we will be complete within a moon cycle or so. Leader will go into more details regarding expansion and roles next *Sympos*, so until then, peace be with you."

"And also with you" came unanimously.

Moshe hoped that whoever would occupy those remaining seats deserved it.

"Cache!"

Abigail yelled out the command ferociously. It stifled the Kohen long enough for ten of Ecclesia's newly discovered dissenters to gallop their way across the room while the remaining ten grabbed torches off the pillars and readied themselves for combat. The Kohen leader appeared neither outraged nor roused. If anything, Reenu thought he seemed reluctant as he and his men advanced towards their would-be captives.

A couple of them walked directly to Reenu. Hands still above his head, the one on Reenu's left pulled out some rope while the other held has baton in between a state of action and ease. Their placid manner was enough to confuse Reenu, who nearly believed their aim was unthreatening. Either way, it didn't matter. They lost the benefit of the doubt when they hurt his friend.

Reenu kicked the rope-bearing Kohen in the stomach. He bent over backwards, but not before Reenu was able to wrench the rope from his hands, which he used to block the oncoming overhead baton of the other Kohen. Reenu quickly wrapped the rope around his baton, yanked it to his right, and then swung it back around so that it met the Kohen with a loud crack across his nose. Reenu's opponents were still committed to finishing the fight, but he sped past them as they got back up. He had made eye contact with Matthias, and he wasn't about to let him go.

Matthias' eyes shone with fear. He was not

did he really not expect to fight

armed, and his plan of retreating towards the entrance was now compromised by the anger in Reenu's eyes. Matthias still grimaced through the aches of his wounds from The Last Call as he gracelessly hobbled away. He knew he was now being hunted by a starving predator, so he attempted the tried-and-true tactic of weaker prey: deflection.

Reenu followed Matthias' finger and found that it pointed straight at a convulsing Amaru.

On the other side of the room, those who followed Abigail's command had made it to their destination. A couple of them had been knocked down by flung batons, but the rest pulled apart a weak spot in the wall. Makeshift spears of greasy, moist wood and jagged ends were systematically tossed to everyone who was willing and able to attack. It happened to be everyone. The final item to be recovered was a jet-black, heavy sphere attached to a chain. It was handed to Abigail, who held it like a relative last seen long ago.

"Amaru!"

Reenu scrambled for his lover-friend, who was once again direly injured, helpless on the floor. There was no blood this time, but her eyes had rolled back and she would not stop shaking. Reenu looked around in desperation. He knew no one would be able or willing to help at the moment. He didn't know what to do to help her himself. Another frantic scan of the room and he saw a recess in the wall where someone was taking out a ball and chain. He picked up Amaru, who had traded her convulsions for unconsciousness, and rushed towards it, dodging a couple baton swings and the flailing of a burning Kohen on his way. He hid Amaru in the alcove and turned around. If she could not get any help right now, it would be his job to make sure she did as soon as possible. As far as he could tell, his best chances lay with interrogating one specific traitor. Reenu ducked a baton on his left, blocked a punch on his right, and swung his roped baton down hard on a Kohen before him. All the while, he never ceased running. Running towards Matthias. A few more maneuvers and he would be on him.

Abigail had three Kohen before her, odds which she found entirely exciting.

"Come on you little Leader-cocksuckers! I've got another ball for you to fondle!"

She looped the leg of the one who was closest to her with the chain so that he was stretched into a deep lunge. She then shattered his knee with the ball. His painful scream became exaggerated as she leapt off what remained of his knee so that she was above the other two Kohen. She straddled the face of one of them while piledriving the other's with the ball. Her final stunt with this trio was falling backwards, bringing the Kohen down with her, and introducing her ball to his spine. She then got up, grabbed a nearby spear, and stabbed each of them through their chests.

Abigail wiped splattering blood from her chin. Even though she enjoyed her odds, she saw her comrades struggling with the same or worse. She looked and saw one of them surrounded by four encroaching Kohen. He fanned out his torch to keep two of them at bay, but the other two swiftly tackled him and started their flurry of baton strikes.

They would never succeed being so outnumbered, no matter how tough they fought. It is for that reason that she resorted to her next command.

"Darkness!"

And it came with a single, collective huff.

Reenu stopped at its suddenness. He looked around for some source of light; his eyes were not adjusting quick enough. He had placed a hand on Matthias' shoulder, and he was winding up for a well-deserved punch when the flames went out. There! The faint gleam of daylight was coming from

they must have left the hole uncovered

the entrance hall. He also saw Matthias scrambling that way.

The cries of the Kohen affirmed Abigail's foresight before her eyes did. Hers were a people adapted to the darkness. What some may have seen as an unfortunate fall was presently a gift. She heard blood spill out and felt the floors become slick with it. One of the Kohen tried scaling the wall and he even threw his baton so that it hit the ceiling, but he was dragged back down and punished for it. She saw that their other advantage was in their brutality. The Kohen were beating the dissenters into submission, but the dissenters were killing. There were about seven or eight dissenters staggering across the floor from their wounds; there were twice as many Kohen motionless. The fools. It would be their demise.

Reenu grappled Matthias' crutches away from him and the two collapsed together. Reenu mounted his foe and started striking his face in the open-palmed "push" way that he does. Matthias was feeling the pain, but his face did not show it.

"How could you do this to them?!" Reenu yelled. More pointedly, "To me?"

"I could not explain it all, kid," Matthias calmly said.

Another push-punch from Reenu. "You better try!"

Reenu held his hand back in a readied position to show he would not let up if need be, but he would end up never striking Matthias again.

"She's fucking lying, Reenu! There is no *KAMNOS*!"

Reenu let his hand slowly fall.

"What?" Reenu asked, breathing quicker. "How could you know that?"

"He doesn't."

Reenu turned to see Abigail holding her ball and chain. There was menace in her eyes, like a wolf ready to pounce but waiting for some invisible signal.

"You can't trust what he says, Reenu. He betrayed us all. This blood is on his hands. Kill him."

Reenu looked back at Matthias. There was no plea in his eyes. He was like the sheep who realizes the impossibility of escape. Fate accepted.

"I...I can't."

"What do you mean?" The wolf found a more appetizing prey.

Reenu suddenly discovered that he was now the one between a rock and a hard place. He would have to choose his words carefully in order to not make another enemy. But the more he thought, the more he recognized that there was no amount of reasoning or explanation that would satiate her. Bloodshed was the only answer. He resignedly looked back at Abigail, and that's when he saw who was just beyond her, and was well-pleased.

"He doesn't. He never has. And *we* don't. Not anymore."

Amaru placed a delicate but confident hand on Abigail's. The one with the ball. What Amaru thought was a peacemaking gesture led to Abigail tightening her grip from underneath her.

"Then you alone will lose." She said this as she spread out her arm towards the rest of the room.

Less than half of the Kohen were still standing, but the dissenters were still nearly unfazed. In fact, roles had reversed and the ones being rounded up were the Kohen themselves - a majority huddled together in one corner of the room in a defensive position. Intricate baton swings were preventing any penetrative attacks, so the dissenters stood back a bit. Then, one of them raised her spear. The others all did so. Reenu realized they were about to launch their weapons. A unified throw would slaughter the rest of the battalion. But just as the self-starter pulled hers back, ready to throw, a large rock landed on it and snapped both the spear and her arm in two, replacing them with a solid beam of light. Everyone in the room looked up.

The rock came from the ceiling.

Slowly, another rock tumbled down, crushing the leg of a dissenter.

Then another rock.

And another.

And then the rest of the ceiling caved in.

Moshe stared at the beige ceiling in his bedroom.

He hadn't seen Fila in a couple days, which was odd. They had grown accustomed to meeting at noon and spending time together until sundown. Then Moshe would go back home, despite Fila's prodding to prolong their engagements. Mostly, Moshe just didn't care to stretch out under The Tree for that long. But he was also learning how to deal with an emotion that he was unaccustomed to: boredom.

At the *Sympos*, Moshe caught Shedim before he was able to sneak away. He asked if he could work at The Citadel. Shedim blinked a few times at his candidness before a simple

"No."

When Moshe protested, Shedim explained that newcomers shouldn't just expect to be able to work for the *Symvoul*. There was a process to these things. Moshe said he was willing to man the lowest position there, he just wanted to be a part of great governance. Shedim's eyes gleamed. He told Moshe that he should ask him again next *Sympos*. Moshe asked if it would be helpful for him to directly ask Leader next time, which elicited a slightly more emphatic

"No."

Shedim did offer him a tangible piece of advice, however. He suggested that he take the time to get to know his new friend. Fila was a model citizen and a lovely lady to be with. So that's what Moshe did for the next few days. He didn't even venture to meet his actual neighbors; he became so engrossed in learning Ecclesian culture from the blonde dame he was fated to meet. Until yesterday, when she wasn't at The Tree. And he lay in beige ever since.

He knew he shouldn't have been wasting so much time. But he also didn't feel the pull he felt when he first made it to Outer Sanctum. No desire to meet unknown brethren and discuss The Manual. No desire to discover the luscious fruits and delicacies that lined the streets. He figured that maybe that's what boredom is. Not a lack of options, but a lack of desire.

The doorbell went off. It was still a frightening sound, as pleasant as its two-note descent tried to be. It was so immediate and loud, it felt more like an alarm than a tone of welcome. Moshe leapt to his feet and was downstairs in an instant.

When Moshe opened the door, Fila let herself in immediately. It was dark outside the first time she entered Moshe's house.

She resolutely walked over to Moshe's living room couch and planted herself on it. The bob of her hair bounced with each firm step. Moshe knew she was upset, but he couldn't help finding that involuntary gesture cute.

"Fila, where have you been?" Moshe asked.

She turned her head and shot him piercing eyes.

"Do you have anything to drink?"

"Sure," Moshe answered.

He walked over to his kitchen and poured a glass of water. Fila watched him before deciding it wouldn't do.

"No, no," she insisted. "Something stronger than that. You must have wine, I'm sure of it."

"Oh," Moshe said. "I'm not sure, I wasn't aware of...that."

As he was finishing his statement, Fila bent down to reach a drawer at the bottom of his island that he didn't know was there. In a few swift movements, the two of them were sipping a full glass each. Well, Moshe was sipping. Fila was nearly gulping.

She was filling up her second glass when Moshe placed his hand on hers to get her attention.

"Fila," he said, looking into her eyes. "Where have you been?"

Fila finished filling her glass and took another sip before she verbally responded.

"I've been wasting my time." Another gulp.

Moshe leaned back against his island.

"Well, me too. But only because I've been wondering where you are. Worried, even."

She eyed him as she held her glass to her lips.

"Sure, Moshe. You're worried, Shal was worried, Eras was worried. You're all worried and you're all the same."

She turned away from him. Moshe put his glass down.

"What are you talking about?"

She turned back, her lip trembling now.

"Moshe, I don't want to find someone I can live with. I just want to find someone that I can't live without. Eras and I got along so well, but *clearly*, he has...different tastes. I've been spending time with Shal lately, but he's just...disinterested, I guess. And..."

Fila stood there for a second before choosing her glass over more words.

Moshe understood now, at least partially. He had a feeling, but he certainly didn't want to assume anything, not so early on. And he also didn't understand why.

"And you've been thinking that maybe I could be that person for you?"

Fila put her glass down so she could hold her head in her hands and shake it.

"How can I know that?" her voice muffled. "I've been wrong too many times. They've told me someone would come. They said I shouldn't worry. I'm in paradise now, it's only a matter of time. 'You'll know when you know.' But...*how* do I know when I know?"

She was fighting back a sob, and Moshe gave her the time to do so. He tried to give her wisdom, some kind of apt answer for the situation. But it seemed like an impossible question. He certainly didn't have to deal with it before. All he could do was look at the facts and hold her hands, even though his left one couldn't do so.

"Fila, you have been such a comfort to me these last few days. You've taught me a lot. You've been such a companion. You're fun, yet you somehow don't grow tired of me. You're beautiful. You're a wonderful person - there's plenty for me to find attractive in you."

Fila's body loosened upon hearing something nice about her for once. But she still held her well-earned anxieties with her.

"Moshe, you see what's on the surface, what I've presented to you. But you don't know my past."

"Trust me," Moshe said, the beginning of a chuckle in his voice. "If there's anyone with a past to forget, it's me."

Fila heard those words. She really heard them. There was a darkness in them. Foreboding. And adventure. Excitement.

And then:

"Fila, maybe it's time we let both of our pasts stay where they belong. And start something new."

Fila felt her entire body tremble in anticipation, and the way Moshe didn't shy away from the force of that feeling. She felt the honesty in his light brown eyes. He smelled the beauty of her fragrant, soft skin.

They fell into each other in that kitchen, and let something new take place.

Reenu looked across the room at Amaru. She was in the other group. The dissenters had been split into two groups of twelve. De-armed and defeated. Bound by rope and circumstance. Daylight got into Reenu's eyes and he looked away, nearly blinded by it. After the ceiling collapsed and effectively ended the rebellion, thirty more Kohen swung down on ropes, coordinated as ever. Reenu saw the roots above and smelled the soil he had once spent a night with. It was the Apago Forest, where he and his friends were momentary prisoners once before. This time felt more perpetual.

When he turned to hide from the sun, he saw Abigail just a few feet away from him. Most everyone there had their heads sunken in surrender or their bodies tense with fear. She was not like anyone else. She held herself up straight on her knees, chin pointed up and eyes set squarely on the Lead Kohen. From Reenu's position, she looked ready to either pounce upon him or take whatever discipline she would be dealt with defiance. Whichever came first.

The Lead Kohen was wiping the blood and gore off of his baton. Suddenly, he struck it hard into the floor. It cracked under the weight of his strike, and he solemnly left it standing there.

"We did not desire to use that much force," he relented. "Our reinforcements up top were a last resort."

Reenu looked around at the impenetrable circles of Kohen that surrounded the two groups. They left no space between them, no more room for successful dissent.

"A maneuver like that could have been costly. Too costly. We put you all in mortal danger. As well as ourselves."

A pause.

"We are fortunate to have escaped with our lives. We who remain at least."

Reenu looked around. Aside from the Kohen who died in combat, everyone else remained. When the roof started collapsing, he saw both sides come together in sheltering formations: huddling up and keeping their heads down, guiding each other to get underneath protective debris. Everyone except Abigail.

"We have all been given a second chance. And...we think that even dissenters like you deserve one."

The air in the room changed, and it was not just from the fresh supply that was let in from up top.

"Whatever the reasoning for your...political positioning is, it could be entirely valid. I can see why the struggle to be a citizen could be disgruntling. Rejection hardens the spirit, for better or worse. To some extent, you cannot be blamed for reacting instinctually. However, you are now being given a choice. You can all agree - and it must be unanimous - to stop meeting and give up your plans...or one of your groups *will* be punished."

Reenu didn't know these people well enough to tell whether or not they would consider such a proposal, but he could sense it. The Lead Kohen allowed a minute of silence so they could truly let their situation sink in. After some time, he opened his mouth to tally the vote.

"That's not a real choice, it's a fucking ultimatum."

The Lead Kohen turned his head to find where that line came from, but he already had a feeling where to go.

"That's what you people do," Abigail said. "You monopolize and demonize so that whatever binary you construct is really just one viable option. Don't call it a choice."

The Lead Kohen slowly walked over to Abigail. Every step was felt and seen by all. Reenu tried to look at Amaru but her visage was blocked by the backside of a Kohen. Then the Lead did something surprising. He got down on his knees and sat back, making himself even a little lower than Abigail.

"There is always a choice," he said softly. "You can do what's right and be rewarded. Or do what's wrong and risk retribution. That is how justice and order work."

"If it were so simple," Abigail retorted. "But it's always more complicated than that. We are people of competing wants."

"That's why we need people to rule us."

"That's why our rulers are so shitty."

"They can't be right all of the time."

"So they make furnaces to burn away their reminders of that?"

Abigail's eyes were blazing, but the Lead looked at her with pity.

"You know that isn't true."

Abigail pulled her head back. She looked at the people who listened to her every word.

"True. Hmph. Of course it's true. Whether or not it's real doesn't make it any less true."

Leaning against the room's entrance, Reenu saw Matthias shift his body a little, as if preparing himself to leave. The Lead noticed and nodded.

"Abigail, do you want to tell us your plan now?"

Abigail's eyes lit up with fire again.

"Or risk retribution?" The Lead asked.

Abigail looked around at her followers once more. The fire didn't leave her eyes until they met Amaru. She was awake and alive, but just barely. It was then that Abigail understood how dire the conditions were. She must relent.

"We are under the Apago Forest for a reason. Not only would we be hard to find, but it was the easiest way to accomplish our goal."

The Lead tilted his head back and lowered his eyes.

"Which is?"

"...make *KAMNOS* come true."

Reenu's heart sank. It was not unlike the feeling he had when they burned the bodies of their captors so long ago. Or when he heard the crack of Amaru's temple coming from Moshe's fist. It was not so much the shock of the revelation, but the comprehension that Amaru must have been emotionally devastated by it. The blow of deceit coming from the only person here she fully trusted. Believed in, even. And the fact that he couldn't be there with her or even see her as it happened.

"Explain," demanded The Lead.

"We were going to burn it down, you dumbass," Abigail answered, not liking his tone. "We've been tunneling our way up. In the middle of the night, we'd set fire to the trees. News of it would spread instantly, and it wouldn't take much rumor-spreading for a *KAMNOS* spill-over to be considered the source. Easy shit."

"And what would the point of that be?" The Lead questioned, frustration spreading across his facial lines.

"...you need a fire so that more people see the light."

"How can you so carelessly deny compassion for yourself and others? 'There is good in store for you if you would only trust.'" The question was genuine.

Abigail thought. She carried a look of pensive doubt, but it melted into bored disinterest.

"Ask your fucking Leader the same thing."

The Lead sighed. He put his thumb and forefinger to his mouth and emitted a sharp whistle. The Kohen surrounding the other group prodded their prisoners into standing and started walking them out of the room one by one. Amaru's group. Reenu tried standing up himself before he felt a baton gently force him back down. He saw Amaru as she left the room, but she could not turn her head to see him.

"You made your choice, Abigail," The Lead said nonchalantly. He started writing on a pad that one of his cohorts gave him. "It's unfortunate that it affects so many others."

The remaining Kohen gave each of their hostages a swift smack to the head with their batons. It left them all groaning on the floor. Once The Lead was sure that the group he secured for justice's sake was far enough away, he and the rest of the Kohen grabbed the ropes that led to the Apago Forest and kindly made their exit.

Abigail casually walked to a sharp piece of rubble and cut herself loose. Then she went to the remaining eleven to set them free as well. She asked each of them if they were fine before moving on to the next one. Reenu was the only one who didn't affirm her.

Reenu looked around at the room one last time before he would never come back. Silent tears streamed down his face. It was a mess of blood, bits of bone, broken spears, stained rock, scattered debris, doused torches, and heavy despair. The sun was nearing its setting, and the few rays of light that still hit the room only made it look more ominous. Reenu felt a twisted joke

it's the chaos she always wanted

rise within himself, but he denied it any room. He briskly walked toward the entrance, prepared to be rid of these people forever. But he stopped. Abigail deserved to hear something from him.

There were so many things that Reenu wanted to say to Abigail. He wanted to question her decision, defy her leadership, disagree with her plan, make her realize what she had done. But only one question seemed pertinent.

"Alright, Abigail. What's next?"

- -

Moshe opened his eyes. He was once again staring at the same beige ceiling, but it was no longer boredom that he felt. It was something lighter.

He turned his head, expecting to see Fila beside him. She was not there, but one of his other senses assured him of her nearness. The smell of something good concocting downstairs lured him into the kitchen. There she was. A picture of his ideal other: spatula in one hand, pan in the other, four timers intricately set up, and the utensils she had finished using already washed. She was doing a lot but she could manage herself. Moshe found that to be more attractive than anything else. And it didn't hurt that she let her robe reveal more than usual.

"Good morning," Moshe said with a smile.

Fila returned the gesture, pretending not to notice him until he greeted her so that she could show him the full extent of her grin. They exchanged a kiss and then Fila pushed Moshe away to the table. She wanted him to know that she could handle everything.

Moshe sat down and closed his eyes. Everything about the present tense was nice. He tried a little, but he couldn't think of another time where that statement was true. He acknowledged that there were some great experiences and laughs and love shared with the people in his past. But there was always a danger there, too. Being on the run from scavengers or wolves or the sun. Having to look for sustenance or navigate living without it. The worry of planning ahead. The negativity that permeates that kind of desperate lifestyle.

right now...everything is nice

The first timer went off.

Moshe heard the slight clink of the plate before he opened his eyes and saw it before him. He didn't know what it was but it was beautiful.

"Thank you for preparing firstmeal," Moshe told Fila.

Fila laughed. "Firstmeal is an Outer Sanctum word. We call it breakfast."

Moshe smiled and started eating voraciously.

Fila giggled amidst a mouthful of her own. "Moshe, don't spoil your stomach! You can take your time, there are a couple more courses coming."

Moshe slowed down exaggeratedly and Fila rolled her eyes.

"Sorry. I'm just...really hungry, I guess."

"I wonder why," Fila said with a wink.

They enjoyed their first course silently after that exchange. Fila finished her plate before Moshe did,

ironic...or hypocritical

but it was only so she could attend to finishing the second course. She started washing her plate when she remembered what she wanted to talk about.

"Oh. Moshe. There's a few things I wanted to run by you about the rest of the week."

Moshe perked an eyebrow. Fila had never seemed like the type to look ahead. Each of their days had been spontaneous and unplanned so far. He didn't mind it, though.

"Okay. What were you thinking?"

The second timer went off. Fila got to plating.

"Actually, for today at least, I'm thinking we can take it slow if you want. No need to rush. But tomorrow, preparations will need to be made. I mean, it will be the week's end after that so there won't be a-"

"Preparations for what?" Moshe asked.

Fila tilted her head. She held a full spatula in one hand and it nearly slipped out of her grasp but she was able to barely recover and land it on the plate. She giggled slightly.

"Moshe, please. No need to be funny. I know you have a bit to learn still, but you *obviously* know The Manual."

Moshe felt a pang of insult in his chest, and he wasn't about to let it sit there.

"Of course I know The Manual."

Fila paused, confused at the situation. "Then...you know what has to happen within three days."

Moshe pushed his chair back and turned so he could face Fila more fully.

"No. I don't. Just tell me."

Fila pushed the plate aside.

"Well, last night we came together."

"Yes."

"Our bodies united."

"I know that, Fila."

"So we must have our *gamosnio* within three days."

Moshe firmly walked towards Fila until he was in the kitchen beside her.

"What are you talking about?"

The third timer went off. Fila went to stop it and then proceeded to empty another pan, but Moshe held her arm so that she couldn't.

"Fila, talk to me. What is this *gamosnio*?"

Moshe felt Fila's pulse quicken and observed her chest inhale and exhale more rapidly. Like a sheep who knows they've been caught. Or learns they're all alone. She led Moshe to the living room and opened up a copy of their sacred text.

"Here in Makao 2," Fila pointed to the words so Moshe could follow along. "'When a man lies with a woman, it is a holy unification. The only way it is broken is if it is not affirmed within three days.'"

Moshe remembered this passage now. It was part of what planted the thought that having multiple loves was problematic. He tried not to think about that right now. Or them.

"There's nothing about a *gamosnio* here," Moshe negated.

"That's just the word we call the affirmation it's referencing. It's a public ceremony that seals our love and makes us an everlasting couple."

Moshe was confused, but he saw the trouble he was in. So he threw out whatever rebuttals he could.

"We never talked about that in Outer Sanctum."

"I could see why. Those people want to be with anyone and everyone. They don't understand the virtue of commitment."

Moshe realized that they were holding hands as they went back and forth. He pulled back thinking it was inappropriate to be physically connected while being intellectually disparate, but he saw that he left some hurt on Fila's face with the action.

"That could be true for some of them. But it seems like a vital concept to just overlook."

"Perhaps there are some...misinterpretations happening on that side of The Wall. We should bring that up at the next *Sympos*. Because this is really one of the fundamentals of Ecclesian society. Everyone does this."

Moshe was taken aback. His body reacted similarly.

"Fundamentals? One of the fundamentals of Ecclesian society is based on a couple of lines in one book?"

Now Fila was taking offense.

"It may just be a couple of lines, but it is the very *spirit* of The Manual! Longevity in exclusive embrace. It's the life we are all called to lead. It's how we survive as a people!"

The fourth timer went off. It drew their attention long enough for a break in the argument to surface. But they stayed where they were and let its shrill accents ring out.

Moshe massaged his temples. Fila couldn't understand why this was such an issue for him. He was already an Ecclesian, why was it so hard to accept this new life? That verse about the sheep returning to its *casu* had never felt so true. But it still seemed odd for Moshe to be so...resistant. He had accepted everything prior whole-heartedly. He appreciated structure and even felt undeserving of the city's glory. The problem couldn't be with the rule...

Fila understood. It was the age-old explanation, after all.

"Moshe...do you not want to be with me?"

Moshe slowly looked up at her. She expected to see regret or shame or even indifference like she had seen on so many lovers prior. But there was none of that. Only something like the beginnings of rage.

"This is not about you, Fila. Not at all. I had no idea this whole thing existed. Truthfully, I would not have slept with you had I known the consequences. Not because I don't think you could be a great partner. But you only *could* be. How can I *know* that in the course of a few days?"

Fila stifled her tears because she needed Moshe to hear this.

"But Moshe, that's the law. If you let three days pass...well, that's shameful. We *have* to have a *gamosnio. Everyone* does it."

Moshe exhaled. "And there's the real problem. Like I said, it's not about you. But if I didn't know about this apparently fundamental law...what else could I be wrong about?"

The *whoosh* of flames. Moshe and Fila rushed to the kitchen to put out the burning pan. Moshe threw the pan on the floor. Fila ran to the restroom. Moshe started pillaging his pantry for something to put the fire out with. He stopped when he realized he didn't know where something like that would be. It was all foreign to him, the inner workings of his own house. Fila returned with a hefty bucket of water and doused the flames until they became steam. There were a few embers left so Fila stepped on them. They persisted. She became more and more aggressive in her stamping. They persisted. Fila would not give up. She howled and howled as energy and frustration unleashed from within her. Moshe just stood there.

Moshe and Fila sat at The Table. Duman, Apa, and Eras were with them, and the fivesome were engaged in heated but playful conversation.

"Baradiddles, all of them!" Duman burst out in comical rage as he swigged once more.

The other four perplexedly looked at each other.

"Duman, I swear-" Eras started.

"Oh, but you really shouldn't," Duman interrupted and burped to equally healthy laughs from Fila and Apa. Eras rolled his eyes and allowed his hands two blasé claps.

"Very funny coming from the guy who's clearly making up these four-syllable words. For all we know, half of them could be swears!"

Eras' eyes lit up when he spoke, as if the thought completed itself when the words came out. Duman had to laugh at the accusation. Amidst their amusement, Eras shot Fila a side-eyed glance that she definitely caught and held.

"But what you *can't* charge me with..."

When Duman returned to his original point is when Moshe fully checked out. It was all nonsense, anyway.

Wasn't it just last week that Fila had an undeniably awkward interaction with Apa and Eras? And now she talks to them like they've been friends their whole lives. Completely ignoring the gamosnio. Two days ago it was the end of the world if we didn't have one. But now it'll be swept under the rug. Of course, eventually, it will have to come up. We can't save face forever. But maybe that's what everyone is doing. Are all the conversations happening around this Table just fronts for people to show they're doing okay? Even Duman? I have yet to see him this side of The Wall without a drink in his hands. I can't even remember the names of half the people I've met tonight, but Fila made it a point to show me off to all of them. As if we are what matters. Her hand just grazed Eras'. I wouldn't usually think anything of it, but this woman is more crafty than she seems. Every motion of hers in the past week has been calculated. De-

signed to make me fall into her restrictions. But it's not real, she has to see that. Savyer...am I doomed to always despise the ones I grow close to?

Moshe blinked. Some change in the decibel range made him come out of himself. He realized his remote companions were all looking at him intently.

"Sorry," Moshe tried recovering. "Did I miss something?"

Their stares were blank yet concerned.

"I just asked if you were still hungry, sweetie? You haven't touched your plate at all."

Fila's hand covered his. Her voice dripped with niceness. The kind that you have to accept.

"I guess not," Moshe said. He cracked a fictitious smile and grabbed his plate. When he stood up, he wasn't sure if he would stop at the trash dispenser. Maybe he would continue to the doors. And then The Wall. And then Outer Sanctum's gates. And then to whatever else in the world there could possibly be. But he didn't even make it to the trash dispenser when the servers ushered him back to The Table. Leader was here.

Moshe looked around but didn't see Leader anywhere. He only saw Shedim make his way to the podium. But he was grateful for the news. He could handle those around him letting him down. Maybe they had plenty of their own learning to do still. That seemed to be a theme. But if there was anyone who could be counted on, it had to be Leader. The one in charge of such a thriving city. The one so closely related to Savyer himself. Shedim tapped on the microphone a few times, bringing it back to life.

"Ecclesians, it has been too long. We know that Leader has been doing good work while he's been away, but even so, it can be painful going too long without him. So I must get out of the way immediately. Here he is: Leader Saios."

Shedim bowed and scurried away back to his front-row seat. Everyone stood up and started voraciously clapping. Moshe was happy to follow along this time. Everyone was overjoyed. Fila grabbed Moshe and kissed him, and then Eras did the same to Apa. From somewhere else came brass fanfare. It was not unlike the notes from The Wall, for it actually expanded upon that musical idea. Then, from the shadows behind the podium, he emerged.

Moshe couldn't figure out what was different about him. Physically, everything looked the same. The jaw, the curls, the purple, gold, and white. The undoubtable smile. But even though Moshe had only seen him once before, he felt so very familiar. Comforting.

"My people, my people. How I have missed you so." Leader waved his hand vertically so that everyone would sit down. It reminded him of the trumpet players he and Fila saw on the corner the other day. There were four of them, but a fifth waved a stick around. Fila explained that he was someone who made sure the musicians stuck together. Dictating how fast they would go, how loud they should be.

"Bad news first, as always," Leader said. An instantaneous thickening of the air.

"You have all heard about the meager defiance that was forming underground. It's been taken care of and will no longer be an issue."

Fila gripped Moshe's hand. Duman put his cup down, finally. Moshe tried not to gulp. Why was this bad news?

"This is good for Ecclesia," Leader admitted. He started to slowly pace back and forth in front of the podium. "Doubt is the enemy of faith. My story tells me so. All stories do in some way. And what our Outer Sanctum brothers and sisters need is more belief, not less of it. And I believe that this was a victory for them as much as it was for us. But...in a small but significant way...there is loss."

Even in his mostly incoherent state, Duman detected something. Something that led him to stand up and half-stumble towards the front.

"Shedim should have *never* told you about this incident. For a number of reasons, but mostly this. If you, my people, are ever at even the slightest risk...I believe it is *my* duty to tell you so. To keep you properly informed. This 'rebellion' - a word that overblows their significance and should have never been used - was never a real threat. That is why I planned to tell you about it afterwards instead of preparing you for what was to come. And yes, Shedim is my Head Stomio. It is his responsibility to inform you when I can't. But that entails relaying information to you *in the way that I would*. What he did instead was plant seeds of unnecessary worry in your hearts, and that's..."

At this point, Leader turned to face Shedim directly. He took the moment to gather his emotion. Everyone was expectant, though none more so than Shedim. And Duman standing behind him with two Kohen.

"Shedim, you have grown sloppy in your tone, attitude, and word choice. This is not your first offense and you know it. You must be reprimanded, friend."

Shedim felt the presence of the Kohen behind him. His initial reaction was resistant. But he considered the stakes and the situation. He stood up and walked away willingly. Duman took his seat.

There was silence for a while, but plenty of thoughts brewed. Leader chose not to say anything. He wanted the weight to be felt. And then:

"I would have handled that matter with Shedim alone, but I wanted you all to see that we cannot allow for such mishandling of roles. Those lines are not meant to be crossed, for the good of all. Do not worry, everyone. Shedim will not be treated harshly, just fairly. He is not fired. You will all see him again soon enough. But he needs to take the time to remember. Remember how he got to be in such a position. Remember what it takes to be an Ecclesian. It's something we must all be reminded of daily."

One clap. Then another. Then five more. Then the room became full with applause. Leader waved it down.

"No message tonight. Just remember. And let's move on to a more exciting development: Expansion!"

Leader pulled out a bottle from behind the podium and popped it open. Shouts and cheers.

"That's one thing that Shedim *was* right to hint at."

There were more laughs at that then Leader anticipated. He waited.

"Anyway, as The Table nears completion, we are ready to reveal our plans for expanding the city walls. This is an all-hands project that will require much from each of us in order to work, but when we are done, our glorious city will be more spacious than ever before!"

Hoots and hollers.

"Picture it, fellow followers: being able to spend your days with friends and loved ones in a newly renovated Apago Forest!"

Oohs.

"Or playing *tosbala* with your neighbors without worrying about how close you are to accidentally breaking one of their nice lawn sculptures!"

Aahs.

"Every facet of Ecclesian life will be bigger and, subsequently, better. We will enjoy a freer freedom, one that we've all earned together!"

The cheers wouldn't end. To Moshe, it was nauseating.

"What about The Table?!"

Moshe didn't mean to sound angry, but he had to stand up and yell in order to be heard. Everyone else went deathly quiet. Leader calmly analyzed Moshe's demeanor and smiled.

"Two interruptions in two months? Is Duman rubbing off on this city?"

Laughs and laughs and laughs, but none were harder than Duman's roars. Moshe felt sheepish, but he was strengthened when he saw Leader wave him on.

"If everything is getting bigger," Moshe cut above the noise, "then The Table will as well, right? And that means more seats."

Now Leader was the only one clapping.

"That right there is an Ecclesian heart, everyone."

Now there were some polite claps.

"A concern and grace for others. Your name is Moshe, right?"

Moshe nodded.

"I've learned about you. This concern of yours fits right in with your reported character. Well, Moshe, I was prepared to mention it later, but I will address it now, for your sake. The answer is...possibly."

Moshe felt a hand on his side. It was soft and gentle in its plea for him to have a seat. A few nights ago, it was all he wanted. But now he shook it off.

"I don't know you well enough, Leader," Moshe said. "Is that a real answer?"

The air thickened again. Leader laughed again.

"You are asking a complicated question. Expanding The Temple requires material that we do not currently have."

"Maybe they don't have to sit at The Table, but there would still be room for them somewhere in Inner Sanctum, right?"

Moshe had done a lot of sitting on the sidelines lately. He didn't feel like backing down anymore.

"Technically, sure," Leader answered. "But the tradition Savyer instituted is that the amount of seats at The Table is the maximum number that Ecclesia can boast and still flourish. Everybody knows that."

"So what?"

Gasps!

Moshe knew he had to backtrack. He didn't mean to say that, but he saw that his fist was clenched. He breathed in and out three times.

"Obviously Savyer, tradition, and The Manual are all integral to Ecclesian life. But isn't it The Manual itself that says 'the letter of the law is forfeit in the face of love?' What more Ecclesian act is there than to sacrifice for those beyond The Wall? Expansion sounds great. Having more of this good life sounds like it would be better. I think we all deserve that, even if I don't know if I've personally done enough to deserve it myself sometimes. But happily working on bettering life for ourselves feels like a betrayal of the very same law that got us here. So...which part of the law do we follow?"

Eras and Apa both looked at Fila, deeply disturbed. Fila sank in her chair, hoping that she wouldn't be noticed. Everyone else looked to Leader, horror on their faces. Still, many hid the inclination for this kind of drama deep within their hearts.

Saios wanted to stop pacing, so he unhinged his jaw and rotated it from side to side. This Moshe kid was interesting. He had a fire within, and Saios respected that. It was something that he felt many an Ecclesian could use. But fires are dangerous. They must be tempered in order to be used properly. Was there a way that Moshe could be tempered? He realized he was thinking about the future when the present required his attention. What did his people need from him right now? That was the bottom line. Savyer once taught him that when making a tough decision, look at the facts and go from there.

Fact #1: Moshe is disrupting an otherwise beneficial *Sympos*.

Fact #2: Moshe, a newcomer, is suggesting a radical change that he knows nothing about.

Fact #3:

The lines are not meant to be crossed.

Chapter 11: Patiently

Two Kohen delicately lifted the bag off of Amaru's head now that she was indoors. She scoffed to herself. It wasn't so long ago that she was in a similar position, but congratulations to her! She had graduated from being detained by volunteers to the real deal. True professionals led her by the hand like she was an Ecclesian dignitary instead of the opposite. Last time she was able to maneuver her way through the ordeal with a cunning tongue. She contemplated whether that could work here or if more physical means were suitable. Then she contemplated whether any attempt at escape was worthwhile in the first place. Why run? What was out there waiting for her now?

She was being walked down a hall of windowless doors that disassembled any sense of time. It was just the three of them as far as she could tell. No sign of any other rebels. Their steps echoed repeatedly; that was all that could be heard. Amaru reasoned that she could easily slip through the Kohens' respective grips, slam their heads against the walls, and take off running even in her weakened state. But where would she go? They stopped before one of many indiscernible doors.

"We apologize, Ms...?" started the Kohen on her left.

"Amaru," she said with a steely look.

The one Kohen exchanged a glance with the other, but they were both content with letting it go.

"Amaru. Please note that we truly do not want to keep you here; it will only be temporary."

"Why?"

The Kohen appeared slightly startled.

"Well, we will only keep you here until we have what we need."

"Which is?"

"Nothing of your direct concern. We just need you here. You'll see that it's not all that bad. Think of it like a timeout. Your parents ever put you on one of those?"

Amaru just looked at them, her lips pulled back and her chin extended in silent defiance. The other Kohen grew uncomfortable.

"Ahem, I'm sure you were a good child, Ms. Amaru," he said before swinging open the door.

Inside were seven equally divided cells. The five nearer to the entrance were empty and

from lack of use or the opposite

clean. Each of them had a wool blanket, a wool pillow, and a hole in the floor. Hers even had the slightest vent for sunlight bordering the ceiling. But those minor amenities were overshadowed by the indifference of the metal bars that housed them. Still, it was quite a step up from the torture and slavery of the captors from her past life.

The uncomfortable Kohen unlocked the way to her new home while the apologetic one led her in. She sat with her back against the beige brick wall. In the cell to her right was a man whose left leg was obviously shorter than his right. Amaru knew she had seen him before, but she didn't care to think about it currently. Besides, he was staring at her with something of a strange, crooked smile. Diagonally across from her cell was another being, though she couldn't tell the gender from their positioning. They were huddled to themselves in the farthest corner, motionless other than the soft peaks and valleys of regular breathing.

"Someone will bring meals at sunrise every day. But like we said, don't get too comfortable. You'll be out soon enough."

But Amaru was already staring straight ahead at the floor in front of her. She was determined in her unresponsiveness. Not because she didn't want to give them any information or let them inside her head, but because they didn't deserve to talk to her. No one did. They weren't her friends. No one was.

"Peace be with you," both Kohen said. This elicited a short, wheezy laugh from Amaru's strange neighbor. Both Kohen bowed slightly in confused respect and left.

"Letting you leave already? Haven't heard that one before," the man said. Amaru detected age in his voice. "I can't tell if that means you did nothing wrong or everything!" Another wheezy laugh cut short as he quickly recognized his line wasn't funny to his newfound audience.

"Of course, maybe they don't know that the promise of freedom is the worst form of slavery. Or maybe they do."

Amaru didn't budge.

A few hours passed. Amaru was still where she was, though she had to suppress her leg from starting its habitual bouncing a number of times. She thought that the tedium of inaction would have been easier for her - she had just spent a week healing in nothingness, and she had not even fully recovered yet. Letting time waste away should have been familiar at this point, but this was different. Her time with Reenu was that of inevitable mourning while simultaneously being taken care of. She realized that she had taken it for granted - she should not have been so callous towards him while he was going out and coming back to tend to her needs. But here, there was no one. And she was no longer mourning. Like Abigail said, it was time to fucking do something. Mandatory mourning passed into restless abiding.

Amaru leapt up. It shook her elderly neighbor, who had nodded off to the point of snoring. She started pacing and he started observing her. She felt his invasive eyes. She turned and looked at him and his crooked smile. Neither said anything, and that only added to her *what's the point of this*

frustration, but she didn't want to give her unwelcome acquaintance any kind of communicative satisfaction. She looked away and stared at the wall she had leaned against. She thought of something. She placed her head against it and tapped. The sound was muted, but it didn't feel like very robust material. Pulling back her fists, she got to work.

Punch.

Punch.

Punch.

Punch.

It was starting to hurt, but she could have sworn that some of it was coming off and embedding onto her knuckles.

Punch.

Punch.

Apparently it was blood, not the wall.

PUNCH!

PUNCH!

PUNCH!

CRACK!

"Aagh! Fuck!"

Amaru felt a snap in the smallest finger on her right hand and promptly pulled back. She gingerly held her hand and cursed herself.

"Woman, the brick won't budge," came that old, neighborly voice. "But neither will you, it looks like. You should conserve your energy *and* your mind and quit that nonsense."

Amaru turned so that her back was towards the man. She looked down at her hand. There was nothing nearby that could help her with it. She looked down into the hole in the middle of her cell and saw water. She contemplated "icing" it, but the smell was revolting. In the morning, someone would be by with food. Would they be willing to bandage her up? They had been peculiarly kind so far. She could use that. They would come in with the bandage, and then Amaru would beat them unconscious against the bars. With the door unlocked, she'd run, find a way out, and then...

i don't know

"How do you know?"

Enough time had passed that the question felt like it was for the air, which is why the beggar didn't recognize its intended target.

"How do you know?!"

It also didn't help that Amaru insisted on keeping her back towards him as she asked.

"Know what, miss?" The beggar ventured.

"That the brick won't budge."

The beggar shifted his weight onto his shorter leg. The stronger was growing weak.

"Oh, I've been here before. Plenty times. Seen a lotta attempts in plenty different ways," he said matter-of-factly.

Amaru's eyes tightened. She heard the third member of their prisoner party move slightly. After her yelling and the ensuing conversation, they must have been awake.

"Why?" Amaru asked.

"Why not?" the beggar said with a snort. "This is the closest I'll ever get to Inner Sanctum. Much safer and cleaner for a character like myself. More stable, too."

Amaru put her hand down and rested it gently at her side. Something about this man felt perceptive and practical. She tried not to like it.

"Then why not leave Ecclesia altogether?"

The man wheezed again. "Well, maybe you have forgotten or maybe you ain't take the time to really look at me yet, but I'm in no shape to be leaving any time soon."

Amaru reddened and was glad she was faced away from him. But in here, the stakes were low. She figured she might as well air out another embarrassing thought.

"How did you..."

"Get crippled?" He knowingly concluded. It was not Amaru's question, but it was just as interesting.

"Well, I was born with it. My father said that when I was enterin' this world, he grabbed both my feet and saw that- er, wait. That's not true. Maybe it happened when I tried to scale The Wall and landed straight on my left. Stunted it a couple inches just like that. I think? Eh, whatever. Don't make a difference, really."

"One was determined before you were born and the other was an accident," Amaru countered. "Why wouldn't it make a difference?"

"Hmm. They both were, if ya think about it," the beggar replied. "Besides, people don't know one way or another when they see me. They'll treat me the way they do all the same. *That's* why it don't matter."

Amaru sighed. Her finger was throbbing. Swelling already.

"What have you done to change that?"

No response. Amaru let the question be. It was a foolish, impolite thing to say, anyway. Not that she ever cared for social graces, but that was one thing The Manual impressed into her. It wasn't the duty of the afflicted to make others see them, it was the duty of the more fortunate to see. But someone was always more fortunate. Still no response. Had she offended the man so deeply that he shut himself off from her? He - the closest thing to a comrade? The silence grew until the throbbing in her pinky was audible.

A strange, throaty murmur grew in intensity from behind her. The beggar was

are you fucking kidding me

snoring. Amaru whipped her head with abandon, concern for pinky completely evaporated. She was rewarded with that homely, crooked smile.

The beggar pushed out a mixture of wheeze and cough that sounded painful but was apparently out of hilarious joy. Amaru leered at him and turned back around.

"Whoo-hoo, thank you sweetheart. I needed a real laugh; it's been so long. But that's the answer to your question. You trick 'em. You trick 'em into seeing you."

Amaru didn't react for a couple seconds, but then she set free a laugh of her own. It was small and distant, but it led to another wheezer from the old man.

"I have another question for you, then. You said to conserve my energy and my mind..."

Amaru felt a tremble in her voice. She looked at the shine of the blood on the wall.

"...how do I stay sane?"

The beggar deliberated whether or not Amaru meant in here or out there, but he reckoned that one answer fit both locales.

"Well, talkin' helps."

A portly woman got up early for a special reason: she had recently turned her life around. Years in Outer Sanctum, and three children via two fathers later, she finally understood that *she* was the problem. She was used to blaming circumstance, but now that she was taking responsibility, things were really changing. She was especially determined to be a better mother. Today, just as the sun was rising, she woke up her youngest, and the two of them left their tent for a brisk walk-and-talk. Nothing too long or too deep, just a casual, agreeable activity that was apathetically interrupted by violent, unrepentant, steadily intensifying moans of pleasure.

Ambree heard angry woman shouts from outside her tent but she pressed on. She would damn well finish at this point. She embodied a confidence that was new and freeing, just like the experience she was currently having. She still considered herself asexual when it came to her relationships with others - this activity was purely biological. No longer was she concerned with the looks she got or the complaints she heard. No longer was she captive to the beauty standards of others or even herself. She had finally turned her life around. And nothing got her off more than her own bald head.

She had recently made another important self-discovery as well: she was fine with living in Outer Sanctum. The tents were her home, the mansions were not. She had spent so much time trying to fit into that golden Ecclesian standard, but with all of that shape-shifting, she would have to give up too much of her self, her desires, and her personality. In trying to become someone else, living amongst the tents helped her see who she really was. And she was finally content. Especially now that she was *actually* in love.

"I'm leaving," Arah said as he promptly entered the tent.

"Aaaaah!" was Ambree's climactic response. She felt her body convulse and instinctively clench the used maroon robe beside her.

"What?! Where are you going?" Ambree heard excitement in her voice that she was steadily able to curb.

Arah got on his knees and scooped some water to his mouth. The motion generated ripples that distorted the image of Ambree's bald head, much to her annoyance. Arah looked up at his partner, their faces within kissing distance of each other. He knew she was developing into someone new, and though he had only known her for a month or so, he was proud of her for that. He was sorry he would have to miss whatever came next.

"Ambree, you know I can't stay."

Arah stood up and walked over to his rocks. He flipped them over and examined each one. He would need to travel light, so only the most suitable weapon would do.

"Wrong," Ambree responded. "I very well know that you *can*. And it's what we agreed to. We threw away our *senti*, but staying here is fine. It's perfect, actually. We can be happy."

Arah found it. One side was as pointed as could be expected, it was just a little longer than his hand, and there were slightly jagged edges that ran underneath. He hoped to never use it, but he was no fool. There would be a need for it where he was going. He held it in his right, felt the strength that its forceful use would convey. He loosened his grip and let it fall to the floor. With a frown, he replied.

"Right. We *can* be happy. We have been, I have been. Thank you for being a part of my life during this time. I needed you, you know that. But I don't want to - I can't - even live off of *the scraps* of this polluted place. I keep thinking...about that trio. Moshe's the name of the tallest one, right?"

Ambree nodded so that she could bite her tongue.

"I keep thinking about them," Arah continued on as he looked blankly at the rocks. "I never knew them, and I guess you only met Moshe once, but it was clear that they were inseparable. Every time I saw them, there was joy and trust on their faces. What a rarity. But that fight...if Ecclesia's draw is poisonous enough to break even them apart...it just feels wrong to be supplied by her consequences."

Ambree was sad. Her heart was heavy, but she was a veteran in the field of heartbreak. She knew that it was necessary to look past it in order to see the end without bias. And Arah was right. He had to leave. She squeezed his hand, smiled through moistening eyes, and gave him a nod. She directed his hand back towards the jagged rock. Arah's face expressed a similar emotion as he picked up his wilderness companion.

"Are you going to look for him, then?" Ambree consciously asked.

Arah nodded. "As much as I owe you for getting me through his loss and back on my feet, I owe him even more. He gave me direction. It was his insights that gave you that, too. If he's out there, maybe I can pay him back..."

Arah looked down and let a shroud of despair overcome his eyes.

"...and if he's somewhere here..."

Arah's lip wavered. He didn't know what to say. Ambree tilted his head up so that they were face-to-face once more.

"Then I'll let you know when I see him," she finished for him.

Arah let out a laugh that carried some of his misgivings, but not all. He nodded repeatedly.

They kissed goodbye.

"When it was the three of us, I was never worried, even as slaves. Crowds made me...anxious, but they always have. But since..."

Amaru pointed falteringly to her temple.

"...I don't know. Something's wrong."

The beggar sat cross-legged and nodded several times. He rubbed his grizzled chin and let time sit between them. It was his favorite remedy.

"Well, of course something's wrong: your family's broken."

Amaru let that thought in. It was true. She hadn't put it that way in her mind yet, but the imagery revealed another layer of why everything felt so complicated now. But the beggar wasn't done.

"Your family's broken and you're afraid."

Amaru stood up straight. She had pressed herself against their cells' neighboring metal as their conversation progressed. This man had a soothing, paternal way about him. Part of it was her realization that there was no reason to hold information close anymore - there was nothing else to do, anyway. But he also ensured her that it was safe to do so. It might have been his warm brown eyes or the careful yet fluid way he talked. It might have been the silly tufts of white hair that sprung from the back of his head or that perpetual grin that was finally getting to her. But this was a man she knew she could trust. Even if they weren't on a first-name basis yet. Trust or not, she knew his last words were dead wrong.

"Afraid?" Amaru repeated incredulously. "I've never felt that. Of what?"

The beggar's eyes flared with intrigue. "This partner of yours that betrayed you...you've never experienced that level of doubt before."

Amaru let out her trademark scoff. "Doubt and fear aren't the same. Of course I doubt. I doubted Ecclesia from the beginning. It's how I live. How I stay prepared."

"But doubting someone in your circle - doubting a bond that you never thought could be broken - that's something you could have never prepared for."

Amaru slumped back against the metal.

The beggar stretched out his legs as best he could. His good one was falling asleep.

"And now," he said. "Your mind is looking for something to hold on to. That's why you punched the wall even though you really know that there ain't no way it would budge."

Amaru started to pace, but she stopped herself. She saw the blood again, now encrusted into the wall. She kept her back towards the wise man as she decided to turn the tables. She had had enough questioning of her motives for the night.

"Sir, what's your name?"

He had an instantaneous response for that one.

"Doesn't matter anymore. A name is for others to call you by."

another thing that doesn't matter

His answer was accompanied by an elongated, phlegmy cough. Amaru witnessed that she was really getting used to his company since even his coughs were unalarming.

"What should I call you then?" Amaru asked as she locked eyes with him.

"Eh, what everyone else does. The beggar's fine."

They passed smiles to each other and Amaru assented.

THUD!

Arah had heard the gates of pearl close many times before, but never had they sounded so purposeful, so resolute. And never had they closed with him on the outside.

The noonday sun beat down ferociously. Arah felt beads of sweat form and fall within seconds. There was no direction other than the straightforward one: follow the road out until it was no more. Arah clutched his rock tightly and walked.

He assumed that's what the beggar would have done, at least. The safest path was the clear one. If his memory served him right, he would eventually get to trees. He couldn't imagine his mentor making it any farther than that, and the security and shade they would provide made sense as a place to call home for a bit. He made it past the dead palms and ascended the hill. Arah looked back at Ecclesia, convinced it was the last time he would see her. She really did look glorious from the top of the valley. He felt a tear evaporate from his cheek, his heart stricken with a melancholic weight. As poisonous as his old home became for him, there was still something beautiful in its midst. It was truly unlike anything else in the wasteland, and he was grateful for that. He wished everyone there would somehow find peace, and then he continued on his way.

Just before sunset, Arah made it to thickening forest. His feet became immovable burdens, but he didn't want to waste any time. He ought to look for the beggar while there was still light. He climbed the nearest tree, mainly using his arms to propel himself upwards until he got a good view of the area. No sign of any life, but there were plenty of bushes. Perhaps his mentor was hiding amongst them for cover.

The bushes were prickly to the point of being impossible to breach, so Arah cut down a branch with the jagged end of his rock in order to poke into them. He considered just yelling out his name, but he didn't want to alert any wolves that might be nearby. Or worse yet: people.

He found nothing in the bushes. At a couple points, he felt something firmer than leaves but softer than ground, so he repeatedly jabbed them, thinking that if someone was in there, they would have cried out in pain. But he never got any response, and when he looked inside, all he saw was black.

Arah sighed. His hope was waning. He realized that he had honestly expected to find him already. It just felt like that was what was going to happen. Then they would survive on their own together. He hadn't anticipated being truly alone. Even though he often felt alone in Outer Sanctum, he was steadily surrounded by people. His mind would have to adjust if he were to keep a healthy level of stability.

The sun had set. Arah knew he would have to start a fire soon, but he decided to sit down and do something he hadn't done in a few weeks first. He began to meditate. Surprisingly, it was an easy habit for him to drop. Maybe it was because the cognitive dissonance of Ecclesia grew too loud. But now, all there was was quiet. And if he were to ever find his friend, it would be with a clear head. And after fifteen minutes, his clear head told him to start a fire.

Arah cut down enough branches to last him for the night. He didn't want to ignite anything where he was at, though - there were too many bushes and too high a chance for the fire to burst into something wild. So he put his heavy rock down, picked up all the wood, and took it somewhere safer.

When he returned to the bushy area to retrieve his increasingly useful tool...it was not there. Arah put a hand through his hair. It was as long as it had ever been, but it was also stickier than it had ever been. He thought of the days when its gloss was his primary concern. He wrapped it up tight into a bun close to his head, for it was what he did when he felt the threat of danger.

He knelt and analyzed the immediate ground. When he dropped the rock, did it bounce into one of these bushes? He put his hand in to look for one, but it got scratched up. He couldn't afford any open wounds. He would have to come back here and look when the sun returned.

The moon was full. Arah returned to his temporary campsite and was relieved to see all of his compiled wood still there. The plan was to use his rock for ignition, but he would have to make do another way. Minutes later, Arah sat by his fire.

Alert. But exhausted. Arah never let his eyes fall as he continuously scanned the trees and open space that surrounded him, but his body was definitely worn out from the work of the day. He had forgotten how much was corporeally required of him just to survive out here. He felt his stomach *actually* grumble. It shocked him. He had trained his body to rely on less and less sustenance as time went on, but now he wondered how long it would be before he *needed* to find something to eat. Would he have to go out beyond the woods in order to find some sheep? Would that be giving up on his search? There was no way the beggar was out in the full desert. But it had been ages since Arah had had sheep. It sounded really good just to be able to peacefully feast on some actual meat...and then wrap himself in their soft wool...as he let the evenings fade and let himself drift...off...to...

When Arah awoke, there was barely an ember before him. The moon was still full. Wind was blowing. He sat up quickly and expectantly. But there was no one and nothing around. It was completely dark. Except...

There was light just a few hundred feet away. He couldn't tell from the distance, but the way it flickered suggested a fire. He couldn't confirm that, though, because whatever the light emitted from was blocked by a person clad in complete white.

Arah scurried over to hide behind a tree, out of sight. He peeked around the other side. He still couldn't make out enough detail, so he risked a nimble rush to a closer tree.

The person was kneeling by a fire. Their back was toward him. Arah wondered if they even knew of his nearby presence, but he couldn't risk it. He crouched and started sneaking the other way.

That's when he heard the wolf howl.

He pressed himself against the ground. Somehow, the howl had come from the side of the forest that was closer to Ecclesia. He turned his head to look back at the person with the fire. They were standing up and looking out. They were concerned, too. After a tense half-minute, the person returned to their seat, though clearly more agitated now. Arah thought he could hear them grumble something to themselves.

Arah considered the possibilities. Going away from the person meant going towards the wolf. He could try to hide beside a bush for the night, but that offered little security. The wind had picked up so that it nearly mimicked the howl of the wolf. Arah's body shivered. Maybe he could get close enough to the fire to warm up a little? He had been assuming the worst, but maybe this person was friendly? And if they were foe, maybe it would be better for Arah to get the jump on them first? And who knew how many other wolves were out there? Arah stealthily made his way towards the fire.

With how perilous his situation was, Arah tried to shake a fearful thought from his mind, but he just couldn't. As time went on, he felt how low the beggar's chances of survival were. His heart despaired. He began to hope that his mentor was somewhere in Ecclesia all along. Though he did not know what that could mean.

Arah now stood thirty feet behind the person in white and their fire. He heard their low, gravelly voice more clearly:

"...last time I ever use a sheepskin for that...Koja shouldn't have crossed me...now look at this mess...clean it up, clean it up..."

Words came in between inexplicable throat noises.

fuck this

Arah took a step back.

He felt something fall over his head, and before he could look at it, he was suspended in the air.

His hands went to his throat, where rope constricted him captive. The small person in white slowly stood up and turned to face him. They were sane and somber. Arah looked up and saw the rope wrapped around an overhanging branch, firmly secured and prepared to take life. Outside of the flickering flames and Arah's gurgling, it was utterly quiet. Even the wind died. Arah tried to pull at the rope but it was hopeless. He let his legs flail so he could at least turn himself around and see where the rope ended.

Figures of darkness stood before him, hooded and clad in complete black. Solemn as their white counterpart.

"Engh...gurg...ungh..."

Arah's choking throat couldn't emit any words of desperation. Words that he hoped would convince them to spare him. To change their minds. To let him live.

Soon, darkness was all that he saw.

And that darkness, pairing perfectly with the balm and heat of the fire, reminded him of one thing as he faded into void.

KAMNOS

Amaru woke up to the jump of a throbbing
must have slept on it again
headache. She had always been one to sleep on her stomach, but she
knew she couldn't afford the luxury anymore. Not until her temple was
fully healed.

The real ache of it was that it had only been a couple hours. She
could tell by the royal blue coming from the vent. It was fairly bright,
but she deduced that that was due to a full moon. She felt no rest in her
bones, only an agitated emptiness.

The beggar was sleeping soundly: flat on his back, his limbs sprawled
out as much as was diametrically possible. Amaru
wish i could be that comfortable here
smiled. But then she felt another pulsation. She was growing antsy
in her confinement, so she started pacing. As necessary as their conversation was, she didn't feel the need to leave any less urgently. Should she
do her best to fall asleep so that when someone came by in another four
hours, she would be refreshed enough to strike? That ran the risk of her
being woken up by them and feeling groggy, or even missing her chance
altogether. But if she stayed awake and the throbbing continued, she
might be too exhausted to-

The beggar started coughing in his sleep. It distracted Amaru from
her thoughts, but she tried to make nothing of it. But before she could
resume her plotting, she noticed something. The coughing wasn't stopping. Maybe that was normal for a wheezy old man, but it sounded
strange. It wasn't scratchy, it was husky. It had substance. Like he was
choking
Amaru ran to the metal bars that stood between them. His body had
instinctively curled up, but he was still asleep. His head shook violently
as the choking deepened, bits of spittle and other debris making their
escape from the sides of his mouth. Amaru shook on the bars before realizing the futility of her actions.

"Hey!" she screamed out. "We need help! The beggar...is..."

She feared the worst. Whether or not anyone was coming, she had to take action. Nothing could be done about the bars, but maybe the beggar was wrong about the brick. Amaru scurried over to the part of the wall that separated their cells and followed through with her initial plan.

PUNCH!

PUNCH!

PUNCH!

CRACK!

PUNCH!

PUNCH!

CRACK!

Punch.

Punch.

punch.

"What did I tell you?" came a weakened, wheezy voice.

In the furor of her fists and grunts, Amaru hadn't noticed that the beggar sat himself upright. The choking had ceased. Bile and water were strewn about him, but his breathing had returned to what was normal for him.

"What the fuck was that?!" Amaru concernedly yelled at him.

The wheezy laughs were back. "I don't know. Another first for the night. But I'd say you're worse for wear more than I am."

Amaru saw that most of her fingers were mangled, cut up in bloody remnants. Adrenaline carried her beyond pain for now. But it would really fucking hurt soon enough. Whatever, she would not let the attention be turned to her right now.

"Are you not even a little concerned, you crazy old man?"

The beggar grinned. "Patience. All things happen when they mean to. The sooner you get comfortable with that, the less your hands will bleed."

Amaru did her best to show off her middle finger, but all she could offer was a half-cocked gesture. Another slice of wisdom from the sage. But she wasn't in the mood to learn.

"All things?" Amaru retorted. "No. For some, maybe. But you're willing to say that even the injustices of Ecclesia are *meant* to happen?"

"The universe will work itself out *in time*. It always does." The beggar's response was sturdier than usual. His tone suggested Amaru had hit a sacred nerve.

"Ah yes, even for those who suffer? Or...die?" Amaru said.

The beggar wiped some of his bodily grime off his robe. "Death is always thought of as something made out of venom, when really, it's the antidote. Trust me, miss, evil won't last past its due."

Amaru looked down at her busted fingers. She didn't buy it, and he probably knew that, but it was nice to hear someone put a label on what she was feeling. *Evil*. And to be optimistic about its end...it wasn't much, but it lightened her spirit.

Suddenly, another strange sound entered the room. Amaru and the beggar looked at each other in confusion. It was low yet coarse, the sound of suppression. It maintained a rhythm that slowly sped up and slowly got louder. The heaving of weeping. Amaru pinpointed its location: their third neighbor. Neither of them had given this being any thought since they began speaking. But he let his limbs unfold as he rolled over to face them. Amaru couldn't believe her eyes.

Moshe was against the metal bars that imprisoned him, cross-legged and red-eyed.

Chapter 12: The Business

23, 8 DBK

Ambree lay on her side in her empty tent. She had done so for nearly two weeks, only venturing outside for sustenance. Even then, she would stockpile enough *casu* to keep her home as long as possible. It still amazed her how easily perverse men would give up their rations for a fleeting glance at her exposed breasts. Some even made weekly dropoffs at her tent in exchange for groping. She had yet to let any of them sleep with her, though; the *casu* provided her more than enough self-loathing.

The ease of returning to old habits was frightening to Ambree. It was a lifestyle that was still within her. It was comfortable, and maybe finding something comfortable again was necessary for coping. She had no desire to go out and meet people. Self-discovery and inner freedom were overrated when people kept staring at your damned head for the entirety of a conversation. Some even avoided her altogether because of her baldness. She had no desire to read any of the writings that the beggar gave to Arah which he then left with her. There was a time when his thoughts were liberating, bonding devices for her and her love. But now, she simply had no desire for anything.

She tried to figure out where things went wrong. Yes, leaving was right for Arah, but it was clearly not right for her. Too many bad memories lived outside the walls, worse than the ones she made inside. Why did he have to leave? She understood why, but what about her? How were her needs being taken care of now? Ambree felt a low rumble rise in her stomach. She rolled over and lethargically extended a hand towards the small mountain of *casu* that sat sludgingly beside her. She shoveled it into her mouth. Why would anyone value her needs when she didn't do so herself?

Like a twitching in her eye, an image flashed by unexpectedly. The day before Arah left, they talked about establishing some kind of discussion group. The beggar had often told him that community was important. *As screwed up as everyone is, well,* everyone *is.* It became a favorite adage of theirs to repeat, but Ambree was inspired to take it further. Their tent would be available to whoever wanted to have a more open dialogue about The Manual, Ecclesia, and life in general. The goal wouldn't be to convert anyone to their line of thinking, but to allow people a reprieve from the pressure of Outer Sanctum life. Perhaps they would, in the process, find others who *did* feel similarly. It was an exciting prospect because it was both dangerous and good. Arah shot it down once he realized how treacherous it would be to invite people into that kind of space. He told Ambree that their relationship was more important to him than the peace of strangers. They both let the idea go, but it was a cause that she still held hope for. It was the type of fire that she could use right then.

"ECCLESIA IS A BUSINESS, NOT A PARADISE. ECCLESIA IS A BUSINESS, NOT A PARADISE. ECCLESIA IS A BUSINESS, NOT A PARADISE..."

The oddly shrill boom of the amplified voice startled the *casu* right out of Ambree's hand. It slopped onto her face and into her nose.

"Gurgh," Ambree coughed out as she wiped away the junk, disgusted.

"ECCLESIA IS A BUSINESS, NOT A PARADISE. ECCLESIA IS A BUSINESS, NOT A PARADISE. ECCLESIA IS A BUSINESS, NOT A PARADISE..."

The voice raged on, becoming more passionate with each chant. It became accompanied by a mixture of angry, confused voices and clamoring footsteps. The day had just dawned, this was not exactly how people appreciated waking with it. But Ambree could tell there was curiosity in some of those voices. Including hers.

After cleaning herself up a bit, she stepped out of the tent and headed east with everyone else.

Reenu sat in hiding. The ash of years' past threatened to invade his lungs and provoke a cough, though he doubted that anyone would hear him over

"ECCLESIA IS A BUSINESS, NOT A PARADISE. ECCLESIA IS A BUSINESS, NOT A PARADISE. ECCLESIA IS A BUSINESS, NOT A PARADISE..."

anyway. The muscles in his shoulders were beginning to cramp, but the nearing footsteps and voices told him he would not have to stay still for long. A few more minutes and he would be running for his life. He allowed himself to think back on two nights prior in order to get his mind off of the various aches in his body. When Abigail stopped, he would re-focus on the present.

"What's next? Why do I always have to have the fucking plan?"

Reenu instinctively winced at Abigail's bitter reaction. If he wasn't in the thick of it himself, he would have recognized the actual pain and loss in her voice. This wasn't the rugged revolutionary of five minutes ago - seeing the remains of her implicitly drafted soldiers and freeing the ones who still stood had changed that to some degree. But Reenu was in quite a depth as well.

"Are you kidding me?" Reenu's voice was subdued with the question, but it possessed the kind of muted tone that carries an unnerving menace under-

neath. It caused Abigail to look up at him, which was fortunate for her because it gave her enough time to dodge his downward swing.

"You brought all of that destruction onto us. All of it. Did you not consider that you might fail?"

"What was I to do? Let them take us all *away*? Might as well take out a few of the Leader cocksuckers while we had the chance."

"Maybe there wasn't much you could have done," Reenu conceded. "But there's got to be something we can still do, right? You're not going to just give up."

Abigail slumped her head back down, apathy returning in full force.

"I won't fucking let you."

Abigail's head shot back up.

"Look at you, kid," a wry smile growing across her face. "Might make a mean rebel after all."

Reenu shook his head. "Not like you. Just...not ready to let Amaru..."

Abigail nodded sympathetically. "We can work with that. Alright, so, I fucked it up, it seems. But you're right - there's got to be something we can still do. So how do we figure that out? My usual plan of attack is to think a step ahead of the enemy. Let's start with looking at their last step."

Reenu digested Abigail's suggestion. "Why would they only take half of us? What good does leaving some do?"

"Bait. They want to lure the rest of us in, thinking that we'll stage an attack on Inner Sanctum in order to get them back. But the fact is they're probably..."

Abigail bit her tongue, and Reenu took note. It wasn't like her to use tact.

"We can't do that on our own," she said. "It won't save them; it'll just imprison us as well."

"If we can't storm Inner Sanctum...what can we do here in Outer?"

Abigail pointed to her head approvingly.

"You're catching on quick. Recommence!"

As battered as the ten men that still stood were, they hastily got back to their original seats, ready to receive whatever information was coming their way.

"We've been patient," Abigail started. "We've allowed the hopefuls to live in their status quo. We've recruited the ones who will listen, but it doesn't seem *like most of them will. And since our plans for Inner Sanctum will no longer do..."*

Abigail pointed above her to the south.

"...I think it's time we take the fight to the streets. PLT."

The men raised their spears in approval. Reenu still had his improvised rope-and-baton, but he left it at his side.

"Pali, you said you've seen Duman teaching someone at Ecclesian Essentials recently, correct?" Abigail asked.

"Fight? Those hopefuls are innocent," Reenu purposefully interrupted. "I don't see how violence against them will do any good."

The men lowered their spears so they were merely half-raised. Abigail looked annoyingly at Reenu, but she was prepared to clarify.

"No, we won't be violent towards them. But we will be...burning bridges and turning over tables, so to speak."

"The sun's barely out!"

"What's the meaning of this?"

"Don't make me into a bad neighbor!"

The megaphone's resonance was now completely replaced by complaints. Reenu shifted his legs into a more readied position.

The time for turning was nearly upon them.

Abigail cursed her luck as she estimated that less than half of Outer Sanctum's residents had gathered in front of her. It would have to do.

She put the megaphone down...

And just stood there.

The morning mob's cries began to settle into confused murmurs. A young, freckled brunette spoke out:

"Anything you want to say to us besides...well, you know..."

Abigail stood still.

Another voice yelled:

"Hey! Aren't you the bitch who ruined The Last Call?"

Everyone around him shushed and booed his vulgar mouth, though Abigail could see that his insight was changing faces. Still, she made no movement. A middle-aged man near the front decided that he had been out in the boorish sun long enough.

"Let's go back home, everyone. Just a lousy waste of time..."

Abigail saw two Kohen making their way through the departing crowd. From what she staked out a half hour ago, they were two out of the five that she wanted to be there. The other three must have kept their post at The Wall. She could work with that. She picked the megaphone back up.

"You there! Brunette with...apparently with a twin. You asked if there's anything I want to say to you. *Of course fucking not.*"

A handful of people gasped, but most of the hopefuls had heard and, though it would take some prodding for them to admit it, used a taboo word or two in their time. The Kohen, however, sped their gait.

"I have no words for any of you," Abigail continued. She started to pace back and forth as she went. "You have failed to see how the Ecclesian system has failed you, but you press your noses in your Manuals and keep trying anyway. Idiots and fools! There's a difference between stubbornness and blindness, and none of you seem to know it..."

The Kohen began pushing their way past people.

"Not even your own bloodshed would convince you. Lucky for you, *we're* not interested in that."

The crowd started rambling amongst themselves, some even looking at each other with suspicious eyes. It stalled the Kohen long enough for Abigail's closing statement.

"It's so easy to draw a crowd," Abigail said, nearly laughing as she did so. "Disappointing, but obvious. No, if violence won't do, the only thing that could is to hit you where it hurts: your poor little tummies."

The Kohen now stood before Abigail, batons drawn, just in time for them to see Reenu and five others fly out of the Torched Tents beside her, weapons in hand. They raced northwest, dedicated to their destination. The Kohen's heads were turned long enough for one of them to be pulverized by Abigail's ball-and-chain. Abigail wrapped the chain around the other's neck and kicked him onto his knees. With a crowd of seven hundred before her, Abigail yanked the chain until she heard a satisfying crack, and released.

The crowd broke off into a fearful frenzy, everyone clawing their way back to safety, back to what they knew. Abigail, blood pumping with adrenaline, picked the megaphone back up.

"ECCLESIA IS A BUSINESS, NOT A PARADISE.
AND YOU ARE THE PRODUCT."

Three Kohen stood at The Wall. For two of them, it was their regular shift. It was a banal duty, but an important one. Most days, hopefuls kept to their regimen - it was really only on Last Judgments that some became rowdy enough to require Kohen services. But today was differ-ent. That's why the third of them was there. He looked to the east and nodded.

"Here they come. Once they pass us, head to EE with the dampening cloths."

Reenu ran fast and light; there was no need to be concerned about *scraping*, he only felt adrenaline and the rush of displaced air pressing past him. It reminded him of a past life - the company was different, but that in itself was somehow exciting. He had never done anything without Amaru or Moshe by his side. And the five men that presently ran behind him, well, he trusted them as much as anyone. There was no relationship, but a common drive: to introduce The Troei Café to chaos.

"Hey!" shouted one of the Kohen as they raced by The Wall.

Reenu was innately composed of obedience, so his head turned to face the interjection. He thought he recognized one of the Kohen, but it caused him to slip on a drop in the road. His five acquaintances pressed on towards their goal. Reenu dipped deeper into his adrenaline in order to catch up.

"And now you are fully knowledgeable, fully energized, and fully prepared to be the new First Attendant at Ecclesian Essentials! Congratulations!"

Duman hugged his protégé tight and jumped up and down ferociously.

"Oh, my goodness," muffled the smothered protégé, who was more interested in breathing than celebrating in that moment. "Thank you, again, Duman. For all of your instruction. It really is an honor to take over for you."

Duman released the young adult and smiled cheekily at him. He saw a tract that was tilting out of place and frowned.

"I see you actually missed one, Cleo," he blandly intoned as he put the tract back in its place.

Cleo gulped. "I-I'm so sorry, Duman. I don't know how I missed-"

"Not to worry, not to worry," Duman assured him, back to his cheery state. "You still pass the inspection, of course. Not everything is going to be perfect when you start off. But we must always aim for that golden standard, my boy! *Nevertheless, I'll do my best-*"

"*That's all we can do, yes? Yes!*" Cleo finished with Duman in unison.

"Perfect!" Duman replied. He headed for the door.

"Oh, Duman?" Cleo said.

Duman stopped.

"This transition has been so fast, I've wondered, but I haven't asked. What is this new position you're taking on?"

For once, Duman wanted to make this quick. He stood where he was and didn't turn back.

"Why do you wonder, Cleo?"

Cleo was thrown off-guard by the fiery tedium in Duman's voice.

"Oh, I just was curious. And I'm sure it's time-consuming, but I was hoping you would still be able to help me if I needed it. Just for the first few weeks..."

Duman breathed in and out.

"You know everything I know. Anything else can only be learned on the job. Okay?"

Cleo gulped again. "Sure, yeah, that's fine. Thanks again..."

Duman opened the door and then turned around. He couldn't let this final interaction end negatively. He smiled.

"And to answer your fair inquiry...there actually *is* no new position. Not yet."

The others had already gotten to trashing The Troei by the time Reenu arrived. Benches were tossed here and there. One of them had strewn the contents of the trash receptacle all across the grounds. But Reenu saw that they had yet to adulterate the serving area, so he decided to make himself valuable.

Reenu grabbed stacks of trays and threw them over his shoulder. He slathered a couple in *casu* and the other menu item (he realized then that no one ever asked for...whatever it was), and flung them about. Glass once separated the servers and those unfortunate enough to get served, but no longer. Reenu smashed it with repeated swings of his rope and baton and hopped inside.

It was then that Reenu noticed a server was still on-duty. The one he was all too familiar with. Her eyes were finally animated.

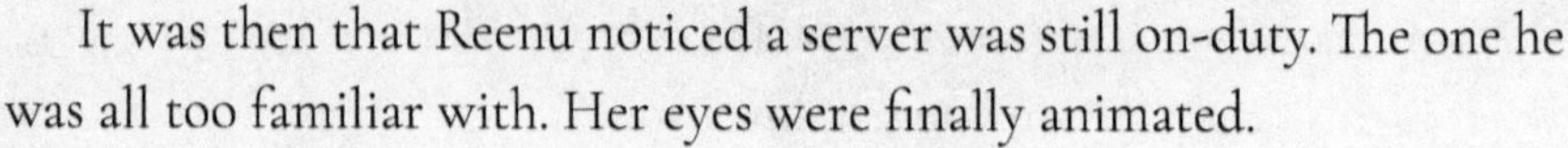

It had only been a half hour, but Cleo mentally patted himself on the back for not messing anything up as of yet. That didn't stop him for sweating like a merino at noontime, though.

He had heard a ruckus coming from the northeast. Some kind of yelling or chant that was drawing quite an exodus of people. But no matter what, it wouldn't draw him from his post. He couldn't let Du-man down.

"help! i need help!"

Cleo gulped.

Where were those cries coming from? Cleo squinted and scanned the landscape.

"help...please..."

There! Just across the way, he saw a small hand extended in the air. It must have been a youth, but the rest of him was hidden behind a slight drop in the road.

No matter what, Cleo would not leave his post.

"please...can anyone help me?...i'm hurt..."

Cleo looked back and forth. Well, the shop would still be in sight. And it would be obvious if someone came to the gates...

The pleas were replaced with literal cries.

"Um...don't worry! I'm coming!"

The server shielded her face from Reenu and started whimpering.

"Please, sir, please don't hurt me!"

Reenu recovered from the surprise of seeing her and dropped his rope baton.

how threatening I must look

"Oh, no, I-I don't intend to. I didn't realize anyone-"

"Please, sir," the stout woman said. She had backed herself into a corner and slumped down. "I've served you almost every day, what have I done to earn this punishment?!"

Reenu held his hands up. "No, no, nothing, of course not. This isn't about you."

He took a step towards her. The woman burst into sobs. He took a step back. She couldn't listen to him as she was. Reenu considered heading back outside and finishing the job

but I've got to make this right

He squatted down to her level.

"You're right," he said in a soothing voice. "You *have* served me almost every day. And...I still don't know your name. What is it?"

The woman lifted her head from her hands and rubbed her eyes. "Leilah."

"Leilah," Reenu continued. "I appreciate all you've done for me and this community. It's worthwhile work, really. Remember all those weeks ago when you said it wasn't your place to change how things are done?"

Leilah thought for a moment and then slowly nodded.

"That's...completely fine," Reenu admitted. "But I think it's *my* place to do so. That's all this is. No harm will come your way. But I do suggest you go back to your tent. Things are...riotous right now."

"Hey! Kid with the scars!"

Reenu turned and looked towards the shattered glass. A woman who was as bald as she was beautiful leaned with her arms against the serving area.

"If you're with them, I'd like to join."

Cleo skittered over to the source of the cries. It was a youth after all, though the development of his muscles and faint facial hair showed that he was on the verge of becoming a man. He was doubled over and rocking back and forth in clear pain.

"Son, what's wrong?" Cleo asked him.

"Engh, it's my ankle," the young man said. "I fell and twisted it. I don't think I can walk back to my tent."

Cleo cleared his throat. "Uh, well, I might be able to help you. But how far is your tent?"

"It's ten rows up and three over. Can you walk me there?"

Cleo frowned. He pointed behind him. "I'm sorry. I'm actually on-duty at EE. I can't leave, but–"

"Please, sir! Almost everyone else is gone, it seems."

Cleo tried to look around, but the young man pulled him down to his face.

"Please! It hurts so much…"

Cleo started sweating. He felt hot.

"Ok, well…maybe I can ask someone in one of these nearby tents if they can walk you. I'll just tell them…"

Cleo paused. He realized he didn't know something yet. How rude of him.

"Forgive my manners, my name is Cleo. Son, what's yours?"

"Epi."

That brief interaction was all it took for Pali, Via, and Krati to introduce the tracts and goods inside of Ecclesian Essentials to torches. They then fled to the safety of their tents and parents. Cleo felt the heat and smelled the fire before he heard its flicker. He turned around and sank into utter misery. Ecclesian Essentials was already half-engulfed in flames.

"Duman, forgive me," Cleo said in a low, defeated whisper. "Epi, we've got to get out of here."

But Epi was gone, too.

In addition to her ball-and-chain, Abigail kept the megaphone with her as she sprinted towards The Wall, though she almost wanted to abandon it. She had insisted that the plan was to give the hopefuls a final chance, but she didn't think that portion of it actually mattered. They were all a bunch of wannabe goody two-shoes sheep.

Abigail saw smoke coming from the south. The little ones did their job. Good. If she had it her way, they would have joined in on what was coming next, but someone mentioned that they were only kids. Reenu sided with them, and she didn't have enough of a wolf in the fight to push for it. As it was, they would manage just fine.

Abigail was fifty feet from The Wall, where a lone Kohen stood before it like a shepherd thinking he could defend his entire flock. That much she was prepared (and excited) for. What Abigail didn't anticipate, however, was the identity of that lone Kohen.

Slowing herself to a moderate gait, Abigail ignored the evoking itch to feel the back of her scalp. The last time she saw those fierce eyes was when they stared her down with murderous intent.

"I've learned that your name is Abigail," the Kohen said. "Mine's Jaben."

Abigail took constant, exact steps towards Jaben. "Who'd you hear that from? My friends in your prison?"

Jaben held his arms with the undersides outstretched. A gesture of peace, he hoped.

"I am a changed man..."

Abigail scoffed and spit.

"When I pulled you down, I hated you," Jaben said. "It was silly and childish of me. Now there are no longer any hard feelings within me, and I hope you can say the same. But I will defend these gates and these people with my life if I must."

Abigail didn't really care about this man. The hair-pulling was annoying and painful, but truth be told, he helped give them the cover they needed. But it was the audacity of his supposed transformation that doubled her resolve. She knew he was the same man who once hated her. Still hated her. She dropped her megaphone so she could hold her weapon with two hands. She gripped it tight and snarled.

"Then you will lose it."

"Hey, Prax, this is Ambree. She wants to help out."

Reenu stood with his five acquaintances and the woman he just met. The Troei was a certified catastrophe of *casu* and equivalent garbage, and they were about to evaluate a job well done when Ambree showed up. Prax, surprised by her presence, looked her up and down and shook his head.

"It's fine, miss, we'll manage on our own," he said as he turned to leave. The others started to take off, but Reenu wasn't ready.

"Wait, guys, hold on. Am I missing something? Ambree wants to join us. Isn't that what we want?"

Four of them froze in place and looked at Prax. He motioned for them to continue on without him. He took Reenu aside.

"Reenu, in case you weren't aware, we are in the middle of something-"

"Something where the point is to help others see the light."

"No, the point is to tear down Outer Sanctum's structures-"

"So that others get on our side. Apparently, it's working."

"Regardless, Abigail wouldn't want another variable to be thrown into the mix. We don't even know this person. They need to be properly screened before-"

"Were *you* screened, Prax? Was *I*?"

"Not in the strict sense, but relationships must build before trust happens. Especially in an operation of..."

Ambree waited as long as she could, but she was done having her life be directed by the whims of men. She would join the cause whether they liked it or not. She ran where the other five ran: The Wall.

Abigail blocked a flurry of swings from Jaben's baton and kicked him back a few steps.

"Military training do you well? Ready to kill?" she mocked in between a couple hooks that he successfully dodged.

"The desert taught me offense," Jaben said. "Under Lieutenant Zacchaeus, we only learn defense."

"Sheepshit," Abigail spat out.

In all fairness, it *was* one of the more arduous battles of Abigail's life. After the hooks, Jaben uppercutted his baton into her chest and pushed her away. Slightly dazed, she came back with an overhead swing of the ball-and-chain that he sidestepped. Each swing of hers he had been able to block. She was doing the same, but she realized his attacks were much more...cautionary. It alarmed her that he could have done real damage if he wanted to. His plan was to tire her out. The only time she was able to land anything was when she thrusted her weapon at his shoulder. He was able to maneuver out of its path, but her forward momentum accidentally forced her elbow into his chin and he fell backwards before quickly recovering. That's when she knew how she would win.

Abigail backed up a few steps, almost bumping into The Wall behind her. Jaben did the same, readying himself. With a demanding cry, Abigail charged at Jaben with another overhead swing, but just as she lifted her ball-and-chain and Jaben raised his baton in defense, Abigail kicked him between his legs. Jaben doubled over from the shock, and Abigail grabbed dirt from beneath him and flung it in his eyes.

"Aargh..."

THWACK!

Swinging a baton around aimlessly is poor protection when blinded. Abigail took the opportunity to level Jaben's head with a strong swing of her executor. He collapsed to the floor facefirst.

But it wasn't over. Not for Abigail. She brought her weapon down on his back four more times in quick succession, to varying levels of crunching gratification. She landed on his back, felt blood splatter onto her knees, and pulled his head up. With both arms around his neck, she felt whatever life was left in him start to slowly ebb away-

"Abigail! Let him go!"

Abigail looked up. In front of her was Reenu, a woman she had never seen before, and the rest of her crew right behind them. Further back was an ever-growing, nosy crowd at a distance that was safe enough and still properly tantalizing.

"We don't need to go all the way. The point has been made," Reenu insisted, eyes wide.

Abigail became aware of how hard she was panting. Whatever. If he wasn't dead already, he'd surely be incapacitated for life. That was good enough. She shoved his head down and stood up.

"The gates?" Reenu asked.

Abigail looked to the left. The Wall was operated by looped chains on each door that could be pulled from either side of it. It required two people at once in order to be opened. Abigail and Reenu made their way while everyone else watched in anticipation.

Before she got to her side, Abigail picked up her megaphone. She uttered out a final speech as she pulled on her chain.

"YOU PEOPLE...ungh...ARE GETTING ANOTHER CHANCE. ONE THAT YOU DON'T DESERVE. IF YOU THINK...agh...THAT I'M ON YOUR SIDE, YOU'RE WRONG. I'VE MERELY GOT BUSINESS...mmf...TO ATTEND TO HERE. BUT NOW THAT THE WAY

IS OPEN, COME AND SEE HOW GLAMOROUS THIS LIFE YOU PINE FOR REALLY IS."

They pulled until the chains locked in place. The bulk of the doors prevented them from seeing beyond from their vantage point, but the way was open. Abigail looked across at Reenu...and smiled. They had actually done it. They were going to save their friends and plunge Ecclesia into anarchy. And it was all thanks to her.

Reenu smiled as well, but that changed once he looked back and saw fear on Ambree's face. Prax and the others had placed their spears on the ground. Everyone else stared at what was beyond The Wall. Reenu and Abigail whipped around the gates and beheld fifty Kohen led by Lieutenant Zacchaeus. They turned around in hopes for a way out, but they saw that the rest of their crew now had batons pointed at them. Prax had Ambree on her knees and rested his baton across her shoulder. Reenu looked at Abigail once more. Perhaps she had another layer to her plan, another answer to this confounding question. But all he saw in her was something he had never seen in her before: complete defeat.

we thought one step ahead, but they, two

Fading in from void, but only slightly so. Wherever Arah was, it was not much brighter than unconsciousness. Either that or he was going blind.

Arah felt with his body that he was lying prone against a wall, arms held up above him. He tried to sit himself up and brought his hands down to his neck and recoiled immediately. Bruised and swollen. His hands clinked in the midst of that motion. Heavy chains. They clinked loudly.

"hey-"

Arah heard from somewhere he did not know. The voice sounded friendly, but desperate. Arah made no response. He would not be tricked again.

"hey, are you awake now? how are you feeling? i saw the bruise ring around your neck when they brought you in...they did...they did the same to me..."

The voice whimpered as it whispered. Sniveled, even.

Arah heard sincerity in its tone, but how easy was it to fake concern? He still couldn't deny that his heartstrings were being pulled, much like how it felt as if the skin of his wrists was being pulled out of place. He adjusted his seat to ease the strain, but the tiniest of clinks was the result. Arah heard much louder clinking follow, though he still could not pinpoint its location. Wherever they were, the walls echoed.

"good, you can hear me!"

The voice was much more excited now.

"listen to me, please. my name is Bukshee. i was a Kohen-in-training but I...I just fucked it up. i don't know why *you* left the city, but that's why I did. why the fuck am I telling you this? right, I need to be honest with you if I expect you to trust me, which I *need* because...shit, how long has it been? must be over a month. but I don't think I have much time left, and it would have been even less if you hadn't shown up when you did. but we've got to get out. we've got to figure it out together. they only come down every...shit, how do I know? there's no sun, no moon, no food, only this horrible, horrible darkness!"

Bukshee devolved into incoherent crying. Arah was beginning to tell which direction he was in, but he sounded far away. The room must have been as large as it was irredeemable. And judging by his unseen companion's fragile mental state, he was probably right. They had to get out.

"hey, Bukshee," Arah whispered back. "where exactly are we?"

The voice that answered had to be Bukshee's, yet it was now gravelly and deep. It was just as quiet as his whisper, yet it now permeated the whole room with dread.

"You know where we are."

Arah heard muddled scuffing from above. Footsteps. Then there was jangling that led to the heavy, screeching opening of a door. The footsteps were descending.

Wherever Bukshee was at, Arah no longer knew. The terrified being went completely silent. All was completely silent. Except the footsteps.

The deceptively warm glow of torchlight made the first appearance. Then the man behind it. A blackhooded figure shone his torch over a body. Arah presumed the body to be Bukshee's, though it was as still as death. Blackhood stood there for a moment until he was satisfied. He bent over and whispered something into Bukshee's ear. Then he walked directly to Arah.

Arah contemplated Bukshee's behavior. Should he have played dead as well? It might have been safer. But he wanted to be able to see his surroundings, and the presence of torchlight may have presented him the only opportunity to do so. And he wanted answers.

Blackhood kept the torch high and close to him, so Arah wasn't able to see much. He first noticed something circular on the otherwise barren ceiling, some kind of grate. It surprised him that there weren't any gates or dividing walls. If this was a prison, where were the cells? He also estimated the room to only be about fifty feet wide and long, suspiciously small. It was the nature of the walls that must have disoriented the sound - they were made of the same reflective pearls as Outer Sanctum's gates, though much grimier and unconsidered than even *casu*. He had yet to see what was ground-level.

Still silent, Blackhood knelt before Arah. He wore black mesh that confounded his face and its features. He wanted to be covert. Given the circumstances, Arah was surprised that he himself wasn't completely terrified. All he felt was an insatiable, foolish desire to belittle his oppressor.

"Don't need the rest of your friends to take down one man now that he's in chains?"

Blackhood tilted his head to the side, pondering. Then he caught on.

"We do not know one from the other. Safety in unknown numbers." His voice sounded like monotonous metal.

Arah found that strange. "What do you mean? You don't know who you're working with? How can you trust them?"

"We all serve Leader...even if he doesn't know it. We are Kohen, individually hand-picked by another to fulfill this unpleasant duty. We understand its gravity."

"Why are you even telling me this?" Arah found his captor's confidence annoying.

"Because you will never leave *KAMNOS*."

Arah couldn't hide the shudder that his body required of him. Blackhood had no reaction.

"No point in denying it when there's no reason to keep up appearances, is that it?"

Blackhood had no reaction. Arah stared at where his eyes would be for an indeterminate amount of time.

"You have eaten your last meal. You have seen the sun for the last time. You have seen the moon for the last time. You will die here with time. Please forgive us. It must be this way."

Blackhood stood up and walked towards the center of the room.

"Forgive you? What the fuck?" Arah was incredulous. "Why would I-no, why would *you* do this to people? Remind me again where in The Manual it says that-"

"Why did you leave?!"

Arah held his tongue. Not only was he struck by the question, but it was the first shred of emotion that he heard in Blackhood's voice. It was hoarse and thick. It struggled to find its way in.

"No one leaves Ecclesia for the wasteland. Unless there is a problem. We can't let anyone believe that. Because then they will stop believing in hope. And they will die out there. So you must die in here as an unsung hero, a sacrifice for that hope. Have no fear, we shall not burn you. The rumors are not true: Ecclesia does not run on that kind of fuel. I've already told you its currency. But the rumor does its part to keep that currency alive. So we keep it alive. Peace be eternally with you."

Blackhood brought his torch to the floor. It lit something. The spark spread until it covered some of the surface and burst into flame, lighting up the room. Arah was momentarily blinded by its brightness, but when his eyes adjusted, he saw that the burning material was a person. Long since dead. The smoke that left the body didn't stay; rather, it escaped with its gauzy scent out through the grate in the ceiling to be harvested and released at random throughout Outer Sanctum. Arah's eyes adjusted further, though he wished they hadn't, because they revealed to him exactly how the Kohen were able to keep the rumor of *KAMNOS* alive.

There were at least a dozen bodies there with him, all in varying states of decay, all emaciated from starvation, and all fulfilling their potential as sacrifices for hope.

Chapter 13: Zacchaeus

72, 71, 70, 7, 6, 0 DBK

Reenu slid down the burning decline, unable and unwilling to stop himself. Sand invaded previously unsoiled parts of his body, but he hadn't the strength to prevent its raid. He rolled forward until he finally collapsed headfirst at the bottom of the desert valley.

"Reenu!" Amaru yelled before she went after him. She tried taking large hops while still maintaining her balance, but the unforgivingly cumulous sand toppled her over as well. She too hadn't the stamina to fight back.

"Goddamnit," Moshe said to himself from the crest above. His friends were being foolishly unsafe, but he knew it was only out of exhaustion. They were usually much more cautious. Still, there was something inviting about falling down the way that they did. To just allow his body a moment without resistance, a moment where it would be carried without any inflicted direction. But they also could have broken their necks, considering how fragile they had all become. He would have to be more deliberate in his steps.

When Moshe reconvened with his friend-lovers, Amaru had already patted out most of the arid beads from Reenu's person.

"You have a burn here, here, and here," Amaru told Reenu while pointing at his side, tricep, and inner thigh. "Dammit, Reenu, you need to be more careful."

Moshe scoffed. "You didn't fall much better, Amaru."

Amaru tightened her eyes in readiness for objection, but she saw Moshe nod towards the back of her shoulder. A burn, of course.

"At that point, I had to go after him."

Moshe nodded and looked off towards their goal. The valley was vast, a two-hundred-foot chasm that separated them from a world they had never known before. It was no wonder that their captors never went beyond its bounds. But that was how they knew they were headed the right way.

"Let's cross to the other side and spend the night at the base there. Should be able to get enough shade so that we won't burn when the morning comes."

"Spend the night?" Amaru rhetorically asked. "It's barely noontime. We should try to push ourselves and climb out of here."

Moshe shook his head. "I doubt we can in our state. Better to rest and recover as much energy as possible."

Amaru let go of Reenu's hand, which she had instinctively been holding in between hers.

"That's exactly fucking why we've got to push ourselves. Moshe, we haven't eaten in fifteen days. I don't know how many more days we-"

"I know, Amaru," Moshe interrupted. The sun was hot, but he kept his cool. "First thing we'll do once we're past The Divide is find some food. There's bound to be untapped resources on the other side."

"If that's the first thing, what's the second? How will we know where we're supposed to go? Will there be signs that say 'PARADISE: HEAD DUE EAST' or some shit like that?"

Moshe looked at his two companions as they sat beneath him, looking up with the eagerness of an unsuspecting sheep. He started laughing and kissed both of their heads. Amaru and Reenu looked at each other, confused and concerned by such a rare event.

"You and your questions, Amaru," Moshe said between near-snorts.

"What's so funny?" she asked.

Moshe started to compose himself. "I...I don't know. Just seeing you two...here in The Divide...we're really doing it. We're going to make it."

Neither Amaru nor Reenu were comforted by Moshe's explanation. He realized he must have appeared like he was losing his mind, laughing in such a dire time. But he wasn't, he definitely wasn't. He sobered up.

"If there are no signs, we'll do what we've been doing. Follow the waste - it'll lead to something eventually. Amaru, how much sheepfat is still usable in that skin?"

Amaru turned the skin inside out and scooped the remains.

"Just a handful."

Moshe nodded a few times. "Rub it on your burns, should be enough. Then let's get to the other side."

That night, the trio camped at the base of The Divide. Amaru and Reenu were wrapped in each other's limbs, buried a half-foot deep in warming grains. The wind was nearly howling; it had picked up over the last couple of nights, though Moshe knew it could still get much more biting. He would have joined his friend-lovers, but he couldn't sleep. He thought too much. About the journey and its perils so far. About how he was the one that convinced them to come along in the first place. That meant whatever happened to them was his responsibility. He knew that they were close, really close. This was as far east as anyone he knew had ever been. Whether that was because all who passed The Divide never wanted to come back or never had the chance to, he did not know. But he did know that their journey would come to an end very soon. All that stood between them and the unknown was an impossible slope of sand.

He looked up at the wall of sand and hated it. It was another opponent, another obstacle. It was another malevolent force that tried to kill him and his companions, another goddamned thing that he had to protect them from. Another impossibility that he had to make possible. He couldn't wait any longer. Even if no one had ever made the climb before, it was no matter. He would be the first. And he would return by morning with a bounty that Amaru and Reenu would rejoice over - the sustenance they needed to complete the journey with him. He fucking got this.

Moshe ran straight up the slope as fast as he could, his arms in swift conjunction with his legs. He made it fifty feet up before the sand gave in and pulled his steps into itself and downwards. Then he tried racing with all four limbs on the ground: more stability, more support. But now it was his left hand that got pulled in, and when he struggled to release it, he tumbled over backwards until he landed on his back with a thud. The sound stirred Amaru, and by the time she cleared the mist of half-dreams from her eyes, she saw an agitated Moshe sliding back down. He backed up and prepared a running start before he was made aware of his risen friend.

"Moshe, what are you doing?"

Moshe realized he was panting hard and did his best to stop it, but not before Amaru could ask another question.

"Wasn't it your idea to rest so that we could recover?"

"Yes," Moshe admitted, "but I realized that an attempt in the cool of dark would be worthwhile. And...I couldn't sleep, anyway."

With that, Moshe ran at the slope once more. This time, he only made it twenty feet up before he met with another tumble. Amaru sat up, causing Reenu to awaken with a slow yawn.

"Moshe, you've done so much to keep us safe lately. More than either of us could ever repay you, and I'm sure that's what you're trying to do right now. But maybe some sleep would be what's best for us all, including you. Especially you."

Amaru may have had a point, but it didn't matter. Time was running short for their bodies' internal clocks, and Moshe couldn't just wait patiently for them to expire.

"One more try," he said.

Moshe ran up the slope once again, but this time in a zigzag. He did all that he could to avoid the soft spots in the sand...and it was working. He was more than halfway up the slope, so focused on his task that he didn't hear the growing, obnoxious bleating of twenty sheep from above. He did notice, however, when one of those sheep seemed to hover bottomside down next to him. Moshe's eyes turned up slowly as he saw a string of attached sheep lead to someone waving at him from up top. From where he was, he could not tell if the shepherd was a man or a woman, but the shining white of their clothing nearly blinded him. And theirs was the friendliest voice he had heard in all his life.

"Hello, good sir! My name is Mahu. I'm a recruiter from Ecclesia, and I would like to escort you and your company to paradise!"

Reenu, Abigail, and Ambree were being escorted to prison. With bags on their heads, they couldn't have known that for sure, but they all felt it to be true. What they couldn't have guessed was that it was about to be-

"Quite crowded in here, huh, Lieutenant?" said the burly Kohen who was manhandling Reenu, his voice preempted by the jangling of keys and the grating of a door.

Suddenly, Reenu felt the bag lift up and off of him. His first sight gave him more delight than he could have expected.

"Am-...Katir!" His friend-lover was laying down in her cell with her arms behind her head. Reenu also saw that someone else was huddled in the cell next to her.

"No more ruses. Call me Amaru, you dumbass." Amaru said this playfully, but she stayed where she lay as if she possessed knowledge that Reenu was about to discover for himself.

Reenu's chaperone pushed him into the cell across from Amaru and swiftly locked the bars behind him. A hole with putrid water. And also: an unwelcome neighbor.

Moshe sat cross-legged and held his palms open and outward in Reenu's direction. His eyes were big and shone in a way Reenu had never seen from him before. His mouth hung open and his lips held a slight tremble in a way Reenu had never seen from him before. Vulnerability. Reenu let the first wave of instinct pass through him. Then he turned away and saw how his other new jailmates fared.

Abigail was roughly pushed into the cell to the right of Reenu's; her front bars running parallel with the prison's entrance. Ambree was more delicately placed to the left of Amaru; on her left was the final, open cell across from the entrance.

"Six out of seven spots, boss," one of the Kohen said to Lieutenant Zacchaeus. "All the other rooms are full, too. Let's hope there's no more where that came from."

The third Kohen gave a sympathetic chuckle, but the Lieutenant kept his head down. He was clearly sullen, but all eyes that were on him could see that he had something he wanted to say. Instead, he turned around and beckoned for his small troop to exit.

"Zacchaeus! Not even going to say hi this time?"

Amaru was pressed against her cell's cold, metallic door. Both of her previous interactions with the Lieutenant were under wildly different circumstances, but she hoped that this outcome would be at least as positive as the first. She didn't know him well, but she knew something was clouding his valorous spirit. Rather than respond to her, Zacchaeus kept his pace.

"Listen to me, man!" Amaru yelled after him. "You got what you wanted! Besides, you know there's only one shithead who deserves to stay in here! You can take your time with your sentences, I guess, but you should at least tell us *why* we need to stay for now."

Zacchaeus stopped at the entrance. Then he used both hands to close it behind him. The action made him swivel his body around as he did so. Amaru briefly caught his eyes, but not long enough to tell what was going on inside his head.

Abigail remained standing throughout this interaction, her body tensely facing her part-time lover.

"What does he want?"

Amaru turned her attention to Abigail. She felt sheepish - she often did in the presence of the female fighter. She slowly pointed at her chest before admitting,

"You."

Abigail dealt out a scornful laugh and started checking the integrity of her cell: pulling on the bars, pushing against the wall, stomping on the ground. It was not out of drive, however, but the nervous tic of habit.

"Not sure what good that'll do him anymore," she said to herself.

Amaru walked to the edge of her cell. "What was that, Abigail?"

"Nothing, Ms. Sheepsmilk-and-Water."

Amaru wasn't sure what that meant, but the derisive tone was communication enough.

"What is your problem?"

"Whatever problems I've got, you've twice as many, you fucked-up, wishy-washy child."

"Abigail-"

"And now you're in a prison full of those problems! Let's start with your fearless fuckin' leader over there!"

Abigail threw her voice in Moshe's direction, but he was facing the wall so that his back was towards the rest of them.

"Got a taste of the good life but you couldn't keep it down, huh? You choked on it and spit it out, but now there's no other portion left for you. You're gonna fucking starve in here. Or did you two kiss and make up already and this obvious contention is just growing pains?"

Amaru looked away and went to sit down. Moshe put his hands on the wall and let his head fall forward. He started to speak:

"I've tried to-"

"Eh, I don't wanna hear a fuckin' word from you, bitch," Abigail interrupted. "And you shouldn't either, Amaru. Not even if he begs for forgiveness."

Abigail swiveled her attention to the cell besides Amaru.

"Well, well, speaking of begging. Ha! Wouldn't join the cause but ended up in its shit anyway. Now there's no crowd left for you to proselytize to, old man."

Ambree stood up and raced to the side of her cell that joined Amaru's. She moved her head this way and that so that she could see him for herself.

"The beggar? Is he in here?" Ambree eagerly asked.

Abigail was bemused by the new recruit's interest, but not intrigued enough to care.

"Yes, whore, but as usual, he's sleeping, and he surely won't wake for you. Hopefully he never wakes again."

Ambree's interest shifted. "Don't you dare call me that!"

"These cells would be stuffed and overflowing with the amount of men you've taken in. Stuffed like your-"

"You've slept with plenty yourself, Abigail! And not even for love."

Abigail slowly rotated until she saw her objector. Reenu stood up straight with a puffed-out chest pressed against their neighboring bars. Abigail walked over and did the same. She appeared as if she would whisper to him, but she kept her voice loud and clear.

"Yes, but never for currency. That's what a whore does."

Moshe didn't want to move from his place, but his curiosity and conviction had to be satiated. He made an about-face and saw his old tempter. Ambree returned his gaze, and the mess of these penitentiary partnerships worked themselves out in her brain.

"This really is fucked," she said as she changed course and sat back down.

Everyone followed the interaction. All except the beggar, who would sleep soundly through the rest of the commotion. Reenu and Abigail looked to Moshe for an explanation while Amaru closed her eyes and rubbed her temples. Moshe cleared his throat and searched for one.

"She was...my..." He realized any words he chose would be taken the wrong way. He wondered if there was a right way. Abigail didn't wait.

"Whatever," she said. She walked over to the corner of her cell that was the farthest away from any of them. "Now that we're all acquainted, we can be the most fucked-up troupe of merry friends, made happy-go-lucky by forgetting our collective baggage with each other. Or we can all just peacefully, quietly make like the beggar and wait for our sentences. I'm picking the latter because I just do not give a fucking shit anymore."

With that, Abigail stretched out across the floor and covered her eyes with her arms. Ambree huddled her legs close to her chest. Amaru kept her eyes closed, kept rubbing her temples. The beggar kept sleeping. Only Moshe and Reenu remained present, still facing each other. Reenu allowed himself another look into Moshe's eyes. He glimpsed a moment that was pregnant with possibility.

But Reenu shook his head and lay down and tried his best to count sheep and fall into sleep.

"Okay, last one...here we go...almost there..."

Mahu and Moshe held on to one end of the sheep caravan which extended down the cliffside just enough for Amaru and Reenu to climb it. Once they were all safely atop The Divide, each helped pull the sheep back up with them. The effort was enough to get them all panting. All except Amaru, who sniffed a couple times and showed Moshe three fingers on her left hand. Moshe nodded subtly.

*"Great, great, looks like we're all accounted for. Thank you guys for - *whew* - thank you guys for helping. So, as I was saying, my name is Mahu, and wha-"*

While Mahu was catching their breath, Amaru slipped around their back, pulled back their arms, and locked them together as she collapsed to the floor. Reenu hopped over to them and grabbed Mahu's legs by the ankles, keeping them pinned down. Successfully subdued, Moshe walked over and knelt by them. Mahu was struggling to break free, but Moshe placed a hand on their chest and said,

"Relax and we won't hurt you."

Mahu stilled expertly. Moshe raised a brow.

"Who are you with?" Moshe asked.

Mahu looked at Amaru and then Reenu with worried eyebrows.

"I was happy to explain that I'm with Ecclesia, a walled-off city in a valley not too-"

"We've heard," Moshe interrupted. *"But who are you with...currently? You're not out here with twenty sheep and supplies on your own."*

Mahu gulped. *"We recruiters split up just before dawn in order to cover more ground, but we always meet back at the edge of the forest by nightfall. I've gone a little farther than usual since we're expanding beyond The Divide soon. Though, at this rate, I'm not likely to make it back until maybe tomorrow's nightfall..."*

Moshe heard what Mahu was saying, but his mind became preoccupied with their face. Long eyelashes, but a rugged chin. A delicate nose, but almost muscular cheeks. Their expressions were forgiving yet assertive, and there were no breasts where Moshe first placed his hand.

"Are you male or female?"

Mahu blushed, clearly thrown off-guard by the inquiry.

"Um, it's complicated. If it makes you feel better, you can refer to me as you would a male."

"Hm," hmmed Reenu, as if both confused and curious. Moshe was mostly just confused, so he lowered his right eyebrow, took his hand off of Mahu's chest, and thought up a different direction.

"Why are you recruiting? Is there a war we should know about?"

"No, no war," Mahu insisted. "We recruit people to come live with us."

"Mm," mmmed Amaru, as if both doubting and interested. Mahu picked up on that and tried to look up at Amaru to address her, but as soon as they tried, Amaru moved her shoulder into their head, keeping it down.

"Sorry, I won't make any more movement," Mahu said, which would prove to be true. "But it's true. We were once inhabitants of this world, but now we are citizens of another - one that's good enough to deserve the title of paradise. There is a process to becoming a citizen, but all are welcome and encouraged to try the narrow road. And we go out in search of others because we do not wish for any more to perish. The world has enough of that already, does it not?"

Moshe sat back in a more relaxed pose and breathed in and out deeply several times. He wanted Mahu to believe that he was mulling it over so as to draw out their intentions more clearly. It was what they were searching for, but who was to say that this wasn't just some opportunist capitalizing off of the rumors? Mahu was too unassuming, and unassuming people don't last long. Unless they lived most of their lives in paradise.

"This isn't how I envisioned us finding Ecclesia," Moshe admitted.

"Oh?" Mahu said, intrigued. "How did you envision it?"

"We would have preferred to scout the place out. Make sure the rumors are true. Now we'll be led right in on the word of someone we just met."

"Not to worry," Mahu soothingly said. "You can do so if you'd like, though the walls are so tall I'm afraid you won't be able to scout much other than from the distant view at the top of the valley. But allow me to at least guide you to the forest, and then I can just point out the way from there. I don't have to go *with you all the way, but I can help. Oh! You'll just need to know the password to get in: salvation. And you can have a sheep or two if you'd like."*

Reenu's stomach growled and his grip slightly lessened. Moshe noticed that Mahu didn't budge an inch. He would have asked Reenu his opinion, but he knew that the kid would always lean towards naiveté. He looked to Amaru instead for the opposite counsel, but her face was a blank slate. It would be up to him then. That's fine, he already knew what to do. They would tread carefully with this person and be sure to ask a plethora of questions. The first sign of danger and they would tie them up to one of their sheep and roll them down The Divide. Either way, Moshe would make sure that he and his friends would at least get sustenance out of this.

"First, we'll need to eat," Moshe said. "That'll give you the opportunity to explain some things. Right now, I'm wondering...what's a forest?"

Mahu's smile bordered on condescension, but it was pulled back from the ledge by the authentic joy they felt from the chance to make new friends.

Ambree found that she was dealt the least favorable cell. Not because it was any less lacking in luxuries - if that's what a lone waste hole could be labeled - but its diagonal position from the entrance meant newly penetrating light and the authorities who brought it would always observe her first.

"The *Symvoul* apologizes for this midnight disturbance," Lieutenant Zacchaeus said as he gruffly swung his way in. The light from his torch blinded Ambree, but it was the apathetic clanging of the door that woke most of the others. The Lieutenant took a couple of limping steps before continuing his announcement.

"Newbies, expect a routine daily visit with firstmeal. But we thought it courteous to keep you all updated as to your fates now."

Amaru sat up and searched The Lieutenant's face. Still empty. But perhaps she had gotten through to him a little.

"There is no update…"

Amaru sat back. Reenu kept his eager stare that was more of a glare. Moshe rubbed the sleep from his eyes. The beggar slept.

"…but there will be soon. For now, I've come to let you know that someone else will be watching over you in my stead."

Amaru sat back up. "Why? What about this job is uncomfortable for you?"

Lieutenant Zacchaeus grit his teeth and stared straight ahead, avoiding eye contact. "Not to worry, you'll be in good hands."

The Lieutenant stepped to the side and let Matthias walk in front of him. Crutches nowhere to be found, he held his head high in the face of his captives. The Lieutenant continued his introduction.

"Now, it's to my understanding that most of you already know Matthi-"

A couple of breakneck actions ended with Matthias nearly meeting unconsciousness. Abigail dropped from the shadows above and enclosed Matthias' neck with her arms. Reenu realized she must have pressed against the corner wall of her cell in order to keep her body up against the ceiling. Abigail repeatedly banged the back of Matthias' head against her cell door until blood appeared; then, she pulled him against the bars and made no indication that she would ever let go.

Almost as breathlessly, Lieutenant Zacchaeus cycled through until he found the right key, placed it in Abigail's door, and flung it wide. This flung Matthias towards the room's sole exit, where he gasped for breath and tried to recover. Abigail now stood face to face with the Lieutenant.

No one interrupted the standoff. A clever decision was all that stood between Abigail and freedom. A maneuver, a well-placed jab, a distraction - all were options that she had the time to analyze and consider. Which would be the move that she could successfully pull on the Kohen captain? But all that came of it was a staring contest. And he won. Abigail started to weep mutedly, her body nearly convulsing in its restrictions. She did not want to dissolve into sobs, so she went back into her cell and muffled her cries with her reddened arms. Everyone stayed still for a moment, and then the Lieutenant cleared his throat and closed the cell.

"It's likely now that someone *else* will be by in a few hours with first-meal," he blankly said as he turned the key.

"Lieutenant, listen to me," Amaru said, her voice tempered by what her eyes just saw. "We're sorry for what just happened, but trust me, it won't happen again."

Lieutenant Zacchaeus looked at Amaru and scoffed. "Speak for yourself."

"I am," Amaru said. She gave the Lieutenant a stern but compassionate look. "But I also know we all just want this to be done with. Forgive us for being restless. I know your duty is hard, and we'll respect the process from here on."

Zacchaeus stared at Amaru. He knew she was sly, and for that, he didn't fully believe her. But no one had ever acknowledged the gravity of his position before. His face made like it was going to crack a smile, so instead, he held out a hand. Amaru shook it through the bars. Zacchaeus turned around and gave Moshe something of a wink.

"Listen to her."

With that, he helped Matthias to his feet and left.

Ambree turned and turned and tried to make herself comfortable. Abigail stopped crying, but kept her arms where they were. The beggar continued to sleep. Moshe looked at Amaru, who had taken a seat against her wall and was looking down. Moshe felt something brewing within that The Manual warned him about, but its potency overcame his thought space like the smell of burning. It was pride.

"You handled that well," Moshe told her.

Amaru kept looking down.

"Said what she had to."

Moshe turned towards Reenu. He was the one who responded, but his eyes were fixed on Amaru.

"It was also the right thing to say," Moshe insisted.

"How do you know? Is it in The Manual that you're supposed to suck the dick of your oppressors?"

Moshe was taken

change happens quick sometimes

aback. He wanted to demand respect, but he knew there was cognitive dissonance in that impulse.

"No, but it does say to meet people where they are at. That's how you reach them."

Reenu said nothing. Amaru slid until she was lying flat against the ground. She closed her eyes and ended her part in the conversation. Moshe tried to think of how he could follow his own advice. How could he make things the way they once were? What was it they wanted from him? What was something he never gave them back then?

"Reenu," Moshe started. "Don't you want to know how I ended up in here?"

Reenu kept his eyes on his lover-friend, vowing within himself not to give Moshe the release he was seeking. He did flick his hand towards him, however, so regardless of how ambivalent he felt, Moshe was pleased enough by the indication to continue on.

"I talked back to Leader - to Saios, that is." Moshe let the statement marinate in the air. He searched Reenu's face in hopes for a reaction of realization. But instead, he saw a snarl being held back. Reenu turned his face away.

"Sounds like you had a hard time," he said.

Moshe shook his head even though Reenu couldn't see it. "In front of everyone. They want to expand Inner Sanctum without any plans for expanding The Table. Everything about life there is already so easy and complacent...I thought they would see my point. But...I don't know what it is. It's like time well spent made them forget what life beyond is really like. And, clearly, there isn't any room for critique in their plans, either."

Reenu vigorously turned his head around and stared Moshe down with a ferocious glare and parting words.

"Sorry it wasn't what you wanted."

Moshe was frightened. This anger was novel - or had it been bubbling underneath all along? He couldn't have known; he hadn't paid close enough attention. But it made him realize that Reenu didn't want dirt on him. His old friend didn't want to know how he had failed. Reenu put his head to the ground and covered his exposed ear with his hand. Moshe's gaze lowered until it found the waste hole. The only aberration in an otherwise smooth, unseasoned floor. The liquid in it was murky, but scentless. Moshe wondered if his cell had ever been occupied before or if he was her first. It hit Moshe that what he had done to his friends was far worse than what they did to earn their captivity. And now it seemed certain that he had permanently lost Amaru, and Reenu was quickly falling in line. He didn't blame them, but it led him to believe that there was only one route left for him to take.

Moshe tried to keep his eyes closed, but he knew that was impossible. He was thirsty.

...

A couple hours later, the beggar awoke. He stretched out his limbs and let out a loud, obnoxious yawn. He hadn't felt so well-rested in ages. His eyes naturally inclined themselves towards the vent above Amaru's cell. The sun was about to rise - firstmeal time! The beggar thanked Existence and the nature of her flow for all that was and all that would be.

But the violent retching across from him necessarily interrupted his thoughts.

Moshe was vomiting all over his cell, but all the others were sleeping right through it. Other people? That was surprising, but he appreciated the added company.

"Kohen, help! Everyone - umph, umph - wake up!" The beggar begged coarsely between his coughs.

Reenu was the first to be roused, but he could only let out a soundless gasp at the sight of his neighbor. Moshe had stopped his outpour of brown, sloshy liquid, but continued to gag uncontrollably. His face was turning blue.

"Fucking sheepshit!" Amaru yelled out when she saw Moshe writhing on the floor. "Zacchaeus, Matthias! Get in here!"

Ambree came to and joined in the cacophony as well. Abigail remained neutral. Suddenly, Lieutenant Zacchaeus burst through the door with Matthias right behind him. They dropped several platters of food, and Zacchaeus reached for the keys and something else he pulled out of his pocket. Amaru saw that it was faded green like a dying tree. The Lieutenant opened Moshe's cell and splashed his way to his prisoner. He got down on hands and knees with him, forcing Moshe to chew and swallow a dull green substance. It only took a minute for the impulses and adrenaline to die down.

"What the fuck was that?!" Amaru yelled, voice nearly cracking.

"Lieutenant, is Moshe going to be ok?" Reenu concernedly asked.

The Lieutenant bit his lip and refused to nod. The stench from what he sat in was settling in his nostrils.

"He can tell you himself."

Moshe was still breathing heavily, but he looked at Reenu and Amaru with shame in his eyes.

"He drank from the waste hole. The boy tried to kill himself," the beggar said. He gave Amaru a knowing look. She remembered what had happened a couple nights before.

"Moshe," she said like someone testing the waters. "Why did you do that?"

It was the first time Amaru had cast her eyes Moshe's way since she knew he was there with her. Since he had split open her temple. Moshe wished he could commemorate the occasion with a better answer.

"It's the only way to get your attention."

"Are you fucking serious?"

The Lieutenant stood up and walked out of the cell. Amaru rolled her eyes and started pacing. Reenu winced hard and sighed. The beggar observed. Abigail and Ambree began to lose interest in the self-pity.

"Lieutenant Zacchaeus, hold on!"

Moshe put all of his strength into the exclamation; he had a confession to make, but it was not only for his superior.

"You must know...I killed the recruiter: Mahu."

The sun became the moon became the sun, but Mahu hardly took a break from speaking outside of the occasional bite of sheep jerky (an incredible snack, they would come to find out). Amaru was thoroughly annoyed by nightfall, but it certainly lent credibility to their role as a recruiter. If most Ecclesians were like Mahu, she would have a hard time getting along with them, but at least they would be harmless. Reenu, on the other hand, became infatuated with Mahu. Reenu's greatest penchant was for learning, and Mahu's endless reservoir of esoterica, regarding topics such as different kinds of stone, holidays, and the color green, was proving to be quite the delight. Moshe himself felt no real threat emanating from behind Mahu's blithesome temperament, but the tall, decrepit brown towers in front of them hinted that it was their end of the road.

"Trees," Mahu informed, interrupting his own exegesis on the questionnaire all potential citizens are asked. "Well, dead ones, at least."

"That why they're not green?" Moshe asked.

All of Mahu's enigmatic facial features seemed to lift at once. "Quick learner, you are," they said with a wink.

Moshe nodded and tried to smile, but he wasn't quite there yet. "That mean we're at the forest then?"

Mahu nodded fervently. "It will grow much thicker and greener as we go along, but, yes, here we are!"

Reenu put his arm around Amaru's waist and pulled her in close for a kiss on the cheek. She resisted his cheer at first, but smiled back eventually. Moshe handed Mahu a deadpan stare, who returned his look with a confused one until they realized what it was for.

"Right, well, I'll be off then."

Reenu stopped hugging Amaru and perplexedly looked at Mahu, who was already gathering their remaining sheep and supplies. Mahu made their way to each of them and extended a hand. A strong grip, Moshe noted.

"Moshe, Amaru, Reenu, it really was a blessing to meet each of you. I hope you feel the same, because I'm sure we'll be seeing each other again very soon! And remember: peace be with you!"

"What are you doing?" Reenu asked, sharply enough to demand the attention of all.

Mahu blinked twice. "Oh, no, Reenu, you're supposed to say 'and also with you,' remember?"

"Why are you leaving?" Reenu asked, just as sharp.

"Reenu," Moshe said, taking control. "That was the deal. Mahu guided us to the forest, and we're very grateful for that, but now that we know where we're going, we'll head to Ecclesia our way."

"So you trust Mahu enough to help us some, but not enough to go all the way? Ecclesia is still a day's journey away in a direction we can't know for certain."

Reenu had put his foot down, now standing with his chest out ever so slightly. Moshe would have thought it was cute if his own frustration wasn't mounting. Mahu sensed the tension.

"Hey, Reenu, it's fine. I understand that Moshe's just being precautious-"

"Paranoid might be more like it," Reenu said sternly. "Moshe, Mahu needs to head back to stock up anyway, let's just take them with us. At least a little longer, we're headed into unknown terrain."

foolishness! don't you see that this tactic is exactly what an expert scavenger would do: the hand of a friend is a liability

Amaru bounded over to where Moshe stood. She put a hand on his shoulder and whispered into his ear:

"look, I'm not sold on Mahu either, but maybe the smartest thing to do would be to keep them with us...they were the one that suggested leaving once we got here, after all..."

Moshe grimaced. He cursed himself for letting the situation sour. He didn't like the position they were in: risk accompanied both routes. But to keep the peace and to keep the danger within throat-slitting range, he acceded.

"Mahu, you can stick with us, if you would like. But I would still prefer to approach Ecclesia on our own once we are close enough."

Mahu's fervent nod returned. "Absolutely! Now, come, we've an hour or so before sundown. Then I will show you how to start a fire."

What Mahu said was true: the forest became dense with itself, even to the point where telling time from the sun above was unattainable. No one noticed *until a passing remark from Reenu interrupted another one of Mahu's regional tales.*

"Ooh...getting chilly..." Reenu said, rubbing his chest.

Mahu froze in speech and movement. "Reenu, you're right. How could I have let the hours slip away? I suggest we split up."

Amaru rolled her eyes and sped over to where Mahu stood. She picked them up by the scruff of their robe and pinned them against the nearest tree.

"What are you talking about?!" Amaru yelled.

"Sorry, sorry!" Mahu cowered. "Let me explain, please. We need to find wood that's suitable for a fire. That'd be easy enough here, but we don't have any sharp tools to help, so already-fallen wood will have to do. That might take some time, and it's getting late, so it might be best to double our efforts by splitting up."

Amaru looked at Moshe with disapproving eyes. He shared her sentiment, but found a way down the middle.

"Amaru, let him - er, them - go. Stick with Reenu and I'll stick with Mahu. We'll split up, but we're to remain in each other's sight. Understood?"

Everyone saw the peace-making wisdom in the decision. They tied their supplies with the sheep and went. Minutes later, Moshe looked fifty yards to his left and saw Reenu scanning the ground while Amaru kept her head high and alert. They were a good pair, a good trio altogether. Mahu had become considerably quieter, understanding the delicate line of trust that they walked.

"Mahu," Moshe said. "You've been kind enough to answer all our questions and maneuver through our...aggressive precautions..."

Mahu picked up some wood and kept their face towards the ground. "All part of the job."

"Of course. And you've told us story after story of your time in Ecclesia. It all seems quite grand, but I feel that there are some holes you've yet to uncover."

Mahu dropped the wood and stood up. Moshe expected more of the same apologetic demeanor, but he was given something else. The face of one who had been disrespected one too many times.

"Ask anything you'd like, Moshe."

Moshe did. "The questionnaire: that's all there is between us and paradise?"

Mahu didn't back down or lead with narrative frills. "No. There's much more. But nothing dangerous or even close to being as inhospitable as your current life. But it's all designed to test whether or not you are worthy."

Moshe had a feeling. "Of joining the high and mighty?"

"Of taking what's yours."

"Baaaaa!"

"Moshe!"

Moshe threw his head west. It was quite a bit away at this point, but he saw that Mahu's sheep and their feeble supplies were being torn to shreds by a pack of wolves. Amaru and Reenu had already started racing over there. Moshe looked fiercely into Mahu's eyes. He saw an even greater level of concern than he had.

They took off as quickly as they could. Mahu fell behind for a few moments, but struggled to keep up.

"Moshe!" Mahu yelled. "Call them off! It's a loss, but we'll be fine once we make it to Ecclesia tomorrow!"

Moshe pressed on. Sheep were sheep.

Five wolves ravaged one side of the sheep caravan. Tied together, the sheep were helpless to move, so they could only make noise. The wolves had already carved out the bodies of three sheep; they made their way inwards rapidly. Reenu slid to the other side of the sheep and picked up their supplies and sheepskin. He passed one to Amaru and put his on.

"Let's untie a few and lead them away!"

Moshe and Mahu caught up and Reenu handed Moshe his sheepskin.

"The wolves don't know we're here yet! Let's save a few while we can."

Moshe nodded and Reenu went to one end of the sheep line. He was immediately pounced upon.

"Reenu!"

Moshe and Mahu ran to save him. Reenu held the wolf's head and struggled to keep it away from landing a bite in his flesh. The wolf chomped near his ear. The wolf chomped above his face. The wolf chomped and then nuzzled its nose against his neck, the grand prize for the predator. The wolf opened its mouth once more and then felt the full weight of Moshe's body against its own. Moshe and the wolf tumbled away.

"Are you okay?!" Mahu cupped Reenu's head in their hands and felt him *nod. Just then, the howl of a wolf afar rang through the woods...and was met in response by a half-dozen more.*

"Go, then!" Mahu yelled. "Run away with Amaru and Moshe and I will catch up with you."

Reenu fled. Mahu turned and saw Moshe straddled atop the offending wolf. He had procured a nearby rock and was repeatedly bashing it into the disintegrating skull of his prey.

"Moshe, let's go!"

Mahu saw the bloodthirst in Moshe's eyes and knew he would have to physically pull him out of it. But Mahu didn't see what Moshe saw. On the other side of the sheep line, one of the wolves was chewing through the part in the rope that bound all the sheep together. In a few moments, the rope would be no more and the sheep would scatter, leaving an open path for the rest of the wolves to set their eyes on new prey. So Moshe let Mahu pull him away. Moshe determined that he would indeed go with Mahu, but only for so long. When the two of them were halfway between the wolves and their friends, Moshe dropped. He fell onto Mahu's right ankle. What Mahu said was true: they didn't have any sharp tools. None except the ones gifted by cruel evolution.

Moshe bit deep and hard into Mahu's ankle. Mahu screamed out, whether initially from pain or shock, no one will ever know, but it certainly must have been both when he saw a chunk of his flesh fly from the teeth of his recruit. Moshe pulled Mahu's body to the earth and stepped over him for good measure. Reenu and Amaru turned back when they heard the scream. They saw Moshe with blood in his mouth and his arms flailing, desperately urging them to keep moving. Then they saw a wounded Mahu crawling against the dirt, crying and trying to form begging words but to little effect. Then they saw the pack of five become fifteen and head directly towards Mahu. Then they turned around. They saw no more, but they heard screams and chewing echo in their ears for the rest of the night. In his head, Moshe would come to convince himself that Mahu might have survived; they never saw the body, after all. That was how he would cope with the evil that he allowed himself to partake in, that he forced his friends to bear. He didn't know how the act would change their collective relationship, but he was confident in one thing.

If they got out of the forest alive, Ecclesia would be theirs for the taking.

"They tried to save us, and in return, I brought them down. I guess Mahu did save us in a way, but their sacrifice was not their choice. So, Lieutenant, you can keep me in here until I rust. I'm a killer."

Lieutenant Zacchaeus inadvertently took a limping step back. The mystery was solved; he could finally tell Mahu's family what had become of their child and sibling. The burden he had carried since he first learned of Mahu's disappearance just a couple of days after The Last Call was finally lifted, by Moshe of all people. He was appalled - not by the act, but by the admission itself. Yet he could tell that the confession of guilt was not for him. Reenu and Amaru were at the edges of their cells.

"I convinced myself that you had not seen what I did," Moshe said, his eyes flitting back and forth between Reenu and Amaru. "But I knew you had. You never said so explicitly, but I never let you. I broke our vow. I abandoned you even before I left for Inner Sanctum. I...I had a dream once, way back when we lived in our parents' territory. In it, I saw these strange, airy, angry circles hovering around you two. Dark, black things. But then I was taken to a place where I saw...your children. And they had the circles too, but they were lighter in tone. And then I saw *their* kids and the circles were even lighter. I saw generation after generation grow and build and live together until the dark circles were completely gone. This dream...it's what stirred within me the desire to leave. I woke up with the thought that even if what I had to do to get us here was wrong...eventually, being here long enough would make it right. Now I see that could never be true. I hurt you both, and to both of you, I'm so very sorry. Eternally sorry. I couldn't face it until now because I needed this to work. Now it's all crumbled. And all I know is that anytime I was acting out of fear, it would not lead to the better choice, but the safer one."

Moshe stopped because he couldn't go on. He had never let himself deeply feel his crimes until he spoke them aloud. He hung his head until he fell towards the floor and began to sob. He wanted to ask for their forgiveness, but how could he? He was the most undeserving one in the room. He felt a hand envelop his. Reenu had reached through the bars, fervently nodding in consolation.

Ambree cried a more audible reaction. Abigail put her fist on her chest. The beggar smiled. Amaru shook her head.

"Moshe, you tried to kill yourself in order to get our attention," she said. "You're *still* doing all that you can to maintain control. I used to think that when I would get something wrong or disagree with you, that it was because *I* was messed up. No, it's the other way around."

Reenu let go of Moshe's hand, conflicted.

"I understand," Moshe agreed as he wiped tears away. "It's something in my nature, something that might never change. I understand that I've done too much for our relationship to be like it once was. But do you think you could ever forgive me?"

Seeing him in his brokenness, a brokenness that he finally admitted to, Amaru felt empathy deliberately making its warming return.

"Maybe someday."

It was all Moshe could ask for.

The Lieutenant tried to discreetly wipe his eyes, but everyone noticed. He pulled on Moshe's cell door, double checking that it was locked, and motioned for Matthias to lead the way in their exit.

"Zacchaeus, maybe you didn't hear me right," Moshe told his superior. "I'm the villain. I'm the only criminal here. Well, except for Abigail, maybe."

Abigail held up a solitary finger from the other side of the room. "Fuck you, too. And just for the record, I don't forgive you either. Nor you, Matthias."

Matthias glared at Abigail, but he felt guilt as well.

"Everyone else...their only crime is their identity," Moshe continued. "They are not made for Inner Sanctum, and that's completely fine. You know that. I could tell from that night in the forest that you disagree with how things are run. You may be a leader, but you've got your own conscience. You've got to find a way to let them go. And they'll be free to live their lives wherever they choose."

Zacchaeus felt the stare of his underling from behind his back.

"It's more complicated than that."

"Zacchaeus, I don't know you well," Amaru jumped in. "But I know that what Moshe says is right. You're not like the rest of them. You feel what we feel. You can come on down and be with the rest of us. You know something isn't right. You've got to learn to live with yourself."

Zacchaeus purposefully looked at every face in the room. He wondered how the conversation had shifted its gaze onto him and his faults. He knew how Ecclesia functioned better than any of them, yet they had enough of an inkling to suspect her problems were systemic. Little did they know that there would be a *Symvoul* meeting later that afternoon, but it felt like fate for them to confront him in this way. With abandon to worrying about what Matthias might say or do, he made a commitment.

"Well, I got y'all together again, didn't I? I'll see what I can do."

<hr>

Time. What is time? The indefinite, continued march of existence. A constant that can be so variable. Those above believe time to always be the same. Sun, moon, repeat. But without those sacred points of reference, who can know anything about its passing? Perhaps a God who's abandoned his creation in fear of what they've become. Arah's crazed grin burst through his cracked lips as he contemplated this irony. He had all the time in the world to think these thoughts, but the suffocating darkness would never allow him the knowledge of how much time he spent doing so. And who knew how much time he had left, anyway? He chuckled to himself.

He rubbed his thumbs along the defined indentations he once called ribs. There was once actual meat there; he was once a strong lad, if he remembered correctly. He had a much brighter future at one point. He chuckled again, his ribs barely managing the pressure. As simple as it was, there was something comforting in the repetitive motion he made with his thumbs. At least in the darkness, he could easily imagine that the contact came from someone else. Ambree, or anyone, really. He didn't even have to close his eyes.

Meditation was of no use; Bukshee's fading whimpers always got in the way. Reflecting on the beggar's principles didn't help either, they faded and were replaced by hunger. The first couple of weeks (he presumed) were excruciating in their vacuum state. But it always amazed him how quickly the body adapted. There was liberation even in nothingness. He was beginning to see that there was nothing he could even try to worry about. No more people to take care of, no more morality qualms to consider. Just waiting for whatever would come next.

There were footsteps making their way down once again, but Arah barely noticed them. They matched the stilted rhythm of his heart beating loudly in his ears. Soon enough both would slow down.

The torch told him how bleary his sight had become. He tried rubbing away the lack of vision. Two blurry figures stood on the other side of the room. One of them lightly kicked the body of Bukshee.

"A tragedy, this is. He had such potential in life. I know he would have cherished the opportunity to make things right. But in death, his body will serve Ecclesia much better than he ever did."

Arah saw that it was not the torchbearer who said this, but his much shorter and rounder companion. A companion who was not cloaked in black at all, but a glaring white with purple trim.

"We still have that one, sir," the torchbearer said. He pointed at Arah.

The two of them walked his way. The torchbearer held his flames close to Arah's face to check if he was awake and still sane. The dignitary stooped until he was level with Arah. Arah felt his body snap out of delirium instantly. Somehow, the distortion of time had caused him to nearly forget the sound of that voice, but when coupled with that sweaty, pinkish face, he remembered all that there was to remember.

"Hello, my child," Duman said serenely. The fresh gashes on his face and the flickering fire gave him a ghastly visage. That of one whose soul had long since expired.

"You may have thought your life to be over. But today, all things have aligned to give you a purpose far greater than you could have imagined. You have been chosen to fulfill a prophecy begot by Savyer himself."

- -

Days passed. Each of the six were wide awake and hungry, but silent. There was not much to say, and the blooming of a low, constant brr held their collective attention. By the time the first of them awoke - Moshe - it had already started, but its continuous growth was undeniable. Speckles of sharp frequencies popped up here and there; they didn't detract from its menace. The buzzing became so ubiquitous that no one heard the footsteps.

Lieutenant Zacchaeus swung the prison door open like change was coming. Everyone except for Abigail gave him their gaze. Behind him followed Matthias.

And another Kohen.

And another.

Until there was one standing in front of each of them.

Moshe stood up to face the Lieutenant from the other side of the bars. Right eyebrow cocked, he stared directly into Zacchaeus' eyes. There was nothing there.

Instantaneously, all of the guards swiftly unlocked and barged into the cells, approaching their assignments with cuffs of steel. Ambree was turned around and placed against the wall. Abigail gruffly flipped herself over from where she lay, but Matthias swung his baton across her back anyway. Amaru fought back and yelled obscenities, but her Kohen was a foot taller than the rest. Reenu backed up a few steps, but his submission didn't de-escalate the situation. The beggar lifted his hand up in hopes for help getting to his feet. The Kohen placed only one cuff on their respective prisoners before bringing them out to the hallway.

Moshe kept staring at Zacchaeus, passively allowing his restraints to be put in place. He knew there was no point in resistance. Zacchaeus mouthed reluctance, but it mattered no longer.

The haze of the outside buzzing had become clearly defined: the expectant, impatient cravings of a crowd.

Chapter 14: The Front

Leader, your anxiety is admirable
terror itself is in danger of full bloom
it's not enough to just pull at the weeds
Savyer, I wonder if I've failed you
all will be well in the Sanctums
let's see what the wolves decide

Zacchaeus looked at the seven who stood with prisoner hands before him. All bound and blindfolded together by chain and circumstance. The fallen leader led the bystander led the great deceiver led the self-abuser led the firm believer led the traveler led the blind follower. Their sequence was intentional: Moshe was in front, yes, but binding the beggar directly to him would slow down any thought of swift escape. After that, each person was separated from those they were close to. He hoped Leader (and Duman especially) would overlook the arrangement. He knew the three silent ones would. He assumed it to be a technicality - this was the more logical order, anyway - but he could no longer confidently claim to know either of their expectations. In any other context, Zacchaeus would have commended his men for successfully subduing and correctly organizing the prisoners, but his mind could not escape yesterday's *Symvoul*.

They turned the last corner of the tunnel, a final stretch into the light. He watched as four out of the seven tried to shield their eyes from the forgotten countenance of the sun. Their heavy, insufficient chains made the amenity an impossibility. The only ones who made no attempt were Moshe, who positioned his body to protect the eyes of the beggar, and, of course, Abigail, stubborn as all *KAMNOS*.

what was Duman thinking

Duman's voice had moved beyond the reverberant echoes within Zacchaeus' head and now boomed throughout the tunnel. He was telling of the dangerous types of people who hid within Ecclesia's accommodating walls. He was reading the *prophecy*. With each stanza, he took the time to elaborate on its poetry and his domineering interpretation. It was clear that he was doing his best to temper the nervous excitement in his voice, but the crowd was already consuming his diction with haste. Zacchaeus saw horror spread across the faces of the emaciated one from *KAMNOS* and Reenu as they learned who they were according to the scripture. Ambree and Amaru looked much more offended.

What could he do? What could he say? The wheels were well in motion, they had been since Shedim shredded Duman's face. Sympathy in scars. The crowd would only be satisfied with results from a justice that they were currently being convinced was necessary. They were at the edge of the tunnel now. If the crowd wasn't so fixated on Duman, they would have seen their prey entering the light of day. Zacchaeus had never concerned himself with power and its endless plays, but here he was, *the fucking Lieutenant*, and his concerns had been so easily tossed aside for those of the newcomer. It wasn't right, but what could he do? As they waited for the cue, Zacchaeus glanced at his men. Seven of them stood alongside the prisoners, excluding Matthias and himself. The ratio was one to one, but the dynamics certainly weren't even.

"Kohen, relent!" Zacchaeus shouted.

It was not the assigned protocol, but each of the Kohen followed their orders and stepped away from the prisoners. Zacchaeus walked up to Amaru and placed something in her palm.

"*Chorto*," he whispered as if she knew what it meant. "For whoever wants it."

Amaru was confused until she angled her eyes downward, barely able to peek underneath her blindfold. The dull green substance. She knew what the exchange meant for Zacchaeus, the inherent risk he took in allowing his men to witness their fraternization. If he couldn't prevent the pain that was coming for them, at least a small act of defiance could lessen it. Maybe that was worthwhile in and of itself.

Duman had finally arrived at his favorite line, and he made sure to savor the delivery.

"Ladies and gentlemen, have we got a show for you!"

The crowd erupted. It was their cue.

He let Matthias lead them out into the haphazard devices of the throng, knowing that his final efforts would not be enough to save them.

Duman ate it up. In his heart, he knew that the crowds cheered not for him...but they might as well have! It was he that successfully educated them on the pressing need for justice. It was he who reminded the city of her values and reinvigorated her commitment to them. It was he who now stood in the skybox overlooking The Kolosaio with Leader seated beside him. Shedim was slinking around in the sunken tunnels somewhere, completing whatever menial busywork was befitting of his character. Duman was the Head Stomio now. And why shouldn't he be? Who knew the people and what they wanted better than he did? Who was more devout to The Manual and Savyer than he? Why, not even Leader-...no. He didn't like that thought. He shouldn't have thought it. But who was the one that convinced Leader to move? Certainly not the three silent ones. Duman's eyes lit up when he saw Zacchaeus' broken protégé wave at him from the ground one hundred feet below him.

"And here they are! The criminals themselves!"

Inner and Outer were united in their jeers. Duman had turned the seven prisoners into a single enemy. He felt something pass through his chest briefly. He did not particularly know most of them, but Moshe...nothing burdened his heart more than wasted potential. But he had a judgment to pass. Matthias guided the group in a long amble towards the center. The jeers did not let up even as they arrived at their destination. Duman cleared his throat.

"Everyone, please, listen to me!" And they did. "By this point, you are all well acquainted with the crimes of these...criminals. You understand what needs to happen next, but that does not make it any easier to see. Prepare your hearts as best you can."

Many hung their heads in reluctant expectation. Somewhere in the middle of them all, Adah and her twin Adinah did so as well, though for differing reasons. Adah could not believe that the friends she once knew had become such brutes. Adinah believed it, but she still feared what they would have to do next.

"The Table," Duman continued, letting emotion seep in. "Our symbol of faith, hope, and love. Our greatest triumph. It is the place where many of us hold sacred conversations and bountiful jollifications, and many of us still will soon enough. *All* of us hold it high above all else in our hearts...all except the seven who stand before it now."

Matthias rapidly yanked each blindfold off and pushed the chain gang forward so that they all doubled over onto the waist-high structure that was before them. They all struggled to stand up as the thousands around them cried out in anguish.

"They stomp on The Table now," Duman cried out, "but it was their subversive actions beforehand that had done so already. Their feet dirty her beautiful wood now, but it was their corrupted hearts that have made her unholy."

Anguish returned to jeers, but Duman held both arms high above his head to regain their attention. They would need to hear his final condemnation.

"Do not despair, fellow followers. This sorrow lasts for but a moment. As quickly as they have soiled The Table, so too will she be made holy once more...very soon. But first...we must get rid of this present darkness. Wolves for wolves!!!"

While they were standing themselves up, Moshe observed that Matthias had sped away as quickly as he could back to the two-person wide opening in The Kolosaio's wall. He saw Zacchaeus shoot him a final look of penitence as he momentarily closed the stone door on them. It was the only opening he could find, and now it was sealed, with horizontal bars at eye-level so one could look through if need be. It didn't take much for Moshe to discern how helpless they were. The lowest tier of the crowd was still twenty feet above them. They stood atop the chair-less Table amidst a barren scene, completely at the whim of those not in chains, though it was not until Duman uttered his final statement that he was met with those whims. The stone was re-opening, snarls escaping from behind its hidden boundaries. The stone was re-closing, but escape was now the last thing on their minds.

Seven wolves rushed towards them with vicious roars and famished stomachs.

"No..."
"What the-"
"Shit."
"Wow..."
"Fuck me. Fuck us."
"Oh, inconsistent Duman, doesn't this make us sheep?"
Moshe looked to his right, his eyes made incredulous by the beggar's statement. The beggar responded with a slight wink sent his way.
a wink? does he not see what we're all seeing?
Then the wolves were at their feet.
Two had sprinted ahead of the others, fixating themselves on Reenu

and Arah since they were the closest prey. They bumped forcefully against The Table, their heads ramming into its skirt. The Table didn't budge, but the sudden shock of flashing teeth knocked Reenu back, bringing Arah down to his knees with him. Reenu's head banged against the other side of The Table and dangled over its edge.

"Shit, man, here!"

Arah extended his clamped hands towards Reenu's arm in order to pick him up, but the movement brought Amaru down towards him. She recognized his intentions and was able to adjust her center of gravity before the other dominoes fell into place. One of the wolves saw Reenu go down and rushed under The Table in order to get to him. Arah pulled with enough torque to slide Reenu just out of reach of the wolf's jaws. Then the other five rammed themselves against The Table.

The entire line of prisoners shook this way and that from the impact. They were able to stand each other upright eventually, but panic had already claimed their minds.

Reenu started hyperventilating; Arah was holding his hands and shouting vaguely reassuring sentiments, but he was shouting them so that his failing body and nerves could also believe the words. Amaru's hands were dripping, and the inability to pace only compounded the stress building within her. Ambree and Abigail were equally frozen. The beggar could no longer stand, so he sat himself down and lifted his arms above his head so as to not burden the chain that bound them. Moshe gulped and cleared his throat. He stuck his head out so everyone could see him.

"Everyone, we need to calm down! These animals will only be more excited by-"

At that moment, one of the wolves backed itself up and leapt particularly high. High enough to get its forelegs onto The Table. Ambree shrieked as it scratched up Moshe's shins.

"Fuck!" he yelled out as he kicked the wolf in the face several times before it hopped back down. The beast and its companions were undeterred, though.

"Let's huddle together!"

Moshe helped the beggar move inwards towards everyone else. Their bodies met in the center, the safest place possible for the time being. Blood trailed from Moshe's legs and stained the dark grey wood he stood on.

"One of them is wounded," Duman boomed from on high, "scratched by the instinctual attack of a wolf, *but it is precisely he who scratched and attacked me!*"

Gasps!

"Look on my face and see this truth!"

Most of the crowd turned to see Duman, but many remained stuck in the trance of upcoming bloodshed at The Kolosaio's core.

Moshe forgot the pain in his legs momentarily.

"Are you fucking kidding me, Duman? You liar! What happened to-"

But Moshe could only be heard by those in chains, as the roars of the crowd and the wolves were deafening.

"Fuck it," Moshe lowered his voice. He stuck his head forward again. "Listen, I know we're not all friends, but we'll never get the chance to be if we don't figure something out now! If anyone has any ideas, don't hold back!"

They jumped into action. Reenu and Arah put their hands together before yanking them back as hard as they safely could. Arah had to stop after a couple attempts - he hadn't the energy or muscle to do much at a single time. Amaru smushed the sweat from her hands all over her manacles. Ambree put hers around the back of her neck and started pulling, and the beggar stood as best he could so she could try it. All their attempts bore no fruit.

Moshe kept an eye on the wolves. None had yet been able to pounce back onto The Table, though not for lack of trying. They were as tenacious and full of stamina as they were fifteen minutes ago. But when one of them was able to get paw on tabletop, another's bum-rush would knock it off. They stumbled over each other more often than not. In that sense, they were their own worst enemy, their primary obstacle keeping them from a feast.

Suddenly, Moshe felt weight shift downwards towards his right. He turned and saw that Abigail had sat down. Indifference hadn't left her eyes for a few nights, but he would have expected such danger to do something to her. But now, her apathy could be the death of them, so he wouldn't allow it to stand any longer.

"Abigail! Get up!"

She stared straight ahead.

"Abigail, you've got to fucking get up! You're weighing us down!"

Still nothing. Unmoved. On either side of her, Ambree and the beggar were brought to their knees. Moshe took a step towards fixing the problem...

"Aaaahhooooohh!!!"

A wolf leapt up and sunk its canines into Abigail's bent knee. The shock stirred a cry out of her, but the pain prevented her from action. Ambree took another knee and grabbed the wolf's mouth. She tried lifting the jaws apart, but the animal stared straight ahead, unmoved. Ambree felt awful about what she would have to do, so she gave Abigail a warning.

"I'm sorry Abigail, this is going-"

"Just fucking do it!"

Ambree ripped the wolf loose and tossed it off The Table. The beast took with it muscle, sinew, and flesh, and left the inside of Abigail's knee white with exposure. Ambree grimaced at what she saw, but what was even more horrifying was Abigail's face. No scream emitted from it, just a mouth agape, a throbbing vein threatening to pop underneath her red curls, and the smallest, most frightened pupils.

"Savyer above," Arah absently said and trembled. Reenu tried not to vomit.

Amaru saw someone she once called lover, someone she once aspired to be, currently as vulnerable and weak as she had ever seen...and remembered what she had in her hands.

"*Chorto*," she muttered to herself. Hastily, she stepped past Ambree. "Abigail, take this."

But when she opened up her hands, she forgot how moist they had become. The *chorto* slipped out of her grasp, hit The Table, and bounced into the middle of the pack.

"No..." Amaru said in disbelief. "No, I...Abigail, I'm so sorry."

Moshe stared at the seven wolves before them. They reddened their faces with the remains of Abigail's knee, but it wouldn't be long before they sought seconds. Moshe raised his fists to his chest and his voice to the heavens.

"HOW?! HOW IS THIS JUSTICE?! HOW CAN YOU PEOPLE READ THE MANUAL AND WATCH THIS SUFFERING WITH THE SAME GLEEFUL EYES?!"

The crowd's roar did not let up, but Duman could see Moshe's gesturing and decided to be safe rather than sorry.

"Ehmhm, blood is starting to be spilled, but it could never match the blood spilled to build The Table and all of Ecclesia! Verily?!"

"VERILY!"

"Verily?!"

"VERILY!!"

"Verily?!"

"VERILY!!!"

"LISTEN TO ME, WE-"

"Verily?!"

"VERILY!!!"

"DAMMIT, LISTEN TO-"

Moshe's voice gave way. His throat was coarse with dehydration and overuse. But yelling was all that he could do. He knew each passing minute was a minute less of chances. But nothing they could physically do would save them: he would have to convince the Ecclesians to let them go. So he would keep yelling. He would yell until one of his many adversaries bit out his neck.

"Moshe!"

Moshe looked down and saw the surprising source of the call: Abigail. She looked faint and pale, but Ambree had ripped off the top half of her robe and wrapped it around her knee to stanch the bleeding. She had just enough might to speak and turn things around.

"There's a microphone under The Table."

Moshe raised an eyebrow. "What's a micro-"

"It doesn't fucking matter!" Abigail interjected, impatient even in her failing state. "But it will make you loud enough to hear. I stuck it there the night of The Last Call."

Moshe and most everyone else had more questions, but they would only get to them once it was safe to do so.

"Where is it?" Amaru asked.

"A quarter of the way down. Over on Reenu's side," Abigail said, pointing.

Everyone faced that direction and saw the scared face of the only one in a position to save them. They could try to swap positions, but that would put someone too close to the wolves. Reenu winced so hard his eyes started twitching. Moshe saw the face of someone he once knew so well. Someone so good and so loyal, he realized then that Reenu had the strongest character of them all. He only lacked one thing, something that Moshe would finally offer to him: courage.

"Reenu."

Reenu looked all the way down at Moshe.

"You're the best *scraper* I know!"

Reenu held the gaze for a couple of seconds because he knew he would treasure the moment for the rest of his life. Then he smiled and beckoned them to come his direction.

"Let's go!"

The group made their way down.

"The criminals have decided to make a move," Duman said for all to hear, but he couldn't hide the puzzlement in his voice. "I'm not sure why...but of course, I could never grasp the absolute *depravity* lurking within their minds! Regardless, they shall not escape justice! Verily?!"

"VERILY!!!"

Reenu stood at the spot Abigail mentioned. He told Arah what he would need him to do. Arah's knees wobbled in anticipation, but he nodded. The rest of the group, aside from the beggar and Abigail, took the risk of becoming bait. They held themselves threateningly close to the edge of The Table, jumping back and forth in order to keep the wolves teasingly interested. But it worked.

With his head poking over and under the edge, Reenu saw the mic. He wouldn't be able to reach it with his hands, but he had always felt that he was much more capable with his feet anyway. He looked back at Arah.

"Alright, Arah, you got me?"

Arah nodded and tightened his grip on their shared chain with his meatless fingers.

Reenu swung out and felt the microphone with his feet, but was unable to grasp it. The motion took Arah forward a step, but he held fast.

"Shit," Reenu said as he swung back up.

"What, are you not able to get it?" Arah asked through panting.

"I think I can but-"

"Then just do it, man! I can't hold you up forever!" Arah proclaimed with a somewhat encouraging pat on the shoulder.

A few feet down, Ambree narrowly dodged a bite. She saw that Abigail had been inching a little too far forward, so she pushed her back to relative safety.

Reenu swung again. This time, he was able to grasp the microphone properly, but as he was swinging back, he felt his body get lower to the ground. Arah had slipped and now dangled one leg next to him. A wolf jumped up and landed in his lap, scratching various parts of his face and chest. He wrestled with its forelegs, but his compromised pose left him without any room to use his weight. Jaws opened wide across his face.

Amaru punched the wolf in the nose and lifted both Arah and Reenu back onto The Table.

Arah's panting intensified. "Thanks..."

"Reenu, pass it over," Amaru replied.

On its way to Moshe, Abigail flipped a switch on the microphone. When Moshe held the cylinder in his hands, he looked confused.

"How do I make it work?" he asked.

"Just speak into it."

Far out of the range of the crowd's audibility, Duman expressed his concerns to Saios.

"Leader, we should send a message to Zacchaeus to increase security. If they make a run for it..."

"Duman, you worrywart, I appreciate your concern, but be not afraid," Saios reassured him. "The only way they could escape is if someone let them. But I will send a message to the Lieutenant if need be. Either way, keep doing what you're doing; the crowd loves you."

Leader was right. Duman beamed. The three silent ones remained as they were, sitting just behind Leader, not even in view of the crowd below.

"The prisoners have stopped their march, perhaps they have realized its futility. Justice is nearly upon them! Verily?!"

"VERI-"

"Hello- well, fuck! It works!"

The crowd went silent when they heard the unexpected boom seemingly come from all around them. Duman and Leader looked down in worried awe. Even the wolves were startled into a collective whimper and momentary silence. Moshe breathed deeply. In and out. Everyone heard it.

"Listen to me."

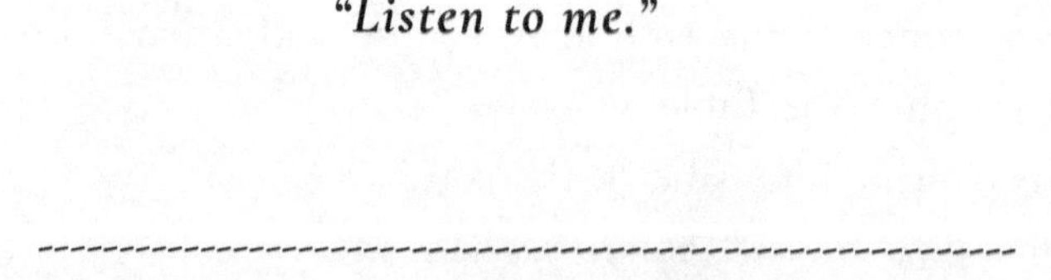

Lipos had considered not attending what everyone was calling "The Krisi at The Kolosaio." The hype was truly injecting a vital dose of excitement into Outer Sanctum, but he was feeling lethargic. He had been feeling that way for most of his life, but it was destructively amplified when the one he considered his only friend decided to leave him. He didn't really understand why, but he knew it was his fault. He tried to make friends with some new arrivals, but even though there was kindness in their voices, he could tell by how their bodies moved that he was off-putting to them. Maybe he shouldn't have asked for the remains of their *casu* so often. But since then, he actually hadn't eaten. It had been at least ten days; he conserved energy by not moving at all. He was woken earlier than usual the morning of The Krisi, so he determined to fall back asleep once the marching had passed. But someone stopped at his tent. They encouraged him to come along. A stranger. His stomach protested, but then he realized that this was an Inner Sanctum event - maybe *psomi* was on the menu! He didn't know what to expect; no one knew anything outside of it being some kind of purification event. But he certainly couldn't have known that what he heard and saw that day would give him what he needed: freedom.

"What could I say to convince you we deserve freedom?"

Moshe pondered this aloud with a confidence he hadn't felt since pre-Ecclesian times. He knew exactly what he would say.

"I could try to convince you that Leader Saios and Duman are wrong. My crime? I only asked Leader a logistical question. Nowhere in The Manual does it say that is outlawed. But why would you believe my word over theirs, right? They say I was threateningly violent in my disrespect. Maybe they're right."

Duman turned to Saios. He always had something to say, but now he was nearly whimpering, mouth wide and empty. Sweat permeated his body like sheepskin, but Saios was as cool as he could be. He knew what was happening had to come to pass. If they tried to shut Moshe down now, the people would only grow more suspicious. Duman couldn't tell, but Saios was actually gritting his teeth.

"But what about everyone else here beside me? I could go over each of their individual 'crimes' and, even though some of what they have done is worse than what others have done, I could logically and faithfully establish why some other form of judgment might be more suitable."

Abigail mustered up a laugh. She knew passive-aggressiveness when she heard it. Fuck him. Ambree had been so invested in Moshe's words that she had forgotten that she was soothing Abigail by rubbing her back, but it was at this time that the wolves themselves stopped being invested in Moshe's words. They resumed their attempts at consumption. Everyone took a step back and readied themselves for when one or many would break through. Moshe paused when he saw this, but the beggar squeezed his hand and urged him to proceed.

"But this isn't about justice, is it? You have gathered together not for the sake of righting wrongs, but for one purpose: unity. To be united for or against something is more powerful than being right about it. And you're not the only ones here that are united. Let me assuage your doubts and fears, there is indeed something that each of my friends standing above these wolves has in common. We are all different."

Even though he couldn't see her, from where she sat, Fila felt that she had never seen Moshe so clearly. He wasn't the sensitive, noble man she once assumed him to be, he was an attention whore! He was loving this spotlight! It didn't matter that he had embarrassed her in a deep, public way; soon enough, everyone would be able to see through this dignified guise he was putting on. But she was curious as to where he was going. She kept her arms crossed and waited.

"I came to Ecclesia because I believed in hope. I had to. And I brought the two most important people in the world with me so that we could have that hope met. But...somewhere along the way, it became about something else. My desire to keep them safe devolved into a desire to keep myself socially sound. I betrayed them, and I have to live with that. If there's any debt I owe today, it's that. I have no excuses, but maybe that's just what happens here. Ecclesia is clearly a system made from love and peace, but in order to keep it safe, sometimes we have to betray those very values."

Reenu held back tears. He had already mentally accepted Moshe's repentance, but hearing him admit his transgressions to everyone in the city...well, now his body believed him. He could tell by the quiver in her lip that Amaru did, too.

"Look at The Table. It is long and wide - there is much room for many people, but soon, it will be full. And then what? And what are we filling it with? Who are we filling it with? Look at the ends. The Table has corners, edges. But when we round them off, there's less room for all of us. This is what I learned when I became a citizen of Inner Sanctum, but I know you already know this to be true. You can follow all that The Manual commands, but this isn't about The Manual. You all know it well; it is not your belief that should be questioned but the way in which we handle such belief. You can give yourself away to friend and enemy alike, but if you aren't 'in,' you aren't in, and this is where you end up. What can I say to

convince you we deserve freedom? It's not about that. What can I say to convince you that we ALL deserve freedom?"

Shedim walked briskly, excitedly through the tunnel, for he carried with his gait orders from Leader. Duman had to stay where he was as the face and the voice for the public, which meant it was up to him to relay instructions to Zacchaeus. It was truly an honor. Or at least, that would be the story he told anyone who asked him about it later. The reality was that this was his chance to right some wrongs, and he had to take it, orders or not. Of course, he would never tell anyone on the *Symvoul* that he knew about the microphone under The Table. He had thought about it, but this was working in his favor better than he could have expected. One day, he would reclaim his position from Duman. That annoyingly joyful little man seemed as clean as they come, but *no one* was as crafty as Shedim. He would find the dirt he needed soon.

Eight Kohen instinctively stood in a defensive line behind Zacchaeus until they saw who it was that approached. Good. News of his assault had not spread far. Zacchaeus was observing The Krisi from the ground level door. Shedim found it odd that the Lieutenant had not returned to the Skybox with the rest of the *Symvoul* and that he was incessantly rubbing his left leg, but there was no time to thoughtfully evaluate such behavior. Shedim strode until he was alongside Zacchaeus.

"Lieutenant, I hope these men with you are some of your bravest."

Zacchaeus kept his eyes fixed on the potentially grisly scene before him. He was annoyed by how Shedim handled himself the night prior, and he was annoyed to see him now. He knew the ex-Head Stomio hated it when people wouldn't look him in the eyes after he addressed them, so he intentionally kept his face forward.

"They're the only ones I'd trust to handle wolves. So what do you think?"

Shedim shook the irksomeness aside. "Good. Because you'll need to send some of them out there."

Zacchaeus relaxed the tightened face muscles he was using to squint.

"What in the world are you thinking, man?"

"This is a direct order from Leader," Shedim obstinately affirmed. "This vile speech is taking too long. He's getting...a little restless. Send someone in to assist the wolves with getting atop The Table."

Zacchaeus shook his head but kept his voice low. He didn't need his men to hear this.

"That's far too dangerous. These Kohen are brave, but even *they* couldn't complete such a task unscathed."

"Then they shall be scathed."

Shedim was not going to return to Leader with the news that he couldn't get the self-appointed job done. But Zacchaeus didn't verbally respond. He only gave his analog a disgusted look and returned his gaze to The Table.

"Leader told me you would resist."

Shedim let the thought and its implications marinate with silence. Zacchaeus slowly looked back at Shedim. He didn't know if he believed him, but the very suggestion of perceived insubordination meant he had to proceed with caution. If anything, Shedim's admission meant that he had an inkling as to how Zacchaeus was feeling. He was listening now.

"If you don't want them to get too close, have them stand from afar and launch their batons at the prisoners. I'm sure they can be precise."

Zacchaeus cursed himself. That slithery tongue had slipped itself into a solution. If he resisted now, his loyalty would be in question. But Zacchaeus was still not ready to commit. He needed more time.

"Don't you know how this will look to the people? One of our men actively attacking the prisoners? This only works if they understand that this punishment is inevitable, not forced."

that ought to do it

Shedim slowly raised his hands to his hips and cocked his head.

"These are Leader's orders. You understand what it means if you refuse them?"

That question was all that he needed. Zacchaeus took a step towards Shedim and put himself within an inch of his face. He pressed a finger into his rival's chest.

"I will *not* sacrifice my men for this. I followed the plan, we all did. They shouldn't have to suffer and die because it isn't working out. It will be what it will be."

Shedim leered at Zacchaeus. He held out their near embrace and anticipated fear replacing defiance in the Lieutenant's eyes.

It didn't happen.

Shedim took a couple steps back and turned around.

But.

No.

He was *not* going to return to Leader with the news that he couldn't get the self-appointed job done.

With a swift, hushed about-face, Shedim leapt at Zacchaeus.

"Aaaahhhh-"

THWACK!

He was halted by a fist to the nose.

Shedim crumpled to the ground and writhed in muted pain.

Zacchaeus breathed in and out rapidly as his adrenaline naturally slowed itself. He looked down at Shedim and then up at his Kohen. They had readied their batons, but now they looked at their leader with wariness. They replaced their batons at their sides, but Matthias kept his hand on his. Zacchaeus wondered what they thought, but he did not dare ask. Instead, he just nodded and fixed his eyes back on The Table.

"Oh look, Shedim. Moshe just finished his plea. Nothing to worry about any longer."

The silence grew uncomfortably long. The wolves still nipped at their feet, but the pangs of hunger outlasted the hunger itself. The growls and barks had ceased. Up above, Duman's heart inflamed as he wondered if Zacchaeus would open the door. Was a rebuttal expected of him? Below, the crowd wondered what would happen next. What could? At the bottom, Moshe and his friends started to believe that escape was near. Who would provide it?

"Guys, look," Ambree said in a slightly hushed tone so that the microphone wouldn't pick it up. "The wolves are tiring. Maybe we should hightail it out of here while we have the chance."

"Ambree, we'll only get out if someone lets us out," Arah reminded her. "But after that...I've got a good feeling."

Arah cracked a grin and a nod at Moshe. Moshe realized he had not looked at "the traveler" before. He was curious how long he had been in a cell. Aside from the clearly fallen-out remains of hair and the black-blood lips, he could tell the man was once handsome. They would be friends soon enough.

"And it looks like someone's gotten up to speak," Reenu said with a pointed finger.

They all turned to see.

The young woman seemed kind enough from where they stood. It was hard to make out the details, but her shoulder-length blonde hair was endearing. Yet she shuddered as she stood. The beggar thought it might have been the result of strong emotion. Moshe knew that to be the case, but he did not know which way her feelings now fell.

With all of her strength, Fila let Ecclesia know that Moshe was a

"LIAR!!!"

The scream was louder than Duman, louder than the crowd, louder than Moshe even. It took so much out of Fila's body that she collapsed back into her seat and was washed away by hysterical tears. Recovering from the startle of the outburst, Duman found himself very pleased. All of Inner Sanctum knew and loved Fila - their sympathy was already hers - and to all the Outer Sanctum degenerates, well, all they saw was a poor, traumatized blonde. Smiling, he cleared his throat and prepared to capitalize on the momentum...

But the crowd had already swallowed it.

The Kolosaio re-erupted all at once, as if picking up from right where they stopped. The harsh noise shook the wolves out of their stupor and reignited the fire in their bellies. Their paws left deeper marks on The Table, and they almost collectively realized that digging in would chip away at the protection of their prey. Pieces of The Table started to go flying, and the chain gang took a couple steps backwards. Recalibrating his mind and analyzing the situation, Duman abandoned all of his typical eloquence and linguistic frills for a massive chant and a raised fist.

"LIAR!"

"LIAR!!"

"LIAR!!!"

Pressure came from every angle; the prisoners were sure to implode. The microphone's whine grew to a piercing volume. Abigail leapt up from where she sat, yanked it out of Moshe's hands, and turned it off.

"Of all the fucking things right now, I don't want a fucking microphone to be what kills us by popping our brains out!"

Abigail yelled loud enough for Moshe to hear, but he was too dazed by the ringing to notice. He looked around, seemingly aimlessly. He mouthed a question to himself, causing the beggar to perk up both eyebrows.

Amaru despaired. She had been in countless lethal situations with Moshe and Reenu before, but none had ever felt so suffocatingly futile. But as those memories sifted through her mind, she knew she had to do what she had been unwilling to. She let go of her spite. She let go because she remembered a time when Moshe always provided them the best way to go.

"Moshe! What do we do?!"

But he wasn't listening. He was looking around.

A flare of familiar irritation flashed through Amaru's insides.

"Dammit, Moshe, don't ignore me now! We *need* you!"

But Moshe continued looking, and the beggar looked with him. Up into the crowd. After the ringing subsided, Moshe found that the loudness of the crowd was only the result of the silence prior. In reality, they weren't more deafening than they were before his plea. In fact, they were less. Moshe and the beggar observed that a good portion of the crowd remained silent, pensive. Not most, but enough. But the volume of those around them would always drown out their diversity. They needed a final push.

"What can I say?..." Moshe's question to himself trailed off.

"They've heard enough words."

Moshe looked down at the answerer beside him. In the beggar's eyes was the kind of peace that Moshe had been searching for ever since he set off for Ecclesia.

"It's time to make our bed. I'll go first," the old man said, each word like a sigh of relief. "Then you'll hold them off."

Moshe gulped and nodded. He was afraid, but it wasn't the fear he had been feeling. Not the kind that locks one up, but the kind that tells the truth. Moshe realized Amaru was yelling at him.

"-than a foot left! Moshe, we've-"

Moshe saw that the wolves had chewed nearly a third into The Table. Such a shame that it would need to get rebuilt.

"My friends and those who could have been, here's what's going to happen."

Everyone listened.

"We are going to lower the beggar to the wolves."

Bewilderment spread across the faces of the uninformed five. Ambree in particular was disgusted.

"Shut the fuck up, Moshe! You're telling me that we're just going to let the most vulnerable-"

"After the wolves...gnaw through him, you five will still be chained, but I will be free. I'm going to run in the opposite direction and you are going to run for the door."

Amaru was appalled. This was the kind of suggestion she would have never expected to hear from her old leader. She held back a fluttering lip.

"Moshe...the door is sealed. We won't make it out, regardless. Let's just take them all on together."

Moshe felt his eyes cloud. He shook his head.

"Amaru, you learned so much from me. I should have lowered myself and learned more from you. It's our best chance. And even if none of us make it, it's what *they* need to see. If we all fight and all miraculously survive, the crowd will only be more enraged. There will be no hope for change."

Moshe pointed at the undecided above them. They all began to understand, but Abigail wasn't having it.

"Moshe, look at this!" He looked at her wrapped knee. The robe around it was soggy with blood. "They don't deserve to see!"

Moshe felt her pain, but he couldn't help but stifle a somber laugh.

"Abigail...weren't you listening? We *all* deserve to see."

Abigail sat with the thought. No one wanted to agree to what they would have to do, but there was no more dissonance. Ambree helped Abigail up, and she and Moshe held the beggar on either side.

"Beggar," Moshe said, almost out of obligation. "Peace be with you."

The language he had only recently said with conviction now felt a little silly leaving his lips. But the beggar loved it. He let out his last wheezing laugh.

"And also with you, son. Thank you for helping me mean something."

Moshe smiled, glad that the beggar was the most accepting of this path. Then he remembered something.

"Abigail, turn the microphone on. They need to hear it, too."

The chants of "LIAR" died down. Fila never even participated in them after her initial cry. Although the moment was the emotional release she craved, she now felt empty. Nothing was resolved. Duman, on the other hand, had spirits renewed. Admittedly, he wished it to be done with already so he could get back to more personal matters, but it was his job to keep the flame going. He returned to his combative commentary.

"These immoral fiends would much rather The Table be carved up by wolves than to accept their punishment with digni- what's this? They've lifted up one of their own...the...uh, the beggar...and-"

The microphone's screech shut Duman up. The sound of starving wolves filled The Kolosaio. Then it was the sound of teeth on flesh. Then a woman's wail. Then the crunch of bone. All mixed with the horrified exclamations of a crowd. Duman knew he had to keep going, but his stomach disagreed. He vomited right next to Leader's chair, but Saios barely even noticed. He gasped along with the crowd. The three silent ones disappeared.

As soon as he could, Moshe pulled his freed portion of the chain away.

"Abigail, toss me the microphone."

Abigail did so. Her and the other four now stood further from Moshe than they had been since being in cells. He looked each of them in the face. Reenu couldn't verbalize anything, but his stream of tears said plenty. Arah looked dutiful. Amaru mouthed a simple phrase, one of their shared favorites, and Moshe nearly changed his mind from that alone. But he saw the solemn gratitude on Ambree's face. And the genuine determination on Abigail's. And he was resolute. So since he wasn't graced a private moment with his lifelong friends or a lasting conversation with any of the others, he would have to settle for something that they all needed to hear.

"Goodbye...run!"

One giant leap off The Table and Moshe found himself in the middle of the wolves. Five of them immediately recognized the presence of an easy snack, but the other two were still feasting on the remains of their first victim. As the five enclosed upon Moshe, he swung his confined hands and brought his chain down hard across the backs of the other two. The one closest to him managed to tear open his left calf and scratch up his torso. But now he had their attention.

Moshe aimed for the one farthest from The Table and barreled right through it. With a roar, he lowered his shoulder into its jaw and felt teeth break from the impact. He stumbled over its body, recovered, and ran.

All seven wolves chased after him. The crowd heard an equal mixture of their barks and Moshe's grunts. Some speculated where he was headed, but Moshe knew there was nowhere to go. It was all just buying time.

"Let's go!" Abigail exclaimed, shaking the group out of their unified disbelief.

They all hopped off The Table one by one. Ambree and Amaru steadied Abigail in between them, so Arah and Reenu made sure to amble at a pace that they could keep up with. But it was only a few seconds before Reenu stopped them.

"Wait," he muttered, holding up a hand. "The chains are too noisy, might alert the wolves. Hold them close."

Everyone did so. Amaru was amazed that Reenu gave the command without a tremor in his tone, even as tears still passively fell down. It didn't surprise her that he noticed the chain noise, though. He was the best *scraper*, after all.

They quickly but cautiously headed for the sealed door.

Somehow, Moshe found himself at the wall opposite the door. He assumed it was adrenaline that brought him there safely, but he realized running could only last so long. He could better serve his friends and prolong their chances by utilizing the remainder of his energy to fight. He turned around to face the wolves.

The first one leapt at his face, but he held up the metal between his wrists and pushed it away in a dazed state. The second was not far behind, and it tried the same thing. This time, its teeth got entangled in Moshe's metal, and he used the momentum to lift the wolf over his head and toss it behind him. A whimper accompanied the bulk of its body hitting the still wall. The third one went low, but Moshe leapt over and past it. His motion carried him into pinning the fourth one down onto the ground and choking it. He swung his legs out in front of him and brought his heel down onto the fifth one's skull, cracking it in the process. He used his other leg to jab at the sixth and seventh, keeping them away until he felt life leave the one he had pinned.

Moshe scrambled up into a warrior's pose. Blood still pulsed out of his shins and calf, but the rest of it did not belong to him. He felt thrill course through his veins.

But then the second one bit his ankle.

Reenu's guidance brought the prisoners within a hundred feet of the door. He appreciated making it this far, but he had no idea what they could do next.

"We're almost there!" Arah proclaimed.

"Then what?" Abigail sourly countered. "We just gonna bang on the door and ask to come in?"

Amaru felt the contagiousness of Abigail's discouragement until she saw what was peeking at them from the door. Eyes. She couldn't be sure, but judging from their faint shade of green, she had a feeling she knew who they belonged to.

Zacchaeus saw the prisoners headed his way and felt a confused lump of dread within his throat. He wasn't stunned that they had made it. He saw it all. He watched the heart-rending but necessary sacrifices.

No, he was stunned by the elation he felt when he saw them. He placed a hand on the door's grip.

He felt another hand grip his.

Shedim stared him in the eyes.

"What are you doing?" He asked without hiding the threat in his voice.

Zacchaeus felt his dread dissolve into panic, but then he noticed the bruising that was forming around Shedim's eyes. It was then he resolved that he would finally quit backing down.

"Letting them in." Shedim intensified his grip, but he left his hand where it was.

"Now why the *fuck* would you do that?"

Before Shedim knew it, Zacchaeus swung his hand off the door's grip and flailed it outwards, leaving Shedim exposed. Zacchaeus grabbed his ridiculous shoulder pads and pulled down so that his knee pummeled Shedim's stomach several times. Then he ripped the shoulder pads off and threw Shedim away, causing him to stumble backwards until he crashed on the floor.

"Slither off, old pal. The front's over," Zacchaeus said as he swung the door open.

The prisoners didn't even have to slow their stride.

They stood before Zacchaeus, regaining their breath and realigning their beliefs. Amaru tried to express her gratitude, but she was speechless.

"If helping you out is all it takes to shut you up, I would have never put you in a cell," Zacchaeus casually said.

Amaru smiled.

"Here," he continued. "The keys to freedom."

The prisoners started unlocking their shackles and rubbing their irritated wrists, but it wasn't long before they each had a baton in their face.

"Kohen, what is this?" Zacchaeus asked them.

"The Head Stomio ordered us to send them back out there, sir," said one of them.

Zacchaeus looked past the Kohen, but Shedim was nowhere to be seen. Zacchaeus sighed. He knew where he was headed.

"Stand down, men," Zacchaeus dismissed.

"But, sir, the-"

"*He* is no longer the Head Stomio, but *I* am still your Lieutenant. For now, at least. If you have a complaint with me...take it to Duman."

The Kohen hesitated but obeyed.

A blaring shout of pain filled The Kolosaio. Everyone in the tunnel looked past the door to see its source. From their perspective, they couldn't make out the details, but they knew what was happening.

The ankle-biter was the beginning of Moshe's end. He fell to one knee and hot dust infiltrated and burned his open shin. Wolves know a vulnerable foe when they see one. The first one sunk its teeth deep into his shoulder. He shook it off and elbowed the ankle-biter until it let go, but the three in front of him pounced. Moshe fell onto his back. A flurry of bites and scratches slowly turned Moshe unrecognizable. He kept punching and tried rolling away repeatedly, but each attempt was dismantled by another wound. They chewed through his arms, but not his shackles, leaving them dangling by his side. At one point, Moshe was able to rise above it all. He stood up amongst a heap of his own gore and tightened his muscles as he let out a yell. But one of the wolves leapt and bit out his neck, opening up a stream of blood and bringing Moshe down for the last time.

All were calcified. The prisoners were frozen. Zacchaeus sympathized. He hated that Moshe's friends had to see such a violent demise, but they couldn't grieve just yet.

"Matthias, come here."

Matthias dutifully approached with a hand on his baton.

"You are all well-acquainted with one of my finest new Kohen," Zacchaeus told the group. "He will guide you out and get you through the gates. Shedim will be back soon, so best leave now. Go on."

Matthias took his hand off the baton. He grumbled as he saw Abigail smirk at him. Finally, she knew physical pain like he did, but that didn't lessen the animosity he felt towards her. He would follow this order, but he would make sure that it was his last. They all thanked Zacchaeus, but as always, Amaru wanted more.

"Why are you helping us?"

Zacchaeus shook his head and looked away.

"I should have helped you a long time ago. I knew when I met you that you three would change things. Wisdom, remember?"

Reenu allowed himself a slight smile at the memory.

"But I was scared. Change is scary. I fought against it this whole time, but...Moshe did it. He got on my nerves some...so of course he was the one who helped me see the light."

Amaru swallowed her emotion. After all they had been through, it was over. But it was also just beginning. They would soon greet the desert like an old, annoying friend. Where would they go? Who else was waiting for them? She had no other leads. Nothing else was out there. The only difference the past three months made was now they knew. They knew Ecclesia was too good to be true for them, and they were all the more cynical for it. And now, they lost a friend. She knew that Moshe didn't see it that way, that he died believing he was paying back a debt. But knowing what was ahead of them, Amaru wondered

did he pay too much

As she opened her mouth to say her last goodbye, Zacchaeus turned his head back towards The Kolosaio. She did the same.

What she saw made her see that it had all been worthwhile.

The crowd saw and heard it all. Inner Sanctum. Outer Sanctum. None could peel themselves away from the sanguinary carnage. For some, it was petrifying; others took morbid delight. After the last bit of flesh was consumed, stillness reigned. The wolves quickly fell asleep, content. But they were just as quickly awoken by shouts of fervor. No single individual started the movement - dozens of Ecclesians made their way down from their seats and onto the ground level all across The Kolosaio simultaneously. Many fell badly, breaking bones at the bottom. Thirty men, women, and children overtook the wolves, invigorated by the chance of a lifetime to succeed against them. Even more took to The Table, chewed and worn as it had become, and overturned it. They ran madly for the door. All of the babel distorted reality, but after the masses escaped, it became clear that the vast majority of citizens still sat where they were. Awaiting further instruction. Receiving it in the form of fire. Many escapees headed for the gates, but some stopped by Inner Sanctum homes to loot, destroy, and utilize whatever would help them burn it all down. Not all were from the other side of The Wall; some true Ecclesians joined in as well, tired of their concrete lives. The Kohen stood their ground for as long as they could, but those who didn't get out of the way in time were promptly trampled. The Citadel was broken into out of curiosity more than anything else. Branches were snapped off of The Tree of Origin to be later fashioned into weapons. No one fucked with The Troei. People stopped by their tents for what little possessions they had, but they were just as eager to incinerate those wretched abodes as well. Then there were the entrance gates. One particularly emboldened ex-Ecclesian pushed his way past everyone. He had always wanted to pull the lever. He did so with such vigor that it broke off.

The gates of pearl opened, and they would not close again.

Coda: The Second Birth

...

When the sun hit her eyes, Amaru awoke.

...fuck...it's today...fuck...

It was days like this that she appreciated the narrow cutout in the wooden roof above them. She didn't exactly appreciate how involuntary it was to wake with the dawn, but being late today would have been even worse. Now she had time to clear her head and focus her thoughts. The cabin's emptiness informed her that Abigail was already out and about. If she could help it, Abigail avoided all help getting around, but that usually meant getting up before anyone else. Amaru figured she was likely seeing Ambree one last time. That helped, too.

After pushing the wolfskin covers aside, Amaru rambled on over to the far corner of their room. She proceeded through a circuit of push-ups, sit-ups, and rock lifts. The rock felt heavier than usual. As she lifted it above her head one last time, a pastiche of nostalgia, regret, and intense physical strain threw a roar out of her. The rock crashed on the floor and scuffled its gray surface. Amaru fought to keep herself from crying.

She looked at their water supply. Abigail had grown accustomed to Amaru using her share for washing her now shoulder-length hair, but she would probably never like the fact. In light of today's announcement, it made sense that Amaru would try to look decent, but she needed strength moreso. She tied up her hair and took a few sips.

Perhaps Amaru should have taken the usual time to meditate, but she thought it would be best to check on everyone else's mental health above her own. Spirits needed to be high. So she swung open the door and wore a smile.

Their place was at the western perimeter of Profana. There were no gates or strict borderlines, but Amaru wanted to be stationed there since that was where retributive threats were most likely to come from. For today, however, this meant she was on the exact opposite side of where she would need to be in an hour's time. It was a blessing, really; she wanted to bask in the scenic route if she could.

The sound of falling sand clumping as it hit more sand was the first thing to greet Amaru that morning. This pleased Amaru, for it meant progress was being made. Pali, Via, Epi, and Krati were digging competitively under the direction of their silent overseer.

"Babu! Come here!" Amaru barked out in mock alarm.

All five of them lifted and turned their heads towards Amaru, relaxing when they saw her. Amaru waved at them and shook her hand forward repeatedly, suggesting they resume. When Babu reached Amaru, the two grabbed each other's forearms in tender greeting.

"Working the boys hard, I hope?" Amaru asked, grinning.

Babu nodded with an equivalent grin.

"I suppose I should call them men now. Either way, looks like this might finally be it," Amaru said. The two of them looked back at the diggers and the sand they were heaving over their shoulders. Moist, dark brown. Babu nodded but Amaru didn't notice.

"Babu, I hope you understand how important this is," Amaru continued. "This could save us. It's not as flashy or exciting a duty as what other bands do, but I think it is the most important one. That's why you're in charge. I'm proud of you, friend. I trust you."

Babu nodded and swiped at his eyes. It was true. Amaru had come to value their friendship more than any other. He was a caring, selfless person, everyone knew that. Amaru especially enjoyed that he didn't talk back. When Babu wiped away oncoming emotion, he also tapped at his left eyebrow and grinned again. Amaru playfully shook her head. The giant was also curiously impish.

"It'll grow back someday!" Amaru insisted as she lightly jabbed at Babu's stomach. But she knew it wouldn't. The changing of months had proved that multiple times over. The same went for her crooked knuckles.

"Alright, friend," Amaru said with the knowledge that playtime was over. "I've got to get a move on. Make sure your men catch a breath soon. Time is short. I'll see you then."

Babu nodded as the smile on his face left with Amaru.

The next stretch of Amaru's walk was composed primarily of living areas. Some people preferred the security and structure of wooden homes like the one she and Abigail stayed in. Oddly enough, most stayed in bundled-together twigs. Amaru didn't understand that. They seemed uncomfortably similar to the uncomfortable tents they used to know. But it was their choice. Some even chose to live without a roof, sleeping on sand and looking up at the distant stars at night. Wondering what inhabited those realms. Regardless, one thing everyone agreed on was that each home would be at least a minute's walk from the next.

Someone was galloping towards Amaru's position from behind. Amaru quickly spun around to find a disappointed Diora.

"Dammit," she said, trying to subtly catch her breath. "One of these days, I'll get you."

"Not unless you get a new pair of feet," Amaru joked. She surprised herself at her own joviality this morning. Perhaps it was deflection.

"You bitch," came Diora's response. "I've been training with Reenu as much as I can."

Amaru tilted her head from side to side. He *was* the one to learn from.

"Maybe he's a bad teacher then." Amaru resumed her walk with Diora by her side. "What have you got?"

Diora cleared her throat. "Unfortunately, not much. It's like the sheep have all but died out or migrated away or something. The latter would be more useful, but there haven't been any tracks that we can find. Wolves, on the other hand, have fuckin' multiplied like maggots. Venandi thinks that the den he found holds like thirty of them."

Amaru winced. "That would be unusual. So much for Savyer's Oasis, huh?"

Diora remembered the story that Lea - er, Saios - would tell about a place where Savyer would retreat to in times of stress. Due to the facts that Saios burned most of it down *and* that they decided to head in the same eastwardly direction after The Krisi, they realized that they could theoretically be standing on those very same grounds. But they could have never known.

"I agree," Diora said, "but it *could* explain where the sheep are ending up."

There was silence between them for several paces. Amaru didn't like where this report was headed.

"What do you suggest?" she asked.

Diora straightened her spine and let her chest elevate. "I think we've got to attack. Even if the sheep issue isn't related to this den, killing these wolves off would be huge for our supply. Of course, we couldn't do it with the regular five. We might need to make an exception here and get as many people in on it as possible. And here's something that would help: Rixi and Venea have been working on this airy poison thing in their spare time-"

"Diora!" Amaru interjected. She was accosted by memories of the last pack she had to deal with. Seven on one. Her temple throbbed as she tried to cool down. "Sorry. I just don't think we're there yet. Let's re-evaluate in two weeks."

Diora frowned. This was a mistake.

"I understand your concern, Amaru. But the longer we wait, the less of a chance we have."

Amaru used to appreciate Diora's tenacity. Now it only added to her throbbing. But she had as much of a voice as anyone else did.

"Okay. If you believe in it, bring it up at the send-off. After they leave, of course."

Diora nodded vigorously.

there, that's that...time to change the subject

"Breakfast is almost up. Can you go remind everyone that we'll be meeting in...shit, I guess thirty minutes?"

"Sure."

Amaru finished the walk with Diora to the food area. The Profanans had decided not to name the structure, but rather, to refer to it as whatever meal was currently being served. This morning it was Lamb Platters, Leilah's specialty. Amaru and Diora stepped inside and saw that mostly everyone was there. Diora went ahead with her announcement, but Amaru wasn't listening. She was scanning. Once she saw that the two people she was looking for weren't present, she quietly snuck away.

Ten minutes later, Amaru arrived at her least favorite structure. It was smaller than a wooden home, but its modest stone pillar dignified its apparent value. The only stone on the grounds - Amaru felt it a waste, but enough people didn't. The door was open, which meant people were inside. Two stepped outside as Amaru stepped in, people she didn't really know. They smiled at her but Amaru kept her eyes away. The room was bare of furniture and would have been completely dark were it not for torchlight at its northernmost wall. The torches lit up a mural. This mural depicted history as they knew it, starting with blank wilderness. Small groups of people came next, followed by Prames and the beginnings of Ecclesia. Savyer graced the middle of the wall, drawn as the largest being upon it. After the depiction of a full Table came the Kolosaio with a fiery red question mark over it. Arrows pointed into nothingness from that point on. The Profanans had decided not to draw anything else until a new climactic event transfigured their calendars. Maybe today was the day. Some used this room for reflection. Some just used it for the quiet. But a few others did what the two in front of Amaru were currently doing. Kneeling down with their faces prone and hands on their own copies of The Manual were Adinah and Reenu.

Amaru waited for them to finish. She knew Reenu wasn't so devout that he wouldn't be time-conscious. Still, she waited longer than expected. Eventually, the two of them slowly rolled their backs until they sat up straight and tall on their haunches.

"Find what you're looking for?" Amaru impetuously asked from behind them.

But in their current states, Reenu and Adinah would not be goaded.

"'To search is folly-'" Reenu started.

"'For peace is always present,'" Amaru finished without rolling her eyes. "I remember."

Adinah held an awed, slightly gaping smile as the two of them turned around to face Amaru.

"I'm impressed, Amaru. I would not have guessed that you are familiar with Paroi."

ah, yes...the backhanded compliments never cease from your mouth, you-

"Adinah," Amaru acknowledged her with a nod. "Hope you two had a restful night. We should be on our way, so if you're ready to go-"

"Amaru."

Reenu said her name and stole her gaze with his own. Ever since leaving, they had drifted. Other people filled the various gaps in their lives: Abigail, Adinah, really any of the fifty others as well. Like went with like. They both knew what was happening, but neither spoke of it. Bringing it up meant they would have to deal with more than just what was going on between them. Both were usually content with leaving the past where it was. But all it took was a shared look for everything to come back to the surface.

"Are you okay?"

Amaru's hands started to sweat. She looked away. Despite it all, Reenu was still the only one who could see past any facade she constructed. Abigail had her moments, but they were usually sexually charged. Reenu had always been more holistic. That's why she left. And why she felt so agonizingly seen now.

Reenu extended a hand.

"Maybe you should sit with us for a moment?"

Amaru knew what the invitation meant. She shook her head no even as she wiped her hand against her sheepskin clothes.

"You know I've never believed any of it."

Reenu shrugged his shoulders. "It's not perfect. Nothing is. No one is. But it can be good."

Amaru searched for one last excuse. "Well...I don't have a copy."

Reenu smiled. "You can use mine."

Amaru relented. She felt the weight she bore shift ever so slightly from her back to theirs. She placed her hand in Reenu's to keep from collapsing just as much as it was to give in. There, the three of them prayed alone together.

They ended up being the last ones to arrive, but Amaru didn't mind this time. She needed the scenic route that morning. Outside Profana's easternmost home were the rest of her fifty inhabitants. Amaru quickly found Abigail propped up on her two wolfsbone crutches and greeted her with a long kiss. They exchanged words that were lost amongst the murmurs of the crowd. It was only a couple of minutes before the doors of the home they stood outside opened up.

Arah was the first to exit. He kept his chin high as he descended the front steps. Amaru remembered those glimpses she caught of him back before they even met at The Krisi. He was a specimen then, but now she felt that this was the fittest she had ever seen him. There was meat on his bones, his lips were clean, and his hair had grown back, though he now kept it at a close buzz. The only thing that didn't heal was his nose, and not just because of the wounds the wolf had inflicted. A year ago, he cut it off. He told everyone who asked that he felt it to be an unnecessary appendage, but Amaru knew it was so that he could forget. Ironically, the action is what made everyone remember, though all Profanans had grown accustomed to the look by this point.

Arah did not walk alone. Attached to him was Ambree, who was clearly more forlorn. She tried not to look back at the fifty who stared at her like she was a reluctant bride looking for a way out of her vows, but her eyes darted towards them a couple of times. Eight more people filed out, and it soon became apparent that they held hands as they went. They were bound by circumstance, so why not make that symbolic bond physical? It was an act of both acceptance and defiance, one that Amaru respected even if it frightened her a little. If they were to be cast out, the only way they would get through it was in unity.

The ten of them lined up opposite the fifty and stood still. Varying levels of animosity permeated the air, but the overwhelming spirit of the crowd was sentimental. It was the end for some, but a new beginning for all. There was something exciting about that. Awkwardness also persisted, as no one had exactly written out the procedure for something like this, the first of its kind. Abigail nudged Amaru, indicating that she should get on with it. She was right. Amaru pushed her way through the crowd until she stood between the ten and the fifty. She tried to position herself so that she could face both sides equally, but she realized that she would just have to pivot occasionally if she wanted to address them all. She pulled out the scroll she had been hiding and let it unravel itself. It shook within her hands. Whatever calm her recent meditation was supposed to instill in her had vanished. Her palms threatened to dissolve the written words before her, but that was a small concern. She had the lines memorized; the scroll was just to look official and have something to hide behind, but for that purpose, it was not enough. This was a speech she never thought she would have to give.

how in fuck did Moshe do it

She thought of the night prior.

The warmth of the fire complemented the solitude quite nicely, but it was still not enough to ease the slight in her heart. She had walked until the sun went down just to ensure that no one followed after her, but the tension was something she could not leave behind. Amaru stoked the fire with a twig and watched its rapid ascent be quickly consumed by the night. She tried to breathe. Of course, she couldn't stay for long. She would have to get up earlier than usual tomorrow, but clarity always came when no one was around to dispel it. Unfortunately, it didn't last long enough.

"How's Abigail?" Reenu asked from a few feet away. Those quiet feet.

Amaru would have been angered if it was anyone else.

"Her pride hurts more than her knee," Amaru said matter-of-factly.

Reenu sat down. "That heals quickly with her. Still, I'm sure she's shocked you came down differently than her on the naming poll."

Amaru dully stared into the fire. "We had to call our home something eventually. At least it's badass."

"Yeah, that helps," Reenu agreed. "She'll come around at some point..."

Reenu shifted his left and then his right leg. Amaru had noticed the development of this new habit came along with Reenu growing more confrontational as of late.

"Will she be by your side tomorrow?"

Amaru kept her eyes forward. "She has to be. She knows that."

Reenu planted his hands firmly on his legs. "What about Arah and Ambree?"

"I didn't make these fucking rules!"

Amaru suddenly faced Reenu and buried her hands in the sand in an act of ferocity. She let go of the twig in the process and lost it to the fire. But Reenu wasn't intimidated. His motivation was also frustration, but it came from elsewhere.

"No one's saying you did, dumbass! It's the hard thing to do, but it's also the best option. Of course the people who were 'picked' disagree now."

picked...does he know...

The fading fire wasn't enough to make Amaru's palms sweat, but the implication of Reenu's words definitely were. She looked at him in anticipation, not willing to admit to anything before her suspicions were confirmed. Fortunately, Reenu was a friend.

"You're fortunate that I was the only one who noticed the switch. But we all have to live with it."

Amaru felt anger flare up again, but then she noticed how close their faces had become. Reenu cooled down as well when he noticed. Amaru returned her gaze to the embers.

"You know I couldn't let her be one of them."

Reenu nodded. "Technically, this makes sense for everyone. But the principle of your tampering...I'm not going to judge you. Just be careful."

Amaru allowed herself to breathe. She didn't know why she expected less of her once friend-lover, but it was comforting to know that he wouldn't expose her. If anyone else knew that she traded Abigail's fate for Ambree's...

"Thank you...I...I just hate having to be the one who makes these damned announcements. It feels like people think the decision comes from me. I hate crowds."

Reenu fell back onto his elbows. A little release of aggression was all he needed to relax.

"Honestly, I'm glad it's not me," he said almost teasingly.

Amaru scoffed. "Thanks, asshole."

"But you are definitely the best fit for the job. You always have been."

"Eh, I think Abigail has an easier time saying shit people don't like."

"She does. But she doesn't care enough. You need to say the hard stuff because you care. People will feel that."

Amaru reflected on that thought for a moment. Reenu was probably right. She was the balance. Wisdom. Then she said something that only they could share. She finally spoke up.

"I wonder how Moshe was always able to do it."

Reenu sat up. This was what he was hoping for.

"Well, he certainly wasn't perfect."

"And I've got the scars to prove it," Amaru retorted. They smiled at each other as she went on.

"But he bore the weight for so long. All on his own. If it wasn't so fucked up, it would be kind of admirable."

Reenu reflected on that thought for a moment. Amaru was probably right. Moshe was their center. They had tried to pretend that wasn't true for so long, but it was undeniable. Building Profana together often felt aimless without that unifying soul. It's why Reenu had gone back to The Manual: to search for that motivation hidden within its roots. To feel connected again. Time would tell if that would work. But Reenu realized something new.

"The memory we have of him...it's not all that different from Ecclesia."

Amaru blinked in confusion. She wasn't following.

"I mean..." Reenu continued. "There's good that he did. There was some good in Ecclesia. There's bad in both as well. Differing degrees obviously, but maybe instead of condemning one or the other, what we should do instead is see what we've learned from them."

Amaru felt that anxious tension bubble within her. She hadn't stopped to think that way. She was once called wise, but ever since Moshe's death, she didn't care about what she had learned. Ecclesia was a corrupt empire that she would never revisit...but others she now lived beside loved it anyway. Moshe was a broken soul that did so much to wrong her...yet she loved him anyway. Both needed fixing. Maybe one was a harder problem to solve than the other, but that didn't have to mean that it was lost.

Amaru picked up her sheepsquil and parchment.

"As you all know...with the influx of last month's arrivals, we've reached max capacity. It was decided very early on by the initial adhocracy of ex-Ecclesians that we would not exceed fifty inhabitants on Profana's grounds...however, it was not decided what we would do when the time came until last week. Unlike the tyranny under which most of us once resided, Profana has no council, no officers, and no one above the other. We all have natural talents, but we cycle through roles in order to learn from one another and avoid any semblance of power. But that is why it also takes time for decisions to be made, so I hope we all can forgive ourselves for allowing our resources to squander the past couple of weeks. It was decided by majority vote that we would...say goodbye to ten selected at random, not showing preference to those who have helped out the most or even those who have been here longest. Sticks were drawn yesterday, and those who drew the ten shortest...have complied, gathered their things, and are now prepared to leave. Last night, we graciously allowed ourselves the opportunity to say goodbye, so there is no need to do so now...but maybe we should conclude this matter with a reminder. Why did we decide to do this? Couldn't we just expand and make things work? Indeed, it is a hard decision, but it is also the best one for all. Though it has been hundreds of days since The Krisi, those of you who came out of Ecclesia must remember her complications. She offered promises she could not deliver. Inner Sanctum was a true haven, but only for a select few. Only for a certain type of person. That was the result of power, people being in charge, officers. Resource scarcity bred inequality. We cannot allow that to happen to us. From one perspective, you might say we are making the same mistake that Ecclesia did. What is the real difference between this vote and their gatekeeping? As we learned from...as we learned from Moshe, Inner Sanctum *was* indeed planning an expansion. But it was not an expansion of The Table, their symbol of welcome and inclusion. No, it was an expansion of their own property. Who's to say that if we were to set ourselves up like them that we wouldn't make the same choice? We *cannot* become too big to not fail. The most just thing to do for everyone's sake is to give these ten brave souls a chance to make it out there with some of our wood, food, and water and keep ourselves from power. Of course, they can always visit. We hope that trading becomes a mutual route between us, and we will never forget the value of the relationships we've made. But for now, there must be a separation of time and space. May peace leave with you as you find yourselves a new home."

The ten stood and stared at the fifty for a piercing minute. They *had* all complied, but not all agreed that it was a choice. Arah peered at Amaru with vacant eyes. Ambree's eyes filled as she searched for Abigail, but she was nowhere to be found. Both sides had agreed to not speak, so after a minute passed, the ten turned around and walked away. They went hand in hand for a number of footsteps before Arah stopped to let out a terminal denouncement of his own.

"And also with you."

Then they left.

The fifty stood there for several more minutes, unsure of what to do. Amaru had done her part, it was not her job to tell them to go about the rest of their days. It was no one's job. She could only stand there, halted by uncertain emotion. At some point, the first person left in search of an early lunch. One by one, people started filing away. Amaru determined to stay until she saw the ten fade completely into the horizon. She kept her eyes forward even as Reenu and Adinah came and arranged themselves on either side of her.

But as the ten disappeared, something curious replaced them.

Far, far to the east came a color no one had witnessed in the skies before. Gray. The three who provided the shade's distant welcome were puzzled as to what it could be. What it could mean. Whatever it was, the Profanans did know a couple of things with certainty.

They would always be heard.

There would never again be a Table that told them otherwise.

They would no longer be the faceless.

Acknowledgments

They say you're supposed to keep this section of your book down to a single page, but I have a feeling that we need a little more space than that to do this even a fraction of justice.

God, in whom I live and move and have my being.

Charles Haynie, what I hear of you is more legend than reality, but it was the act of reading your book that assured me I would one day write my own.

Dad, your affinity for English and your disciplined work ethic is the foundation that writing all these chapters required.

Kimberly Rose, your initial approval of Chapter 2 in January 2019 was all I needed to keep pressing on with writing. And your love is all I need to keep pressing on with living.

Kenny, talking through the plot with you first and foremost was in every way the right move. I respect your thought process and artistic taste to death.

Matthew, your natural creative spirit and robust world-building is what inspired me to think bigger. And it's why I realize that a sequel is not only necessary, but possible.

Jordan, our conversations are always aimless yet purposeful, and it is your existence that proves to me that there will always be someone who wants to hear what I have to say.

Carlitos, our talks at Grandma's were the beginnings of me being ok with deconstruction. Who knows if reconstruction could have happened without them?

Jerome, Andrew, and Brett, our DnD campaign was inarticulate and far too long, but it was where Moshe was born and first challenged to live in a world outside his own.

Stephanie, Bekah, Nate, Mary, Rick, Uncle Matt, Bo, Gabe, Chloe - you are the people that have convinced me that the system I was in was worth saving even when I found that I could no longer stay in it.

Daniel, Austin, Matt, Cedric, Garrett, Justin - you are the people that let me escape it.

Grandma Enriqueta - a song, a chapter, and a character come straight from you. Wisdom, always.

Abbi - a song, a chapter, and a character come straight from you as well.

Rose, the only way that I can visualize the previous one hundred and eleven thousand words is through your beautiful handiwork.

To all my other friends and family, even if you did not contribute directly to the creation of this story, you have contributed directly to me and who I am. You have earned your place here. Particularly Isaiah, whose friendship was often all I had as a child. And my mom, whose sacrificial nature is part of the answer to the grand question that this book poses.

My time working in a megachurch filled with good people and careless oversight is the input that induced an output of songs, characters, plots, themes, and imaginary conversations. For that, I must be grateful.

To the spiritual leaders and doubters that have inspired me and carried me through reconstruction - The Liturgists, BadChristian, Dan Koch, Pete Enns, Corey Farr, Peter Rollins, Matt Hauge, Craig Anderson, & Rumi - you have given me the language I needed to process the world. And permission for the lack of it.

To those at IngramSpark, thank you for the tools necessary to make this a physical reality.

To those who donated to the Indiegogo campaign, what an honor and a responsibility it is to bear the financial gifts of others. I hope it was worthwhile.

And, of course, to the reader...thank you. Two and a half years ago, I could not have conceived of what committing to a project of this length would entail, but I've found that when you believe in its meaning, the commitment comes naturally. As a creative without a following, I've always been content with making things that no one sees, but this story is the first one in my life that I deeply need to be known. You are fulfilling that part of me, and it's a humbling, life-breathing prospect.

May we always seek to better the systems we are placed in, whether through small reforms, complete upheavals, and sometimes, even leaving.

Verily?